THE SCUM VILLAIN'S SELF-SAVING SYSTEM

CONTENTS

Contents based on the Pinsin Publishing print edition originally released 2017

6

Jin Lan

THREE YEARS went by in the blink of an eye.

During these three years, other than occasionally asking Liu Qingge for assistance in clearing his meridians to treat his poison, requesting medicinal prescriptions from Mu Qingfang, and briefly visiting Qing Jing Peak to arrange leveling missions for his disciples, Shen Qingqiu spent most of his time wandering about the outside world.

He passed the days leisurely until an urgent notice from Yue Qingyuan arrived to suddenly summon him back to Cang Qiong Mountain.

As the Qing Jing Peak disciples had seen nary a shadow of their peak lord in such a long while, for his return, they gathered at the mountain gates well ahead of time to welcome him. As soon as they saw Shen Qingqiu steadily climbing the mountain steps, they all flocked toward him, clothes rustling.

The one leading them, Ming Fan, had by now become a lanky young man; though you couldn't say he was extraordinarily handsome, his features could still be considered neat. Anyhow, the sharp mouth and sunken cheeks he'd had in his youth were no more, and gone was that petty cannon fodder's face that had been so obvious at a single glance.

Even more striking was Ning Yingying, who had become a lovely young lady with a splendid figure. Upon seeing Shen Qingqiu, she rushed over and grabbed his arm, pulling him up the Heaven-Ascending Stairs.

While being greeted by a sweet-smelling maiden was indeed a wonderful thing, Shen Qingqiu unfortunately couldn't enjoy it, especially because Ning Yingying had developed quite nicely. No longer was she that dainty and delicate little girl of the past; sometimes her chest would accidentally brush against him. In fact, it did so until Shen Qingqiu, face still expressionless, was streaming with cold sweat. He had once again thought of those two long chains of posts in *Proud Immortal Demon Way*'s comment section—the ones demanding Shen Qingqiu's castration.

"Shizun, you're always away from the mountain," Ning Yingying said, cutely vying for his attention. "Your disciples all miss you so much."

"This master has also missed you...all," Shen Qingqiu said affectionately.

That's not right, he was thinking. *Shouldn't the one you miss be Luo Binghe? Why are you thinking about a scum villain? And as one of Luo Binghe's wives, weren't you originally supposed to suffer five continuous years of sleepless nights and lack of appetite, becoming all emaciated and stricken with grief?*

Why does it look like you've become plumper instead?!

The disciples escorted Shen Qingqiu to Qiong Ding Peak. In Qiong Ding Peak's Main Hall, eleven peak lords had already all sat down. One or two trusted disciples stood behind each peak lord, with the exception of Liu Qingge.

Traditionally, Bai Zhan Peak's modus operandi was a hands-off, "shepherd-style" of education; everyone trained on their own. The peak lord would occasionally pop up to beat up a bunch of disciples, but other than that, they generally wouldn't teach anything else. This continued until a disciple could fight off their master, at which point the master handed over the title of peak lord. Thus, Liu Qingge naturally didn't have any trusted disciples.

Shen Qingqiu greeted everyone in turn, then sat in the second seat, which was for Qing Jing Peak, while Ming Fan and Ning Yingying stood behind him. Across from him were Xian Shu Peak's Qi Qingqi and Liu Mingyan.

Yue Qingyuan had yet to announce the start of the meeting, so Shen Qingqiu opened and shut the folding fan in his hand, playing with it while he looked around at all the peak lords and their disciples. He found himself thinking that if Luo Binghe were still here, no one else would be standing behind him. Neither would there be any question as to who was the most outstanding disciple of Cang Qiong Mountain Sect's next generation.

His thoughts were still running wild when Yue Qingyuan spoke. "Does everyone know of Jin Lan City?"

"I've heard a little about it," said Shang Qinghua. "It's located in the Central Plains, where the two great rivers, Luo and Heng, meet. The city values trade; it's said to be quite prosperous."

Yue Qingyuan nodded. "Correct. Jin Lan City is accessible from all sides by both land and water, so merchants from all over have always gathered there. But two months ago, Jin Lan City shut its gates. Not only are the gates impassable, not even letters can be relayed."

A healthy, thriving trade city shutting its gates with no warning was like a financial center abruptly breaking off all relations with other branches—it was illogical. There absolutely had to be more to it.

Shen Qingqiu lifted the teacup by his hand and scraped at the tea leaves on the surface. "Zhao Hua Monastery is nearest to Jin Lan City, and my impression was that they share a very close relationship. If something did happen, the masters at the temple would have realized something was wrong."

"Correct," Yue Qingyuan said. "Twenty days ago, a merchant from Jin Lan City escaped the city via waterway and rushed to Zhao Hua Monastery to cry for help."

If he was using the word "escaped," it seemed that the situation was genuinely serious. The entire hall grew solemn.

"That middle-aged man was the owner of Jin Lan City's first weapons shop. Over the years, he had often gone to Zhao Hua Monastery to pray and burn incense, so quite a few of the temple's monks knew him.

"When he arrived, he was swathed entirely in black cloth, with only half of his face exposed. He was already wholly exhausted by the time he reached Zhao Hua Monastery, and he collapsed on the mountain steps as he told them repeatedly that there was a terrifying plague within the city.

"The monks guarding the mountain immediately carried the man into the main hall and reported the event to the head abbot. But by the time the head abbot rushed out with several other masters, it was too late."

"He died?" asked Liu Qingge.

"The merchant had by then decayed into a skeletal state."

Hadn't Yue Qingyuan just said that the man had exhausted himself by the time he reached the Monastery gates? How could he have become a skeleton in the blink of an eye?

Shen Qingqiu muttered, "Shixiong said that the merchant was swathed in black cloth? From head to toe?"

"Precisely. During the wait, a monk tried to help him remove the black cloth. However, whenever they touched him, he wailed in terrible pain, like his skin and flesh were being ripped off, so they didn't dare remove it by force.

"The masters of Zhao Hua Monastery were deeply disturbed, and after discussion, they sent Master Wu Chen and several Buddhist elders to investigate that very night. As of today, they have yet to return."

Compared to Shen Qingqiu and his cohort, the masters of the "Wu" generation were uniformly higher in seniority, and their cultivation wouldn't be lacking either.

Hence, Shen Qingqiu was a bit flabbergasted. "Not a single one came back?"

Yue Qingyuan solemnly nodded. "Huan Hua Palace and Tian Yi Temple have also sent ten-odd disciples each. They met with the same result: no one returned."

Three of the four major sects had been dragged into this mess, so naturally Cang Qiong Mountain couldn't just passively observe. No wonder Yue Qingyuan had sent an emergency summons.

Indeed, Yue Qingyuan said, "With no other choice, our fellow cultivators from the other sects sent Cang Qiong Mountain an urgent letter with an emissary, pleading for our assistance. We will certainly lend it. However, this is a serious situation. I'm afraid there may be petty ne'er-do-wells of other races fanning the flames to stoke this incident, stirring up havoc. Some of us will go, but some must stay behind to guard the peaks."

In other words, to prevent a situation like the incident with Sha Hualing, when they had been completely vulnerable.

Needless to say, "other races" could only refer to the demon race.

Liu Qingge was the first to say, "Bai Zhan Peak is willing to escort Mu-shidi to the city."

Since there was a plague, Qian Cao Peak's Mu Qingfang definitely had to go.

Shen Qingqiu looked at these two: one who was responsible for making his medicine, the other responsible for clearing his meridians. Both were leaving, and Shen Qingqiu didn't have a protagonist's halo with which to protect himself. What if there was an unexpected accident? This was really too concerning. How could he *not* do his part to watch over them?

So, he hurriedly added, "Qingqiu is willing to go as well."

"My original plan was for you to watch the mountain," said Yue Qingyuan.

Of course Shen Qingqiu knew how to deal with him: all he needed to do was endlessly pester Yue Qingyuan.

"There's no need for Zhangmen-shixiong to think me so fragile. Even if Qingqiu is untalented, he knows a few things about demons. If they really are the ones making mischief, I can still be of some assistance."

The walking demon encyclopedia—both the original and current flavor could definitely live up to this title. After all, there was that stack of records and ancient books in the back of Qing Jing Peak's Bamboo House, the same ones that hundreds of generations of peak lords had to read in full before they were allowed to succeed the position.

Yue Qingyuan thought for a while. If he let Shen Qingqiu go with Liu Qingge and Mu Qingfang, it would be far easier for Shen Qingqiu to suppress the Without a Cure poison still within his body. Also, if they got into a fight, the Bai Zhan Peak Lord could protect him.

Therefore, in the end, everyone was divided into three groups. The Liu-Shen-Mu trio would clear the way as the vanguard; they would go to Jin Lan City first to investigate. The second group would wait outside and act in accordance with their report. The third group would stay and keep watch on Cang Qiong Mountain.

The situation was urgent, so there was no time to leisurely take a carriage or boat. Though Shen Qingqiu disliked flying on his sword, he knew that at a time like this, he needed to keep up with everyone else's momentum.

Thus, the trio flew out on their blades. Before half a day had passed, Shen Qingqiu gazed downward from above the clouds, took a deep breath, and yelled to his two sect siblings, "The Luo and Heng River junction is right below us!"

When they looked down from a great height, they indeed saw the two rivers meeting each other like a winding pair of endless, thin silver ribbons. The water sparkled under the sunlight, akin to a haphazard dance of silver scales.

One of the two rivers was the one Luo Binghe had been placed into after he was born, left to drift downstream: the Luo, from which his surname derived.

The trio chose to descend at a wide and level hilltop. From there, they could faintly see the curling eaves of far-off Jin Lan City, its tightly closed gates, and the raised drawbridge.

Shen Qingqiu lowered the hand with which he'd shaded his eyes. "Why didn't we fly straight into the city?"

"In the past, at Jin Lan City's governor's request, Zhao Hua Monastery cast an enormous barrier covering their airspace," Mu Qingfang explained. "It prevents immortal swords or anything with spiritual or demonic qi from passing through. They'd be forced to veer off course."

Shen Qingqiu had personally witnessed Zhao Hua Monastery's barrier-casting abilities with the group of barrier masters employed by the VIPs at the Immortal Alliance Conference. If they ever ranked second, no one would dare claim first, so Shen Qingqiu didn't ask further questions.

Since they couldn't descend by air and couldn't enter through the gates, there had to be some other means of ingress. As it turned out, Yue Qingyuan had briefed Mu Qingfang about the situation in detail, and he guided the other two through a forest. From within the shade of the trees, there came the murmur of flowing water. That sound emerged from a low cave.

Mu Qingfang waved the others over. "There's an underground river here. It leads into the city."

Shen Qingqiu understood. "That weapons merchant escaped through here?"

Mu Qingfang nodded. "Several merchants who participate in black market dealings use it to meet or smuggle goods through it. Not many people know this route, but because that weapons merchant had a good relationship with several of Zhao Hua Monastery's masters, he once disclosed a few things to them."

The cave entrance was covered in vines and stood only as tall as their chests. They had to stoop to enter. After walking for a while, they finally felt the ceiling rise, and the sound of flowing water began to gurgle. Several battered, worn-out boats were anchored by the riverbed.

Shen Qingqiu chose a slightly better boat that at least didn't leak, then flicked his fingers. The lamp hanging at the bow flared with light. After looking left and right, he found only one oar.

Shen Qingqiu made a gesture of request toward Liu Qingge. "We'll be going against the current, so rowing into the city will require the person among us with the best arm strength. Shidi, if you please?"

With a dark expression, Liu Qingge took that long, thin boat oar and diligently began to use it as a punting pole. With each stroke, the boat leapt forward an incredible distance. The lamp at the bow creaked and swayed jerkily.

Shen Qingqiu pulled Mu Qingfang over to sit down and glanced at the glittering water by the boat. He could even see several fish happily swishing their tails as they swam by. "This water is so clear," he said idly.

Right after he said this, something much larger drifted along after the swimming fish. Face-down in the water was a corpse.

Shen Qingqiu shot upright in his seat.

Fuck, fuck, fuck, a floating corpse! I just said "this water is so clear," and you reward me by drifting over a floating corpse?! Do you have to be so heavy-handed when you slap my face?!

Liu Qingge used the oar to hook the floating corpse and flip it over: it was actually another skeleton. They hadn't noticed earlier because its entire body, including its head, was swathed in black cloth. Also, as noted, it had been floating face-down.

"Mu-shidi, do you know if this world has a kind of plague that can make a person instantaneously decay into a skeleton?" Shen Qingqiu asked.

Mu Qingfang shook his head. "It's unheard of."

Since they were moving against the current, they would be pushed backward unless they kept advancing. Having stayed still for so long, their little boat had already moved a distance back.

Liu Qingge picked up the oar again, and after a moment, he spoke. "There's more ahead."

Sure enough, five or six more floating corpses drifted toward them from up ahead, one after another. All were skeletons swathed in black cloth, just like the first.

While Shen Qingqiu fell deep into thought, Liu Qingge abruptly stabbed the long oar into the nearby stone wall. The thin and brittle bamboo actually stuck straight into the solid, seamless stone. This stabilized the boat, fixing it in place.

Shen Qingqiu had also sensed something was wrong, and he sprang to his feet. "Who is it?"

A sound of hurried breathing came from the dark depths before them; the lantern at the prow of the boat faintly illuminated a human silhouette. Then they heard a youth's voice say, "Who are you? What are you doing, sneaking around in this underground river?"

"You're here too. I'd ask you the same," said Shen Qingqiu. Though he stood on a broken-down little boat, between his teal robes, black hair, and the longsword hanging at his waist—not to mention his every movement, so calm and composed—he still possessed quite the immortal's demeanor. Shen Qingqiu had by now become an experienced poser, and had managed to put his own spin on the badass act.

As expected, the youth hadn't anticipated someone so high and mighty. He balked for a long moment before shouting, "You should leave! No one is allowed into the city!"

Liu Qingge humphed. "You? Who could you keep away?"

"There's a plague in Jin Lan. If you don't want to die, then get out!"

"Young man, we are here precisely for that reason..." Mu Qingfang said gently.

When they refused to leave, the youth yelled angrily, "Do you not understand human speech? Hurry and get out! Or else I won't be so polite!"

Before he finished speaking, he was attacking them with a spear, ferocious like a tiger and heartily intimidating.

Liu Qingge let out a disdainful laugh, and he pulled the bamboo oar out of the wall. With a flick of the pole, the youth was sent flying into the river. Yet the boy continued to spit and curse even while splashing about in the water.

"Should we fish him out?" asked Shen Qingqiu.

"What for? He's young and full of energy. Let's go." Liu Qingge continued to push them forward.

The trio exited the underground river, and the illicit boat drifted back into the darkness along with the current. The exit was at the city's most overgrown pond, and not a single person was around. After they walked toward the center of the city for a while, out of nowhere, a set of footsteps caught up to them from behind.

The bedraggled youth charged forward and yelled at them, flustered and annoyed. "I told you not to enter the city! What use is it to have you here?! So many people have already come, saying they were going to save us from the plague. Head monks and big shot Daoists, Hua Palace—whoever! In the end, none of them were able to leave! You're looking for death!"

So this young man had ambushed them in the dark with their best interests in mind.

"Then since we have already entered, what do you think we should do?" Shen Qingqiu asked.

"What else can you do?" the youth replied. "Follow me and don't run around! I'll take you to the old monk."

The trio had no objections. None of them were familiar with Jin Lan City, so of course it was best to have a guide to stop them from any accidental detours.

Shen Qingqiu looked down and asked, "Young man, what is your name?"

The youth puffed up his chest. "My name is Yang Yixuan. I'm the son of the owner of Jin Zi Weapons Shop."

Was it possible that he was referring to the weapons merchant who had risked death to bring word to Zhao Hua Monastery in search of aid?

As Shen Qingqiu appraised the youth, Liu Qingge asked, "What are you looking at?"

"The way I see it, this child can exchange a few blows with you and has a pretty good temperament," he replied. "Both traits are hard to find. He's a promising talent."

"What does that matter? I don't take disciples. Too bothersome."

As they walked into the main part of the city, more and more pedestrians began to appear. But this "more" was only in comparison to the previous empty streets. At most, there were only three or four silhouettes per street, and all were buried in black cloth from head to toe, their movements hasty, like birds startled by a bow or fish slipping through a net.

The Jin Zi Weapons Shop was appreciably large. It sat on the widest main road and occupied four storefronts in a row, all connected together into one store. It even had an inner courtyard, inner hall, and cellar.

Master Wu Chen was in the cellar. He lay on the bed, a blanket covering his lower body, and as soon as he saw Cang Qiong Mountain Sect's reinforcements, he began to chant "Amitabha."

"Master, the circumstances are urgent, let's skip the pleasantries," said Shen Qingqiu. "What is this plague raging through Jin Lan City? Why did you enter but never leave, without even sending a message? And why is everyone wrapped in black cloth?"

Wu Chen forced a smile. "The answer to all of Master Shen's questions is in fact one and the same."

As he said this, he lifted the blanket covering his lower body. Shen Qingqiu stiffened. Underneath the blankets there lay only a pair of thighs: from the knees down, everything had disappeared. Where there should have been a pair of calves, there was nothing.

"Who did this?" Liu Qingge asked stonily.

Wu Chen shook his head. "Not 'who.'"

Shen Qingqiu was puzzled. "If not who, then did they disappear on their own?"

Unexpectedly, Wu Chen nodded. "This pair of legs did indeed disappear on their own."

His legs were still swathed in black cloth from the knees up. Wu Chen reached out, straining to unwrap them, and Mu Qingfang hurried to help.

"This may make everyone a bit uncomfortable," Wu Chen warned.

The black cloth was unwrapped layer by layer. When Shen Qingqiu saw what lay inside, his breath stopped.

Great Master, you call this "a bit uncomfortable"?!

The place that should have been Wu Chen's thighs had thoroughly festered, the skin necrotized, into a mass of rotten flesh. After the black cloth was untied, a terrible stench came from them in waves.

"This is Jin Lan City's plague?" Shen Qingqiu asked.

"Yes," said Wu Chen. "When this disease first develops, red patches appear in a small area. After three to five days on the short end—half a month on the long—the red patches expand and fester. After another month, the rot advances down to the bones. In order to delay the progression, one must swathe oneself in black cloth and avoid exposure to light and the elements."

No wonder everyone in the city had bundled themselves up until they were black mummies.

"If the disease develops over a month's time, why did Yang-xiansheng, the fellow who went to notify Zhao Hua Monastery, instantly decay into a skeleton?" Shen Qingqiu asked.

A sorrowful expression appeared on Wu Chen's face. "This old monk is ashamed to say that he only later discovered that the infected patients can survive for approximately a month, as long as they stay within Jin Lan City. But if after they are infected they go a certain distance away from the city, the disease's progression accelerates. My two shidi discovered this the moment after they rashly tried to leave the city and return to the monastery."

No wonder no one could enter and no one could leave.

"What is the origin of the disease?" Liu Qingge asked. "How is it transmitted?"

Wu Chen could only sigh. "This one is ashamed. We have passed a great deal of time in this city, yet still we have not made any progress toward a solution. We do not know the illness's origin, nor its method of transmission. We do not even know if it *can* be transmitted."

Mu Qingfang was shocked. "What do you mean?"

Shen Qingqiu realized something. "Observe the weapon-seller's son: he has been taking close care of Master Wu Chen for a long time, yet he wears not a strip of black cloth. His skin is still intact, and he is quite healthy. If this is truly a plague, wouldn't it be strange that Master Wu Chen had not infected him?"

"Precisely," said Wu Chen. "This one is terribly sorry to have let you all be trapped here."

"You only intended to save people from disaster; there is no need for apologies," said Shen Qingqiu. He noted that Mu Qingfang was absorbed in investigating the festered parts of Wu Chen's leg, like he couldn't smell a hint of the stench. "Mu-shidi, have you made any discoveries? Can you create a medicine to treat it?"

Mu Qingfang shook his head. "This doesn't seem like a plague but rather like..." He looked at the few people around him. "This humble one needs to examine more patients before he can come to a definite conclusion."

Shen Qingqiu exited the cellar, whereupon he saw the weapon-seller's son heading back the way from which they had come in a rage, a longsword slung over his shoulder. He smiled as he asked, "Young master, what's happening?"

"Someone entered the city again," Yang Yixuan huffed. "Those people from Hua-wherever are the most useless. They're all just rushing to their deaths!"

Huan Hua Palace must have sent more aid (i.e., additional victims). But as the boy's face was puffed up like a steamed bun, Shen Qingqiu couldn't help teasing him a bit. "Young man, your martial skills are rather good. Did you have a teacher?"

Yang Yixuan ignored him.

"Let me tell you, you should go find that gege who tossed you into the water today," Shen Qingqiu continued. "He's most formidable. Fighting a few rounds with him will be more effective than learning from anyone."

When he heard this, Yang Yixuan abandoned Shen Qingqiu and ran.

Having found Liu Qingge a sticky new problem, Shen Qingqiu was in a joyful mood. He walked a few steps and turned a corner, but when he saw the scene before him, he stopped in his path.

The city was devoid of life, and the gates of every home were shut tight. Many of those who had been homeless in the first place had nowhere to go, so they could only gather on the street. Before, when carriages and horses had streamed through the streets, people coming and going, these forsaken had been afraid to show their faces. But now with everything so empty, they became fearless. They'd set up a big iron cauldron and piled firewood underneath it, and they were boiling a churning pot of water as some plucked the feathers off a chicken stolen from who-knew-where.

Each person was wrapped in tightly bundled layers of black cloth, but upon seeing Shen Qingqiu, who was extremely conspicuous in their midst, they were not the least bit shocked. Instead, they regarded him like they would a corpse. After all, these days they had seen every kind of impressive-looking cultivator sweep into the city, claiming they would save the rabble. And had they been of any use? They died even faster than the local drifters!

The cook rapped on the iron pot. "Soup is done! Come get your share!"

Many of the drifters lying nearby who were picking at their lice rolled to their feet and gathered around, bowls in hand.

This plague had disrupted the rhythms of the entire city's day-to-day, so this spontaneous communal meal was liable to actually save some lives.

They had to discover the origin of the plague soon. Silently making this resolution to himself, Shen Qingqiu turned to go—only to come face-to-face with a person walking toward him. They held a walking stick, their figure hunched over, the hand holding their bowl shaking so much it was about to slip; they seemed to be an old lady.

Shen Qingqiu moved to get out of the way, but the old lady must have been weak due to age or fatigue from hunger. She tripped and crashed into Shen Qingqiu.

As Shen Qingqiu helped her up, the old lady mumbled, "Apologies... Apologies... I'm old and confused..." She quickly walked past him and away, probably afraid people would take all the soup.

Shen Qingqiu walked another two steps, then balked.

Something was off.

That old lady had looked like the faintest breeze would knock her over, but when her body crashed into him, hadn't it seemed even heavier than that of an adult man?

He whipped his head back around. In that crowd of people clamoring for bowls of hot soup, the "old lady" he had just seen was nowhere to be found.

There was an opening into an alley to the left. Shen Qingqiu dashed into it in pursuit. He just managed to catch a glimpse of a hunchbacked silhouette flashing down the end of the alley.

Fuck me, with this speed, they wouldn't lose to a runner doing the 100-meter hurdles! "Old lady"? Yeah right! I must be blind!

Shen Qingqiu broke into a run and gave chase. Though this old lady was indeed suspicious, could he be blamed for not realizing something was strange right away? Right now, everyone in Jin Lan City cut the same suspicious figure, what with all the walking around while hunched over and dressed entirely in black!

Mid-chase, he suddenly felt an itch on the back of his hand and raised it up to look.

This limb really was plagued with misfortunes. It was this arm that had been poked full of holes by Elder "Sky Hammer" Tianchui, and now it was this hand that had become infected and was breaking out in red patches!

Come to think of it, it had also been this hand that had first clicked on this stupid novel, *Proud Immortal Demon Way*. If only he could chop it off! Ahhhh!

With this brief distraction, Shen Qingqiu slowed a step. Then he sensed someone charging over, sword glare at the ready. With a flick of his fan, he prepared to return fire with a blade of wind and yelled, "Who goes there?!"

The person sprang from a nearby roof to the ground. The two looked at each other, and Shen Qingqiu blurted out, "Gongyi Xiao?"

The youth immediately lowered his sword and responded in more shock than joy. "Senior Shen?"

"It's me. Why are you here too?"

Then Shen Qingqiu remembered that Yang Yixuan had said more of Huan Hua Palace's people had entered the city through the underground river. That must have been the party with which Gongyi Xiao arrived.

"So Huan Hua Palace sent you to lead a scouting party into the city?" he asked.

Gongyi Xiao replied, "Indeed, this junior was ordered to investigate the city, but...the leader is someone else."

Shen Qingqiu thought this curious. Gongyi Xiao was the favorite disciple of Huan Hua Palace's Old Palace Master. Before Luo Binghe appeared, everyone had tacitly agreed that Gongyi Xiao would be the next leader, and even the Old Palace Master's beloved only daughter adored him. Whenever the disciples' generation did anything, Gongyi Xiao was always in charge. Other than Luo Binghe—who could stomp all over this young man with his protagonist's halo—who else could steal such a position?

But at the moment, there was no time to mull it over.

"Let's chase them together!" Shen Qingqiu said.

Gongyi Xiao gave a resounding agreement, and the two leapt forward, side by side.

The hunchbacked figure flashed into a three-story building. Even from outside, a haze of fragrant powder assailed the nose, and as the structure was covered in beautiful decorations, it had to be some sort of brothel. But now there were no joyful voices or laughing conversations, no signs or sounds of prosperity, only a gate left wide-open, the main hall dreary and oppressive.

Holding their breaths and on full alert, the pair stepped over the threshold.

The chairs and tables in the main hall were overturned, leaving everything a scattered mess. Shen Qingqiu gave Gongyi Xiao a look. "Let's split up and search. You check the private rooms on the left, and I'll take the right."

He used his fan to push open the nearest door. He could make out the indistinct form of a person lying on the bed and initially raised his guard, but he lowered it soon after.

It was only a skeleton wearing a colorfully adorned jacket, its head covered in pearls and jade, lying in a serene position. This was likely one of the women of the establishment who, knowing her time had come, had dressed and groomed herself, donned her best clothes, and gone to meet her death in sleep. Perhaps it was the nature of women to insist on bringing their most beautiful selves even to the end. Shen Qingqiu sighed in sorrow, backed out of the room, and shut the door.

Many rooms in a row each contained the corpses of women in formal dress. It seemed like this brothel had practically been wiped out. As Shen Qingqiu was about to push open the sixth room, he heard the sound of movement and human voices from the second floor.

As he flew up the stairs with Gongyi Xiao, Shen Qingqiu stole to the front. But unexpectedly, before his feet had left the staircase, he heard the gentle voice of a youth.

"It's no trouble."

Though it was only three words, as soon as Shen Qingqiu heard this voice, it was as if he had been struck by a bolt of lightning. The fan in his hand cracked under the force of his grip.

For an instant, it was like even his breath had ceased.

He was paralyzed on the steps, but he could already see into the private room at the end of the long, second-floor corridor. A group of disciples dressed in Huan Hua Palace's colors had crowded around a person in the center.

It was a youth wearing black, shouldering a modest, unadorned longsword, his complexion as clear as jade, his eyes like two deep pools of cold starlight, and he was at present nonchalantly moving toward Shen Qingqiu.

He had grown up quite a bit and the feel of his presence was far different from before, but even if Shen Qingqiu were beaten to death, he would never mistake that face—one that could grace the cover of a romance novel, no matter the angle!

At the same time, a familiar voice, which had spent a long time gathering dust, spoke in Shen Qingqiu's head. In a mechanical tone reminiscent of Google Translate, it began to spout off messages like a barrage of gunfire:

[Hello. System activation successful.]

[Universal activation key: Luo Binghe.]

[Self-examination results: Central power source is operating normally and in good condition.]

[Hibernation mode suspended. Normal operation mode activated.]

[Download and installation of update complete.]

Wait a minute, what the fuck, you actually updated?!

[Thank you for your continued use of our services.]

Can I get a refund?

Shen Qingqiu stared at that young man, who ought to have been familiar yet seemed a stranger. His limbs went stiff and his throat dry.

Wasn't Luo Binghe's grand comeback supposed to be five years after his fall?

Wasn't he currently supposed to be inside an endless hell, carving his way through thorns, studying the blade and farming monsters?

Why had his ascension moved up two whole years?!

Why were you so impatient?! If you rush your leveling, you won't have any safeguards, Bing-ge!

Shen Qingqiu had the urge to turn around and sprint down the stairs, sprint out of Jin Lan City, and sprint out of this goddamn world—

But right after he turned around, Gongyi Xiao blocked his path, and the youth just *had* to ask, "Senior Shen? Why are you suddenly turning back?"

You really can't read the room, understand timing, or catch on to faces before you speak, can you, Young Master Gongyi?!

A seemingly gentle voice came from behind him. "Shizun?"

Neck stiff, Shen Qingqiu slowly turned his head.

It was only a simple movement, but right now, it felt like his head weighed several thousand kilograms. At this moment, in his eyes, that perfect face of Luo Binghe's was more frightening than anything in the world.

What scared him even more was the expression on that face. It was neither icy-cold nor a poisonous smile hiding daggers within, but a kind and tender look that could warm its recipient down to their bones.

Fuck—don't act like that, it's terrifying!

The more silky-soft Luo Binghe's smile, the more thoroughly his opponent's soul and body were about to be destroyed. This statement was absolutely not a joke.

Shen Qingqiu's entire person was stuck at the top of the stairs, unable to ascend or descend, his hair rising all down his back.

Luo Binghe strolled over and spoke softly. "It really is Shizun."

His voice was velvety and light, but every word that emerged from between his teeth, and every tap of his footfalls as he took each step, sent Shen Qingqiu's heart through the equivalent of a high-altitude bungee jump combined with an ice bucket challenge.

The guillotine blade was already over his neck; nothing left but to face it.

Shen Qingqiu gathered his composure and steeled himself. His right hand clutched the slats of his fan, the veins bulging faintly, while his left swept up the hem of his teal robes. With a lift of his foot and one more step, he finally made it onto the second floor.

With that single step, he was already about to burst into tears.

Back in the year Luo Binghe had participated in the Immortal Alliance Conference, their eyes had been level with each other's, but now Shen Qingqiu had to slightly lift his head to look Luo Binghe in the eye. He was already coming up short based on force of presence alone.

Fortunately, Shen Qingqiu had been a poser for years now, so he had plenty of experience. No matter how terrified he was on the inside, no matter how turbulent his emotions, his serene, unperturbed expression was solidly baked onto his face.

After a long while, he painfully squeezed out a line from within his throat. "What exactly is going on here?"

Luo Binghe gave him a smile, but he seemed to have no intention of answering. Instead, it was the group of Huan Hua disciples behind him who crowded forward, clothes rustling.

Only now did Shen Qingqiu realize that these disciples' attitudes were completely off. In his early years, Shen Qingqiu had been known in the way of a great and revered scholar, and his name had swept all throughout the land. Even when he met with others of the same generation, it was rare for them to not conscientiously welcome him with respect, to say nothing of a junior from another sect.

Yet these Huan Hua Palace disciples seemed to be full of hostility toward him. Their gazes brimmed with displeasure, and some were already flashing their weapons. Given how Luo Binghe was standing there, perfectly unflappable, this group of perfectly fine youths from a famous righteous sect looked more like a gang of henchmen ready to rush forward and stake their lives for their boss—or like demonic lackeys poised to kill and burn...

Don't you have it wrong, young people? Don't be in such a hurry to be someone's bodyguard, okay?! As if the person behind you needs your protection! It's already pretty good that he's not harming anyone, but the person who really needs protection is me—me!

Realizing that the atmosphere was off, Gongyi Xiao inserted himself between the disciples and Shen Qingqiu. "Put your swords away," he reprimanded them quietly. "What sort of manners are these?!"

They relented and showed some restraint. The ones who'd drawn their swords grudgingly sheathed them, but their hostility toward Shen Qingqiu didn't decrease.

No wonder. Of course Gongyi Xiao wasn't the one leading the party this time. A while back, if the most highly regarded disciple had spoken, none of his fellow disciples would have dared show displeasure. But now Luo Binghe was here, and his post-darkening brainwashing skills were first-rate, so everything inevitably revolved around him. Even after ten thousand years, no one else could ever again become the default leader.

But even though Shen Qingqiu felt like he was about to suffer a concussion from pure shock, he still couldn't figure this out. When exactly had Luo Binghe infiltrated Huan Hua Palace? In the original work's progression, that didn't happen until at least two years in the future!

Both sides stood stiffly for a while, until a graceful young lady dressed in a light-yellow outer robe abruptly emerged from the sidelines. "You still have the time for this?" she said while shedding tears. "Luo-shixiong, he... That scoundrel harmed Luo-shixiong. Can't you focus on finding a way to help him first?!"

Only now did Shen Qingqiu notice a humanoid figure collapsed in the far corner; it was that fake old lady. He looked at Luo Binghe again and saw that a portion of his sleeve seemed to have been shaved away by a sword glare, exposing a small section of his wrist.

Luo Binghe's skin was very fair, so the couple of red spots on his wrist were especially stark.

Shen Qingqiu instinctively let slip, "You were infected?"

Luo Binghe gave him a glance, then shook his head. "It's but a minor wound. All that matters is that everyone is safe."

With that considerate display of selflessness, for a moment Shen Qingqiu could almost believe that the individual before his eyes was still that bleating, grass-loving little lamb who had huddled behind his knees.

However, the Huan Hua Palace disciples really were good at raining on his parade.

"Isn't this just perfect?" one remarked sarcastically. "I suppose Senior Shen's overjoyed that Luo-shixiong was infected by the plague, right?"

Shen Qingqiu was seriously starting to wonder when exactly he'd offended the entirety of Huan Hua Palace.

Gongyi Xiao took in Shen Qingqiu's expression and felt incredibly embarrassed. He turned back to his fellows and scolded them in low tones. "Be quiet, all of you."

As a senior who'd made his name years ago, Shen Qingqiu could never sink so low as to squabble with insignificant youths who'd been brainwashed by the male lead. Expression indifferent, Shen Qingqiu dropped his arm so the sleeve naturally covered the back of his hand that had broken out in red spots after he'd first bumped into the fake old lady.

Pockmarks covered half the face of the disciple who'd spoken; once scolded, he resentfully closed his mouth, his entire expression reeking dissatisfaction.

Then Qin Wanyue spoke. "It's all our fault. Luo-shixiong, if you hadn't protected us, you wouldn't have..."

Shen Qingqiu had already roughly surmised the truth of what was spreading through the city. He could guarantee it on all the youth and frustrations he'd wasted following this twenty-million-word-plus serialization for years.

First, to a mixed-lineage heavenly demon like Luo Binghe, this thing was the approximate equivalent of saline water or glucose—entirely harmless. It might even have health benefits for him!

Second, if Luo Binghe had let others drag him down or been injured for their sake, that was *definitely* a plan of his own design! No need to ponder!

Don't you know that's the fastest way to farm righteous reputation and favor points?

Shen Qingqiu couldn't stand to keep watching the air of heartbroken grief hanging over Huan Hua Palace's party. Of course, what he couldn't stand even more was having this silent stare down with Luo Binghe. It was as if both of them were waiting for the other to speak first.

Instead, Shen Qingqiu steeled himself and prepared to do a bit of proper business. Without another sideways glance, he walked toward that fake old lady's corpse and drew Xiu Ya. With a few slashes, he shredded the black cloth to pieces, revealing the body inside.

As expected.

At a glance, this "person's" appearance was ordinary, and it was impossible to tell if they were male or female. But that wasn't the main point. The main point was this, and it was dreadful: the body's skin was completely scarlet, like the entire thing had been thrown into boiling water and cooked through. Yet rather than having been reduced to a mush, the carcass was whole.

"A sower," said Shen Qingqiu.

Sower was a type of profession among demons. To put it mundanely, as Shen Qingqiu understood it, they were the Demon Realm's equivalent of farmers, farm owners, and wholesale food distributors.

Due to a variety of reasons, including local geography and race, many of the Demon Realm's creatures had rather peculiar biological needs. This included a portion of demons who tended toward hardcore tastes. To put it concretely, they liked to eat rotten things, the more rancid and putrid the better; anything crawling with maggots was considered both an exceptionally exquisite delicacy and abundantly nutritious.

But where could one acquire such a quantity of rotten things?

This was the purpose of the sowers.

The flesh of every non-demonic organism a sower touched and purposefully seeded would, after a short period of time, begin to fester. In days past, this practice had enabled a type of massive communal meal that had been popular on noble estates in the Demon Realm. The estate lord would capture some hundred living people and would corral them in a structure like cattle, then send sowers into their midst. Within seven days, once the victims had sufficiently rotted, the doors could be opened. You could either let the people stumble out and eat them where they fell or walk inside yourself and devour them on the spot.

This manner of...unique dining custom was disgusting in the extreme.

Of course, the ancient heavenly demons from whose lineage Luo Binghe hailed were the most elegant and traditional of the demonic bloodlines—equivalent to the Demon Realm's blue blood nobility; the average demon commoner's B-Point scores couldn't begin to compare to a heavenly demon's. Needless to say, the heavenly demons had not taken part in these faddish tastes.

If not for that, Luo Binghe could be as handsome and rule-breakingly OP as he wanted, but girls would be unable to overcome the physiologically and psychologically taxing challenge this bizarre worldbuilding detail would present to their worldviews—so Shen Qingqiu suspected. Think about it! How suffocating would it feel to kiss him if it were true?! Ha ha ha!

Since sower as a profession was grossly anti-human, it had incited the uncompromising ire of many Human Realm cultivators at the time. Consequently, they had launched a campaign to eradicate all sowers. Quite a few nameless heroes had even risked infection and ended up perishing together with the sowers. Within ten years, sowers had gone almost entirely extinct, becoming rare even within the Demon Realm. It was entirely normal for young disciples and ordinary cultivators to have never heard of them. But whenever he was at his leisure, Shen Qingqiu was in the habit of taking an aged text from Qing Jing Peak's eclectic collection and reading it as a speculative fiction novel, so he understood the situation well.

Unfortunately, this conclusion that he'd come to all by himself, which should have been a helpful contribution, went unappreciated.

"So Senior also knew about the demonic abominations that are sowers," Qin Wanyue said politely. "Luo-shixiong guessed the identity of the culprit a while back. Just now, he explained the relevant information to us in detail."

When she finished, she and all the other Huan Hua disciples directed an adoring, longing gaze toward Luo Binghe, as if his face were emitting thousands of rays of golden light.

It's here! Could this be the legendary "regardless of what the male lead says, everyone else will feel their own IQ and knowledge get absolutely crushed by his words" protagonist halo of wisdom?!

Luo Binghe looked toward Shen Qingqiu and smiled. "Everything I know was taught to me by Shizun."

...The most terrifying thing was that Shen Qingqiu got the feeling that Luo Binghe's face really was emitting a faint glow.

Shen Qingqiu very much didn't want to waste any more time in this kind of eerie atmosphere. However, since Huan Hua Palace had killed the sower, naturally the right to handle the corpse was also theirs.

"If that's the case, may we borrow this corpse for study?" Shen Qingqiu asked. "It's possible Mu-shidi may discover something, and it may assist us in developing a medicine that will curb the epidemic as early as possible."

Luo Binghe nodded. "Everything will be as Shizun says. This disciple will deliver the corpse promptly."

The way that "Shizun" left his mouth every time he said it made all of Shen Qingqiu's hairs stand on end. At last, he acutely understood how characters in the original work felt when facing that dagger-concealing smile of Luo Binghe's.

Shen Qingqiu pulled himself away and flicked aside his sleeves, then left without a second word.

After exiting that abandoned building, Shen Qingqiu fell into a state of devastated psychological shock. His head swam as he walked, his steps unsteady.

Gongyi Xiao chased after him. When he saw that Shen Qingqiu's face was pale, his expression distracted, he nervously said, "Senior Shen, I must apologize. In truth, I knew that Luo-shixiong was with Huan Hua Palace, but our master ordered us to keep it a strict secret and to not let outsiders know. Violators would be expelled from the sect. I couldn't inform you of the situation."

Shen Qingqiu grabbed him. "I have only one question for you: When and how did Luo Binghe end up in your Huan Hua Palace?"

"It was Qin-shimei. Last year, she rescued a grievously injured and unconscious Luo-shixiong on the banks of the Luo River."

Last year. In only one short year, Luo Binghe had kicked Gongyi Xiao off of his pedestal as the most trusted disciple. It seemed that not only had Luo Binghe's annexation of Huan Hua Palace occurred earlier, but his efficiency had improved. Also, Gongyi Xiao really was doomed to be cannon fodder, fated only to be kicked off of various number-one pedestals by the male lead!

"After you rescued him, why didn't he return to Cang Qiong Mountain Sect?" Shen Qingqiu asked.

Gongyi Xiao took careful stock of Shen Qingqiu's expression, and he spoke cautiously. "Once Luo-shixiong was rescued and woke up, he seemed to be unwilling to bring up the past. When he was delivering his farewells, he disclosed...that he wouldn't return to Cang Qiong Mountain Sect and that he hoped Huan Hua Palace would keep his whereabouts a secret. It seemed he intended to wander the world. But our master thinks very highly of Luo-shixiong, so he vigorously urged him to stay. They don't call each other master and disciple, but with the way our master treats him, he's already no different from a succeeding heir."

So that's how it was.

No wonder the Huan Hua Palace disciples had showed such a hostile attitude toward Shen Qingqiu just a moment ago. This act of Luo Binghe's was his standard "trampled white lotus who silently endures."

People had no doubt begun to think: If everything is fine, why would Luo Binghe be unwilling to return? Maybe it's because Cang Qiong Mountain Sect, and Shen Qingqiu in particular, have wronged him. That false news of his death at the Immortal Alliance Conference must be covering up some terrible secrets.

Luo Binghe's brainwashing skills weren't just talk. Having seen how those disciples blindly and fastidiously followed him, Shen Qingqiu knew exactly where Luo Binghe stood with Huan Hua Palace.

A disciple from Sect A took a trip to Sect B. Subsequently, the entire hierarchy of Sect B from top to bottom cried and begged for him to stay, and even hid and concealed him so other sects wouldn't find out. How unscientific and unreasonable. But with the male lead's halo shining down upon the situation, it was absolutely logical!

Shen Qingqiu was silent. Gongyi Xiao thought him sad and disappointed. His beloved disciple hadn't died but had instead preferred to roam around the world instead of returning to see him. Of course this was a painful tragedy. So, Gongyi Xiao offered consolation. "Senior Shen shouldn't pay it any mind. Perhaps Luo-shixiong is struggling with a temporary internal conflict that he's yet to resolve. Before now, he never left Huan Hua Palace's sphere of influence, yet when he heard that Cang Qiong Mountain's Senior Shen was participating in rescue efforts here, he took the initiative and asked to come. Perhaps there's been some turn for the better. Although, my shidi and shimei... Ahem, on this matter, I believe they've misunderstood Senior. I hope you won't hold it against them."

Shen Qingqiu's heart was as choked as a dammed-up river. Sure enough, the positive reputation he'd painstakingly farmed over many years was nothing in the face of Luo Binghe's ability to smear him without second thought. And what a thorough smearing!

But on second thought, this couldn't actually be considered smearing. After all, Shen Qingqiu hadn't been wrongly accused in this case. He had indeed kicked Luo Binghe down into the Endless Abyss.

In the end, he couldn't find any reason to justify or exonerate himself.

"And you?" Shen Qingqiu asked. "Why don't you misunderstand?"

Gongyi Xiao was stunned for a short while. Then he said, "Though I don't know what exactly happened in Jue Di Gorge, I wholeheartedly believe that Senior isn't the sort of person who would harm his own disciple."

As he said this, Gongyi Xiao was thinking back on their meeting in Bai Lu Forest. Specifically, he was remembering the things Shen Qingqiu had accidentally let slip and the way he'd affectionately gazed upon that monster.

Meanwhile, Shen Qingqiu was thinking, *It makes sense. Since we're both cannon fodder fated to fall to the male lead's indestructible body, we're able to understand and sympathize with each other's situations more than anyone else.*

Therefore, both parties were moved.

While they were busy being pleased within their own minds, the group from Huan Hua Palace caught up with them. Shen Qingqiu accidentally glanced back and saw that Luo Binghe was looking over in his direction.

In the brief incense time since his reunion with Luo Binghe, it seemed that Shen Qingqiu's heart had become quite a bit more delicate. It often felt like a small boat caught in a raging sea amidst a storm.

For example, at present, though Luo Binghe wasn't standing anywhere close to him and had maintained an appropriate smile, that pair of cold, pitch-black eyes pierced him with incredible force, making Shen Qingqiu's heart tremble in fright.

Bing-ge, what's wrong now? Even the sight of cannon fodder talking and huddling together for warmth offends you?

Upon arriving at the entrance of Jin Zi Weapons Shop, Shen Qingqiu heard someone inside who was arguing loud enough to shake the roof. This was all thanks to Liu Qingge.

Liu Qingge was responsible for the hard labor, and after they'd separated, he'd gone to capture experimental subjects for Mu Qingfang. With the people in the city so on edge, no one was willing to cooperate. However, at this point they didn't have the luxury to be concerned with consent, so they had resorted to martial power to solve the problem.

On top of that, Liu Qingge had never been the sort of patient person who preferred reason over force. His approach was highly consistent with Bai Zhan Peak's customs: he simply went out and grabbed whoever he saw. In one pass, he had collected more than ten burly macho men, then tied them up by the forge, which had by now become Mu Qingfang's research lab and experimental station. This group of big, strong men were shouting, cursing, crying, and wailing so terribly that no women could have overcome their performance.

Once Shen Qingqiu arrived in the cellar, he explained the unexpected events he had just experienced to his companions. However, for the time being, he didn't bring up that he himself had been infected.

Master Wu Chen once again chanted Amitabha. "Thanks to our fellow cultivators from Cang Qiong Mountain, we've finally made progress on this matter."

"I'm afraid it's not that straightforward," said Shen Qingqiu. "The infected cannot infect each other, and according to Qing Jing Peak's ancient texts, the largest recorded number of people a single sower has infected in one go is only around three hundred. If a population as large as an entire city has been infected, there absolutely has to be more than the one culprit."

Liu Qingge placed his hand on his sword's hilt and stood. Shen Qingqiu knew he was the type to act first and think later, to up and leave without another word. He indubitably wanted to set out and find other sowers this instant.

"Slow down!" Shen Qingqiu said hurriedly. "I still have something else to say."

"Go ahead, Shixiong," said Mu Qingfang.

Shen Qingqiu didn't know how to start, and he hesitated for a moment before saying, "Luo Binghe is back."

There was little reaction. In the first place, of the three, Master Wu Chen was from Zhao Hua Monastery and didn't know this "Luo Binghe." Meanwhile, Mu Qingfang rarely cared about things other than medicine. Thus, it was only Liu Qingge who frowned.

"That disciple of yours?" he asked, stunned. "Didn't he die at the hands of demons during the Immortal Alliance Conference?"

Shen Qingqiu found it was getting harder to explain. "He didn't... die. He came back alive. It's a long story." He stepped forward. "Let's patrol the city first. I'll explain this in detail when we get back."

"All right," said Mu Qingfang. "The earlier we take care of the remaining sowers, the fewer horrors the people will suffer. I should also go check on those patients."

As soon as he spoke, Shen Qingqiu thought of that brightly shining set of silver surgical tools Mu Qingfang always carried with him, which included all kinds of knives and needles. When spread out, they seemed to belong to the scene of a forensic autopsy. There were also hundreds upon thousands of bottles and jars in his infinite storage, with all sorts of labels. The words and descriptions on those labels were just like the flavor and effects of the contents within: stuff that made people go green upon hearing, let alone smelling, that made their courage flee with a glance. In a moment, that group of macho men by the forging station upstairs likely really would blow their lids—and the roof with it.

Shen Qingqiu let out a dry laugh. He was about to follow Liu Qingge out of the cellar when from out of nowhere, his heartbeat suddenly seemed a hundred times louder. His movements also slowed, becoming sluggish.

Liu Qingge sensed that something was off, and immediately asked, "What's wrong?"

Shen Qingqiu didn't answer and only tried to summon a spiritual blast with his right hand. A feeble spiritual flow sputtered through it, forming not a single spark.

Fuck me. Of course I have a flare-up at such an important time. Are you kidding me?!

"Without a Cure," Mu Qingfang said quietly.

Liu Qingge pressed his fingers to Shen Qingqiu's pulse, waiting there for a moment before resolutely pushing him back down into a chair. "Sit here and wait."

Wait for what? For Luo Binghe to show up at their door?

Shen Qingqiu shot to his feet. "I'm going with you."

Liu Qingge never gave others face when speaking. "Don't be a hindrance."

Master, you're the Bai Zhan Peak Lord capable of single-handedly holding off thousands of enemies! How would letting me fly with you be a hindrance?!

"Shen-shixiong, have you taken your medication today? Was it on time?" Mu Qingfang asked.

Shen Qingqiu truly wanted to scream at the heavens: *I haven't given up on therapy!*

I clearly took my medicine on time this month! And I had Great Master Liu help circulate my meridians on time too! Exactly why *would it randomly flare up? It's basically lightning on a clear day—I'm utterly baffled!*

At this moment, the System just had to, of all things, send a sudden notification: [Protagonist satisfaction points +100.]

Get lost! What are you saying with this?! "Whenever Shen Qingqiu meets misfortune, the male lead is extra satisfied"?!

"Shen-shixiong, you must not force yourself," Mu Qingfang added. "Liu-shixiong is also doing this for your own good. Exerting yourself and rushing around during a flare-up is enormously dangerous. You stay here and rest. I'll go prepare medicine. Wait for Liu-shixiong to return, and then he'll help clear your meridians."

Shen Qingqiu stood three times, but Liu Qingge pushed him back down every single one, and Mu Qingfang's tone was that of a man lecturing an unruly child.

In the end, Shen Qingqiu could only helplessly say, "Very well. Liu-shidi, listen to me, a sower's entire body is covered with scarlet skin, and they are highly infectious. If you meet something suspicious that looks similar, don't be rash and get close. Attack from afar. Once you return, you must come to my room without delay. I have something very important to discuss with you."

The last sentence was the most critical; Shen Qingqiu deliberately enunciated the words with added emphasis.

Comradeship is priceless and fraternal love supreme. A thousand days are spent training troops for the sake of one moment. Master Liu, you absolutely must shield me!

After the Liu-Mu pair left the cellar, Wu Chen descended into intense thought. "Immortal Master Shen, don't you think it strange?" he asked. "The Demon Realm was quiet for so long, yet in recent years, there seem to be signs of a resurgence. At the last Immortal Alliance Conference, numerous rare demonic creatures reappeared in the Human Realm. And this incident in Jin Lan City is even more troubling. Sowers appearing now after they were eradicated a hundred years ago? This one worries that this...most likely isn't a good omen."

Shen Qingqiu profoundly agreed. "Master, your apprehensions are exactly why I can't be at ease. And this iteration of sowers are markedly stronger than their predecessors. None of the sowers I read about from a hundred years back were able to prevent the infected from traveling a certain distance from them, lest they undergo accelerated decay."

Moreover, Luo Binghe should have remained in the Endless Abyss for two more years, yet he's broken out early. How could this be a good fucking omen?!

After being infected, Master Wu Chen's martial aspect had been heavily damaged, and the drain on his energy was enormous. Not long into their discussion, he became tired. Shen Qingqiu helped him lie down, then did his best to quietly leave the cellar.

They had hidden Wu Chen within the cellar so he wouldn't be exposed to light or the elements. Shen Qingqiu's actual room was on the second floor of the weapon shop's inner courtyard. Liu Qingge had yet to return, and at this time, it would have been impossible for Shen Qingqiu to sleep even if he'd wanted to. He sat at a table and lost himself in his thoughts.

One moment, he'd think of the little lamb Luo Binghe, who'd always followed him around while calling "Shizun." In the next, he'd think of that black lotus Luo Binghe he'd only just met, who had left him so thoroughly drenched in unease that he wanted to rip out all his hair.

After an unknown length of time, someone knocked on the door twice, neither light nor heavy.

Shen Qingqiu hastily stood from the table. "Liu-shidi? I've been waiting for you all night. Come in, quickly!"

The room's set of double doors flew open.

Luo Binghe stood in the entrance. Behind him was unbounded darkness. His hands were tucked behind his back, his lips curved slightly upward, but his eyes seemed like icy pools a thousand meters deep.

Yet those eyes smiled as he said, "Shizun, hello."

Oh shit, he's here!

All at once, it was as if Shen Qingqiu's brains had started boiling, catching fire with a whoosh.

Fuck! *The Ring* was playing out live right before his eyes!

He grabbed his fan and, with a nimble flip, leapt out the window.

Luo Binghe had finally done away with that goosebump-raising mask he'd worn during the day and exposed his true nature—and he'd come to make his teacher pay.

Shen Qingqiu's flight was an entirely unconscious impulse. The poser habits he'd developed over so many years allowed him to persevere, so that even while fleeing, his movements were easy and graceful. He landed solidly on the ground, and with a tap of his foot, darted away like a flying bird.

Luo Binghe's clear, bright voice pierced far through the air, reaching his ears while carrying a hint of cold, drifting laughter. "During the day, Shizun was so intimate and gentle with Gongyi Xiao, and this evening you lit a lantern, waiting for Liu-shishu until late into the night. What sincere affection. Why, then, are you so distant when it comes to this disciple?"

Fuck, it feels like he's cutting the distance in half with every sentence. This speed is unscientific!

Shen Qingqiu drew in a deep breath, thinking that whatever happened, he ought to find himself some backup first. He shouted from the pit of his stomach, "Liu Qingge!"

Luo Binghe's voice drew even closer. It was no longer as tender this time around, and instead it came with a wintry laugh. "Liu-shishu is embroiled in a fight, so I'm afraid he doesn't have the leisure to come. Shizun, if you have orders, why not give them to me?"

I wouldn't dare!

Shen Qingqiu understood that Luo Binghe must have delayed Liu Qingge by some means. Aid from that quarter couldn't be counted on. He swiftly poured his entire body's spiritual energy downward, hoping to boost his speed.

But of course he just *had* to forget that he was in the middle of a Without a Cure flare-up.

By the time he remembered, it was already too late. In an instant, it was like all the blood in Shen Qingqiu's body had solidified, and his entire form felt suddenly heavy.

In the next moment, a hand flashed forward to clutch his throat and his back crashed hard into a cold, solid rock wall. The pain resonated from his flesh into his spine, his head buzzing.

Luo Binghe was already within arm's reach.

He had slammed Shen Qingqiu into the wall with one hand. The back of Shen Qingqiu's skull rang with the crash, and he swooned. It took a good while before he could refocus his gaze.

Under the streaming moonlight, Luo Binghe looked even more peerlessly beautiful, as if his silhouette had been carved from ice and jade. He pressed very close, and he spoke with slow deliberation. "After so many years of separation, we meet amidst golden wind and jade dew,[1] yet Shizun incessantly calls someone else's name. That truly saddens this disciple a little."

He says he's sad and brokenhearted, but there's a smile on his lips and bloodlust in his eyes. Any way you look at it, he's lying through his teeth!

Shen Qingqiu felt as if his neck were caught in an iron shackle. His throat bobbed with difficulty, and it was hard to breathe, let alone speak. He could still manage to form a sword seal with his fingers, but his spiritual energy circulation was sluggish, so it was pointless anyhow. No matter how perfect a seal he formed, he couldn't move Xiu Ya.

And Luo Binghe was pressing harder and harder, his hand gradually tightening.

Suddenly, there was a flash before Shen Qingqiu's eyes and a giant dialogue box popped up.

This dialogue box was entirely different from the one before. Before, they'd uniformly looked like Windows XP error windows, but now it was subdued, lavish, and sophisticated... Wait, the main point was the content!

[Accept a System tip to resolve the small complication our valued customer is facing?]

You call this a "small complication"?!

Shen Qingqiu mentally shouted himself hoarse, "All right! Is there still an easy mode?! Easy mode please!"

---

1   金风玉露一相逢. From the poem "鹊桥仙," translated as Immortals at the Magpie Bridge, which describes the annual meeting between the Cowherd and the Weaver Girl during Qixi, also known as Chinese Valentine's Day.

[Access privileges activated. Use key item to maintain state of living?]

Shen Qingqiu's vision was about to go dark from suffocation. "There's a key item?! How many B-Points to buy it? Tell me!"

[Item is already in your inventory. Use item "Fake Jade Guanyin" to consume one hundred of Luo Binghe's anger points?]

Oh shit—the only thing Luo Binghe's adoptive mother left to him, the fake jade Guanyin!

Right after arriving in this world, he'd acquired this life-saving item, a high-tier piece of equipment. How did he keep forgetting? He still had this Get Out of Jail Free card tucked away in his bosom.

System, you finally gave a useful reminder!

Shen Qingqiu mentally shouted, "I will, I will, I will!" His throat was about to be squeezed in two!

[Please note: This item is single-use and can consume a maximum of five thousand of Luo Binghe's anger points.]

At the final moment, Shen Qingqiu yanked on the reins. *"Stop!"*

This was Luo Binghe at only one hundred anger points?!

Are you messing with me?! If he's already this tall, dark, and deadly at a hundred anger points, I don't even dare imagine what a vision he'd be at five thousand!

But the point was that if Shen Qingqiu was going to use an item that could potentially negate five thousand points on a situation that was worth only one hundred—and thereby lose the chance to use it ever again—even if it was a matter of life and death, he needed some time to agonize and struggle!

Then again, if things went on like this, it was either death from suffocation or from a pulped throat.

Just when Shen Qingqiu made up his mind, preparing to grit his teeth and use his life-saving item, the hand around his neck suddenly loosened.

There was no way he could get away even if he tried to run, so he could only continue his poser act, pretending to be chill about it. Shen Qingqiu propped himself up on the wall, barely managing to stand upright and not sink to his knees on the spot.

Seconds ago, Luo Binghe had almost choked him to death, and now he was coming over all smiles to help him up, just like in the past, when he had helped Shen Qingqiu alight from carriages or brought him snacks. Shen Qingqiu actually forgot to struggle. All he could feel was that this schizophrenic behavior was making his hair stand on end.

Luo Binghe sighed. "Why did Shizun run so fast? This disciple almost couldn't catch up."

Bullshit. As if Luo Binghe hadn't just spent ages chasing him down in a game of cat and mouse as if it were nothing. He wasn't even short of breath!

Shen Qingqiu panted, then gingerly opened his mouth, his voice a bit hoarse. "You have quite some nerve, returning in such a grandiose fashion. Aren't you afraid someone will discover your true identity?"

Luo Binghe's eyes flashed. "Is Shizun concerned or worried?"

Shen Qingqiu thought this an interesting reply. In these circumstances, was there any difference between "concerned" and "worried"?

He couldn't resist asking, "Unless you think I won't tell anyone?"

Luo Binghe looked at him, then said pityingly, "Shizun, that would require someone to believe you."

Shen Qingqiu's heart thumped.

So this meant that just like in the original work, Luo Binghe was planning to first utterly destroy Shen Qingqiu's reputation, then painstakingly, step by step, force him down the road to ruin, methodically toying with him until he died?

The original Shen Qingqiu had two major scummy qualities:

1) Attempting to get a taste of countless young ladies and married women alike.

2) Murdering tons of his comrades, as well as other people.

But now when Shen Qingqiu considered himself, after he'd taken this shell, he conclusively hadn't inherited these interests and ambitions from the original. Could Luo Binghe still destroy his prestigious reputation and place in society?

[Friendly reminder: Of course.]

"Shut up, okay?" Shen Qingqiu muttered in his head. "You don't need to remind me of reality, thanks."

[You're welcome. No B-Points will be deducted for this explanation.]

Shen Qingqiu directly x-ed out of the dialogue box that had popped up.

He rubbed his throat and stood for a while, then realized that Luo Binghe was actually still staring at him, seemingly with no intention of attacking again.

Still looking? He can't possibly be trying to make up for lost time after our years of separation, can he?

[Protagonist satisfaction points +50.]

"Haven't you been upgraded?" Shen Qingqiu snapped at the System. "Why are you omitting the reason for the point increase? Don't you dare accuse me of farming points later. I didn't even do anything! Where are these points coming from? Also, could you stop appearing for like a second?"

After a while, Shen Qingqiu asked out loud, "What are you planning to do with your return?"

Luo Binghe replied, "I was merely reminiscing about how Shizun had treated me well, and I wanted to return to see you."

Shen Qingqiu automatically comprehended this as a declaration that Luo Binghe had come back to settle old debts.

In this round of question and answer with Luo Binghe, they had actually managed to be something like congenial, so Shen Qingqiu tentatively grew braver. Without changing his expression, he moved his hand to his sword hilt. "Just to kill me? Then what about the plague in Jin Lan City? Has every resident of this city 'treated you well'?"

Who could have expected that as soon as those words came out of his mouth, they would touch some sore spot inside of Luo Binghe. It was like a cold star had fallen within his eyes, and the faint hint of a smile on his face disappeared without a trace.

"Shizun harbors a truly relentless hatred toward the demon race," Luo Binghe said mockingly. There was a hint of forcibly suppressed anger in his voice.

No, I don't, actually.

Luo Binghe clenched his teeth. "No, I should say, a relentless hatred toward *me*."

See, you do understand—wait, what, what, what? Shen Qingqiu was speechless—he'd never said that!

Luo Binghe took a sudden step toward him. Shen Qingqiu's expression quickly became cautious, and he retreated a step. But behind his back was a wall, and so there was nowhere to go.

Their gazes collided in midair. Then Luo Binghe seemed to realize that he was too worked up, and he closed his eyes, only opening them again after a few moments had passed.

"Does Shizun honestly think that I would kill, burn, massacre cities, and inevitably topple countries just because of that half of my lineage?"

Shen Qingqiu could only keep his silence.

If only he had a physical copy of *Proud Immortal Demon Way* in his hand, he would have slapped it onto Luo Binghe's face.

If you have a smoking gun, then use it! The latter part of that twenty-million-word epic was chock full of the ammunition he wanted. With all the things Luo Binghe had done, the phrases "kill, burn, massacre cities, and topple countries," and "not a dog or fowl was spared" were barely even exaggerations for dramatic effect...

When Shen Qingqiu looked down without a single word, Luo Binghe took it as tacit agreement. He sneered. "Then why did you tell me not to put too much weight on race and that no one is intolerable to the heavens? Why say such pompous things?"

His face abruptly grew dark, malice overflowing from between his brows, and he lashed out. "Utter hypocrisy!" he snarled.

Shen Qingqiu had been prepared for this. At this moment, he rapidly retreated, only just managing to dodge. When he turned his head, he saw that the wall he'd just been leaning against had been pulverized.

Though he'd long known that after he crawled back out of a place as brutal as the Endless Abyss, Luo Binghe's temperament would change, he'd never thought it would actually be such an extreme one-eighty. Moody didn't even begin to describe him.

Having known this would come about in the novel ahead of time was one thing, but seeing a once-familiar person change like this was another entirely. It hit Shen Qingqiu especially hard because this outcome was basically his single-handed creation.

It seemed like Luo Binghe hadn't really intended to hit him. After venting his anger with this attack, he calmed down a bit, tilted his head, and reached out, seemingly to grab hold of Shen Qingqiu—so Shen Qingqiu hastily drew Xiu Ya.

It'd been a long time since he'd drawn his sword by hand. Usually, he summoned it with a sword seal. But now that he had no spiritual energy, he could only wield the blade manually. There was nothing to be done; he couldn't just offer himself up for capture. At least in this moment, he absolutely couldn't just sit still and await death.

He'd made a truly gargantuan blunder. He'd thought Luo Binghe would train for the full five years before he crawled out of the Endless Abyss. Who could have guessed that he would activate his cheats to even greater potential and speed up the process by half?

And by Shen Qingqiu's calculation, the Sun-Moon Dew Mushroom he'd been growing as his life-saving trump card wasn't yet at the point where he could use it.

Watching Shen Qingqiu, Luo Binghe slowly raised a hand, letting him see the violet-black demonic energy roiling in his palm. "Shizun," he said leisurely. "Take a guess. If I grab Xiu Ya, how many strikes will it take before it's corroded all the way through?"

No need to guess—I'll bet fifty cents on one strike at most! Shen Qingqiu felt even more miserable.

Luo Binghe took another step closer, and Shen Qingqiu could only raise his sword to take the attack.

He had mentally prepared for Xiu Ya's destruction, but in a blink, as if Luo Binghe had seen something, he started. Then he suddenly withdrew the demonic energy in his palm and caught the tip of the sword with his bare hand.

Shen Qingqiu hadn't thought he would actually cut Luo Binghe. That made this the second time!

In his moment of shock, Luo Binghe chopped down on his wrist. Shen Qingqiu's hand loosened in pain, and his sword fell, whereupon it was sent flying with a flick of Luo Binghe's finger.

Luo Binghe clamped down on Shen Qingqiu's wrist with a single hand, and fresh blood flowed from Luo Binghe's palm, soaking Shen Qingqiu's sleeve. The blood kept flowing and flowing, and Shen Qingqiu started to panic, worried for no reason.

While Shen Qingqiu was still in the midst of confusion, Luo Binghe flipped his hand over. "You were infected?"

Some small red patches were scattered across the back of Shen Qingqiu's hand, a few more than there had been during the day.

Luo Binghe's slender fingers flitted across his hand in a barely-there touch, and the red patches disappeared under his fingertips like ink dropped in water. As expected, a little thing like this was no threat to Luo Binghe.

Luo Binghe seemed to have moderated his expression. "This hand of Shizun's is plagued with misfortunes."

It turned out they had thought the same thing. As Shen Qingqiu took in his spotless hand, he found himself even less able to understand the course of Luo Binghe's thoughts. Given what had made him pause, perhaps this hand had reminded him of the good old days? If Shen Qingqiu thought about it, this same limb had blocked the poisoned armor spikes way back when. Perhaps it had rekindled some old affections?

Just as he wondered this, a fist suddenly slammed into his stomach.

Luo Binghe smiled. "An eye for an eye. Since Shizun sowed the seeds, he should reap the bitter fruit himself. Shizun should personally make up for the wounds he gave me."

Shen Qingqiu assumed that Luo Binghe was venting his anger for the emotional trauma inflicted on him three years ago by injuring his old master in a relatively comparable way. But then there was a sharp pain on his scalp, and his neck was forced to straighten so that Luo Binghe could press his hand to Shen Qingqiu's lips. The taste of blood flooded into his mouth.

Shen Qingqiu's eyes shot wide open as he finally realized that the "wound" Luo Binghe was talking about was the one he had only just left on his hand with Xiu Ya.

Motherfucker—don't drink it, don't drink it, I absolutely can't drink this!

Shen Qingqiu furiously slapped away that hand and bent over to retch up the mouthfuls of blood he had swallowed, but Luo Binghe dragged him back up and continued to pour blood into his mouth.

Luo Binghe further opened the wound on his hand. Hot blood flowed endlessly from it, yet he seemed even happier. "Shizun, don't spit it out. Even though a heavenly demon's blood is dirty, you won't necessarily die from drinking it, right?"

He wouldn't die, but he would live a fate worse than death!

Shen Qingqiu didn't know how he made it back to the Jin Zi Weapons Shop. Even after climbing the stairs and entering his room, he was still in a daze, and he fell straight onto the bed. He could only feel his brain, stomach, and blood churning and seething; *things*

were crawling about back and forth inside them. He restlessly tossed and turned the entire night.

In the distant past, heavenly demons had been able to control their blood after it left their body, and this ability had been inherited by all members of their bloodline. If someone drank their blood, death was indeed not the only possible consequence. Worst of all, said the possible consequences were numerous.

In the original work, Luo Binghe had mastered control of his blood and used it for a wide range of purposes, including poison; he could even fashion it into parasitic mite-like creatures that he could then use to destroy a target from within. He'd also deployed it as a location tracker, a physical means of brainwashing, a sex tool...etc.

Soaked in cold sweat, Shen Qingqiu drifted between dream and reality, and he only fell into a deep sleep at daybreak. He hadn't slept for long when a wave of earthshaking cheers jolted him awake, and he staggered out of bed. As he'd gone to bed fully clothed, he didn't need to dress. Just as he was about to open the door, it flung open itself, and in burst a lively, bouncing youth.

"The gates are open! The gates are open!" Yang Yixuan said, agitated.

"What?"

"Those red monsters were all captured, so the gates were opened! Jin Lan City finally managed to pull through!" Yang Yixuan shouted. Then, at the thought of his father's death, his eyes filled with tears.

Shen Qingqiu's entire body felt awful, and his head hurt like it had been split open, but he still wanted to comfort the youth. Even as he did, he thought: *That was so fast. They were all captured in one night?*

As the gates were opened, the cultivators from various sects who had been observing from several kilometers away all poured into the city, and they gathered in a large open plaza. Mu Qingfang was also there, distributing the medicinal pills he'd prepared. Jin Lan City, which had been wholly lifeless only a few days ago, was now overflowing with joy. Altogether, seven sowers had been captured alive, and all of them were quarantined inside a Zhao Hua Monastery barrier.

Shen Qingqiu saw Liu Qingge looking pensive. He went up and patted his shoulder. "What happened last night?"

Liu Qingge threw him a look, then replied with a question. "What's up with your disciple?"

"What did he do?"

"Last night, he caught five, and I caught two," Liu Qingge said slowly. He stared at Shen Qingqiu. "Exactly what happened during the years Luo Binghe was missing?"

Luo Binghe hadn't just stolen kills from directly beneath the master of Bai Zhan Peak's nose, he'd actually beaten his kill count. This was a devastating blow to the worldview of any heir to Bai Zhan Peak. It was practically a great shame and humiliation!

And aren't these numbers official confirmation that when it comes to power levels, currently the Luo Binghe to Liu Qingge ratio is 5:2...

Suddenly, the nearby disciples tempered their outcry and moved to clear space, making a path. From not far off, the leaders of several sects walked steadily toward them. Yue Qingyuan and Huan Hua Palace's Old Palace Master arrived side by side, followed closely by the leaders of Tian Yi Temple and Zhao Hua Monastery.

Luo Binghe stood right next to the Old Palace Master.

Illuminated by the first rays of the early morning sun, Luo Binghe looked invigorated, glowing with life. When Shen Qingqiu compared himself to his old student, he became instantly depressed.

Even Yue Qingyuan had something to say about it. When he passed Shen Qingqiu, he looked at him for a while and said, worried, "Your complexion is far too poor. As expected, I shouldn't have let you come."

Shen Qingqiu gave him a hollow smile. "It's only because Mushidi's patients were wailing and howling all night. I couldn't sleep much."

Mu Qingfang had finished distributing the medicine. On returning, he also looked at Shen Qingqiu with surprise. "Shixiong, even with all the noise we made, it shouldn't have left you in such a dreadful state after a single night. Have you taken the medication I left in your room?"

"I took it, I took it," Shen Qingqiu said in a rush. *Please don't ask me if I've "taken my meds today" ever again!*

Then a clamor surged from the other side of the crowd. Shen Qingqiu turned to look and promptly wanted to drop his forehead into his hands. A middle-aged man in mourning clothes stood at the head of a large group of men and women, and he insisted on kneeling before Luo Binghe. This was Jin Lan City's governor.

The governor was beside himself with emotion. "Our small town was saved through the sacrifice of many cultivators. This kindness can never be repaid. If in the future you have orders for us, we will fulfill them no matter the cost!"

The corners of Shen Qingqiu's mouth twitched. What a standard plot development. With the monsters cleared out, it was time to collect followers and reap rewards. And at this sort of time, it was always the protagonist alone who stole the spotlight. Anyone else who'd contributed to the effort would be treated as part of the scenery. Even if Shen Qingqiu excluded himself, Liu Qingge had caught two sowers, and moments ago Mu Qingfang had been right there, distributing medicine.

Luo Binghe's response was also bog standard. "Please rise, Governor," he said humbly. "Jin Lan City made it safely through this calamity due to the efforts of many sects working together to support each other. It would be difficult for a single person's efforts to accomplish such."

His words and manner were sincere and appropriate; he didn't diminish his own glory, but with this, the other sects were placated.

The governor was once more bursting with praise. "Last night, I saw this young master single-handedly subduing those wicked things with my own eyes. Such outstanding cultivation. As expected, a hero's nature is evident even in youth, and famed masters raise outstanding disciples! Palace Master, your sect's succession is in good hands."

Upon hearing the words "famed masters raise outstanding disciples," Luo Binghe's smile deepened, and his gaze, intentionally or not, flitted over to land briefly on Shen Qingqiu's face, like a dragonfly touching water. Shen Qingqiu spread his fan to avoid it.

During the praise, the Old Palace Master's gaze toward Luo Binghe was filled with parental affection. Others might not have been able to tell, but Shen Qingqiu was keenly aware that this was the gaze of one looking at a successor-slash-son-in-law of whom one was proud.

Those seven sowers who had been trapped together squawked and shouted, agitating the people.

"How should these vile things be dealt with?" someone asked.

"Shidi, any thoughts?" asked Yue Qingyuan.

Shen Qingqiu muttered, "Qingqiu has seen related records in old texts that sowers fear high temperatures. It appears that only by burning them in a raging fire can we remove their body's infectious ability to bring decay."

This was eminently easy to understand. Sterilization required high temperatures.

Yet one cultivator protested in shock. "How...how could we resort to such a method? If we do this, will we not be as barbaric and cruel as the demon race?"

All too soon, his voice was drowned out by the enraged shouts of Jin Lan City's surviving citizens.

During the days the plague had raged unchecked, the city had lost countless innocent lives, the victim's bodies festering in death in ways too horrible for words. A perfectly fine and flourishing merchant city had been reduced to the horrific sight it was today. At this time, anyone expressing sympathy or advocating for humane treatment of the sowers risked becoming the enemy of the entire population. The handful of cultivators who did so soon found themselves surrounded by roars of "Burn them!" and "Burn anyone who objects alongside!"

Of the seven sowers within the barrier, most of them bared their teeth, cackling with boisterous laughter and showing no signs of remorse. Shen Qingqiu supposed they probably even thought themselves heroes who'd created a bumper crop for their own race. Only a single sower, the most petite of the group, wept miserably.

At the sight of this misery, sympathy swelled in some few hearts.

Qin Wanyue bit her lip, then approached Luo Binghe. "Luo-shixiong, that frail little sower looks so pitiful."

"They look so pitiful" she said. But however pitiable the sower looked, were they as woebegone as those who'd been infected by the plague for no reason, whose bodies had rotted until they died?

Luo Binghe smiled at her but did not answer.

In Shen Qingqiu's eyes, in terms of reactions to girls, this was far too perfunctory. It probably didn't deserve a passing grade. If he thought back on the original work at this juncture, shouldn't Luo Binghe have taken the chance to express his agreement with tender and sympathetic words? How come Luo Binghe's training speed had increased while his girl-wooing skills had decreased?

But what could be done about it when Luo Binghe had a face that, regardless of angle or expression, was always as silky as jade, assured and elegant? Qin Wanyue was momentarily dazzled, and she flung the words she had just said to the back of her mind, content to continue watching from the sidelines.

At this moment, something entirely unexpected occurred.

That petite sower threw itself forward, slamming into the side of the barrier with a thump. Its scarlet face appeared even more sinister due to its wailing and bawling, and it shouted, "Immortal Master Shen, you must not let them burn me to death. I'm begging you, Immortal Master Shen, please save me!"

Shen Qingqiu felt like some string in his brain had suddenly snapped.

Who the fuck are you?! What's with randomly throwing yourself around and calling for Immortal Master Shen? I really don't know you, okay?!

From all across the plaza, thousands of eyes summarily landed on Shen Qingqiu.

"We were only following your orders," the sower continued to wail. "You never said that we'd be burned!"

...WTF!

What a ridiculous development! And on top of that, it was such a basic, crude accusation. Shen Qingqiu felt like he was drunk.

But the Old Palace Master's response made him feel even more inebriated. "Shouldn't Immortal Master Shen provide an explanation for this exclamation?"

Such a low-level trick, yet someone had still believed it!

"Yes!" someone echoed a second after. "An explanation must be provided."

And it wasn't only one person!

The Twelve Peaks rallied together against outsiders. As soon as these words were spoken, quite a few of Cang Qiong Mountain Sect's cultivators revealed expressions of displeasure. Yue Qingyuan was even more direct: his face became stony.

"Anyone with eyes should be able to tell that this thing is unhappy about its impending death," Qi Qingqi said scornfully. "It wants someone to share its fate, so it's obviously framing him. All demonic evildoers are the same. Yet some people are still taking the bait—how utterly laughable!"

"Then why has it made no other claims and instead focused only on Immortal Master Shen?" the Old Palace Master asked lightly. "This point is worth considering as well."

Shen Qingqiu was wholly defeated by this logic. According to that line of thinking, any time someone was singled out and accused of something, the question of their innocence was "worth considering." The bar for framing someone was way too low.

Luo Binghe spoke not a single word, though he stared over with rapt attention. Perhaps it was only Shen Qingqiu's imagination, but he kept feeling like those pitch-black, star-like eyes were full of smiles.

In the original work, Shen Qingqiu became unpardonably loathed due to the slaughter of his own sect sibling: he personally murdered Liu Qingge. But in the present, Liu Qingge was standing right next to Shen Qingqiu. If someone tried to beat him up, Liu Qingge might even protect him. So obviously he couldn't be charged with that crime!

Could it be that, no longer stained all over by crimes he hadn't committed, he'd be slandered to the point that it made up the change?

Given Luo Binghe's character post-darkening...that wasn't impossible.

A Huan Hua Palace disciple suddenly stepped forward, his face decorated with a few pockmarks. This was the disciple who'd ridiculed Shen Qingqiu in the abandoned building the day before. He bowed before he spoke. "Palace Master, this disciple has just discovered something and isn't sure if it's appropriate to say."

"If you have something to say, then speak," Shen Qingqiu said expressionlessly. "You've already opened your mouth, so why even say that you're unsure if it's 'appropriate' to do so? How insincere." Wasn't this disciple slapping his own face?

Said disciple likely hadn't thought a senior would scold him. His face flared between red and white, until even the pockmarks changed color. But he didn't dare snap back and only glared viciously at Shen Qingqiu. "Yesterday, this disciple and several sect siblings all realized that there were a few infected red patches on Senior Shen's arm. We saw them very plainly, but if you look today, those red patches have all disappeared!

"Cang Qiong Mountain Sect's Senior Mu said himself that the pills he provided the city were created on the spot and that they need twenty-four hours to take effect. It's even possible that they *won't* be effective. Luo-shixiong took the cure right in front of us, and the red patches on his hand have yet to fade. So why has only Senior Shen recovered so soon? His red patches have fully disappeared. Whatever the reason, this disciple thinks that highly suspicious!"

Shen Qingqiu sighed internally. He should've known that Luo Binghe wouldn't remove the seeds of decay out of kindness.

"My shidi oversees Qing Jing Peak," Yue Qingyuan said steadily. "As a peak lord, he has always been a model member of the sect. His moral character is noble and unsullied; this the entire sect both knows and understands. For everyone to believe such baseless claims so easily—you're far too susceptible to provocation."

Shen Qingqiu's face was going to turn red.

Shixiong, don't do this—are you for real? If you're speaking against your conscience just to protect me, I'll feel really awful! Whether it's the original flavor or the current one, I bet neither of us can even touch the edges of "noble and unsullied moral character." Well, no, the original flavor could definitely touch the last word.[2]

"Is that so?" asked the Old Palace Master. "That differs from what I've heard."

Shen Qingqiu's heart sank. It seemed like this was the day that he would be thoroughly dragged through the mud. He still narrowed his eyes. "Since when did hearsay from other sects become the basis for conclusions on the moral character of the heir of our Cang Qiong Mountain's Qing Jing Peak?"

"If it were only hearsay, of course we would not trust it so easily. But this information came from one of your esteemed sect's very own members." The Old Palace Master looked all around him before he continued. "Everyone must know that it is common for

---

2   In the original text, "noble and unsullied moral character" is 品性高洁, but 性 when taken out of context can also mean "sex." Therefore Shen Qingqiu jokes that the original flavor might not match the entire phrase, but with his various scandals he definitely matches that word alone.

each sect's disciples to form friendships with one another, so hearing some rumors and gossip is inevitable. However, the matter of Peak Lord Shen deliberately abusing and doing grievous harm to the disciples under his care? This alone ought to render him unworthy of the phrase 'noble and unsullied moral character.'"

Shen Qingqiu's head was going to swell.

Grievous harm to the disciples under his care? This one was true. During Luo Binghe's early developmental period, Shen Qingqiu had mistreated him in every imaginable way—his glorious deeds using the protagonist as child labor could have filled a tragic novel of great suffering all on their own. The number of other disciples Shen Qingqiu had harassed or even driven out because of their talent also numbered high enough to rival a gymnastics team. It was just—the one who'd grievously harmed them wasn't *him*, it was the original flavor!

"Since you are aware they are only rumors and gossip, you must be aware that they do not merit discussion," Yue Qingyuan said solemnly. "It's true that my shidi doesn't typically like to pamper his disciples, but to accuse him of grievous harm is too much."

A soft, sweet voice broke in. Qin Wanyue had reached her limit; she had to speak up for her beloved. "Then may this woman ask Sect Leader Yue: Would ordering a youth in his teens to face a demonic elder with hundreds of years of training, one who wore armor covered in poisoned spikes into battle, not count as persecution and grievous harm?"

This time, Shen Qingqiu couldn't just chill prettily on the sidelines and listen. "Whether it counts or not, I do not know," he said in an even tone. "But what I do know is that an instance where a shizun intercepts a suit of poisoned armor, pushes aside his disciple,

and shields him with his own body probably can't count as persecution. What do you think, Luo Binghe?"

Of all the cultivators present, some looked astonished to hear
this name, and many of those were from Cang Qiong Mountain
Sect. Some had merely been suspicious when they'd seen that face,
such as Qi Qingqi, who was now stunned in shock.

As for a certain member of the logistics team, who'd nearly fallen
to his knees on the spot upon entering Jin Lan City and coming face-
to-face with Luo Binghe, after his heart had undergone a torrential
bout of rain and wind, he'd since become calm and composed.

Because Shen Qingqiu had often punished Luo Binghe in the
past, Yue Qingyuan had also seen him a few times, but that had
been while Luo Binghe was still young. Afterward, Shen Qingqiu
had elevated Luo Binghe and often sent him away from Qing Jing
Peak to handle all sorts of tasks, which had made it harder to actually
meet him. At the Immortal Alliance Conference, although he'd seen
Luo Binghe's face in the crystal mirror, it had only been for a brief
moment, and the mirrors hadn't been especially clear.

So, Yue Qingyuan actually hadn't recognized the shining,
handsome young man at the Huan Hua Palace Master's side as
Shen Qingqiu's own "beloved disciple." Before this moment, Yue
Qingyuan had heard that the Palace Master's most highly regarded
disciple was also his most senior, so he'd mistaken Luo Binghe for
Gongyi Xiao. Thus, at the moment when Shen Qingqiu pointed out
the truth, he too was stunned.

From amid the crowd, Luo Binghe stared at Shen Qingqiu with
an unwavering gaze. Shen Qingqiu tilted his head and snapped open
his fan. He actually had a mind to smile back, though it might have
only looked like a taunting curl of his lips.

It would have been nonsense to say he wasn't a bit mad. Shen Qingqiu admittedly often worried about his own life, and he had a lot of opinions about Luo Binghe, but that time he'd blocked a blow for Luo Binghe had been pure instinct. Although, Luo Binghe probably wouldn't have needed anyone's help to escape danger. So really, from every angle you could think of, Shen Qingqiu was the one who'd been most screwed over by those three matches—and here they were actually trying to use them to smear his reputation! He was furious.

Luo Binghe said slowly, "The kindness Shizun showed by protecting me with his own body...I will never dare to forget it."

"It's really you? Shen Qingqiu, didn't you say he died?" Qi Qingqi said in disbelief. She looked at Luo Binghe again. "Since you're alive, why didn't you return to Qing Jing Peak? Don't you know that because of you, your shizun was out of—"

Shen Qingqiu hastily burst into a fit of dry coughs so violent that Qi Qingqi had to stop and stare at him.

Shen Qingqiu had a profound desire to bow and beg before her. He had a premonition that the next words he had been about to hear would undoubtedly have been "out of his mind with grief." Fucking hell, he never wanted to hear those words again!

A wave of goosebumps hit him. If Luo Binghe heard those words, he'd laugh hard enough to crack that Platonic ideal of a male lead's face!

"This is exactly what's so inexplicable," the Old Palace Master persisted. "He plainly did not die, so why did you insist that he did? And why was he not willing to return when he apparently had the option to do so?"

Shen Qingqiu was sick of this bad faith tone. "If he wasn't willing to return, there's nothing I could do. He may come and go freely as he pleases; it's all up to him. If the Palace Master wishes to say something, please say it outright."

The Old Palace Master smiled. "Peak Lord Shen knows what I wish to say, and anyone here with a clear mind must also understand by now. It's true that these demonic sowers should be annihilated by fire, but if there was someone directing them from behind the scenes, exacerbating the situation, we certainly cannot let them get away with it. They absolutely must explain themselves to the whole of Jin Lan City."

With these words, he successfully stoked the flames of hatred within the Jin Lan City survivors. Having just suffered a great calamity, they were already terrified and bitter, itching for a target at whom to direct their rage. Quite a few people began to raise their voices in a clamor.

"Shizun loathes evil," said Luo Binghe. "When it comes to demons, he only hates being denied the satisfaction of killing them personally. How, then, could he collude with them?"

This appeared to be him speaking up for Shen Qingqiu. However, he was the only one present who understood the true meaning behind the words "when it comes to demons, he only hates being denied the satisfaction of killing them personally."

Having nothing to lose, Shen Qingqiu cut straight to the point. "Luo Binghe, right now, are you a disciple of Qing Jing Peak or a member of Huan Hua Palace?"

The Old Palace Master sneered. "After all this, Peak Lord Shen is once again willing to recognize this disciple?"

"I never expelled him from my tutelage," said Shen Qingqiu. "Since he is still willing to call me 'Shizun,' he must surely be willing to acknowledge me as such."

He said these words purely with the intention of aggravating Luo Binghe, but it seemed he didn't succeed. Luo Binghe's gaze flickered, and perhaps it was an illusion, but it seemed as if his eyes had somewhat cleared.

Within moments, the crowd had split into two defined camps. Sparks flew through the air, charged with the hostility of an imminent battle. As for the sowers who had instigated this conflict, they were now forgotten on the side. No longer did anyone care about how they were dealt with.

Then there came a woman's sweetly charming voice. "Shen Jiu... Are you Shen Jiu?"

Upon hearing this name, Shen Qingqiu's serene and placid countenance nearly fissured into the Great Rift Valley.

Fuck! Are the heavens determined to finish me today?! I'm done for. It's that woman. It's Qiu Haitang!

In the original work, Qiu Haitang's appearance meant only one thing, and that was Shen Qingqiu's complete and utter fall from grace.

Though Qiu Haitang was no longer a girl in her prime, her face was still as fair as a magnolia flower, her makeup vibrant and beautiful. Along with her slender figure and full bosom, her looks were verily striking. And since her looks were striking, she naturally couldn't escape the fate of becoming a member of Luo Binghe's harem.

The problem was that she'd once had an affair with Shen Qingqiu.

Congratulations! Having had a dubious relationship with *two* of a stallion novel male lead's wives, the original flavor Shen Qingqiu could be considered undoubtedly unparalleled! At least in all of the stallion novels Shen Yuan had ever read, there was no second to be found!

As one could well imagine, this was unequivocally the reason for that second massive flood of "Castrate Shen Qingqiu! Castrate or we unsubscribe!" comments in the reviews.

A raging barrage of "fuck, fuck, fuck, fuck" to the nth power bombarded Shen Qingqiu's mind.

Steps away, Qiu Haitang held her sword across her chest, as though if it came down to it, she was ready to kill him before slitting her own throat. "I'm asking you a question! Why do you not look at me?"

Big Sis, how could I dare look at you? You're here for my life!

An expression of touching sorrow filled Qiu Haitang's face. "So that's why. No wonder. No wonder I searched for so many years but still never found you again. I see, you'd already flown to the summit and become the aloof and lofty master of Qing Jing Peak. Ha ha, how splendid!"

Shen Qingqiu really didn't know where to look or what to say, so he just stared straight ahead, doing his best to keep his expression impassively detached.

Everyone was whispering amongst themselves.

Yue Qingyuan said in a low voice, "Qingqiu, this young lady…is indeed a former acquaintance of yours?"

Shen Qingqiu's heart flooded with tears. *Shixiong… Don't ask me anything more…*

"Former acquaintance?" Qiu Haitang continued sorrowfully. "I am not only a former acquaintance. This man, who looks so dignified, was once my childhood sweetheart…and I am his wife!"

When Luo Binghe heard this, his eyebrow began to twitch madly.

No! You're inarguably Luo Binghe's wife! Wake up!

"Eh? Is this really true?" Shang Qinghua said in surprise. "Why have I never heard Shen-shixiong mention it before?"

Shen Qingqiu curled his lips at him, giving him a fake smile: *Can you stop adding fuel to the fire?*

Who created this awful melodramatic content for the purpose of cranking up Shen Qingqiu's scum and hatefulness points, huh? Yet you have the nerve to just stand back and enjoy the show?!

And all of you over there—aren't you cultivators? Why do you love gossip so much? Go away, go away, get out, out, out!

Qiu Haitang sneered. "He's a beast in a man's clothes, a degenerate wearing a cultured mask. Of course he wouldn't mention his shameful deeds."

Master Wu Chen had interacted with the trio from Cang Qiong Mountain for some time and received Shen Qingqiu's care, so he had a favorable impression of him. Previously, when Cang Qiong Mountain Sect and Huan Hua Palace had been arguing, he had been unable to interject, but he spoke up now. "Amitabha, if this benefactor has something to say, please explain it properly and explain it completely: blind accusations do not invite confidence."

Shen Qingqiu wept to himself. *Master, I know you're doing this for me, but if she explains it completely, I'll suffer even more. What I'm truly worried about isn't having done shameful deeds, it's taking the fall for ones I didn't!*

Just like that, Qiu Haitang became the focus of everyone's attention. Face flushed red with emotion, she puffed out her chest and said loudly, "If a single word I, Qiu Haitang, say from here on out is false, may my heart be pierced by ten thousand of the demons' poisonous arrows, and may I be undeserving of a peaceful death!" She pointed straight at Shen Qingqiu, fury burning in her eyes. "This person is now Cang Qiong Mountain Sect's Peak Lord of Qing

Jing Peak, Shen Qingqiu, the widely renowned Xiu Ya Sword. But no one knows what kind of *thing* he used to be!"

Her language was rather harsh, and Qi Qingqi's shapely willow-leaf brows rose in anger. "Watch your words!"

Qiu Haitang was now some sort of Hall Master in a small, random sect, so when rebuked by a leader of a big shot organization like Cang Qiong Mountain, she unconsciously backed up a step.

But the Old Palace Master said, "Peak Lord Qi, there's no need for anger. Why not let this young lady continue? We cannot silence people's mouths."

Qiu Haitang looked at him and clenched her teeth, the hatred in her eyes overcoming the fear, and her voice once again grew loud. "When he was twelve years old, he was but a slave my family had purchased from traveling child traffickers. As the ninth child in that band, he was called Xiao-Jiu. My parents saw that the traffickers had abused him and thought him pitiful, so they brought him home, taught him how to read, and paid for his food and clothing—kept him warm, fed, and free of worries. My brother also looked after him, and they were exceptionally close. When he was fifteen and our parents passed, my older brother became the head of the house and freed him from his slave contract, and even recognized him as a foster brother. And I, because I had grown up with him, was deceived... I really thought...that we genuinely loved each other... So we were betrothed."

Shen Qingqiu stood there, forced to listen to "his own" dark history alongside thousands of people. The thousands of thoughts in his mind had transformed into tearful silence.

Tears began to well up and overflow in Qiu Haitang's eyes. "The year my brother was nineteen, a wandering cultivator came to our city. He saw that the area had an abundance of spiritual qi, so he established an altar at the city gates. Any young boy or girl under the age of eighteen could go there for a spiritual evaluation. That cultivator wanted to select someone with exceptional talent and take them as his disciple. As he knew immortal techniques, everyone in the city admired him, and Shen Jiu also went to the evaluation altar. His aptitude was good, and the cultivator settled on him, so he joyfully came running back, wanting to leave my family.

"Of course my elder brother did not agree. In his eyes, cultivating toward immortality was purely a pipe dream. Not to mention, Shen Jiu and I were already betrothed, so how could he abandon his family and leave now of all times? He and my elder brother had a great argument, and afterward, he lost all his cheer. We thought he was only temporarily depressed and that after he thought it through, he would naturally come to accept it."

Then her expression abruptly changed. "Who could have known? That very night, this man finally revealed his ugly nature. He lost his mind and killed my brother and many of our servants all at once, leaving bodies scattered all over the estate—then disappeared from the city with that cultivator the same night!

"After this calamity befell my household, as a lone weak woman, I was powerless to support it, and just like that, a large estate fell apart. I searched and searched for this nemesis of mine for many years but never found any leads. The cultivator who'd taken him as a disciple had been killed many years ago, and the dead end became even deader... Had I not come to Jin Lan City today, I fear I would have spent my entire life not knowing that this vile ingrate, who killed his benefactors with his own hands, had actually managed to climb all the way up to the position of peak lord in the number one sect under the heavens! Though he is much changed from when I knew him... that face, I could not mistake that face even if it burned to ash! I am not afraid to speak the name of the cultivator who incited him to murder either, for they are a murderer of countless innocents, whose name has been on the wanted list for years: Wu Yanzi!"

This Wu Yanzi was notorious, with innumerable misdeeds to his name. When it suddenly came forth that one of the twelve peak lords had been his disciple, everyone was horrified. But amid the sea of sighs and gasps, Shen Qingqiu found himself growing calm.

Deep down, he was actually a little skeptical. Qiu Haitang relayed a compelling tale full of ups and downs, but the experiences she described weren't free of logical holes. Shen Qingqiu didn't mean to discriminate against the original flavor, but the novel had always tried its hardest to illustrate the unlikable traits of Shen Qingqiu's personality: pigheaded, petty, tactless, uncharismatic, antisocial, and a sham. With that kind of disposition, it was hard to believe that the young Shen Qingqiu had endeared himself so totally to people entirely unrelated to him that they would treat him as family.

Unfortunately, no one else was able to catch these sorts of details.

At first, Shen Qingqiu had been afraid of this plot line, yes, but not *especially* afraid. There was no definite evidence to prove these stale old events had occurred other than Qiu Haitang's testimony, so he'd figured that as long as he doubled down and refused to confess, he could make Qiu Haitang wonder whether she had accused the wrong person. The whole affair would be no more than an indistinct smear on Shen Qingqiu's character background.

It wasn't like there was anything he could do to change what had happened. Shen Qingqiu truly had wronged Qiu Haitang. But that was the original flavor Shen Qingqiu! The new guy didn't want to carry the black pot of blame! He would have preferred to compensate her properly at a different time and place.

And anyway, he hadn't killed Liu Qingge, nor had he molested Ning Yingying. He'd done nothing at all to warrant a fall from grace like unto a hundred-floor skyscraper toppling in a single night, nothing to warrant being chased down and beaten by the masses.

But everything was different now.

The problem was that all of the indistinct smears on his reputation had massed together. First, the sower had accused him of treachery, then came the Old Palace Master to guide the case, and now Qiu Haitang had appeared to denounce him. All this could, together, serve as proof of his dishonorable character. A scum of a man who pulled a hit-and-run on his lover *plus* a traitor colluding with the demon race *plus* a disciple of a wanted fugitive—what an excellent example of making something already perfect even more so, like adding flowers to brocade.

As things that seem to be perfectly aligned by pure coincidence accumulate, people no longer take them to be coincidental.

"Sect Leader Yue, favoritism has no place when one deals with this kind of matter," said the Old Palace Master. "Otherwise, word may get out that a magnificent sect like Cang Qiong Mountain harbors such unsavory characters. How would you explain yourselves to the masses?"

Yue Qingyuan showed no reaction. "So what is the Palace Master saying?"

"As I see it, let us make temporary arrangements for Immortal Master Shen in Huan Hua Palace. A decision can be made after the matter is thoroughly investigated. How about it?"

Everyone knew what these "arrangements" actually meant.

Beneath the foundations of Huan Hua Palace's residence for short-term stays was the Water Prison. Its terrain was complicated, made even more so by Huan Hua Palace's maze array. This secret array of theirs was on an entirely different level from the ones they used to keep non-cultivators away from the palace. On top of that, the interior of the Water Prison was heavily guarded, and it boasted a complete set of torture chambers and related equipment—incomparably professional. Without exception, every single person incarcerated within that place was a cultivator guilty of terrible crimes, their hands dyed in blood, or one who'd violated the most serious taboos.

To put it simply, Huan Hua Palace's Water Prison was the public prison of the cultivation world. In addition, whenever some cultivator was under suspicion of endangering the Human Realm, they would be sent to the Water Prison to be held in custody while awaiting their trial. This joint public trial would be held by the four major sects before they delivered their final sentence.

Liu Qingge sneered. "Done talking?"

He had patiently listened to this nonsense for too long already, and his heart had been seething with anger for ages now. He grabbed Cheng Luan where it was on his back, his stance poised for a fight. Across from Cang Qiong Mountain Sect, Huan Hua Palace's disciples also drew their swords, one after another, glowering just the same.

"Liu-shidi, stand down," said Yue Qingyuan.

Though Liu Qingge was unwilling, if he absolutely had to obey someone, he would only concede to Yue Qingyuan. He forced his hand away from the hilt of his sword.

As he stepped back, Yue Qingyuan nodded. "These sorts of accusations cannot be made so lightly."

The all-black longsword at his waist abruptly sprang an inch from its sheath, revealing a blindingly snow-white blade.

In an instant, it was like an invisible net had been cast over the entire plaza. The spiritual energy within that space roiled restlessly like the tides.

The incessant hum from Yue Qingyuan's sword sounded like it was droning within the ear itself. A number of the younger disciples instinctively covered their ears, their hearts pounding relentlessly.

Xuan Su!

Everyone was floored.

The reason Yue Qingyuan had ordered Liu Qingge to step down was so he could step up to fight himself?! Unbelievable!

Reportedly, ever since the Cang Qiong Mountain Sect's Peak Lord of Qiong Ding, Yue Qingyuan, had succeeded his position, he'd only drawn his sword twice: once during his succession ceremony and once when he'd battled a descendant of the heavenly demon bloodline (incidentally, Luo Binghe's dad).

Xuan Su had only been drawn an inch, but everyone suddenly understood why. If one wished to sit at the top of Qiong Ding Hall, a calm and mild temperament assuredly wouldn't get you there on its own.

"Formations!" the Old Palace Master called.

Was this the cadence of an imminent battle? The demons hadn't even fought their way into this mess, and the humans were ready to start fighting amongst themselves.

Knowing the situation would only worsen, Shen Qingqiu promptly removed his sword and threw it in front of him. Xiu Ya stuck straight up in the ground before the Huan Hua Palace Master.

Giving up one's sword was equivalent to surrender—an agreement to comply with the verdict. The Old Palace Master snatched up the sword Shen Qingqiu had turned over and waved his sect members back to their places.

"Shidi!" Yue Qingyuan murmured quietly.

"Shixiong, there's no need to say any more," said Shen Qingqiu. "Those who are clean will remain clean no matter what. Qingqiu is willing to accept arrest."

Between the Old Palace Master's senility clamping down on the notion of his guilt and the combo attack of the sower and Qiu Haitang, being imprisoned was just the last nail in the coffin.

Anyway, this sequence of events had unfolded in the original work. Shen Qingqiu had thought he could avoid it before, but he hadn't expected things would still circle back to this set plot arc. Why force Cang Qiong Mountain and Huan Hua Palace to have a falling out as well?

Shen Qingqiu persisted, "Saying more will help no one. The truth will prove itself."

After he spoke, he didn't look to see Yue Qingyuan's expression, but swept a glance at Luo Binghe.

He saw neither joy nor anger on that face; Luo Binghe stood steadily in place, cutting a clear contrast with the cultivators swaying and covering their ears all around him.

After some time, Yue Qingyuan finally sheathed his sword. It was like that giant net was drawn away from the air.

Shen Qingqiu turned toward Yue Qingyuan and gave him a deep bow. When he thought about it, he'd made a lot of trouble for his Zhangmen-shixiong. He was honestly ashamed.

Qiu Haitang was still sobbing incessantly. Qin Wanyue walked over and tried to comfort her. "Miss Qiu, whatever the state of affairs, the three sects will give you an answer."

She said "three sects" to wholly exclude Cang Qiong Mountain, making her position clear. Qiu Haitang was moved, tears in her eyes. She looked up to thank Qin Wanyue, but upon seeing Luo Binghe standing alone to the side, she couldn't suppress the blush that suffused her cheeks.

Shen Qingqiu internally rolled his eyes. Theoretically, he was getting cucked right in front of his face. So why didn't he feel even the slightest bit unhappy?!

A group of Huan Hua Palace disciples led by Gongyi Xiao walked up to him. The lengths in their hands were all too familiar.

Hello, immortal-binding cables. Goodbye, immortal-binding cables, thought Shen Qingqiu, mentally waving as he did so.

"Senior Shen, my apologies," said Gongyi Xiao, sounding honestly sorry. "This junior will treat you with due respect. Before the truth comes to light, I will not let you suffer any slight."

Shen Qingqiu nodded, though he spoke only a couple of words in reply. "Thank you for your trouble."

What use is it if you're the only one treating me with due respect?

One look at the expressions on those Huan Hua Palace disciple faces and he knew every single one was itching to eat him alive. After all, Huan Hua Palace was the sect that had suffered the most serious casualties at the Immortal Alliance Conference. There was certainly more suffering to be had.

With his torso bound by immortal-binding cables, Shen Qingqiu felt his body grow heavy. When Without a Cure intermittently flared up, he only felt the circulation of his spiritual energy become congested—like if the connection was bad, but if you smacked the remote, you could still make do. Once the immortal-binding cables were fastened, his spiritual energy was completely obstructed, reducing him to an ordinary mortal.

"We shall set the date of the trial to one month from now, what does everyone think?" said the Old Palace Master.

"Five days," said Liu Qingge.

The longer Shen Qingqiu was imprisoned in the Water Prison, the more various tortures he would have to bear. The five days Liu Qingge demanded was the least amount of time into which the preparation procedures for the trial could be compressed.

The Old Palace Master was, of course, unwilling to compromise. "If it is so hurried, I am afraid there will be many oversights."

Zhao Hua Monastery were professional mediators. One of their masters suggested, "What about ten days?"

"Seven days," said Yue Qingyuan. "No longer."

With all the sect leaders haggling, Shen Qingqiu began to feel like he was standing in a food market. However, he had his own considerations and hurriedly cut in, "There's no need for more back and forth. Listen to the Palace Master's plans. One month."

If he could delay things further, it would be better for the growth of the Dew Mushrooms. He shot a look at Shang Qinghua out of the corner of his eye and raised his eyebrow.

Understanding his intentions, Shang Qinghua let his hands fall in front of him, subtly making a gesture of "no problem, leave it to me."

However, the success of this plan depended on if Shen Qingqiu could really last a month in a Huan Hua Palace thoroughly under Luo Binghe's control!

7
Water Prison

"**P**LEASE WEAR THIS, Senior Shen."

As soon as Shen Qingqiu lowered his head, a strip of black cloth covered his eyes.

In truth, this action was entirely superfluous. Given the hundreds of twists and secrets of Huan Hua Palace's maze array, even if Shen Qingqiu held a video camera for the entire trip and recorded everything, he probably wouldn't remember how to enter and leave.

The air in the Water Prison was damp, the ground slightly slippery. With his eyes blindfolded, his only choice was to let the escorting disciples lead him.

"Gongyi Xiao," he said.

Gongyi Xiao had been following close behind him the whole time, and he quickly answered. "Senior?"

"While waiting for the four sects' joint trial, am I allowed any contact with outsiders?"

"Only those with Huan Hua Palace's authorization pass[3] have free passage inside the Water Prison."

Therefore, it would be a bit difficult for Shang Qinghua to visit and discuss the plan to use the Dew Mushrooms. Shen Qingqiu thought for a while, then asked, "How were those sowers dealt with?"

---

3   腰牌. *This was a metal plate carved with a person's name and position. Usually worn on the waist, it was often used for authorization checks for entering restricted areas.*

Gongyi Xiao faithfully answered in full. "After they were burned, the masters from Zhao Hua Monastery took them back to perform rites for their souls."

From the side came a disgruntled voice. "Shixiong, why are you telling him so much? Now that you've entered this Water Prison, could it be you still think to leave?"

Such a familiar voice... It was once again that pock-faced disciple who seemed to have a grudge against him.

"Don't be rude!" Gongyi Xiao scolded him.

Shen Qingqiu smiled. "Currently, this one's identity is that of a prisoner. There's no need to scold him. Let him do as he wishes."

As he spoke, they arrived in the place where he was to be held in temporary custody. After the black cloth was undone, his vision became faintly brighter, and he saw that they were standing before a giant stone cave.

Below them was a dark, murky lake, while dim yellow torches were scattered unevenly on the surrounding walls. The flames reflected in the water, where they danced wildly with the ripples. From the center of the lake jutted an artificial platform of white stone. Sparkling and translucent, its color was almost like jade; it had no doubt been made out of a special material.

Gongyi Xiao took out a ring of keys and felt about an area of rock. After his hand performed some sequence, the sound of gears turning came from the lakebed, and up rose a stone path that led directly to the platform at the heart of the lake.

Gongyi Xiao said, "Senior, if you please."

That pock-faced disciple picked up an ordinary stone. "Watch!"

He threw the stone into the lake water, and it floated without sinking. After a moment, there came a sizzling noise, like meat grilling on an iron griddle. The surface crawled with bubbles, at which point the stone rapidly corroded and dissolved until it vanished completely.

"This particular prison doesn't get used often," the pock-faced disciple said gleefully. "Anyone who wants to escape or break someone out from here is dreaming! Deluded!"

Shen Qingqiu was astounded by the ferocity of this liquid. If someone took a tumble into that lake, it was likely not even their bone shards would remain.

Wasn't Huan Hua Palace a famous righteous sect? Where were they sourcing so much of this ferocious, obviously illegal liquid?!

As Shen Qingqiu walked along the stone path, he was especially careful. If he were to slip, he wouldn't have any fun at all. Once he arrived on the platform at the lake's center, Gongyi Xiao turned the key again, and the path leading to it once again sank back into the lakebed.

Shen Qingqiu sat down on the stone platform and observed his surroundings, secretly trying to determine if a sword could render all this corrosive lake water pointless. He'd just had this thought when Gongyi Xiao pulled on a mechanism next to the keyhole.

From above him there came the gurgling sound of flowing water. Shen Qingqiu raised his head just in time to see dark and murky water descend all around him, forming an airtight curtain that hemmed him in on the twenty-by-twenty-meter stone platform.

I was wrong! Forget about people, even a fly wouldn't be able to leave, okay?!

Huan Hua Palace's Water Prison's reputation was well justified. No wonder all the sects had unanimously elected it to serve as the public prison.

Shen Qingqiu knew that someone would definitely come looking for trouble, but he hadn't expected it to happen so fast.

He was woken by a basin of cold water woke splashing all over him.

Shen Qingqiu jolted up, freezing. At first he thought he'd
dozed off and fallen into the lake. He shook his head and blinked
as hard as he could. The sensation of icy lake water in his eyes was
supremely uncomfortable, and only now did he become certain
that he had been doused with ordinary liquid. The hundred and
eighteen immortal-binding cables twined around his body might
have been incredibly thin, but they firmly shackled his meridians,
binding him tightly until even his blood flow was restricted, so
his cold resistance had greatly decreased. He couldn't stop himself
from shivering a bit.

The water curtain around him had stemmed, and the adjustable
path connecting the stone platform to the outside world was now
raised.

His vision gradually cleared. Turning it upward, he first saw a pair
of dainty, exquisitely embroidered shoes, then looking up further,
the pink hem of a skirt.

In the end, he beheld a maiden dressed entirely in pink and be-
decked with jewels, with shapely brows and almond eyes, a metal
whip over her shoulder. She was staring at him.

Shen Qingqiu internally rolled his eyes.

Luo Binghe was really too good at tormenting people; these
wives of his were enough to make a person beg for mercy. It was like
he was on a horseback "flower"-viewing trip: they popped up one
after another, and each gave him more trouble than the last.

*There's no need to keep turning up! I'm not the original flavor—
I have no interest in molesting beauties, okay?!*

The maiden pointed at him with her whip. "If you're awake, don't
play dead. This palace mistress has things to ask you!"

With her seniority and her ability, irrespective of how wretched
Shen Qingqiu might be at present, she could never have the right
to interrogate him. So, Shen Qingqiu said, "This doesn't seem like
something the Little Palace Mistress should do."

The pearl on the Old Palace Master's palm and the apple of his
eye, the unruly head of Luo Binghe's harem, spoke without the least
bit of courtesy. "Enough with the blather! Since you know who I am,
then you must also know my reason for coming."

The rims of her eyes reddened, and she said through clenched
teeth, "You Demon Realm colluder. You vile, despicable traitor to
your own comrades! The heavens have eyes. Now that you've fallen
into this palace mistress's hands, I will make you pay!"

"I don't remember admitting to collusion with the Demon Realm,"
said Shen Qingqiu.

The Little Palace Mistress stamped her feet. "You think that just
because you haven't admitted to it, I can't teach you a lesson? You're
a long-famous senior, yet you were still so cruel, so ruthless to Luo-
gege. Naturally, you would be capable of doing things like colluding
with the demon race as well."

*Genetic inheritance is truly powerful. With this logical prowess,
you're undeniably the Old Palace Master's child by blood!*

Shen Qingqiu was silent for a while, then said, "Did he really say
that I was cruel and ruthless to him?"

The Little Palace Mistress's delivery was beautifully passionate.
"Luo-gege is such a good person, so of course he wouldn't *say* it.

The wounds he's suffered are all hidden within his heart, where no can touch them, where no one can see them... But do you think that just because he doesn't say it, I wouldn't be able to tell? Have I not eyes nor heart?"

...

These heartfelt feelings... Shen Qingqiu's entire body felt like it was about to burst from all the oversharing.

Is this a motherfucking poetry recitation contest?!

He really didn't know whether to pound the ground in hysterical laughter or to start crying hot tears.

I'm sorry! I know laughing at a girl who's sincerely expressing her profound love is terrifically rude! But this is really way too embarrassing! It's basically humiliation play!

Though Luo Binghe's harem was vast, it was honestly a barely functional mess with all sorts of personality types. This was the result of biting off more than you could chew, valuing quantity over quality. It was also the result of Airplane Shooting Towards the Sky's insistence on writing a stallion novel despite being a shitty otaku who'd barely ever touched a woman's hand.

Serves you right, ha ha ha ha!

"What kind of expression is that?" the Little Palace Mistress said with sudden suspicion.

Shen Qingqiu swiftly pulled himself together, checking to see if his face had just been stretched in a grin. Offending this brat wouldn't yield any good results.

As expected, the Little Palace Mistress flew into a rage. "Were you laughing at me just now?"

The Little Palace Mistress had originally been in love with her childhood sweetheart, Gongyi Xiao. But after Luo Binghe appeared, all her passions had surged toward the male lead. There was nothing to be done about it; since ancient times, in a war between a fated love and a childhood friend, the fated love's victory was never in doubt.

This kind of setup—where the target of affection changed one way or another—was actually incredibly common in stallion novels, because there were many cuckold fetishists in the world: whether it was cucking others or being cucked themselves, they derived a strange pleasure from this type of plot. The person whose affections drifted would, of course, believe that they hadn't done anything wrong because they were pursuing their true love, but eventually the guilt would weigh on their conscience. Whenever they saw someone's expression grow a little off, they would feel like that person was laughing at them.

Just so, the Little Palace Mistress's shame became anger. She swung her arm and the whip cracked forth.

That whip's momentum was immense, its crack shrill beyond compare. Shen Qingqiu's spiritual circulation was obstructed by the immortal-binding cables, but his agility had yet to deteriorate. He rolled along the floor, and the whip just happened to smash down less than a meter from his foot.

The smash sent rock shards and pulverized dust flying from the stone platform. In a half-kneel, Shen Qingqiu steadied himself.

Holy shit, what's a young maiden doing, using this kind of barbed iron whip?! It doesn't fit your image!

What fit even less was the fact that, in the original work, the Little Palace Mistress's refined iron whip had only been used for attacking love rivals. It was a tool for fighting over men and getting into b-[beep-] fights, only ever used to hit pretty women if Luo

Binghe stared at them for too long—so why was it being used to hit a man?!

Your whip is crying, can't you hear?! And I've had enough! Can you stop giving me this kind of script?!

Having missed, the Little Palace Mistress's rage grew. With a sweet-sounding cry, she pulled back her whip and retook her stance. The stone platform was only so large, and Shen Qingqiu was moreover tied up, so however fast his reflexes were, the whip's wind inevitably grazed him and ripped his clothes in several places, though it had yet to do him real harm.

After continuous dodging, he was soon backed to the edge of the stone platform. No matter where he looked, he saw nowhere to retreat, meaning he could only directly take a lash. Shen Qingqiu clenched his teeth and braced himself, shutting his eyes and waiting for the pain to strike.

But even after waiting for some time—a long time—he felt no physical pain.

He quickly opened his eyes, and his heart instantly sank.

Luo Binghe was gripping the whip's lash in his bare hand. Two masses of ghostly, pitch-black fire seemed to burn within his eyes, both cold and terrifying. "What are you doing?" he asked, enunciating each word, his voice frozen down to its core.

The Little Palace Mistress hadn't noticed him appear and started in fright. But what truly scared her was that frigid, severe expression she'd never seen before. She shivered despite herself.

Ever since they'd become acquainted, Luo Binghe had always been incredibly kind, good at coaxing and lifting moods. Never before had he turned this manner of murderous gaze upon her. The Little Palace Mistress found herself backing up several steps as she stammered, "I...I...I asked Daddy for the authorization pass so I could interrogate him for a bit..."

"The joint trial is in a month," Luo Binghe said frostily.

The Little Palace Mistress suddenly felt aggrieved. "He's hurt so many of my shixiong and shijie—so many!" she shouted. "And he was terrible to you! What's wrong with me teaching him a lesson?!"

Luo Binghe yanked her whip clean out of her hands, treating the sharp barbs like they were nothing. He didn't seem to use much strength, but when he relaxed his fingers, he revealed that the refined iron whip's segments had been reduced to a pile of metal scrap.

"Go back," Luo Binghe said impassively.

Having just watched a beloved possession be reduced to a handful of tiny fragments, the Little Palace Mistress let out an "ah" in outright disbelief.

Sobbing, she pointed at Shen Qingqiu, then at Luo Binghe. "You, you're going to treat me this way? I'm angry for your sake, yet you won't let me touch him?"

Luo Binghe gave her no answer and threw the shards of the destroyed whip into the lake. The hissing sounds as they corroded filling their ears, unending.

The Little Palace Mistress's lip trembled. In that instant, she suddenly felt that what Luo Binghe actually wanted to crush mote by mote, until he threw it into the corrosive lake...was her. And this was not remotely a joke.

Filled with sorrow and indignation, Little Palace Mistress yelled, "I was doing it for you!" Then she turned and fled in tears.

The script is wrong! Shen Qingqiu howled internally. *The fuck?! Motherfucker, something's gone wrong—*

He hadn't finished before Luo Binghe's gaze shifted to him.

Shen Qingqiu felt like his teeth, stomach, and balls were all aching from stress. At this moment, he'd have preferred to receive a hundred and eighty lashes from the Little Palace Mistress's whip. At most, it would be a surface-injury kind of ache—and it would still be better than being with Luo Binghe in an enclosed area while every bit of his body hurt!

The two of them looked at each other in silence for a long time, then Luo Binghe took a step toward him.

Shen Qingqiu unconsciously maintained a distance between them, his manner aloof.

Luo Binghe's outstretched hand halted in midair for a while, then he withdrew it. He humphed. "There's no need for Shizun to be so wary. If I wished to do something to you, I wouldn't need to touch you at all."

Hugely true. A single drop of heavenly demon blood inside one's stomach was akin to a time bomb planted within one's body, only the possibilities were unlimited. If Luo Binghe wanted, a crook of his finger could puncture Shen Qingqiu's intestines and destroy his stomach, or cause him enough pain to make him wish for death.

Shen Qingqiu sat back down in a meditative pose and lifted his eyes to meet Luo Binghe's gaze.

One month.

No matter what, he had to hold out for one month. Afterward, he'd be a bird soaring high and free.

A big whatever to all this crap! Who gives a shit?!

The two of them were silent for a while.

Shen Qingqiu deliberated for a moment before he said, "If you do wish to do something to me, there's no need to rush. If you wait until after the joint sect trial, my reputation will be ruined and I'll have no chance to turn things around. If you wait until then to settle all debts, wouldn't you have a just reason to do so, and won't it be powerfully satisfying?"

He spoke these words totally based on his understanding of the original Luo Binghe's way of thinking. Logically, it should have been an excellent argument in accordance with Luo Binghe's tastes.

Unexpectedly, not only did Luo Binghe's expression fail to clear, it became even more bitingly cold. He narrowed his eyes. "Why is Shizun so certain the joint trial will find him guilty?"

"That should be a question for you, shouldn't it?" asked Shen Qingqiu.

"For me?" Luo Binghe repeated. He laughed forbiddingly. "Again, me."

Shen Qingqiu had no words for him.

This Jin Lan City plot line was a new addition. In the original timeline, Luo Binghe would have still been leveling up underground at this moment, and he never would have appeared at all. Thus, Shen Qingqiu didn't have the advantage of an omniscient POV. But Airplane Shooting Towards the Sky had guaranteed one thing: after Luo Binghe completed his leveling process and returned to the surface, every scheme and murder had something to do with him. However you thought about it, he was more suspicious than anyone.

Luo Binghe's expression was sullen; he paced a few circles back and forth, his hands behind his back, then sharply turned around and said in a bitter tone, "I dare ask, Shizun, are you going to blame every last one of the demon race's sins, their murdering and marauding, their crimes and evil deeds, on me?"

Shen Qingqiu furrowed his brow.

His lack of answer made Luo Binghe lazily clench his fist. "Once, you clearly trusted me so much, but now you suspect me of harboring ulterior motives at every turn. Is the difference between realm and race so profound that it could so wholly change your attitude toward someone?"

Shen Qingqiu was simply unable to hold back. He gathered his courage and said, "If that's the case, I also have a question for you."

Luo Binghe tilted his head. "This disciple is listening."

"If you deny harboring ulterior motives, for what reason did you turn Huan Hua Palace to your side?"

Why wasn't the male lead following the original plot? Having suffered the constraints of the System and the plot himself, Shen Qingqiu had to ask this question.

Luo Binghe started to move his lips as if he were about to speak, but in the end, he hesitated to open his mouth.

Shen Qingqiu was a bit surprised. "You can't answer?"

Where was that silver tongue capable of taking on the entirety of Cang Qiong Mountain with eloquence alone? Was this the cost of going through the Endless Abyss plot arc too speedily and not properly training and XP farming? Luo Binghe hadn't sufficiently leveled up his speech skill tree.

"Shizun doesn't trust me either way," said Luo Binghe. "Whether I answer or not, what's the difference?"

In the shadowy Water Prison, the water reflected the trembling firelight. Shen Qingqiu's heart seemed to tremble along with it.

After facing each other in silence for a while, Luo Binghe suddenly said, "But I hope Shizun can give me an honest answer to one question." Pursing his lips, he stiffly added, "Just one question."

"Speak."

Luo Binghe sucked in a light breath. He said quietly, "Do you regret it?"

Shen Qingqiu closed his mouth and did not reply; his eyes moved, looking Luo Binghe up and down from head to toe. This "do you regret it" was all he'd said, nothing more.

He had to be asking if Shen Qingqiu regretted kicking him into the Endless Abyss.

Nonsense. Of course he regretted it—his intestines had twisted into knots with regret. But what did Luo Binghe mean by asking this?

Shen Qingqiu's temples were twitching when a giant window abruptly popped up before him.

[Please peruse your choices:

Choice A: Yes. This master regretted it from the start. These past few years, there wasn't a moment that I did not spend racked with remorse, though it was far too late.

Choice B: *(A disdainful laugh.)* After seeing what you've become today, I know there was no need to regret!

Choice C: Maintain silence.]

...How about you go die?

You upgraded, and this *was the fucking update? What the fuck is with those parentheses?! You've even set the tone and expression for me! Do you think we're playing a dating sim?!*

This is worse than the original low-tech version. Quick, who can give me a System 1.0 installation package—I'll thank their entire family!

Shen Qingqiu's face filled with black lines as he complained in his head. "A is way too fake! If I were Luo Binghe, not only would I not believe me, I'd be disgusted. And what the hell is B? Are you sad he didn't snap my neck last time?"

[Please make a selection.]

"C, C, C!"

[Character depth level +10.]

"Can't you tell me how this 'character depth' is calculated?"

So, he gazed fixedly ahead and kept his silence.

Unable to get an answer, Luo Binghe's tightly clenched fist gradually loosened, and he laughed at himself. "I knew the answer, but I still asked Shizun. I'm so stupid."

If Shen Qingqiu hadn't known that Luo Binghe was the power source of all the Systems in this world, he would definitely have suspected that he'd been replaced by his own impostor via transmigration. Which was to say, if not for his omniscient understanding of the plot, Shen Qingqiu would have suspected that...Luo Binghe really was a bit sad.

Silence was golden; more words meant more mistakes. Shen Qingqiu closed his eyes and sat without speaking, his legs crossed.

Facing this voiceless spell, Luo Binghe spoke in a light, icy voice. "Shizun, you were always a man of few words. But you were once willing to say those few words to me, and now you won't do even that." After a pause, his tone suddenly changed, and he sneered. "But it doesn't matter. I have plenty of ways to make you talk."

As this last syllable left his lips, Shen Qingqiu's eyes flew open.

A dense spate of stabbing pains erupted from his abdomen.

Speaking makes you unhappy, refusing to speak also makes you unhappy. Why! What crime did I commit?!

After a moment, the stabbing pain disappeared, and it was replaced by the strange sensation of something crawling inside his blood vessels.

The heavenly demon blood had been in hibernation for many

days, and it had since totally adapted to the environment inside its host's body. Impelled by its master, it had coalesced into insects and was beginning to explore its host's internal organs.

Luo Binghe said leisurely, "Spleen, kidneys, heart, lungs."

As he listed each organ, an utterly bizarre, itching pain would burst from that location. It was veritably both an itch and a pain, like rows upon rows of tiny, densely packed teeth biting down, and it was accompanied by a burning sensation.

Though it wasn't to the point of extraordinary anguish, it was still awful to suffer through.

Shen Qingqiu couldn't remain sitting up any longer, and he folded over at the waist, resisting the urge to curl up into a ball. Cold sweat dripped down together with the beads of water still on his chin.

This action finally seemed more like Luo Binghe's style, but too bad it was being used on him. Fuck, his stomach hurt so much—was this what it felt like when girls got their periods?!

"Shizun, where do you want them to start biting?" Luo Binghe asked warmly.

Nowhere! Wait, they haven't even started biting yet? What will it feel like when they do?!

Shen Qingqiu slapped the System window. "Think of something, okay?! I'm still your customer, right?!"

[Use key item Fake Jade Guanyin? Please note: This item may only be used once.]

"What's Luo Binghe's current anger level?"

[Thirty points.]

"How is it so low? Are you sure you didn't calculate wrong?! This is entirely unscientific!"

Use a godly item that could eliminate five thousand anger points on a thirty-point problem? Absolutely not!

"Are there any other options? What's the second-highest rated method in the field?"

[Activate Small Scenario Pusher?]

From name alone, it didn't sound exceptionally high-tech. But if this was the second-highest rated method in the field, it would do. Shen Qingqiu decisively selected it.

Luo Binghe sneered, "You don't want to look at me, you don't want to talk to me. Do you think I'm filthy?" As he spoke, he took an unexpected step forward and humphed. "If so, I refuse to give you what you want!"

He reached out to grab Shen Qingqiu's shoulder.

As he moved, Shen Qingqiu unconsciously dodged. Luo Binghe caught nothing but a corner of his clothing.

Shen Qingqiu's outer robe had already been ripped to shreds by the Little Palace Mistress's whip. With this tug, over half of it tore straight off his shoulder.

Neither of them could have expected this development. Both were frozen on the spot, petrified.

A basin of cold water had been dumped all over Shen Qingqiu, and even now, his clothes and hair stuck wetly to his fair skin, while strand upon strand of immortal-binding cable as thin as red thread was wound around his body. Even if the shocked expression on his face couldn't have been any more proper, his entire person looked extremely...*im*proper.

Luo Binghe's eyes suddenly opened wide.

He stared for a while, then whipped his hand away and spun around like he had been scalded by an iron.

As Luo Binghe backed away, the blood mites that had been writhing in Shen Qingqiu's internal organs seemed to startle as well. They scattered like birds and beasts, and the sense of blockage in his blood vessels instantly disappeared.

Shen Qingqiu panted, his heart flooding with tears—his period was finally over!

Now how exactly does this Small Scenario Pusher work? Does it just make me lose some of my clothes? Might as well call it Small Stripping Assistant. What's the logic underlying the function? Does it just take advantage of Luo Binghe's physiological disgust upon seeing a man's half-naked body?

Luo Binghe stood stiffly with his back turned for a while, like he didn't know where to put his limbs. Without warning, he tugged off his outer robe at top speed and tossed it behind him.

The robe hit Shen Qingqiu full in the face.

Shen Qingqiu was speechless.

What's the meaning of this?

This scene, these actions, why did they make him so thoroughly uneasy for no discernible reason? He couldn't help but be reminded of that classic bad trope wherein, after a violated young maiden was rescued, her boyfriend draped a warm coat over her...

Shen Qingqiu's hair stood on end. He lifted his arm, letting Luo Binghe's black robe slide from his shoulders.

The soft, fine fabric dropped to the ground, silver light shimmering along the exquisitely sleek embroidery. At the rustling sound, Luo Binghe turned back to look and saw his robe abandoned on the ground. Shen Qingqiu had even cautiously pushed it toward him a bit.

Shen Qingqiu had actually also considered folding it for Luo

Binghe, but he was only thinking about it and hadn't yet made a move to do so. When he looked up, Luo Binghe had already turned around, and his eyes were blinding as they reflected the firelight. It seemed like he was in a fury; the veins on the backs of his hands popped, his fingers clenching and unclenching several times. Then, as if trying to vent his rage, he fired off a succession of spiritual blasts.

He was in fact launching these attacks with no target at all. A few hit the surface of the lake, striking waves of water high into the air. Another hit the wall of the cave, opening a giant crater. Pieces of stone rolled down, and the torches shook and fell into the lake. However, they weren't extinguished, and instead they continued to burn brightly on the water's surface, casting Luo Binghe's face in a flicker of light and shadow, lending him a ghostly air.

Luo Binghe carefully drew back. "I almost forgot. Shizun dislikes anything the demon race has touched."

The oh-so-mighty male lead had given up protecting his image to throw a tantrum for no reason.

How is this any different from a little child kicking their toys all over the place when they don't get their way? You're cutting your own ratings, really.

A perfectly good cave and its perfectly good walls were chock-full of holes before Luo Binghe finally finished raging.

He turned to find Shen Qingqiu still observing him, unperturbed. A vein seemed to jump a few times in Luo Binghe's temple, and he forced out through gritted teeth, "In a month, I want to watch every step of your fall from grace with my own eyes!"

Having thrown down these words, Luo Binghe swept his sleeves and stalked away, slamming a hand onto the mechanism as he exited the cave. With a rumble, the water curtain poured back down.

Shen Qingqiu sat in place, staring upward in bewilderment: He was already a prisoner for Luo Binghe to do with as he pleased—so why was he so angry?

The inside of the cave was dark and gloomy. When the frigid wind blew, Shen Qingqiu's wet clothes stuck to his skin, freezing him until he was shivering in earnest.

To the side, Luo Binghe's robe still lay where it had been tossed on the ground.

Shen Qingqiu's mind wandered despite his circumstances. When Luo Binghe had studied on Qing Jing Peak, he'd never even randomly thrown tantrums, forget about demonstrating such volatile mood swings. But the way he'd looked while shaking out his sleeves and storming off had, unexpectedly, given Shen Qingqiu a shadow of a glimpse of the little lamb he'd once known.

When he returned to himself, his entire body was racked with cold, and he wanted to sneeze. With no other options, Shen Qingqiu's fingertips gingerly closed over that black outer robe, and he hesitantly draped it over himself.

It couldn't be helped. It wasn't like he was being tsundere earlier, just that he had been frankly unable to make himself do this in front of Luo Binghe.

After all, in the original work, hadn't Luo Binghe given girls this exact robe every time after they had sex?!

So how could he wear it right in front of the protagonist?!

Shen Qingqiu had learned that whenever he tried to meditate or clear his mind, there was always some form of outside disruption.

For example, that time at the Ling Xi Caves, and now again in the Water Prison.

The stone path rose, and the corrosive water curtain stopped flowing. Gongyi Xiao hurried down the path. With only a glance at Shen Qingqiu, his feet slipped out from under him.

"Se...Se...Senior Shen, you..." he stammered.

"What about me?" Shen Qingqiu had no idea what was wrong.

Gongyi Xiao had a strange look on his face, like he didn't know whether he should turn on his heel and retreat. He hesitated on the edge of the stone platform without continuing farther. Following his gaze, Shen Qingqiu looked down.

"That robe, isn't it...?" Gongyi Xiao said hesitantly.

Shen Qingqiu sighed. Luo Binghe's outer robe.

Gongyi Xiao finally reacted. He coughed shortly, then asked, "How has Senior Shen been these past two days?"

Shen Qingqiu replied, "All right."

If he weren't so popular he'd have been even more all right. Within the span of two days, three people had already visited. This luxury VIP single room in which he was temporarily detained must be the hottest, most popular suite in the history of Huan Hua Palace's Water Prison.

"I heard that yesterday, Luo-shixiong...was in a terrible rage when he left. This junior was worried that he might have done something to Senior Shen..." As Gongyi Xiao spoke, his eyes involuntarily drifted back to that black robe.

Under his stare, Shen Qingqiu found himself pulling the robe tighter over his chest.

Done what? Luo Binghe had only thrown a tantrum and punched holes all over the place, collapsing half the cave. *What's with that look in your eyes?!*

Shen Qingqiu sighed. "Luo Binghe has really taken to Huan Hua Palace like a fish to water."

Gongyi Xiao smiled bitterly. "Not only that. Luo-shixiong's spiritual power is outstanding, his conduct unwavering, and his actions swift and decisive. Everyone else is left in the dust, so it's no wonder Shizun regards him so highly. If Luo-shixiong weren't so insistent on not taking Shizun as his master, I'm afraid I would never have a chance of becoming head disciple."

Sincere sympathy seeped into the gaze Shen Qingqiu sent toward him.

"This junior came to see you about an important matter," Gongyi Xiao said resolutely. "This morning, Peak Lord Shang requested an authorization pass from my master, but his application was delayed, and he doesn't know when he will be able to get through. He seemed to have some pressing business, and he asked this junior to bring a letter." As he spoke, he reached into his lapel.

Fuck, it really was a letter. And it was only hastily folded twice, without even a wax seal or a sealing spell.

Shang Qinghua, how daring!

"Please relax, Senior, I've already looked through it," said Gongyi Xiao.

Then "relax" my ass!

"However, I couldn't understand what it said."

Shen Qingqiu let out an internal sigh of relief. Good, it looked like he had misunderstood. Shang Qinghua wouldn't fuck up *that* badly. In all likelihood, he'd used a secret code, so there would be nothing to fear even if someone did intercept it.

Shen Qingqiu shook open the paper with two fingers. After skimming it, his face turned green. After reading two lines, his face turned white. All sorts of colors bloomed and intertwined over his cheeks in a lively display.

He was speechless.

This letter was written in English.

No, not quite that: it was written in error-ridden Chinglish. The grammar was entirely Chinese, and any word Shang Qinghua didn't know was replaced by its pinyin equivalent.

"Great Master" Airplane Shooting Towards the Sky: Did you not consider...

What if I can't understand your shit-tier English?!

After puzzling his way through the general gist of the thing, Shen Qingqiu directed some energy to his hand. The paper broke into fragments and fell to the floor like June snow, exactly resembling his currently tumultuous mental state.

As it turned out, it was he who had underestimated "Great Master" Airplane Shooting Towards the Sky.

For Peerless Cucumber's eyes only:

Everything is set, and the preparations are complete. The location has not changed. It's just there was a small mishap with the time. In order to make the Sun-Moon Dew Mushroom mature as soon as possible, I fixed up a little something to promote its maturation—but I accidentally overdid it. Right now, it's as mature as it will ever get, and it will rot in no more than a week. So I hope you can leave Huan Hua Palace's Water Prison as soon as possible. Don't worry, it was only a bit of something like chemical fertilizer, so there shouldn't be any difference when you use the mushroom. Probably.

This wasn't just going off recipe—did the concept of recipes even exist for this guy?

He'd used chemical fertilizer to ripen that all-natural, unpolluted life-form. Fertilizer! "There shouldn't be any difference when you use it" was the sort of guarantee as trustworthy as the ones from used car salesmen!

Gongyi Xiao looked around. "Senior, are you done reading? If you are, please toss the letter into the lake to destroy it. Actually, yesterday, Luo-shixiong gave orders that no one but him was allowed to enter. I must leave as soon as possible so as to avoid being discovered and causing more complications."

Shen Qingqiu grabbed Gongyi Xiao. "Do me a favor."

Gongyi Xiao responded, "Go ahead and ask, as long as I—"

Shen Qingqiu didn't wait for him to finish saying "am able" before he sincerely asked, "Let me out."

Gongyi Xiao was silent until he said, with difficulty, "Senior…I really can't do that."

"I have a reason to insist," Shen Qingqiu said solemnly. "I swear that I don't intend to flee from the trial. After finishing my affairs, I will return to the Water Prison of my own volition to await judgment. If you don't trust me, we can take a blood oath."

One could not renege on a blood oath.

But in truth, after seeing to these affairs, it wouldn't matter whether Shen Qingqiu returned to Huan Hua Palace's Water Prison. So he was, in fact, running a scam.

"I certainly trust Senior, but wasn't detention in the Water Prison primarily your request?" Gongyi Xiao said awkwardly. "Exactly what could be so critical that you would absolutely have to leave? If you're willing to explain, I can report to the sect leaders and seniors participating in the investigation…"

Shen Qingqiu was having some second thoughts: Gongyi Xiao was a Huan Hua Palace disciple, and abetting the escape of a prisoner would be no small sin on any head it lay upon. This was an upstanding youngster. Throwing him to the wolves would be rather unkind. Within this seven-day limit, there were bound to be more opportunities.

Therefore, he changed his tone. "Forget it. It wasn't anything serious."

As he spoke, he struggled to collect all the paper fragments on the ground before tossing them into the lake to destroy the evidence. Because most of his body was bound by immortal-binding cables, movement was immensely difficult. After he shifted a couple of times, the black robe slid off his body.

Gongyi Xiao had originally bent down to help, but when he saw that black robe cast aside on the ground, he unintentionally looked up. His arms and legs went rigid at the sight.

Shen Qingqiu looked at him in askance.

The white garment on his body had been ripped clean from his shoulder; it was obvious at a glance that someone had violently torn it apart with their bare hands. In addition, fragments of fabric that looked like they had been shredded by a whip had been left hanging from what remained. More than a few pale red scrapes were evident on the fair skin exposed by the damage. If one looked closely, they would also detect the faint traces of bruises on his neck that had yet to fade.

Gongyi Xiao received a devastating shock to his worldview.

"Senior... You... Are you sure you're all right?" he asked in a trembling voice.

No wonder Luo Binghe had forbidden anyone but him from entering the Water Prison, even if they had the authorization pass— why he had even confiscated Peak Lord Shang's application.

So it's like this! An insubordinate disciple! Devoid of conscience! Worse than a beast!

Gongyi Xiao inwardly cried tears of blood for Senior Shen.

As for himself, Shen Qingqiu said blankly, "Yes? I'm all right."

Gongyi Xiao was shaken. How... How could Senior Shen have such a tranquil expression even in a moment like this?!

Shen Qingqiu finished tossing all the paper fragments into the lake. "You shouldn't take the words I said just now to heart. You—"

Gongyi Xiao suddenly stood up, turned around, and left.

Shen Qingqiu's face filled with black lines. *I say you shouldn't take it to heart and you just up and leave? Isn't that a bit too brusque?*

But before an hour had passed, Gongyi Xiao returned again, carrying something in hand. He walked over to Shen Qingqiu, unwrapped the seals binding that object, and slashed downward.

With a white flash, the bindings around Shen Qingqiu's body abruptly loosened, and it felt like an electric circuit had been reconnected. He stretched his fingers. His spiritual energy was unmistakably back in operation and flowing smoothly. When he'd been imprisoned, he had been in the middle of a random Without a Cure flare-up, but after two days of being tied up by the immortal-binding cables, the poison had unexpectedly been suppressed again. Was this following the same principle as fighting fire with fire, or how two negatives make a positive?

The immortal-binding cables fell to the ground in pieces. Gongyi

Xiao tossed over the object in his hands, and Shen Qingqiu reached out to catch it.

Xiu Ya!

Holding the sword, Shen Qingqiu was overjoyed and astonished. He looked over at Gongyi Xiao. "I thought this was supposed to be with the Old Palace Master."

"Even if I risk being punished by my master, this junior cannot sit back and remain stoic while Senior is disgraced," Gongyi Xiao said righteously. "I trust you, Senior Shen. Please follow me!"

Shen Qingqiu was involuntarily overcome by a sense of helplessness.

What's this...? I keep feeling like...he seems to have misunderstood something very important... But...forget it... This is fine...

"All right!" Shen Qingqiu said resolutely.

Sure, the heavenly demon blood was still dormant within his body, and wherever he ran, Luo Binghe would always be able to locate him. But that knowledge didn't matter so long as Luo Binghe couldn't chase him there!

"Senior, you... Can you walk?" Gongyi Xiao asked, deeply worried. "Do you need me to carry..."

With a dark expression, Shen Qingqiu took a decisive stride and marched forward, using this action to prove that he could indeed walk, and walk very briskly at that!

Gongyi Xiao started, then promptly followed close behind. Unexpectedly, when they stepped off the surface of the stone platform and onto the path, the water curtain that had been raised rumbled overhead and water gushed down.

Shen Qingqiu, who'd been running quickly, also braked quickly, lest he take the spray head-on. He stepped back onto the stone platform along with Gongyi Xiao, and the water curtain gradually stopped.

It was basically deliberately stopping them from leaving. Wasn't this design a bit too intelligent?!

Gongyi Xiao suddenly understood. "I forgot—once the Water Prison has been activated, there must always be someone on the stone platform. If this person leaves or there isn't enough weight on the platform, the water curtain automatically reactivates, even if the mechanism has been shut it off."

In the past, he'd never had any experiences with helping a prisoner escape, so naturally he hadn't remembered this.

"In other words, one person has to be left on the stone platform before the others can leave?" Shen Qingqiu asked.

Gongyi Xiao nodded.

"Then you stay here."

Gongyi Xiao was silent.

Shen Qingqiu shook out his sleeves and headed toward the path. Behind him, Gongyi Xiao weakly raised his hand. "Senior Shen, even though I am most willing to serve, if you don't have me to lead the way, I'm afraid you won't be able to get out... Ah..."

Shen Qingqiu looked back and added, "Wait for me to return."

Gongyi Xiao stood in place, stupefied. He had a mind to follow, but he was hindered by the fact that he had no way to leave the stone platform, so he could only stand there and wait. A short while later, he heard a muffled sound from outside, and Shen Qingqiu walked back up, dragging a person by the back of their collar.

Shen Qingqiu hauled the still-unconscious pock-faced disciple onto the stone platform, patted Gongyi Xiao on the shoulder, and said, "I happened to see this one on patrol and borrowed him for a bit. Let's go!"

In reality he hadn't just "happened" to see him. There had been four people on patrol. Shen Qingqiu had secretly hidden himself, and only after careful selection had he grabbed this mouthy fellow.

Just now, it had also occurred to Gongyi Xiao to grab a random disciple to use as a weight, but the idea had flashed by only indistinctly. Now that Shen Qingqiu had done it himself—meaning there was no need for Gongyi Xiao to personally knock out a fellow disciple—he breathed a sigh of relief.

As they once more headed toward the outside, shoulder to shoulder, he saw Shen Qingqiu draw that black robe draped around his shoulders tighter, and a lump welled in his throat.

He could only feel agonized. He was already reluctant to see Shen Qingqiu, the leader of a peak, be imprisoned and humiliated. Yet now Shen Qingqiu needed to depend on a piece of clothing from the one who'd assaulted him to cover his body and conceal the marks of that humiliation. How could he not lament in distress?

Shen Qingqiu saw Gongyi Xiao's expression flicker. It looked like sympathy, but also indignation. He could only face turbulence with tranquility, and he kept his expression blank.

Out of nowhere, Gongyi Xiao said, "Senior, please take it off!"

Shen Qingqiu stared. *Huh?!*

Without waiting for him to recover, Gongyi Xiao had already begun taking off his own outer robe. Shen Qingqiu was just considering whether he should toss a spiritual blast at Gongyi Xiao to try and return him to his senses when Gongyi Xiao offered him the outer robe he'd removed with both hands. "Please wear this!"

Shen Qingqiu suddenly understood.

Oh, so that was what he meant. Luo Binghe's clothes were black, but the clothes themselves matched the person; like the male lead himself, they were sophisticated, luxurious yet understated. Obviously, Gongyi Xiao disapproved—wearing such a robe would only draw attention. But changing into a white robe that looked like it could belong to anybody would be more advantageous to their chances of escape. Such attention to detail!

Shen Qingqiu resolutely removed Luo Binghe's robe and changed into Gongyi Xiao's. Before leaving, he thought for a moment, then took the time to fold Luo Binghe's robe. Only after this did he place it on the ground.

Navigation wasn't particularly difficult upon first leaving the Water Prison, but the farther they walked, the more Shen Qingqiu came to appreciate that Huan Hua Palace's maze array was indeed exceptionally terrifying. They traveled through cave after cave, path intersecting with path, and every couple of steps they'd circle around and around, to the point it made his head spin. Despite walking so close to Gongyi Xiao's back, Shen Qingqiu almost lost him quite a few times. If Gongyi Xiao hadn't known the assignments and schedules of the Water Prison's staff like the back of his hand, who knew how many disciple guard patrols they would have run into?

After an hour, they finally made it out of the underground Water Prison. They walked many kilometers more without stopping and entered Bai Lu Forest, until they were about to cross the border of Huan Hua Palace's territory. The Water Prison's alarm had yet to sound, meaning that no one had yet discovered that the prisoner was gone. Luo Binghe's order forbidding all others from visiting the Water Prison had inadvertently greatly aided Shen Qingqiu's escape.

After a short rest, Shen Qingqiu said, "Young Master Gongyi, after this point, you needn't stay to send me off. Hurry back now while we're still undetected." After a pause, he added, "Within seven days, go to Hua Yue City. You'll definitely find me there."

"If that's the case, I won't accompany you any farther," Gongyi Xiao said. "Even though I don't know what Senior intends to do about these future concerns, please be careful. And Senior, please don't worry about the sects' trial next month. It's as you said: those clean will remain clean no matter what. The sect leaders will obviously exonerate you."

Unable to help himself, Shen Qingqiu laughed. First, his dark history was set in stone and couldn't be erased. Second, the trial next month had fuck-all to do with him, ha ha ha ha...

He immediately cupped his hands, carefree and satisfied. "May we meet again."

The road from Huan Hua Palace's border to Hua Yue City ran through the most densely populated and economically developed stretch of the Central Plains. This also meant that an especially large number of secular cultivation sects and influential families were located within the area.

The cultivators of this world highly valued aerial defense. Like in Jin Lan City, they often set up aerial defense barriers over their territories. If an immortal's sword or spiritual artifact flew through it above the speed limit, it would undoubtedly be discovered and reported to that sect's higher-ups.

Obviously, traveling in this way would be like bombastically broadcasting his escape trajectory via megaphone.

Shen Qingqiu flew part of the way and walked another without rest until he finally arrived at Hua Yue City the following night.

His arrival timing was terribly unfortunate, as a festival celebrating the establishment of Hua Yue City was in full swing. The city was adorned with colored lanterns and would be brightly lit the entire night. Soaring dragons and lion dances filled the streets, the drums and music thunderous. People were packed together, vendor next to vendor, peddlers shouldering their poles as they slunk down every street. Practically everyone had poured out of their homes.

Even more unfortunate was that, on his arrival, dark clouds covered the moon. Without the support of sun or moonlight, the chance his plan would fail greatly increased. Anxious about the odds, Shen Qingqiu decided to wait for the time being. At most one day. If after that day, the clouds had yet to disperse, he couldn't afford to care anymore. If the chance of failure remained greater, so be it. A risk would still be better than clinging to an overripe Sun-Moon Dew Mushroom and crying about it. At that point, even if it was cooked and served with alcohol, it would just reek of fertilizer.

As Shen Qingqiu walked cautiously, he occasionally bumped into rowdy children or brushed past groups of laughing girls, and he felt, very slightly, that it really was a pity. If he weren't currently fleeing for his life, he would've liked to take a thorough tour of the city.

Suddenly, several men all dressed in clothes of the same color were walking toward him, longswords slung over their backs. Each one held his head high and chest out. From a glance, one could tell they were arrogant disciples from a random sect.

Though it sounded strange, the smaller and more random the sect, the more afraid their disciples would be that others didn't know they were cultivators. If they could have gotten away with it, they would have emblazoned their clothes with huge slogans.

Shen Qingqiu turned his body in a natural manner and smoothly picked up a demon mask from the side. He placed it over his face, then openly and confidently walked toward them. At the festival, six out of ten attendees were wearing masks; if he mixed in with them, he didn't have to fear drawing attention.

"Shixiong, would that 'Xiu Ya Sword' really sit around in this city, waiting to be captured?" one man from the group asked.

"The four sects sent out the warrant for his capture as one—how could it be fake?" the leader berated him. "Didn't you see how many sects have sent people here to box him in? Keep an eye out. You saw Huan Hua Palace's bounty too. Don't you want it?"

Myriad thoughts filled Shen Qingqiu's mind. It turned out that, without his knowledge, he'd become a wanted criminal.

"It's no wonder Huan Hua Palace put down such a large sum. What happened to them was really just awful..."

The most I did to them was knock out an insignificant disciple, Shen Qingqiu thought. *I didn't do anything else. So how did Huan Hua Palace suddenly become the tragic victim?*

He wanted to keep listening, but they pulled farther and farther ahead, and the rush of people cut him off, so he could only give up.

While he was mulling over whether he should find an abandoned residence to rest, he felt a sudden weight upon his leg. When he looked down, he saw a small child clinging to his thigh.

That child unhurriedly raised his head. His face was pallid, like he was malnourished, but his eyes were both large and bright. They stared straight at Shen Qingqiu as the boy clung to his thigh, unwilling to let go.

Shen Qingqiu patted his head. "Who's your family? Did you get lost?"

The small child nodded, and when he spoke, his voice was meek and sweet. "I got lost."

The child's appearance was naturally endearing, and it even seemed a little familiar, so Shen Qingqiu leaned over to pick him up, letting him sit on his arm. "Who did you come here with?"

The child clung to his neck and pursed his lips. "With Shizun…"

Was he some sect's young disciple? Then if a grown-up came to look for him, Shen Qingqiu was in for a real headache.

But for some reason, the forlorn way the boy said "Shizun" stirred Shen Qingqiu's pity down to the core. He just couldn't harden his heart and toss the child to the side of the road, leaving him to continue huddling miserably. He patted the boy's soft little behind. "Your shizun didn't look after you properly—how incredibly awful of him. Where did you get lost? Do you remember?"

The child giggled into his ear. "I remember. Shizun personally threw me down himself, so how could I not?"

Half of Shen Qingqiu's body went utterly cold.

It was as if what he held in his arms wasn't the body of a young child but a poisonous snake—a massive snake that had wound around his neck and bared its fangs, poised to bite and inject venom into him at any moment.

He abruptly threw aside the person in his arms and turned around, his back covered in goosebumps. The fine hairs all over his body promptly stood straight up.

The entire street was looking at him. The ones wearing masks, the ones not wearing masks. It was like they were suddenly all immobilized, holding their breaths and watching him.

The ones wearing masks were frightening, with their sinister and demonic visages. But the ones not wearing masks were even more panic-inducing—they didn't have faces!

Shen Qingqiu's instinct in that second was to place his hand on Xiu Ya, but he shortly caught himself. He couldn't attack.

This was what he'd once taught Luo Binghe: while within Meng Mo's barrier, to attack the "people" who appeared in the dream realm was to in fact attack your own self.

Cold sweat dripped from Shen Qingqiu's forehead. He had wholly, completely failed to realize that he'd entered this barrier. To be fair, people never remembered when and how exactly a "dream" began.

But he'd been fleeing! Surely he hadn't been so dull-witted as to fall asleep on the side of the road while running for his life?

From behind him there came a tender voice. "Shizun."

Moments ago, when this voice had been by his ear, it had sounded clearly and utterly adorable and innocent. But when he listened to it now, it actually possessed some unspeakably terrifying quality.

"Why don't you want me anymore?" the child form of Luo Binghe asked faintly from where he stood behind Shen Qingqiu.

Shen Qingqiu decisively refused to turn his head and immediately took off.

Though he said that all these faceless people were watching him... No, he couldn't call it watching, because they didn't even have eyes. But their faces still turned in Shen Qingqiu's direction, and he could indeed feel the weight of countless gazes upon him.

Shen Qingqiu pretended he couldn't see any of this and charged straight ahead, thrusting aside anyone in his way. Suddenly, a hand intercepted his palm. He turned his head to look. Though this hand was slim, it possessed terrifying strength, basically like an iron shackle.

A fourteen-year-old Luo Binghe firmly gripped his wrist. On his face was not only the bruising that had never been allowed to heal but an overflowing melancholy. Those pitch-black eyes stared right at him, almost within reach.

You're still coming?!

Shen Qingqiu tried three times before he finally flung off Luo Binghe, then pushed aside the crowd and continued to flee. First was a child, second was a youth—if the adult version came next, he really wouldn't be able to take it!

But this street seemed to go on forever with no end in sight. After a sequence of small stalls on either side, faceless playing children, and demon-masked girls appeared a second time, Shen Qingqiu was finally certain: this dream realm street was looping. Going forward was fruitless.

Since neither forward nor backward would work, he'd blaze a different trail. Shen Qingqiu looked left and right, then darted up to a liquor shop.

Crimson lanterns hung high over the shop's doors, the red glow muted and beautiful, yet the wooden doors were tightly shut. Shen Qingqiu pulled open the doors and had just walked inside when they slammed closed by themselves.

The interior of the house was dark, and a cold breeze blew through it. Rather than being the inside of a liquor shop, it felt more like he'd entered a cave.

Shen Qingqiu didn't think this unexpected. Dream realms couldn't be understood using common sense. Every door had the potential to lead anywhere.

At this moment, a series of eerie noises drifted to his ear.

They sounded like the intensely labored, incessant panting of a person close to death, whose lungs had been punctured—who was in terrible agony.

Moreover, it didn't sound like only one person.

Shen Qingqiu snapped his fingers, flicking a flame forth from his fingertips, and aimed it toward the origin of those strange noises.

The flame illuminated the scene in its entirety, leaving out not a single detail. His pupils instantly shrank to pinpoints.

Liu Qingge held Cheng Luan, the blade aimed at himself, and was stabbing it into his own chest.

His body was stained with blood, large swathes covered with a deep and ghastly red. The wounds weren't just concentrated in one place, and a stream of blood flowed from the corner of his mouth. It looked like he'd already stabbed himself with the sword who knew how many times, yet his expression was both furious and crazed. It was obvious he was delirious, in the midst of a qi deviation.

Beneath the rays of dim yellow firelight, this picture was exceptionally horrifying. Shen Qingqiu momentarily forgot that this was still the dream realm and threw himself forward, wrenching Cheng Luan away. That sword had been staked in the center of Liu Qingge's heart, and with only a light touch from Shen Qingqiu, fresh blood spurted violently forth, filling his vision with red.

At that, Shen Qingqiu's mind cleared a little and he backed up two steps, only to bump into another person.

He jerked his head around. Yue Qingyuan's head was lowered, gaze meeting his.

Though their gazes met, those two eyes were empty and devoid of light. From his throat to his chest, his four limbs and abdomen... were all pierced with a forest of pitch-black arrows.

Pierced with ten thousand arrows?

All at once, Shen Qingqiu understood the meaning of these visions: these were their original deaths.

The deaths that he had been meant to cause with his own hands.

Shen Qingqiu couldn't stand it anymore. He far preferred being outside, getting aggressively stared down by a circle of faceless people, to *this* sort of thing.

He backed up in the direction from which he'd come, and he managed to brush those wooden doors. Feeling as if he'd been granted amnesty, Shen Qingqiu kicked the doors open and rushed outside.

His mind was a mess, his footsteps confused as he tripped and staggered along, cutting a rather sorry figure. Every "person" on the street watched him in a deathly silence, and while he was disoriented, he crashed headlong into someone's chest.

That person's hands swiftly came around to his back, gathering him into their arms.

The other party was a little taller than him, slender and willowy, dressed in clothes as black as ink that exposed only a fair neck. Above that, a sinister mask covered their face.

Shen Qingqiu hadn't yet spoken when a smiling voice came from above: "Shizun, be careful."

He had no need to lift the mask to know whose face lay underneath.

At once, Shen Qingqiu began to struggle. The other party didn't hold him by force, so getting free wasn't difficult. Only after retreating several steps and maintaining a safe distance did he right himself.

"You created this city?" Shen Qingqiu asked.

Luo Binghe casually removed the mask. His expression looked like he was sad that they couldn't keep playing hide-and-seek. "Correct. What does Shizun think?"

Shen Qingqiu slowly nodded. "You truly deserve to be called Meng Mo's succeeding disciple."

To be able to create an illusion this detailed...he feared it was nearly as good as the city Meng Mo had created to trap them in, all those years ago. Furthermore, it had so accurately grasped his lurking fears.

Originally, Luo Binghe's mood had seemed rather good, but on hearing these words, the smile on his lips faded. "I'm not Meng Mo's disciple."

"Didn't you accept him as your master?" Shen Qingqiu asked, slightly curious.

Luo Binghe held his silence for a while before he answered in a peeved tone. "I didn't!"

All right then. If he didn't, he didn't. Shen Qingqiu didn't think there was any point wasting time on this.

"Shizun, if you're willing to return of your own volition, you can ask for anything," Luo Binghe said.

"Are you offering a plea bargain?" asked Shen Qingqiu.

"So long as I don't dissolve the blood mites within your body, it will be futile to flee."

"Oh. Is that so." He smiled. "Then right now, why haven't you personally come to catch me?"

Luo Binghe stiffened, sparks flashing in his eyes.

At this reaction, Shen Qingqiu became even more sure. "Something has gone wrong with that sword of yours, right?" he asked languidly.

The heavens smile down on me!

After falling into the Endless Abyss, while within the stomach of a huge, ancient beast, Luo Binghe had found a mythical sword that had been forged by a master demon blacksmith with an entire lifetime's worth of painstaking labor.

This sword was called Xin Mo: "heart demon."

The name alone tells you that it's something super dangerous, right?!

And that was a must! The stronger the spiritual artifact, the harder it was to control. Since ancient times, Xin Mo had passed through the hands of more than a hundred masters, and all had been blessed geniuses from various races. Yet despite this, none of them had been able to escape the same fate, and they had all died to this very blade—their own sword.

Xin Mo lashed back against its wielder. If you could make it submit, it was a formidable weapon in your hand. But if one day you were unable to control the sword's evil tendencies, you would become no more than another blood sacrifice to its hunger.

Only after starting the Demon Realm arc had the original Luo Binghe gone through his first bout of internal struggles wherein he narrowly escaped Xin Mo's recoil. After that, for the sake of solving this problem, he'd begun a "side plot" that lasted five hundred chapters and involved collecting eight or nine more girls.

But right now, with the plot in disarray, it seemed the recoil incident had also moved earlier.

Xin Mo's recoil was no joke. No wonder Luo Binghe hadn't given chase. He was busy secluding himself to recover, so he was unable to come capture Shen Qingqiu in person.

Suddenly, Luo Binghe grabbed Shen Qingqiu's shoulder and forcefully yanked.

Rip.

Why again?!

Luo Binghe's face was almost as dark as the bottom of a pot. Each word he spat out sounded like he'd first ground it between his teeth. "Even if I can't come in person for now, Shizun shouldn't be too happy."

That doesn't mean you should tear my clothes! Shen Qingqiu clutched the remaining fabric tightly and indignantly said, "What are you doing?! Is this your only method of humiliating others?"

"It was clearly Shizun who humiliated me first!"

[Satisfaction points +50.]

You can add points for that too?! Gross! Why does this feel so sick?!

When Luo Binghe's hand exerted force, the white robe's fabric disintegrated into pieces, drifting away in the wind. His anger still unappeased, he pressed toward Shen Qingqiu. His expression made Shen Qingqiu fear that there would be no end to this. He'd never known Luo Binghe to have crazy clothes-ripping tendencies, but of course he couldn't just sit there and resign himself to it. They exchanged ten or so blows, quick and nimble. Luo Binghe could obviously easily assume the upper hand, but like a cat playing with a mouse, he patiently engaged Shen Qingqiu in close combat.

Shen Qingqiu's movements were swift, but it seemed that in Luo Binghe's eyes, he was always one step behind. When he lashed out with a palm strike, Luo Binghe evaded within a hair's breadth every time, calm and unhurried. Then, as if reciprocating a polite gesture, he perfunctorily returned the blow.

On top of that, the System was being extremely annoying, with satisfaction point notifications ringing without end: +20, +30, +50, etc. The infernal racket flooded Shen Qingqiu's brain. After several back-and-forths, it was Shen Qingqiu's turn to wear a dark face.

Where are you aiming?! Are you messing with me?! Shouldn't the goal of a fight be defeating the other party?!

This wasn't a fight—this couldn't even be considered sparring. It was basically harassment!

As he thought this, Shen Qingqiu's concentration slipped and he used too much force, falling into Luo Binghe.

This, Luo Binghe didn't evade at all, and he let Shen Qingqiu crash into his arms with a thud. His voice carried laughter, like his mood had risen once more. "Shizun taught me this maneuver himself. When it comes to force, there's a time for restraint and a time for release, and one must above all else avoid losing one's balance. How could you forget that yourself?"

At this moment, Shen Qingqiu's mind was bombarded with a colorful explosion of "little beast" ad nauseam.

Motherfucker! This maneuver really was something he'd taught Luo Binghe!

He still remembered that lesson, not long after Luo Binghe had moved out of the woodshed. Though he was blessed with shitloads of raw talent and had come up with a fighting style through random experimentation, other than the handful of cutting and stabbing maneuvers every new disciple knew, he'd known absolutely jack shit about any higher-level techniques.

After watching him practice a series of sword, palm, and foot techniques, Shen Qingqiu had held his forehead for a long time while Luo Binghe awaited his evaluation by his side, as anxious as he was nervous.

Shen Qingqiu had been unable to bear hurting him and, after a long while, had finally squeezed out a single line: "Pragmatic, and quite flexible."

In the name of correcting Luo Binghe's more tragic habits, Shen Qingqiu had put in a great deal of painstaking effort and given him daily private instruction. He had been unable to understand why a nudge wasn't enough. Given Luo Binghe's intelligence and comprehension, Shen Qingqiu shouldn't have needed to tell him anything more than once. But in reality, Luo Binghe was incredibly stubborn. He would immediately forget his lessons, no matter how tirelessly taught, and always used too much force. He had slammed into Shen Qingqiu's arms who-knew-how-many times, until Shen Qingqiu finally became angry.

Are you doing this on purpose?!

Unable to help himself, he had slapped the back of Luo Binghe's head, neither heavy nor light, and shouted, "How is this anticipating and defending against your enemy? You're basically throwing yourself into their arms!"

Only after this did Luo Binghe, face fully flushed, finally start practicing in earnest. He no longer dared to make mistakes so carelessly.

But in the present, Luo Binghe was the one lecturing Shen Qingqiu on his incorrect stance.

What nonsense is this?!

Shen Qingqiu felt like his dignity as a master had been challenged. He was about to counterattack when Luo Binghe's hand trailed downward, following the line of his spine. Goosebumps exploded down Shen Qingqiu's back in its wake.

"Luo Binghe!" he said through clenched teeth.

[Satisfaction points +100! Congratulations!]

Congratulations my ass!

Luo Binghe again plucked away a length of shredded white cloth. "Seeing Shizun in this robe makes me awfully unhappy. It would be better to rip it all off."

Doesn't that mean he won't stop until I'm one hundred percent naked?

"Even if you hate me, there's no need to take it out on this robe," Shen Qingqiu said. "Moreover, it's Gongyi Xiao's!"

Luo Binghe's face fell. "Shizun's the one who truly hates me. You're unwilling to associate with even a scrap of my clothing."

Why?! Why were two grown men neurotically discussing a piece of clothing while surrounded by staring eyes?

Luo Binghe, are you actually the sensitive type? I even patted your robe clean and folded it for you—what more do you want? It can't be that you wanted me to handwash and return it to you personally! Shen Qingqiu thought, his expressions shifting erratically.

"What is Shizun thinking?" Luo Binghe asked at the sight. He added coolly, "If it's about Gongyi Xiao, let me advise Shizun: you needn't think about him anymore."

An ominous feeling rose in Shen Qingqiu's heart, and he asked in a forceful voice, "What happened to Gongyi Xiao?"

Plot-wise, Gongyi Xiao being banished—forced to defend a desolate regional border and deprived of any future prospects—was only supposed to happen after Luo Binghe and the Little Palace Mistress slept together.

But now the plot was jumbled to the point where even Airplane Shooting Towards the Sky, the story's own father, would no longer recognize it. So naturally, any scenario could have moved up.

Shen Qingqiu had yet to hear Luo Binghe's answer when the faceless people nearby stirred.

Originally, they had only vacantly stood there, watching blankly as if they were mentally infirm or doing their own thing. Now they started to steadily gather around him. Shen Qingqiu was squeezed into the center of the crowd, but he couldn't directly blast them away. He looked again toward Luo Binghe, whose brows were tightly furrowed, hand pressed to his temple, too preoccupied to notice anything else—as if he were enduring a mental assault.

Shen Qingqiu had a sudden epiphany. In all likelihood, Xin Mo had taken the chance to lash out and was trying to strike at Luo Binghe's mind. As Luo Binghe could no longer spare the energy to maintain the barrier, the dream realm was beginning to fall into chaos.

If Shen Qingqiu didn't leave now, then when would he get the chance?!

If Luo Binghe couldn't expend any attention to stop him, so as long as Shen Qingqiu faced another illusion and overcame the related fears buried within his heart, he would be able to destroy this failing barrier.

Just like that, Shen Qingqiu left. Luo Binghe's head hurt like it was splitting open, but he was unable to move. He could only yell, "I dare you to take another step!"

Shen Qingqiu took ten steps. Afterward, he turned his head. "How's that?"

Luo Binghe looked like he was about to cough up blood. He ground out each word, one by one. "You just wait and see!"

Shen Qingqiu's gaze didn't falter. He spoke coldly and loftily. "Goodbye!"

You think I'll wait just because you told me to? I'm not an idiot!

To the side, Shen Qingqiu glimpsed another shop. He kicked open the doors and leapt through them. Whatever appeared this time, he was absolutely certain he could face it calmly.

At the very least, his chance of success was higher than when facing Luo Binghe!

The doors closed behind him, and it was like the clamor outside had been severed away by a sharp knife. Within a split second, it was all deathly silent.

Shen Qingqiu held his breath and waited, soundless.

After a long while, it was as if someone had lit a candle, and his surroundings slowly, flickeringly, lightened. Shen Qingqiu looked down, and he came face-to-face with a countenance that was both foreign and familiar.

Before him knelt a frail-looking youth.

The boy wore coarse clothes and was crouched bent over on the ground. It was a crestfallen pose, and his hands were tightly tied with a thick, rough rope. Though his face was deathly pale, his eyes were full of life.

Shen Qingqiu met his gaze, unwavering.

This categorically wasn't Shen Qingqiu's memory, but this face was indeed exactly like his. The only thing it was missing was the polish of time and cultivation; instead, it possessed the inexperience of youth.

This was Shen Qingqiu, yet it wasn't Shen Qingqiu.

If he had to be obvious about it: this was Shen *Jiu*.

Shen Qingqiu abruptly sat up on a wooden slab.

After startling awake, he took in his surroundings, and only then did he realize that he was lying within an abandoned residence.

The sky was already bright, white light streaming through the worn-out window and cracks in the rice paper.

Then he remembered: the night before, he'd wandered at random through the festival, and not long into his wander had really found an old, uninhabited house. He'd originally only intended to rest a little, but by accident he had carelessly fallen asleep, allowing Luo Binghe to catch him within the dream realm.

As Shen Qingqiu considered the illusion he'd seen just before the dream realm collapsed, he couldn't help but sink into thought.

Though his and the original flavor's souls counted as two different people, in the end, he was using someone else's body, so it made sense that there would be at least some influence from the prior owner. What he'd seen in the dream had likely been the original Shen Jiu's childhood memories.

In a way, then, he had cheated his way out, because those memories had absolutely no hold on the current Shen Qingqiu. Thus, he had been able to easily and effortlessly break free of them.

Although in retrospect, Shen Qingqiu thought this fairly suspicious. The Shen Jiu within his dream had been tied up, so he'd assumed it was a memory from the time when Shen Jiu was still held by human traffickers. However, he'd been in a room decorated with a soft carpet, numerous cabinets for keeping valuables, and the walls hung with calligraphy, which had lent it a noble air. It hadn't looked like a criminals' den, but rather had unquestionably been a rich man's study...

In other words, it looked like Shen Jiu had not been as doted upon at the Qiu estate as Qiu Haitang claimed.

Shen Qingqiu hopped up from the bare wooden couch and unconsciously felt up his form. At least all his clothes were still there.

But even though his clothes were intact, he didn't really want to wear them anymore. Though they were on his body, he had an ominous feeling that they could be ripped off at any moment.

Before he'd gone too far through the streets, Shen Qingqiu discovered that more than a few people had poured into Hua Yue City upon receiving notice of the warrant for his capture.

Though many of the cultivators put on an act and didn't wear their sect colors while disguised as common people, when they sat down at roadside stands, their postures were entirely different from an ordinary person's. Shen Qingqiu felt it was too dangerous to go as he was, so he found a corner, smeared his face with dirt, and haphazardly stuck on some whiskers. After making all these preparations, he carefully returned to the street.

When he glanced up at the sky, he saw that the clouds were thin, like they were slowly retreating. If nothing went awry, noon today would be the optimal time.

When he looked down again, a slender snow-white silhouette flashed through the crowd in front of him, fast and light, their profile outstandingly handsome.

Liu Qingge! His hired thug was here!

Shen Qingqiu's eyes brightened, but just as he was about to chase after Liu Qingge, a delicate shout erupted from a nearby tavern.

"What are you saying with your filthy mouth?!"

This voice was clear, delicate, and extremely familiar. Shen Qingqiu unconsciously paused mid-step, the scene drawing his gaze. Right afterward, a sequence of crashes shook the air, and all the passersby cast glances as well.

At this time, another young woman humphed and said spitefully, "What, you have the guts for crime but won't let others talk? No wonder Cang Qiong Mountain produced a degenerate like Shen Qingqiu. Everyone in the sect must be eager to bury their shame, especially Qing Jing Peak. Humph, unfortunately for you, everyone knows what kind of *thing* he is. You think you can hide it?!"

What a venomous tone. The young woman who'd spoken first jumped in to refute her right away. "Shizun absolutely isn't the kind of person who'd do something like this. Don't you dare slander him!"

What young girl would even now speak up for him like so? Who could it have been other than Ning Yingying?

Ming Fan's voice carried into the street as well. "We were only polite to you out of respect for the Old Palace Master. You ought to be more polite as well!"

Though Shen Qingqiu had wanted to go look for Liu Qingge, having urgent matters to tend to, this strange atmosphere made him hesitate for a second. In the end, afraid the Qing Jing Peak disciples would be at a disadvantage, he stayed for a moment and ducked to the side of the building to hide and watch.

There were two distinct camps in this tavern.

One side was led by Ming Fan and Ning Yingying, while a crowd of Qing Jing Peak disciples stood behind them, their every face filled with displeasure. The Little Palace Mistress stood in front of the other side, her hands on her hips as she faced her opponents with a cold scowl. The Huan Hua Palace disciples behind her had already flashed their blades, their glares even more full of fury.

Two young women, one lovely and delicate, the other with gorgeous features, gracefully faced off. Even if the air was filled with crackling, sizzling sparks, the scene was still incomparably easy on the eyes.

Luo Binghe was setting fires in his backyard again. No, even Qing Jing Peak's disciples were involved, and they had challenged Huan Hua Palace. This was the real "enemies meeting on a narrow road."[4]

Shen Qingqiu could guarantee that if he left this scene and walked away right this instant, Qing Jing Peak would definitely suffer more casualties, and greatly. Remember: this Little Palace Mistress was domineering to the point that other than Luo Binghe, there was no one in the world she wouldn't dare hit. Injury and crippling strikes were common dishes on her menu of retaliation!

The Little Palace Mistress humphed. "Not that kind of person? Then tell me, why would he flee in fear of punishment? And he...he... he did *that* sort of thing!" As she spoke, she clenched her teeth in hatred, the rims of her eyes going red.

"Shizun was never convicted. What do you mean 'flee in fear of punishment'?" Ning Yingying shot back. "And there's still no final consensus on who committed those deeds. Our Cang Qiong Mountain never blamed your Huan Hua Palace for being gullible and overly suspicious, or for insisting on imprisoning our Qing Jing Peak's peak lord in your Water Prison without regard for the truth. If not for you, things wouldn't have blown up into the situation today!"

The reason for this b- [beep—] fight wasn't the male lead but Shen Qingqiu?

Shen Qingqiu wiped his brow. *By what merit does this humble Shen deserve this?*

---

4   冤家路窄. An idiom for when you unexpectedly meet your enemies or nemeses. Approximately equivalent to the English "it's a small world," but only for people you hate or who hate you.

At the same time, the dark cloud over his heart that he'd been unable to wipe away grew even darker.

This argument just made it more evident that after he left, something had happened at Huan Hua Palace. And these new grudges and old debts had all fallen on his head.

The Little Palace Mistress flew into a rage—though to tell the truth, Shen Qingqiu felt that she was always in a state of rage.

"So you're saying that our Huan Hua Palace only has ourselves to blame?!" she snapped. "Ah, Cang Qiong Mountain is *so* impressive, so high-up and domineering, so arrogant and unbridled, that not only do you refuse to apologize, you have the gall to be so brazen toward the victims! With this kind of behavior, you still have the face to call yourselves the number one major sect? Preposterous!"

Ning Yingying curled her lip. "Cang Qiong Mountain has already been acknowledged by the masses as the number one major sect. Whether you accept that fact doesn't matter. Moreover, who came at us first and acted *brazen*? Our Qing Jing Peak was eating a perfectly peaceful meal in this tavern. What's your justification for coming up and cursing us out, first saying that you want our whole Qing Jing Peak to kneel to you, kowtow, and apologize for our offenses, then saying that our entire Cang Qiong Mountain should be buried together? Exactly who was being preposterous? Hua Yue City is not your Huan Hua Palace's backyard—or are you saying that the entire world is your house?"

Ning Yingying's voice was delicate and crisp, and Shen Qingqiu was flabbergasted to hear it. How had the innocent, naive, and silly Yingying become so good at catfights? And why was the Little Palace Mistress acting like a beast not properly leashed in her cage, biting at everyone she laid eyes on?

"Our Qing Jing Peak has always cleaved to etiquette," Ning Yingying continued. "Shizun was a proper teacher and said not to bicker with foul-mouthed little children. This is the only reason we've tolerated you thus far. Are you finished? If you are, then leave. Don't get in the way of our meal—I can't eat while looking at your face!" After she spoke, she picked up a cup of tea from the table and splashed it at the other girl's feet.

The Little Palace Mistress didn't dodge fast enough, and a few drops of tea splashed the hem of her dress. "You?" she screeched. "You shrew!"

Ming Fan couldn't take it anymore. Throwing aside his chopsticks, he sneered. "Don't think we're afraid of you just because you're the Old Palace Master's daughter. After all, you're just a little girl relying on her daddy. Neither your seniority nor your cultivation are worth anything—though when it comes to your ability to annoy, you're first-rate. Shrew? The way I see it, you're a bigger shrew than anyone else here. You've lost every last shred of Huan Hua Palace's face!"

Shen Qingqiu was shocked.

Qing Jing Peak's disciples had always been so meek in front of him; they wouldn't even dare fart. If he told them to feed the chickens, they'd dare not walk the dogs too. If he told them to make rice, they'd dare not make congee. Yet it turned out they were actually quite the smack-talkers when let loose.

The Little Palace Mistress's face went white with anger. She'd heard Qin Wanyue say that this soft, bewitching little girl had been sect siblings with Luo Binghe for many years, as well as childhood friends and innocent playmates. All at once, envy and hatred flowed forth from her, and she suddenly raised her hand, a black shadow shooting out from her sleeve like a poisonous snake.

Fuck, she has a new whip!

When the other customers in the tavern saw that it was finally coming to blows, they left at top speed. Although, as they passed Shen Qingqiu, their expressions were unperturbed, like this was nothing strange. It seemed that the residents of Hua Yue City had long since grown accustomed to this sort of scene. The waiter even adeptly stuck a bill on the post before he walked out.

The Little Palace Mistress was the Old Palace Master's beloved daughter. Her martial skills were the product of his hands-on teaching, and her weapons were far from ordinary in quality, the whip's strikes swift and fierce.

Meanwhile, Ning Yingying was the beloved youngest shimei who was pampered by the entirety of Qing Jing Peak; she very rarely encountered danger and had virtually no real battle experience. Her sword waved back and forth, and though she warded off the attacks, a keen eye could see she was having trouble.

For his part, Ming Fan wanted to aid her, but he couldn't get past the circle of the iron whip's dance and could only fret helplessly.

Shen Qingqiu assessed the situation, then casually plucked a green leaf from the flowerpot by his foot, which he sent flying.

The fragile green leaf was filled with spiritual energy. When it collided with the iron whip, there was a piercing crash of something hard on metal. The Little Palace Mistress was unable to see what had gone wrong, but she felt the space between her finger and thumb go numb before her whip slipped from her hand and flew away.

Ning Yingying also started. She'd been about to meet another attack with her sword, but once she saw that the Little Palace Mistress had no weapon with which to block, she hurriedly pulled back, afraid of really stabbing her.

But the Little Palace Mistress had no similar mercy, and her reaction was supremely fast. The second her weapon left her hand, she reversed the momentum of her arm to turn it into a slap.

A smack. Ning Yingying held her face, her head turned to the side.

Fuck!

The five fingerprints standing out on Ning Yingying's face and the cheek already swollen on one side went to show that the attack had been utterly ruthless. Shen Qingqiu's heart ached in terrible distress.

You dare hit a disciple who even I've never touched?!

However, at the sight of Ning Yingying's pretty face made lop-sided—one side swollen, one side smooth, and all over tremendously unsightly—the Little Palace Mistress was enormously satisfied and felt she had vented her resentment. She rubbed her wrist, raised her chin, and laughed. "If your Shizun won't teach you, then let this Palace Mistress do it. Lesson one: One must consider propriety when speaking."

Who the fuck are you, trying to teach my disciples in my place?!

Ming Fan drew his sword. "You bitch! You've gone too far! Let's go all out!"

The Qing Jing Peak disciples couldn't take it any longer. Their youngest shimei had been hit—how could they just let that go?! They yelled and drew their swords, their blades gleaming with dazzling light.

Shen Qingqiu was trying to figure out how to teach the Little Palace Mistress a lesson without inciting greater bloodshed or exposing his location as quickly as possible...when he suddenly noticed that within the crowd of Huan Hua Palace disciples, one person was behaving most strangely and suspiciously.

Shen Qingqiu observed that person for a few seconds, after which his heart thumped.

Not good, he thought silently.

It would no longer be so easy to slip away.

8
Death

AT FIRST GLANCE, this disciple looked rather ordinary. They were mixed in with the crowd of Huan Hua Palace disciples, hunched over and huddling close, gaze flickering around.

Shen Qingqiu only noticed him because his face was one color, his neck another, and his hands yet two more different hues. Furthermore, within this agitated mob where everyone's blood was running hot, he didn't draw his sword or cry out for a fight, nor did he glare at the offending party with furious eyes. Instead, he brushed back and forth through the Huan Hua Palace disciples with his head down, looking just like a pickpocket taking advantage of the ruckus.

As far as Shen Qingqiu knew, only one type of person acted like this.

While Ming Fan was mid-clash, sword ringing and clanging, he looked back and cried, "Xiao-shimei! Shimei, how are you?"

Ning Yingying had halted for a while, like the slap had stunned her silly. Now she finally came back to her senses. Her face was half-red, half-white, expression furious and eyes teary, but she brandished her sword to fight back. She'd suffered this humiliation because she'd been momentarily softhearted. This time, she would show no mercy whatsoever.

The shop's interior descended into a massive brawl. To the side, Shen Qingqiu saw an old cat lazily curl its tail, licking its fur in the sunlight. He scooped it up with a single hand and tossed it into the tavern. Surprised, the old cat screeched and darted back and forth between the two fighting camps. Shen Qingqiu lowered his head and followed it, slipping into the circle of battle.

Once this strange person had mysteriously pushed into the fray, both sides paused. Afraid to harm an innocent, Ning Yingying hesitated slightly. But the Little Palace Mistress didn't have such reservations. Picking her whip back up, she lashed out as before. Shen Qingqiu chased the old cat back and forth through the hall, calling the name he'd given it on the spot.

In the midst of this chaos, Ning Yingying's hands were obviously tied, especially as she was afraid to make a careless move. Yet she kept feeling as if someone was lifting her elbow, then like someone was pushing her shoulder. It was as if even when she didn't move her sword, it still danced, throwing off silvery light.

Suddenly, two smacks rang out, and the Little Palace Mistress held her face, dumbstruck and petrified like a wooden chicken, frozen on the spot.

These two slaps had been much louder and sharper than the one she had delivered to Ning Yingying's face.

Everyone in both camps had seen Ning Yingying's arms fly, slapping first with one hand then the other, giving the Little Palace Mistress two smacks in the face. In tacit agreement, they all stopped where they were.

Ming Fan cheered. "Xiao-shimei, nice hit!"

"No, that actually wasn't me..." Ning Yingying said weakly.

"Don't be scared, it's already done!" Ming Fan said encouragingly. "Everyone knows she started it. You were considerate enough not to hurt her, and she responded with a sneak attack. Serves her right!"

The crowd of Qing Jing Peak disciples agreed, one after another.

The Little Palace Mistress's tears glistened. "You...you...you dare to hit me... Not even my daddy's ever hit me!"

"No, it really wasn't me..."

"It was you!" Ming Fan cut in, scoffing. "Remember, whenever Qing Jing Peak's disciples are bullied, we must return it twofold! If we don't hit back, we'll betray all of Shizun's lessons!"

Shen Qingqiu internally cheered together with the disciples. Good boy Ming Fan had earnestly taken his teachings to heart.

Yes, yes, yes, grudges must be repaid in just this way!

Stealthily, Shen Qingqiu slipped into the group of Huan Hua Disciples and finally caught that old cat, which was still howling and screeching. Regardless of how stupid a person might be, they could still see that something was off with him.

While cupping her two red, terribly cumbersome-looking swollen cheeks, the Little Palace Mistress glared at him, filled with resentment. "Hey! Who exactly are you? Who would dare mess with me like this?"

The Huan Hua Palace disciples surrounded him, yelling, "The Palace Mistress is asking you a question!"

Shen Qingqiu bent over and released the cat. Then he straightened and pointed to the disciple who stood hunched and lurking in the back. "Instead, why don't you ask: Who exactly is *he*?"

All at once, every one of those gazes focused on that person.

The Little Palace Mistress was still in a rage, so at first she only gave the indicated disciple a sideways glance, but the more she looked, the stranger she found him. Leaving Shen Qingqiu alone for now, she turned to the odd disciple and said suspiciously, "Who are you? What are you doing, dressed like that? Are you really from our Huan Hua Palace? Why have I never seen you before?"

The disciple mumbled but couldn't manage a reply.

The Little Palace Mistress turned to her subordinates. "What about you? Do you recognize him?"

Realizing things weren't looking good, the disciple made an eerie sound, which made everyone turn their blades on him.

"Don't get close!" Shen Qingqiu warned with a raised voice. At the same time, he plucked another leaf, then flicked his wrist and sent it forth.

This time both Ning Yingying and Ming Fan saw the way that leaf flew, and they balked. Enveloped in a sword glare's glow, the leaf pierced through the air and sliced open the strange disciple's outer robes, cleaving through his clothes to reveal the skin underneath.

At this, it was like everyone had seen a ghost, and they backed up several steps. Some went even farther, shrieking as they leapt straight out of the tavern.

Scarlet-colored skin.

It was in perfect accord with Shen Qingqiu's guess. To his knowledge, only one type of entity held themselves with that posture: a sower disguised as a normal person.

Only the usually exposed parts of the sower's skin had been painted to resemble the hue of an ordinary person's, and so the sower's cover was blown on the spot. As such, it decided it had nothing to lose and rushed forth with a yell, eyes bloodshot. These disciples were young juniors, so most of them hadn't gone on the recent excursion to Jin Lan City. Therefore they had only heard of this monster and never seen it. Now that a real one had appeared before them—and one that was madly grabbing at whoever it saw at that—they were all scared senseless.

When the sower threw itself toward a Qing Jing Peak disciple, Shen Qingqiu flashed between them and planted a foot in the sower's chest, sending it flying through two tables and spewing fresh blood everywhere.

He turned his head to yell at the group. "Hurry up and leave!"

Instead, Ning Yingying latched on to him, crying and laughing. "Shizun—is it you, Shizun?"

No way! My face is covered in dirt and whiskers and you can still recognize me?

Shen Qingqiu was very slightly moved. However, in this kind of situation, choosing not to leave and on top of that staying behind to be a burden—and moreover calling out his true identity despite his disguise... As expected, she was still dumb.

When the sower tenaciously threw itself toward them again, refusing to relent, Shen Qingqiu pushed Ning Yingying away with a hand as gentle as spring. Then, with the other hand as harsh as winter, he flicked a fire technique at the enemy.

It didn't hit.

No—the fire didn't even come out!

The fountain of blood that had remained dormant and hidden in Shen Qingqiu's throat for many years once more began to stir. He'd had enough of this Without a Cure, the poison that just loved dropping the ball at key moments!

He snapped his fingers continuously over and over, but not a single flame sprang forth. Like a lighter out of lighter fluid, he click-click-clicked away, but there were no sparks no matter how he snapped. While Shen Qingqiu became flustered, the sower lunged and latched on to his thigh.

Shen Qingqiu was struck speechless.

He unthinkingly raised his misfortune-plagued right hand. Naturally, he could already detect three red patches happily taking root and growing at a speed visible to the naked eye.

Not fair! Why am I infected so fast every time?!

Perhaps his rage and sorrow alchemized into a fuse, because with his last snap, an explosive burst of flames finally ignited between his fingers. With a kick, Shen Qingqiu sent the sower clinging to his thigh flying, and he struck downward with a palm alight with raging flames.

The sower was engulfed in a blaze of fire and a series of horrible shrieks.

Ning Yingying and Ming Fan tearfully sandwiched Shen Qingqiu on his left and right. "Shizun!"

The other Qing Jing Peak disciples were about to join in, but they quickly retreated under their Shizun's "go outside and run five hundred laps" glare.

Since his disguise was already a wash, Shen Qingqiu scrubbed and wiped at his face until he recovered his original appearance. "Was anyone infected?" he asked. Then, with a heartfelt tone, he finally said a line he'd always dreamed of saying: "Hurry and take some medicine. You must not stop taking your medication!"[5]

One male and one female voice, one high and one low, sobbed into his ears.

"Shizun, we finally found you."

"Shizun, this disciple missed you so much it hurt!"

Shen Qingqiu hadn't even replied when a cold feeling lanced down his back. He pushed aside his two disciples and sent Xiu

---

5   药不能停, "you must not stop taking your medication!" originated as a slogan to encourage people with depression to not stop taking their medication. The phrase was later co-opted as internet slang as a way to say "there's something wrong with you."

Ya flying out from the folds of his robes. With a clang, his blade blocked the Little Palace Mistress's refined iron whip.

If the Little Palace Mistress could have been considered only temporarily enraged during the recent altercation with Qing Jing Peak, then this time her actions truly brimmed with killing intent. She hacked away with the short whip in her hand like it was a knife or an axe, every move vicious and desperate.

"Are you mad?" Shen Qingqiu asked bluntly. "Where does all this rage come from every day?" He'd long wanted to ask that question!

"You wicked villain!" the Little Palace Mistress shouted. "Return the lives of my shixiong and shijie!"

At first, Shen Qingqiu thought that she was once again grieving the Huan Hua Disciples who'd died during the Immortal Alliance Conference. He would never have guessed what the Little Palace Mistress screamed next.

"Just because Ma-shixiong said some harsh things to you while you were being imprisoned, you—you... He died so horribly, so horribly..."

Who's Ma-shixiong? Could it be that nasty, sarcastic pockmarked guy?

"This Shen didn't take a single life when leaving Huan Hua Palace," he said. "So why are you telling me that he died horribly?" He then turned to his disciples to whisper, "He really died? How horrible was it?"

"He really did die," Ming Fan answered, also quiet. "It was utterly, utterly horrible. His entire body was green and decayed. They say it was a highly toxic demonic poison."

Toxic demonic poison? That very much sounded like Luo Binghe's handiwork.

"Quibbling is useless!" the Little Palace Mistress said. "Today, for the deaths of my Huan Hua Palace disciples, I absolutely must make you pay with your life!"

"This Shen has never been good with poison, and there are hundreds upon thousands of ways to kill your Huan Hua Palace's disciples," Shen Qingqiu countered. "Why would I choose the most cumbersome strategy? I did indeed escape from prison, but how can you prove I killed them?"

"Then can you prove you didn't kill them?" a Huan Hua Palace disciple shouted.

If Shen Qingqiu didn't untangle this, he was afraid that in the future, the two sects wouldn't ever be able to let the matter rest. He deliberated a little, then probed further. "What does your esteemed sect's head disciple Gongyi Xiao have to say about this matter?"

The Little Palace Mistress's eyes went wide; the tears that had originally stopped started to fall once more. "You still dare mention Gongyi-shixiong?" She raised her whip and pointed it at Shen Qingqiu. "You think that just because he's dead and can't testify, you can use him however you wish?"

Shen Qingqiu felt like he'd been struck by lightning.

He caught her whip mid-strike between two fingers. He hoped he'd heard wrong. "What did you say? Gongyi Xiao died? When did this happen? Who did it?"

Even in the original work, the worst part of Gongyi Xiao's fate had been an assignment to Huan Hua Palace's border territories, where he became a trivial character.

"Who did it?" the Little Palace Mistress asked savagely. "You still have the face to ask who did it?!"

Huan Hua Palace's disciples surrounded Shen Qingqiu, robes rustling.

"Kill this despicable villain," the Little Palace Mistress ordered. "Take revenge for Gongyi-shixiong, and for the shixiong and shijie who were guarding the Water Prison. Satisfy their grudges!"

Shen Qingqiu's heart went cold. Could Luo Binghe really have slaughtered every last one of the disciples guarding the Water Prison, including Gongyi Xiao?

And was the loss of those hundreds of lives being blamed on him instead?

"Stupid brat, you don't get it regardless of what we say," Ning Yingying said angrily. "Don't you see that my shizun doesn't know?"

Without hesitation, Qing Jing Peak's disciples entered the fray as well. However, swords have no eyes, so lest Shen Qingqiu wanted to be stabbed, he had no time for careful thought. As this fight wouldn't end if they continued as they were, he leapt out of the tavern, lightly calling back, "Come on out!"

As he'd hoped, both camps followed after him rather than go for each other, every disciple trying to squeeze out the door first.

But as soon as Shen Qingqiu made it onto the main street, he was dumbfounded.

A long row of cultivators dressed in various colors were waiting there, ready for battle, glaring like tigers eyeing their prey.

Fair enough. After all, they'd made such a large commotion in the tavern, it would have been pretty unscientific if they failed to draw the attention of other people, right...?

With a light push of his foot, Shen Qingqiu's steps skimmed the roof tiles, and he landed on the eaves with a flip. He took a deep breath, then yelled from the pit of his stomach, "Liu! Qing! Ge!"

Someone flew up on their sword and angrily denounced him. "Shen Qingqiu, your heart is truly wicked. You purposefully fled to this city, drawing people from various sects here. Was it so you could collude with demons and, in one fell swoop, reenact the tragedy of the Immortal Alliance Conference? Whatever it takes, our Ba Qi Sect won't let you succeed!"

So any and all accusations are perfectly acceptable, huh?!

Shen Qingqiu wasn't even in the mood to rant.

Then from the east came the hiss of a sword glare, followed by a person in white who arrived on a sword, fast as lightning. Mind you, his descent was too forceful, pointlessly whipping up a powerful wind that threw the Ba Qi cultivator right off his own blade.

Liu Qingge stood securely on Cheng Luan with his arms crossed. "What is it?"

Too reliable, Great Master Liu!

Shen Qingqiu said with all sincerity, "Get me out of here."

Liu Qingge stared.

"My poison flared up again, and I can't summon the qi to fly my sword. If you don't take me, I'll just plummet from the skies."

Liu Qingge let out a sigh. "Get on."

The crowd gathered to watch from below berated them without rest, saying things like, "Cang Qiong Mountain abets and shelters evil!" and "Bai Zhan Peak and Qing Jing Peak wallow together in filth!"

But they both pretended that they couldn't hear. Cheng Luan soared into the sky, the wind whistling in their ears, leaving the ten or so cultivators who chased them on swords far behind.

"Where to?" asked Liu Qingge.

"To the roof of the tallest building in the city," said Shen Qingqiu. "After that, please help me hold off these people."

"What exactly is up with you? If you didn't wish to be imprisoned, why didn't you say so earlier? You've made things so troublesome. Besides, even if Cang Qiong Mountain couldn't navigate the Water Prison, couldn't we have just destroyed it?"

"That... There was no need to destroy the Water Prison..."

"Get off."

"I'm only saying there was no need. I'm still grateful for your kindness, so surely there's no need to throw me down."

"Something's coming."

Shen Qingqiu didn't say another word and jumped off at once. The tip of his foot touched tile, and he stooped over on the roof of the building.

Cheng Luan's momentum was incredibly powerful. Liu Qingge and his sword did a dazzling somersault in midair, and only then did he manage to brake, eyes fixed attentively elsewhere. Shen Qingqiu also followed his gaze.

Then he heard a sneer behind him. "Where are you looking?"

Shen Qingqiu nearly stumbled on the spot. That "You just wait and see!" hadn't been just talk.

Then again, since when had anything about Luo Binghe been "just talk?"

He'd actually come to capture him, even braving the risk of Xin Mo's recoil... How deep did his resentment run?

Luo Binghe glared fixedly at them, expression dark, then slowly extended a hand to Shen Qingqiu. "Come with me."

"Gongyi Xiao is dead," said Shen Qingqiu.

Luo Binghe went rigid.

"The disciples guarding the Water Prison are also dead," he continued. "Luo Binghe, over a hundred Huan Hua Palace lives, all so I'd be hated and persecuted. Was it really worth it?"

Red flashed in Luo Binghe's pupils. "Whatever, you won't believe me regardless of what I say," he said icily. "Then there's no need for more pointless chatter! I'll ask again: Will you come or not?"

He stubbornly refused to withdraw that hand. Shen Qingqiu had yet to answer when, out of nowhere, over ten people appeared, hemming them in on the roof while riding their swords.

The leader was again that man from Ba Qi Sect. This time, he'd lowered his center of gravity, basically crouched in horse stance upon his sword to prevent himself from being thrown off balance again. He shouted brashly, "Shen Qingqiu is ours, no one else should even think of—"

Luo Binghe abruptly turned his head and yelled, "Beat it!"

He hadn't even drawn his sword, but from his body a powerful blast of spiritual energy burst forth, and a shrill, whistling shriek filled the ears of everyone on the scene. Every last one of the pursuers, along with their swords, was shoved over to fall several meters away. Half of them even slammed into walls or pillars, coughing up fresh blood.

The Ba Qi Sect had met someone genuinely "ba"-dass with overbearing "qi," and they had been wiped out to the last. The remaining spectators were all terrified. This black-clothed young man's cultivation was undeniably spectacular—how come so few of them had heard of him before?

Liu Qingge pushed Shen Qingqiu. "Go. Do what you need to do!"

"Can you handle this by yourself?!" Shen Qingqiu asked. Five-to-two, ah, five-to-two—he hadn't forgotten these numbers. He'd only called Liu Qingge over to help him fight small fry and give him a lift along the way, not to meet a sudden, unfortunate end!

But neither of these two characters were the sort to in any way listen to others. At the first wrong word—no wait, without even a word, they started to fight.

Cheng Luan was incredibly powerful, but Luo Binghe didn't draw his sword. He concentrated spiritual energy in his hand and used his open palm like a blade to meet it head-on.

Shen Qingqiu knew why Luo Binghe couldn't draw his sword. In a duel between masters, one couldn't afford a single error, and this was the sort of moment when it was easiest for Xin Mo to take advantage of an opening and invade its wielder's mind. If Luo Binghe was possessed with demonic qi in plain view of everyone and his homicidal urges greatly increased, drawing the blade wouldn't be worth it.

Luo Binghe's body actually housed two sets of cultivation systems: one with spiritual qi, the other with demonic qi. Because his dual heritage had successfully integrated, these two systems didn't interfere with one another, each operating in excellent form. When necessary, his left and right hands could even use two different attack types simultaneously in a display of power.

But right now, he couldn't draw his sword, and circumstances made it inconvenient for him to access his demonic qi. Thus, his killing power was diminished. For once, he and Liu Qingge were evenly matched.

Deafening sounds shook the sky above the roof, white arcs and spiritual energy exploding together. Their duel was so fierce that none of the cultivators below them dared to rush in recklessly. Even the most inexperienced and undiscerning rookie could see that if one were to so much as graze either man's roiling, murderous qi, they'd ascend right to heaven without any further need to cultivate.

Their fight was so fierce that Shen Qingqiu actually felt an answering urge—if not for Without a Cure having flared up at such an inopportune moment, he too would have wanted to enter the fray. But it was time. He squinted up at the sky, then leapt to the highest level of the building.

On the highest roof, a gale screamed; it felt like it could blow him right off.

Luo Binghe saw this from afar and was seized by impatience. No longer in the mood to fight, the malevolence in his eyes skyrocketed, and he reached for the hilt of the longsword on his back.

He's actually going so far as to draw his sword here?!

"Luo Binghe, don't be rash!" Shen Qingqiu called in a rush.

"Too late!" Luo Binghe said harshly. With a flip of his wrist, Xin Mo was drawn, wreathed in a dark, billowing qi visible to the naked eye.

Cheng Luan stabbed straight toward Luo Binghe. He gently flicked Xin Mo's blade edge, which was as thin as a cicada's wing. From the center oozed wave after wave of something like a chill, and Cheng Luan came to a complete, uncanny stop in midair.

Never once had Cheng Luan disobeyed Liu Qingge's orders, and he couldn't conceal his shock. But Shen Qingqiu knew that the situation was even more severe.

If Luo Binghe really was hit with Xin Mo's recoil in this place, the lives of everyone on the scene, as well as in the entirety of Hua Yue City and within a fifty-kilometer radius, would be forfeit.

As a last resort, Shen Qingqiu unsheathed Xiu Ya. "Come here, Luo Binghe. Today, we must come to a resolution."

Luo Binghe raised his head and gave him a dark look. In the next moment, he'd flashed forward to around a meter away. Then he raised his hand and drew a barrier that covered the entire roof, isolating them from everyone else. At last he smiled, expression twisted. "Resolution? How can this be resolved? Shizun, at this point, do you really think what's between us can be settled cleanly?"

Why can't it?

Shen Qingqiu breathed in lightly. Though he was clutching his sword, he had no intention of fighting. In truth, wielding this blade at this point would have no effect. "As things are now, there's nothing I can say. Sure enough, even if we scheme until we're exhausted, we cannot outwit fate."

Luo Binghe chuckled. "Fate? What is fate? That which let a four-year-old child be humiliated while no one lent a hand to help? That which let an innocent old woman die of heartbreak and starvation?"

With each line, he stepped forward, menacing. "Or that which let me fight with dogs for scraps? Or let the person I wholeheartedly adored lie to me, abandon me, betray me, and shove me down into a place worse than purgatory with his own two hands?!

"Shizun, look at what I've become. Am I strong enough?

"Do you know how I spent those years within the Endless Abyss? For three years underground, at all times and all moments, my mind thought only of Shizun. I wondered why Shizun would do this to me, why he refused to give me even a single chance to explain or plead my case.

"You want me to concede that this was the fate the heavens ordained for me? I thought for such a long time, and I finally understood." Within Luo Binghe's smile there lay a spine-chilling malice. "None of that is important. It's enough to just do what I want. Fate either never existed at all—or it's something I should trample beneath my feet!"

With the scorching sun overhead, the last wisps of cloud had disappeared without a trace. Sunlight flooded through the entire city, its brilliance dazzling, like the entire land had been strewn with pure gold.

Shen Qingqiu turned his gaze away from the sky. Because he'd been staring straight at the sun, unexpectedly, some tears glistened in his vision.

Even though he'd had no other choice, he frankly was greatly responsible for Luo Binghe having reached this point; he had become a dark young man who thought only of revenge on society. Originally, Shen Qingqiu had wanted to stop Luo Binghe from going to such extremes, but everything he had done had not only failed to have a positive effect, it had actually etched Luo Binghe's hatred and resentment even deeper into his bones.

Luo Binghe saw how Shen Qingqiu's expression softened without warning and couldn't help but startle. However, in that same moment, an incredible pain assailed his head. He clenched his teeth, his hand clutching tightly around Xin Mo, which was trying to break free.

No. He couldn't take the recoil here, at least not at this moment!

To his shock, Shen Qingqiu gently said: "Don't let it overpower your mind."

Upon hearing this voice, in his daze, Luo Binghe was transported to those years on Qing Jing Peak.

It became increasingly harder for him to control himself. There seemed to be a sharp knife churning within his brain, and Xin Mo's black flames suddenly surged.

The assault this time was ferocious. Luo Binghe was in unbearable agony—when unexpectedly, someone tenderly embraced his shoulders.

What followed was a blast of spiritual qi akin to the collapse of a thousand-kilometer dike, like a rainstorm after a long drought. It poured into Luo Binghe's body like a flood, extinguishing Xin Mo's malevolence, with which he had reached a deadlock.

Luo Binghe's breathing evened out, returning to normal, but his heart went cold.

Self-detonation.

Some in the crowd below were already yelling in shock. "Shen Qingqiu self-detonated!"

Shen Qingqiu let go of Luo Binghe and slowly backed away, staggering once.

Xiu Ya fell first. Its master's spiritual energy was gone, and a sword exists with its master. The blade shattered into multiple pieces in midair.

Shen Qingqiu had always been in the bad habit of swallowing his blood, but at this moment, he could no longer choke it down.

Having totally exhausted his spiritual energy, he was now lesser than even a common person, a mere ruined shell. His voice was light and fluttering, the wind blowing most of it away, yet Luo Binghe could hear him just as distinctly as before.

What he said was, "For all that has passed, I repay you today."

Think of it as me doing one good thing at the end.

Then he toppled backward and off the building.

At first, Luo Binghe only blankly watched. Everything playing out before his eyes was now many times slower. Even the moment in which Shen Qingqiu fell slowed until it was crystal clear.

The body dropping in midair was like a bloodstained paper kite. Only when Luo Binghe's body started moving by itself, scrambling to catch Shen Qingqiu before he hit the ground, did he finally discover that Shen Qingqiu's torso was light and insubstantial, his entire body empty, without a wisp of spiritual energy. He truly was akin to a paper kite, liable to be ripped with the slightest force.

In fact, one wouldn't need force. It had already fallen apart.

Luo Binghe was still in disbelief.

Didn't Shizun hate his blood more than anything? Wasn't he unwilling to even be near him, to associate with him at all?

So why, at the last moment, had he so gently helped to contain Luo Binghe's mind, as tender as he had been in those years long past?

Why hadn't he hesitated to help Luo Binghe suppress Xin Mo's recoil, to the point of destroying his own spiritual energy?

All around him, people seemed to be muttering things like "execute the demon," and "eliminate your own for the sake of justice."

Luo Binghe's mind was in a muddle. He could only hold Shen Qingqiu and mumble, "Shizun?"

The Qing Jing Peak disciples had fought the Huan Hua Palace disciples the entire way and finally arrived. Ning Yingying had by now heard that Luo Binghe was alive. She was both surprised by and happy at this sudden reunion, but then she saw Shen Qingqiu, his eyes peacefully closed. The words she'd been about to say took a turn, and she said in a trembling voice, "A-Luo... Shizun... What happened to him?"

Liu Qingge walked forward, a smear of blood lingering by his lips. His expression was heavy as he said, "He's dead."

The disciples were dumbstruck.

"Who killed him?!" Ming Fan suddenly yelled.

The crowd's gaze focused on Luo Binghe.

Strictly speaking, Luo Binghe hadn't killed Shen Qingqiu, but Shen Qingqiu had indeed self-detonated and died before him.

The disciples behind Ming Fan drew their swords, about to attack, when Liu Qingge said, "You can't defeat him."

Ming Fan's eyes were bright red. "Liu-shishu! Then surely Liu-shishu can kill him to avenge Shizun, right?!"

"I can't defeat him either," Liu Qingge said lightly.

Ming Fan choked.

Liu Qingge wiped away the blood by his mouth. "Neither did he kill Shen Qingqiu. ...However, though he didn't kill Shen Qingqiu, Shen Qingqiu did indeed die because of him." Each of Liu Qingge's words was like a knife drawn from a sheath. "Cang Qiong Mountain must avenge this grudge!"

Luo Binghe turned a deaf ear to it all. His mind was entirely a mess and totally at a loss, and he still held Shen Qingqiu's rapidly cooling body. It seemed like he wanted to call out to Shen Qingqiu, to shake him awake, but also didn't dare to, as if he were afraid of being scolded. He murmured, "Shizun?"

"Stop calling him Shizun," Ming Fan snapped. "Shizun can't bear such a burden! My brethren, let's fight together. So what if we can't defeat him, what more can he do than kill us?!"

Ning Yingying spread her arms to stop him. Ming Fan was furious and agitated. He thought that Ning Yingying was still clinging to old affections. "Shimei, look what it's come to. How come you still don't get it?"

"You shut up," said Ning Yingying. "What would Shizun think if you rushed to your death like this? If he heard, what would he say? Shizun would rather be infected than see us taken advantage of or bullied, yet you'd throw your life away so easily?"

All these years, Ning Yingying had always had the charming attitude of a young maiden. At these abrupt, harsh words, Ming Fan halted.

After a long while, tears burst forth and flowed down his face. Sobbing, he wept miserably. "But this... It's so unfair to Shizun... Even though he absolutely didn't collude with demons, everyone kept saying that he did—that he was a killer, a degenerate—and they threw him in the Water Prison... He didn't even get a chance to clear his name."

He choked on his sobs. "Even though he obviously loved this brat so much... At the Immortal Alliance Conference, he bet five thousand spirit stones on him without hesitation—his hopes for him were that high! Whenever anyone praised him, Shizun would be so happy... And afterward, he refused to return Zheng Yang to Wan Jian Peak and insisted on keeping it so he could erect a sword mound on the back of the mountain... He was heartbroken for so long... And in the end, this is what he got!"

Luo Binghe listened in a trance, unsure if this was illusion or reality.

Is that so? At that time, Shizun too was...utterly heartbroken?

Ning Yingying stepped toward Luo Binghe. Her eyes were red, but her words and breathing were steady. "A-Luo, we weren't there for the Jin Lan City incident, but we all heard about it. I don't know why you didn't return to Cang Qiong Mountain despite being alive, and I don't know why you wouldn't stand up for Shizun, and I certainly don't know what happened at the Immortal Alliance Conference. But Shizun's kindness when he raised and nurtured you, and his feelings when he doted on and protected you, those weren't fake. Everyone knows; we saw for ourselves."

After a pause, she continued. "If you feel that the Shizun in the old days didn't treat you well, then think back on the day you lost your jade pendant. Our shixiong inexplicably backed off all at once. You yourself knew there was something strange, right? No one else on Qing Jing Peak would turn leaves into weapons for the purpose of teaching a small lesson."

Luo Binghe involuntarily clutched Shen Qingqiu tighter. He whispered, "I was wrong, Shizun, I really...know I was wrong. I...I never wanted to kill you..."

"My words end here," Ning Yingying declared. "If Shizun really did wrong you in some way, and you can't under any circumstances forgive him, then at least today he finally repaid it all, right? So from now on, you..." At this point, she couldn't take it anymore and turned her head away. "I ask that you...stop calling him 'Shizun.'"

"Repaid?"

That's right. Moments ago, Shizun had said something about repaying him.

Had Shen Qingqiu been saying...that in exchange for pushing Luo Binghe into the Endless Abyss, he would also fall for his sake?

Luo Binghe started to panic.

"I don't want you to repay me. I...I just couldn't get over my anger." He was speaking to himself. "I couldn't get over it. Whenever you saw me, you acted like you'd seen a ghost. Then you would happily smile and laugh with others, when in the past you only did that with me. And to me—you would say only the bare minimum to me. And you kept suspecting me of everything... But I was wrong." He stammered and stuttered, talking as he wiped the blood away from Shen Qingqiu's face.

"You disdained me for being a demon, so I was afraid that if I returned directly to Cang Qiong Mountain, you'd throw me out. I thought that if I took over Huan Hua Palace and became like you, a leader of righteous cultivators, I could maybe make you happy..."

Luo Binghe's voice trembled. "Shizun... I...I really..."

9
Borderlands

Evening came with high wind in the borderlands, whistling through the scattered houses of the little garrison. All down the street, only a single teahouse shone from within. Warm yellow lantern light lent the place a semblance of life.

The so-called borderlands weren't the border between two countries or cities. Rather, they were the border between the Demon Realm and the Human Realm.

The two races belonged to different worlds; for the most part, the Endless Abyss ruptured the space between them. But there were always those few places where the boundary between realms was weak, where time and space were in disarray, and where the residents of the two realms would often end up slipping back and forth between them. On occasion, in some cases, someone maliciously stole across the border.

Few ordinary people were willing to live in a place where the demon race could emerge from thin air and vanish like ghosts, skulking around one day then killing and pillaging the next. Thus, signs of human life in the borderlands only grew sparser by the year. Even when the dimensions of different realms began to intermingle in a prosperous city, the population would usually end up evacuating in a mass migration, leaving behind only the disciples sent by the cultivation world to guard the borderlands.

Lu Liu poured the newcomer a bowl of hot wine as he chatted with the few others gathered around their stove. "Brother, where did you come from?"

"The south."

"Out that way?" A few people looked at each other, their expressions understanding. "It must be hard out there right now."

The newcomer raised the bowl of wine and frowned. "Who said it wasn't? There's a battle twice every three days. No one can endure that kind of torture."

"Cang Qiong Mountain and Huan Hua Palace both belong to the four major sects. Why are they making such a fuss these days?" someone in the corner cut in. "Their disciples can't come face-to-face for a second without getting into a huge fight. Won't their sect leaders control them a little?"

"How long have you been in this damn place, where birds won't even stop to shit?" Lu Liu said. "You've gone too long living under a rock. It's precisely because they have their sect leaders' tacit permission that the disciples have been fighting harder and harder!"

"Why's that? Liu-ge, tell us about it."

Lu Liu cleared his throat. "It's quite complicated to explain: Do you know who the current head of Huan Hua Palace is?"

"I heard it's some kid."

Lu Liu laughed harshly. "If Luo Binghe can be called a 'kid,' then you and I are less than nothing. This Luo Binghe is something else. He came from Cang Qiong Mountain Sect and was even the head disciple of Qing Jing Peak's Shen Qingqiu. At that Immortal Alliance Conference a while back, he dominated the rankings. Now that was truly a sight."

"If he came from Cang Qiong Mountain, why would he become the head of Huan Hua Palace?" a listener said doubtfully.

"After the Immortal Alliance Conference, Luo Binghe disappeared for three years. No one knows where he went or what he did during that time. Shen Qingqiu said that he'd perished, so everyone believed he was already dead. Who could have known that three years later, he'd make a grand comeback—he had even become an influential figure at Huan Hua Palace. Then he forced Shen Qingqiu to self-detonate on the spot in Hua Yue City."

"I never understood that," said the newcomer. "This Shen Qingqiu, was he wrongly accused or did he deserve such a fate?"

"Who can say?" said Lu Liu. "That Cang Qiong Mountain is naturally united against outsiders, and they'll fight anyone who says anything. They've always been like this, holding relations over reason. They won't even let people talk about something as damning as that An Ding Peak Lord, Shang Qinghua, fleeing to the Demon Realm. Huan Hua Palace changed masters not long after that Hua Yue City incident; the Old Palace Master went into seclusion and disappeared without a trace. Luo Binghe took power in his stead and kills anyone who says anything otherwise."

"All because of a dead man?" someone muttered.

"This dead man has made quite a few waves," said Lu Liu. "Shen Qingqiu is from Cang Qiong Mountain Sect, and he was even the peak lord of the second-ranked peak. His corpse should by rights go back to Qing Jing Peak to be interred with the former generations of peak lords. But the problem is, Luo Binghe refuses to return the body."

Everyone was imagining something along the lines of Luo Binghe whipping the corpse or putting it up on display, and their hair stood on end.

"If he refuses to return it, can't Cang Qiong Mountain take it by force?" someone asked. "That peak lord of Bai Zhan Peak is still around."

Lu Liu shrugged. "He can't beat Luo Binghe."

"What?!" The group's worldview was shattered. In the eyes of the world, the peak lord of Bai Zhan Peak had always held the position of undefeatable war god. That this peak lord "couldn't beat" someone or whatever...was honestly unthinkable.

"You don't know?" Lu Liu asked. "Ever since Hua Yue City, Bai Zhan Peak's Liu Qingge has fought Luo Binghe countless times, but he's never won once! And that's not all. Luo Binghe brought Shen Qingqiu's body back to Huan Hua Palace, and only a few days later, he personally kidnapped Qian Cao Peak's Mu Qingfang."

"Qian Cao Peak has always disregarded worldly affairs," someone said. "They help the dying and heal the injured. So how did they manage to provoke this devil incarnate?"

"Luo Binghe took him back to Huan Hua Palace and told him to heal and revive Shen Qingqiu." Lu Liu sighed. "The man had been dead so long, he'd gone stiff. What was there to heal?"

"When I see the two sects fight, Cang Qiong Mountain always likes calling Huan Hua Palace the dogs of demons. Why is that?" the newcomer asked.

"That's because, for some reason, the entirety of Cang Qiong Mountain from top to bottom insists that Luo Binghe is a fiend from the demon race," said Lu Liu. "Numerous abbots of Zhao Hua Monastery have personally testified that spiritual energy circulates normally inside Luo Binghe, but Cang Qiong Mountain still insists on calling him that... Those two sects go back and forth, repaying grievance with grievance, growing their feud larger and larger.

The way I see it, one day, their ships will capsize together and no one will survive.

"So—" In the end, Lu Liu didn't forget to comfort himself. "—being sent to guard the border to be free and idle like us was actually a good thing."

"I really can't understand what's going on with this master-disciple pair, let alone those two sects," the person in the corner said, confused.

"One theory is it comes down to a grudge as deep as the sea. But there's another theory, and this old Lu thinks that one is more believable. Let me tell you all—"

Lu Liu was just about to launch into another round of enthusiastic gossip, when suddenly a burst of knocking sounded outside the door.

Everyone in the room immediately raised their guard. All their mischief and exhaustion was swept away, and each individual readied their weapons and spiritual artifacts.

The borderlands possessed only rare traces of human life, being abnormally desolate. The members of their squadron were the only permanent residents of the entire garrison. The ones who'd gone out on patrol wouldn't have returned so quickly, and the few remaining residents were even less likely to risk death by wandering outside in the middle of the night.

No one inside responded, and after a while there were two more knocks on the wooden door.

"Who is it?!" Lu Liu called out harshly.

Suddenly, a chill wind blew by and extinguished the oil lamps and candles on the table. The room instantly turned pitch-dark, leaving behind only the dull, red light of the stove faintly burning.

The silhouette of a man carrying a sword on his back cast itself through the window paper. The person called in a clear voice, "Liu-ge, it's me. It's too cold today, so I came back early. Open the door and let me warm up with a cup of wine."

The group released the breaths they were holding and cursed.

"Old Qin, you trying to die? Just knocking on the door without a word! If we didn't know better, we'd have thought you were eaten by a ghost!"

The person outside the door chuckled.

Lu Liu felt something was strange, but he couldn't quite figure out what. He said, "Come in!" and opened the door.

A gust of frigid wind swept into their faces, but there was nothing there.

Lu Liu slammed the door shut. "Light the lamps! The lamps, the lamps!"

The newcomer's hand trembled. He turned and formed a fire seal, and the flickering flame illuminated a few silhouettes. He'd yet to light a candle when he turned back around and stuttered, "Liu-ge, I...I want to ask you."

"What are you stammering for?" Lu Liu said, impatient.

"There were only six people in this room, right? So why am I seeing...what looks like seven?"

Dead silence.

Suddenly, there was a loud cry. No one knew who had attacked first, but screams and the sound of clashing weapons rose and fell.

Lu Liu yelled, "Light the lamps! The lamps!"

Everyone hurried to form fire seals, but their movements were too uncoordinated. The flames and silhouettes swayed wildly and disoriented their vision, making it even harder to see who was who.

Afraid of harming their own, no one dared to swing too aggressively, and so the thing that had wormed into their midst took advantage of the chaos. It was like catching fish in turbid water: a claw here, a knife there. As Lu Liu mentally cursed, something suddenly grabbed him by the neck.

His eyes rolled back into his head and his feet slowly left the ground, unable to see what had grabbed him by the throat. Just when he thought his life would end right then and there, the door flew open, and a whirling gale swept inside. Another silhouette charged in.

No one saw how the newcomer fought, but Lu Liu heard an uncanny cry by his ear that sounded like it had come from the thing holding him by the neck. Its grip loosened.

The six people in the room hadn't yet recovered from their fright, and some were lying flat on the ground. This new person snapped his fingers, and the oil lamps in the room lit all at once.

He bent down to study the bodies for a moment, then rose. "They're fine. Just unconscious."

This person was caked in black mud, like he'd just been excavated from a grave, and his face was covered in whiskers that densely obscured his facial features. Despite his lean figure, his face was that of a large, bearded man's.

Lu Liu finally stopped shivering and stared him up and down for a long time before cupping his fist. "Many, many thanks to this distinguished gentleman for your assistance chasing away that creature!"

The new person slung an arm over Lu Liu's shoulder. "This humble one has something to ask."

"Please do."

"What year is it?"

As Shen Qingqiu had tumbled his way down from the mountain, covered in mud, half-rolling, half-crawling, he'd fervently prayed for Airplane Shooting Towards the Sky to be destroyed ten thousand times. Destruction by spiritual energy implosion or by asshole, either was acceptable.

Originally, most of the strategies he'd thought up to preserve his life had involved faking his death.

But what was the point of faking one's death? The trope of plotting a fake death with a puppet or look-alike while allowing the original person to flee had been done to death in TV series!

So the strategy he settled on was dying for real.

That day in Hua Yue City, he really and truly had self-detonated, and even done a good deed along the way, absorbing an enormous amount of the berserk demonic energy in Luo Binghe's body. To say that his meridians had been ground to dust was no exaggeration.

Only by facing death could one return alive.[6]

The Sun-Moon Dew Mushroom was also called the "flesh mushroom,"[7] and this name was entirely literal. Though this mushroom wasn't especially useful for cultivating, it still grew by collecting spiritual energy from nature along with essence from the sun and moon. If you planted its sprout in soil rich with spiritual energy, nurtured it, meticulously sculpted it, and watered it with blood and qi, once it

---

6   *This is a play on a quote from Sun Tzu's Art of War, "Throw them into danger and they will survive; put them on deadly ground and they will live."*

7   肉芝, *"flesh mushroom," is another name for the real life lingzhi mushroom, which the Sun-Moon Dew Mushroom is based on.*

matured, you could cultivate a living body of flesh. The body could grow just fine, but it was impossible to also create a soul via this method. That was to say, you could only grow a soulless, empty shell.

You couldn't find a more suitable vessel.

"Plant a Little Shen in the spring and harvest a Big Shen in the autumn" was no longer just a dream!

But the Dew Mushroom wasn't a Chinese cabbage, something you could simply grow with a handful of fertilizer and water. Shen Qingqiu had destroyed a number of mushroom sprouts before he'd cultivated one that hadn't grown crooked.

A good while back, he and Shang Qinghua had calculated the coordinates to carry out this long-distance operation. Beneath the tallest building of Hua Yue City, they had set up a transportation array, and at the time when the sun was highest, Shang Qinghua had triggered a second array—this one for activation—on Cang Qiong Mountain. The moment Shen Qingqiu's soul left his body, he had been sent into the mature Dew Mushroom, which had been buried deep in the mountains of the borderlands.

Three locations, three arrays. If you connected them with straight lines, they would have formed the most stable shape: an equilateral triangle. Reasonably speaking, it was absolutely stable, absolutely reliable.

The only flaw was a certain person.

"Great Master" Airplane Shooting Towards the Sky was just *too* reliable.

Shen Qingqiu had been worried about flaws like overlarge arms or uneven legs, or a crucial part simply not growing, but none of these problems had occurred. However, sure enough, using chemical fertilizer to mature the Sun-Moon Dew Mushroom had resulted in some side effects.

Just after waking, Shen Qingqiu had waited quietly for a while, but he hadn't heard that detestable Google Translate-like notification.

He internally exploded with joy: *The System hasn't appeared, ha ha ha, the System hasn't appeared! This big shot's changed hardware—I'm not going to reinstall a virus like you, ha ha ha!*

Though he could only rest assured temporarily, he couldn't resist dancing in joy.

Dancing in joy my ass.

His whole body was still buried in the ground. He couldn't move an inch!

For a day, he remained buried, gathering strength from his fingertips until he could finally move his limbs. Only after this did Shen Qingqiu finally, shakily crawl out.

Once he broke through the earth's surface, he didn't even get the chance to revel in the fresh air of freedom before he fell face-first onto the ground.

Ah, this body isn't listening to my commands again. This left him splayed on the mountainside.

Shen Qingqiu spent an entire day walking while doing radio calisthenics, right up until the evening, when his gait finally resembled a normal person's. At least he was no longer simultaneously putting the same arm and leg forward.

The human cast they used had been based on his former appearance as Shen Yuan. It didn't compare to Shen Qingqiu's immortal poise, but it wasn't a bad mortal container. It just had a bit of a certain listlessness—the listlessness of a worthless pretty boy idling his life away. But because he'd used some of his blood while cultivating the Dew Mushroom, a touch of foreign influence was inevitable. When Shen Qingqiu tumbled to the side of a creek and used a sharp mountain rock to scrape away his whiskers for a look, his new face was still three or four parts of ten similar to Shen Qingqiu's. Without a word, he re-pasted the whiskers onto his face.

Finally, after managing to tumble his way to the bottom of the mountain, he grabbed a passerby and asked the year.

Fuck, it's already been five years!

He could understand that right after waking up, his body was uncoordinated and occasionally unable to move because he needed some time to adjust to the new configuration—but only waking up after being buried for five years? What was with this?!

Also, a roast was a roast, but this body was practically bursting with spiritual energy.

The original Shen Qingqiu's body had been quite abundant in spiritual energy when Without a Cure wasn't causing it trouble, but the difference between that and the sensations he had in this one—it was like the difference between two bars of battery (still enough to use) and a full charge (the second after charging and pulling the cord). He would even go so far as to say that he was a *generator*.

Did this count as shedding his body and replacing his bones,[8] changing his tendons and cleansing his marrows?[9]

Was this the drumbeat leading up to his own ascension to OP-hood?!

After so many years, Shen Qingqiu felt for the first time that he'd acquired a lick of the dignity owed to reincarnated transmigrators. For the first time, his unskilled self would perhaps not drag down his seniors in the transmigration regiment!

---

8   脱胎换骨, an idiom describing being reborn as a Daoist, but can also mean "turn over a new leaf" or "change completely."

9   易筋洗髓, refers to 增演易筋洗髓内功图说, a 内功 (martial arts focusing on qi circulation) manual.

When he tuned back in, Lu Liu was rambling.

"These past few years, the demon race has invaded more and more often. All sorts of demons, ghouls, and ghosts have poured into the Human Realm—a major battle is likely imminent... Oh, I haven't yet asked this distinguished gentleman for his immortal name."

The words "Ha ha, this humble one is the untalented Qing Jing Peak Lord of Cang Qiong Mountain, the Xiu Ya Sword, Shen Qingqiu of the Central Plains" veered off course just before they reached Shen Qingqiu's throat.

So close, so close—he'd almost given them his old name. He couldn't think of another name in the moment, and after muttering for a bit, he resolutely said two words: "Peerless Cucumber."

Everything that had happened before was as unto smoke. From today forth, as he walked the jianghu, he would use this ID, which had been plastered all over the comments section for years.

After he spoke, Shen Qingqiu glided away, leaving only a room full of petrified people in his wake.

After a while, the newcomer mumbled, "He just said he was... Peerless... What was it?"

"Peerless...Chrysanthemum?" Lu Liu guessed.

"Wasn't it Peerless Crown?"

"No, no, no, it was Peerless Crazy Flower!"

Shen Qingqiu had walked several tens of feet away, but at the sound of this, his feet slipped out from under him.

Uh, perhaps he would have to think about it some more later. Maybe switch to a different name...

The first step to starting his all-new life would, of course, have to be proceedings with which Shen Qingqiu was most familiar. First, for a prop, he needed a folding fan, one with a white silk base, decorated with an ink wash painting of mountains and rivers.

Shen Qingqiu snapped the fan open and waved it before his chest, sending his long hair and whiskers flying. Perhaps his image wasn't ideal and was slightly unsuited to said prop, but that didn't matter. With a folding fan in hand / Badass act at my command.

Shen Qingqiu placed one foot on a mountain rock and said, "Speak. Exactly what intentions have brought you to infiltrate the Human Realm?"

A crowd of trembling people—ah, no, demons—huddled before him. Though to be honest, from appearance alone there was basically no difference.

"Usually we only...steal small trinkets from the Human Realm and take them back to trade," the frontmost one said, shaking with fear.

The Demon Realm didn't have a common currency, so they often bartered. If something caught their eye, they'd trade for it, or if it didn't, they wouldn't. Between the demon race's questionable skill in craftsmanship and artistic tastes, to them, an everyday piece of Human Realm embroidery was a top-notch artisanal product. Therefore, all manner of ordinary trinkets from the Human Realm were exceedingly popular among demonkind. By contrast, the items they valued least were the various crystals with special effects that were a dime a dozen in their homeland.

But being a dime a dozen in the Demon Realm didn't mean there wasn't a market for them among humans!

Shen Qingqiu snapped his fan shut and spoke solemnly. "This remote and destitute town, where neither birds shit nor chickens lay eggs, has poor production rates and a stagnant economy, and the level of general happiness is lower than average. It is wrong for you to profit from their misfortune."

The minor demon was at a loss. He was pretty sure that in the moment he was captured, this...lofty master had also been stealing— ah, no, borrowing?—clothes, as well as the fan with which he was happily fanning himself.

I was compelled by my circumstances! Shen Qingqiu thought. *Surely you can't expect me to wander around in clothes that had been exhumed from the dirt like some kind of savage?*

However, this actually opened up a new line of thought. These minor demons had never dared to do more than snoop and thieve here and there. But if he could supply them with an honest channel for small goods, perhaps within this world that revolved around cultivation and monster-fighting, he could forge paths into a new frontier based on farming and amassing capital?

Shen Qingqiu irresponsibly fantasized for a while, then felt that if he were to accept underlings, they needed to understand each other's cultural practices.

"Do you eat rotten flesh?" he asked amiably.

The minor demons shook their heads. Shen Qingqiu was about to sigh in relief when the leader effusively said: "My pa said that only the rich and influential can afford rotten flesh."

"Enough."

It isn't at all a question of economic access, okay?!

After climbing to the top of the Demon Realm, Luo Binghe had been more than influential, right? So how come he'd never enjoyed this kind of thing on page?!

After a pause, Shen Qingqiu changed his angle. "What's your name?"

The first one replied, "Six Balls."

"What does that mean?"

"When I was born, my pa held me and said I was six balls heavy."

Shen Qingqiu was speechless. *What balls? Shot put balls or ping-pong balls?! This kind of name is absolutely meaningless.*

The rest of the demons then scrambled to declare their own names, each one more unbearable than the last; they seemed to take much pride in them.

Are the names chosen by demon commoners all this literal?!

Family names didn't exist in demon culture, so the names they chose were daring and audacious, bold and unrestrained. You could tell at a glance that those generals with names that left people speechless, such as Elder Sky Hammer or Elder Single Arm, had started as nobodies and climbed up to the top. But if they came from nobility, such as Mobei-Jun, Sha Hualing, or Luo Binghe's father Tianlang-Jun, their name situation was a little better.

It then occurred to Shen Qingqiu that it was fortunate Luo Binghe hadn't been tossed into the Demon Realm and found there. If he'd been taken in by demon commoners, in accordance with these naming conventions, he might've been dubbed something that made it sound like his parents hated him.

What would he be called? Jade-Faced Little Playboy? Evil Demonic Incubus Spirit?

No, no, no, it needed to be something more earth-shatteringly terrifying.

Then he remembered that in the original story, some girl had bashfully expressed that Luo Binghe's "that" was very "*that.*" With an uncountable harem and innumerable trysts, he could effortlessly pull his trigger in every manner of setting. And even after eons, the gun remained infallible, as vigorous as ever. In truth, the name Peerless Cucumber would have suited Luo Binghe quite well, but since Shen Qingqiu had already taken it, then Luo Binghe might as well be...Heavenly Pillar-Jun?

Ha ha ha ha, fuck! Luo Heavenly Pillar! Ha ha ha ha, how painfully exhilarating!

Shen Qingqiu had been laughing for a while when he abruptly slapped himself.

The fuck is wrong with you?! Getting carried away, using the Great Master protagonist to come up with a tasteless dirty joke in your head! What's funny about this? Don't you get that some people are off-limits for your crass humor?!

The minor demons watched this lofty master first laugh so hard that he fell to the ground, then slap himself in anger. Mystified, they didn't dare do so much as breathe loudly.

Then Shen Qingqiu suddenly stopped smiling and pressed his fan into Six Balls's shoulder, pulling him close. As he did, Shen Qingqiu plucked a sword tassel from the demon's waist. "Where did you get this?"

It was a sword tassel, but it was no ordinary sword tassel.

This decoration belonged to the number one female lead, Liu Mingyan—it was Shui Se's sword tassel!

It was what male and female leads always exchanged as love tokens, you get it? Back at Cang Qiong Mountain, Shen Qingqiu had made a point to take special notice of this one, so it didn't need to be distinctive to stand out to him. How had this thing fallen into the hands of a minor demon in the borderlands?

Terrified, Six Balls responded, "I-I-I didn't steal it, I found it..."

Hit the streets and find me another one then, if it's so easy, Shen Qingqiu thought. "Where did you find it?"

"Th-th-these days, an important person has been traveling the roads at night, though first they send their subordinates to clear the way. We were a little curious and hid by the roadside, then afterward we found this on the road."

The important person the minor demon described had to be someone at the pinnacle of power in the Demon Realm.

This type of character didn't frequent the borderlands; they would only draw attention. In fact, the local environment was most unsuitable for them. Exactly what kind of important person would boldly take over the roads with such swagger, even going so far as to leave behind an intimate item of Liu Mingyan's?

The first possibility that came to Shen Qingqiu's mind was, of course, a certain someone.

He asked, "The important person you're talking about, was it...a good-looking young man?" When he thought about it, he decided against suppressing his conscience and clarified. "Not just good-looking, he's *very* good-looking, *especially* good-looking. Fair skin, pretty face, tall. He doesn't smile often, but when he does, it's exceptionally dark."

Six Balls shook his head, then suddenly blushed.

Why are you blushing? Shen Qingqiu interrogated him for a while, but he couldn't get any answers. He decided internally that this mystery person probably wasn't Luo Binghe.

Luo Binghe carried Xin Mo, and it was a super crazy, ridiculous, huge-ass cheat that broke every single rule. With a casual slash, it could cleave the space between the two realms, and with that slice, you could open yourself a passage through which to enter the

Demon Realm. Luo Binghe would never expend the effort required to make a special trip to the borderlands, let alone to faithfully follow the paths of smugglers.

If that was the case, a problem arose. Demons had passed through the area, yet they had left behind Liu Mingyan's belongings. Could it be that Liu Mingyan had slipped up and been captured?

Shen Qingqiu didn't remember Liu Mingyan, being the number one female lead, suffering such treatment in the original work. What dumbass insignificant bandit would dare touch Luo Binghe's wife?

Furthermore, though the Liu siblings normally each cultivated on their own peaks, the original work had mentioned that their relationship was quite good. Perhaps their sibling bond only seemed distant because neither was the clingy type.

But whether Shen Qingqiu saw her as Liu Qingge's little sister or as Qi Qingqi's beloved disciple, he couldn't just stand aside and do nothing.

Moreover, at this time, the System was (seemingly) unable to threaten him (for now), and thus he had nothing to fear with regard to restrictions or massive deductions of B-Points or whatever. So why not go check it out?

"Where is the rift in the boundary between realms?" Shen Qingqiu asked.

At midnight, Shen Qingqiu hid in the treetops with all traces of his presence concealed, overlooking the area below.

After an unknown length of time, a certain patch of air began to visibly distort.

Shen Qingqiu's eyes lit up. He held his breath, attention rapt, and watched a youth in black rush out of it.

They were a great distance away from each other, but Shen Qingqiu's eyes were incredibly sharp, and he could see the boy clearly. This youth was around seventeen or eighteen years old, with a tense expression on his sharp and handsome face. Actually, Shen Qingqiu found that face somewhat familiar; he just couldn't remember where he'd seen it. Nevertheless, he was certain he had.

Suddenly, a crisp female voice, at once sweet and cold, broke the silent night and echoed through the forest. "Bai Zhan Peak's disciples are truly exceptional. Your body's constrained by a hundred immortal-binding cables, yet you're still able to wipe the floor with a great many of my subordinates and you've fled so far. I truly can't lower my guard for an instant!"

On hearing this voice, realization hit Shen Qingqiu.

A demon who was beautiful, of noble background, and had subordinates, who a minor demon would blush at mentioning—it had to be Sha Hualing.

Sorry! So what if this girl was one of the female leads? She hadn't been around for way too long, and thus he'd pretty much forgotten about her.

If Liu Mingyan had fallen into Sha Hualing's hands, her fate was even more cause to worry. If Sha Hualing settled for slashing up Liu Mingyan's face, she'd be going easy on her.

No wonder this youth's running posture had seemed odd just now, his body noticeably heavy. Shen Qingqiu had only focused on his face before, but now he continued looking downward. As it turned out, there were numerous thin silver wires bound around the lad. The color of his robes confirmed that he really was from Bai

Zhan Peak, but Shen Qingqiu could summon no memory of ever having seen such a young disciple before.

The youth knew he couldn't beat his opponent in speed, so he abruptly braked, his eyebrows furrowed fiercely. "If you want to fight, let's fight!"

There was a flash of gauzy red cloth, and Sha Hualing walked toward him with swaying hips that emphasized her figure. "It took me so much effort to catch you," she said, full of smiles. "How could I bear to fight you? Quickly, why don't you come back with me?"

The youth's temper was violent, and he spat at her.

"You won't?" Sha Hualing asked. "I won't damage your spiritual energy, but chopping off an arm or leg or whatever won't injure that part of you."

As she spoke, her right hand reached out to grab the youth, but before she could touch him, an odd tremor suddenly traveled down her fingers. Sha Hualing assumed she'd fallen for some trick on the youth's part and quickly withdrew. She then raised her hand to examine it. Her five cinnabar-painted nails had been uniformly trimmed a noticeable length shorter.

It was only her nails, and it hadn't hurt in the least, but Sha Hualing's blood went instantly cold.

"Who's there?!" she shouted.

If someone lurking nearby could cut her nails with such ease, then they could just as effortlessly slice open her neck.

Shen Qingqiu was feeling much more relieved as he released a twig plucked clean of leaves.

In truth, he'd just wanted to scare Sha Hualing a little, and while he was at it, keeping her nails so long really wasn't good. Every time

Shen Qingqiu saw them, he was worried they'd break, which made him extraordinarily uncomfortable. Plus, they often scratched Luo Binghe's back into a bloody mess… Even if Airplane Shooting Towards the Sky liked that kind of hardcore flavor, and even if Luo Binghe's healing ability was inhuman, it didn't mean this habit was proper or indicative of a healthy lifestyle.

Sha Hualing's killing intent spiked. She whirled a red cloth and summoned a mass of chilling demonic qi, gathering it around her fingers, and then struck at the youth. This maiden wasn't scared stiff, she was scared *angry*. Truly a character.

Shen Qingqiu had no choice but to leap down from the treetops to drop between the two. He gathered energy in his hand and fired a spiritual blast, directly meeting Sha Hualing's.

He had known that this body was full to bursting with spiritual energy, but he hadn't thought it was bursting to such an extent. Their palms hadn't yet connected when Sha Hualing was flung straight back like a repelled magnet. At the same time, those skimpy clothes tore once more…

Though this was an unexpected bonus, Shen Qingqiu had always insisted on the rule of "Under no circumstances look at an unexpected bonus from women in this world who have above-average looks." He censored it himself.

Sha Hualing was also more than direct. Last time, she had let out some vicious words, but this time, having weighed their respective strengths, she had no words for the occasion and just dropped into a roll. When she lunged into that patch of distorted air, her figure instantly vanished.

Shen Qingqiu tossed his fan several times, channeling spiritual energy into it and transforming the fan into a blade, which he sliced down with a flip of his hand. The immortal-binding cables fell into some hundred pieces.

The youth performed the respectable act of cupping his fist. "Many thanks to Senior for the rescue!"

In turn, Shen Qingqiu performed the respectable act of asking, "You're a disciple of Bai Zhan Peak?"

"I am."

"Under who?"

"My master is the Bai Zhan Peak Lord, Liu Qingge."

Shen Qingqiu was genuinely astonished.

Liu Qingge never accepted disciples. On that Bai Zhan Peak of his, at most there were people equal to him in seniority, and other than that, there were the disciples his shixiong and shidi had taken in. The man himself wasn't interested in teaching. To be fair, what Bai Zhan Peak called "teaching" was just putting effort into beating up on one person in particular...

Shen Qingqiu had some slight suspicions. "What's your name?"

"Yang Yixuan," the youth answered, loud and clear.

Like I said, he looked familiar, so I'd definitely seen him somewhere before, right?

A young child could certainly grow up in five years. Shen Qingqiu looked Yang Yixuan up and down as he thought of how Liu Qingge had sworn that he wouldn't accept disciples because it was too troublesome. But he had in the end, hadn't he!

"Senior?" asked Yang Yixuan.

"How has your Shizun been these past few years?" asked Shen Qingqiu.

At their parting in Hua Yue City, Liu Qingge had lost to Luo

Binghe, and it must have been a true blow. Shen Qingqiu felt he absolutely had to ask after his shidi's current condition.

"He's been defeated in every battle," Yang Yixuan said honestly.

Shen Qingqiu was silent.

The idea that the Bai Zhan Peak Lord could be associated with the phrase "defeated in every battle"... It really made one shake in one's boots.

"Who did he fight?" Shen Qingqiu asked. "Luo Binghe?"

Yang Yixuan humphed. "Who else but that little beast?"

Shen Qingqiu's expression twisted slightly. Yang Yixuan himself was quite a bit younger than Luo Binghe, yet he still called him "little beast." Who had he learned this from?

He didn't yet know that nowadays, whenever anyone in Cang Qiong Mountain Sect referred to Luo Binghe, it was always as "little beast," "demon fiend," or "ingrate." If they called him by his name and added "that bastard," it was considered courteous.

"How did you fall into that demon woman's hands?" Shen Qingqiu asked. "Her words just now were a little strange. What was that 'how could I bear to fight you' business about?"

Yang Yixuan's face immediately flushed red. "If that demon woman hadn't used such devious methods, first disguising herself as a woman who'd fallen into misfortune, then when I became suspicious, suddenly taking off...taking off—I absolutely wouldn't have fallen into her trap and been captured!"

Shen Qingqiu instantly understood. "Look at yourself! Look at yourself. Are you really a representative of Bai Zhan Peak?" he lectured. "Avoiding feminine charms doesn't mean fearing them. So what if she took off her clothes? So what if a maiden stripped right in front of you? Back when your shizun went to fight succubi, their entire cave was filled with unclothed bodies!"

Mind you, at that time Shen Qingqiu had also been there, and true enough, he'd begun to suspect that Liu Qingge was either asexual or impotent...

Yang Yixuan's face was filled with longing admiration. "An entire cave! As expected of Shizun!" Then he said curiously, "Does Senior know my master well? How else could you know of how my shizun fought succubi?"

Shen Qingqiu coughed once. "Old affairs. Old affairs."

Getting back to the main topic: Sha Hualing hadn't just captured Yang Yixuan, she'd likely also taken Liu Mingyan. She would capture Cang Qiong Mountain Sect disciples in such a high-profile manner for only one reason. Something had gone wrong with Luo Binghe.

Luo Binghe's cultivation system was unscientific in the extreme. He had to multitask and coordinate the two systems within him in order to combine diametrically opposed forces into one working network. This meant that his spiritual and demonic qi had to operate as mutual checks and balances against each other. However, once Xin Mo got involved, his demonic qi surged and the balance was lost, throwing the whole into disarray.

In order to resolve this issue, Luo Binghe employed a method that involved looking for human vessels. When the moon was full, he'd search for someone with strong spiritual energy and pass the excess demonic qi in his body to them. In exchange, he absorbed the greater part of the vessel's spiritual qi. In this way, he naturally regained his balance.

However, because Luo Binghe's demonic qi was far too intense, the human vessel would often be left crippled by the energy transfer.

Generally speaking, these extraction implements were limited to a single use.

And of course, Luo Binghe wouldn't do the demanding work of capturing human vessels himself. Naturally, it was Sha Hualing who stored people in cages for him to pick from as he pleased, no explicit orders needed. Luo Binghe simply needed to deploy Xin Mo to cleave open a passage to the Demon Realm on the night of the full moon and grab somebody to use.

The sad thing was that in the original work, Sha Hualing had gone to all that effort, and then Luo Binghe had gotten together with three beautiful nuns from Tian Yi Temple—victims she had personally selected. As one might imagine, Sha Hualing nearly went mad with anger!

"While you were captured, did you see anyone else?" Shen Qingqiu asked. "Where were you held?"

Yang Yixuan shook his head. "As soon as we entered the rift between realms, we were in the lair of that demon woman, Chi Yun Cave. I was shut in a single-person cell and didn't see anyone else."

Shen Qingqiu tossed and caught Liu Mingyan's sword tassel several times. "My guess is that you weren't the only one captured."

He thought for a bit, then decided to go take a look. In any case, tonight wasn't the full moon, so it wasn't time for the extraction. Luo Binghe would be away, busy stirring up havoc and inciting chaos in the Human Realm, so he probably wouldn't come looking to meet with Sha Hualing. And saving Liu Mingyan, who shouldn't have appeared here in the first place, wouldn't count as messing up the plot. Rather, he'd be correcting it.

Yang Yixuan hurried to catch up. "I'll come too! My sword is still in that demon woman's hands."

"You're not scared she'll take off her clothes?" asked Shen Qingqiu.

"There's no way I'd be scared," Yang Yixuan said disdainfully. "Besides, throughout that entire trip she took them off dozens of times. There's nothing remarkable about it anymore."

Shen Qingqiu turned around, speechless. *So the reason she shut you in a single-person cell was actually so she could strip for your eyes only—what an unbelievable bonus. Young man, if you continue at this pace, you'll definitely die to the male lead. How worrisome! You're Liu Qingge's sole disciple!*

Passing through the spatial rift was like passing through a gushing flow of warm water. Once they re-emerged, they were in demon territory.

On the human side, it was already past midnight, but on the demon side, twilight had only just fallen. The air was particularly arid; after standing there a moment, Shen Qingqiu grew a bit dizzy, like he was suffering from altitude sickness. As far as the eye could see, there seemed to be little difference from the Human Realm, although the trees were a tad sparser. Looked like their greenification efforts were a bit lacking.

Yang Yixuan led the way. They passed through craggy stones and soon found the opening of Chi Yun Cave.

It's an honor to see you at last, o cultural monument of the demon race. Seeing it in person, Shen Qingqiu found that sure enough, it was...unique.

It was in the demon race's nature to prefer darkness. Most of their permanent and temporary residences were located wholly underground. When he took in the entire entrance, it seemed to him to be an exceptionally splendid mausoleum.

A tablet inscribed with three characters in twisty red calligraphy erected in front of a big pile of rocks—tell me, what could that be if not a tombstone? Shen Qingqiu thought.

He cupped a handful of spiritual energy, ready at all times to make a mess of any enemy who might show their face. But after he started down the tomb passage—no, the cave entrance—not once did he see any guards. When he thought about it, it made sense. Only demons had ever sneaked into the Human Realm to throw their weight around. What humans would suicidally run over to this side? The demons had absolutely no need to arrange for guards.

The pair stealthily moved deeper. After passing through the stone corridors, they arrived at a large hall.

The hall was carpeted with the intact skins of all manner of strange beasts; at first glance, they seemed to be still alive. Sha Hualing was currently barefoot, pacing back and forth on an enormous tiger skin spread over the floor of the hall.

Shen Qingqiu was worried that Yang Yixuan would recklessly make a sound and alert her. Just as he was about to remind him to shush, he saw that the child had sensibly shut his mouth. Reassured, he turned back around.

On both sides of the hall were numerous cages, each holding tightly bound cultivators in differently colored uniforms. Some looked awfully young, but he also saw veterans. Some were drowsily nodding off, and others were glowering in fury.

Sha Hualing walked over to one of the cages, arms crossed. "You people from Cang Qiong Mountain Sect really are both troublesome and annoying! Capturing two of you took so much effort, and one even escaped before he could be shut away." She clenched her teeth. "If not for—if not for... I'm really itching to break all your legs!"

In this cage, Liu Mingyan sat with her veil covering her face, her eyes closed and legs crossed, impervious to outside matters.

Sha Hualing saw that she was being ignored and smiled coldly. "That thing on your face, don't you ever take it off? Oh, I see, could it be that your face is so ugly that you dare not take it off out of shame?"

Girl...do you know who you'll envy the most in the future? Saying she's ugly is just you giving yourself a thorough slap in the face!

Sha Hualing's woman's intuition was acting up. No matter how she looked at Liu Mingyan, the cultivator irritated her from every angle. She opened the cage, dragged Liu Mingyan out, and yelled, "Kneel!"

Liu Mingyan was naturally unwilling to do so. Though she was thoroughly without spiritual energy, she still stood firm. Sha Hualing pushed and shoved, but she was utterly unable to make Liu Mingyan's knees bend even a little. Enraged to the point that steam came out of her ears, she snatched the veil off Liu Mingyan's face.

In that moment, Sha Hualing's delicate, snow-pale face became even more snow-pale.

Turn around! Turn around! I want to see! Shen Qingqiu howled internally. *Quickly, let me see what the most beautiful woman in this book looks like!*

All these years, he'd been mindful of his status, so he couldn't have just said, "Hey, Shizhi, I heard you're super pretty, so I wanted to look at your face. May I?" That sounded like something a pervert would say when sexually harassing someone. But having spent so long unable to see Liu Mingyan's face, he felt like he was about to burst!

However, before Liu Mingyan could turn and let him experience the joy of a first glance, malice flashed through Sha Hualing's eyes. Her fingers curved into claws and shot toward Liu Mingyan's face.

And thus for the second time that night, Sha Hualing was sent flying, and she was finally unable to stop herself from coughing up a sullen mouthful of blood. A dash of self-consolation flashed through her mind: *At least my clothes weren't damaged this time. I won't need to change again, right...?*

Although Shen Qingqiu had sent her flying, she'd still clawed five gashes into his sleeve. *Didn't I trim those fingernails an hour ago?* he thought, shocked. *Are they capable of unlimited regeneration?*

After tossing Sha Hualing away, he promptly turned his head to look at Liu Mingyan, and as soon as he did, his feet slipped out from under him. In the blink of an eye, she'd instantly put her veil back on—

What's wrong with letting me have a glance?!

Yang Yixuan had found his sword stabbed into a seam in the rocks, and he had already started hacking at the chains on the cage doors with matchless speed. A throng of cultivators swarmed out with each chop.

Then Shen Qingqiu saw three navy blue silhouettes out of the corner of his eye and said with great alarm, "Stop, stop! Don't do anything impulsive!"

Confused, Yang Yixuan turned his head. "Is something wrong, Senior?"

The words had barely left his mouth when Shen Qingqiu realized that he'd already opened the cage at hand, and three dainty Daoist nuns with faces that could have been cast from the same mold rushed out of Chi Yun Cave like a trio of whirlwinds.

Buddy, by haphazardly releasing everyone like this, you've released some people who shouldn't have left!

He had released the three sisters responsible for settling Luo Binghe's demonic qi in the long term!

But the blunder had already occurred. Shen Qingqiu's heart flooded with tears, but it wasn't like he could run after the nuns and stuff them back into their cages. There was no other option; he could only join in releasing people.

As he freed them, he sighed and lamented. He was dead. He'd managed to totally ruin a plot thread—the first meeting between the male lead and three members of his harem. A freak accident had messed up the scenario in which they fooled around and cultivated together. He could only place his hope in that hardworking employee, Sha Hualing, who would bravely go back to war and ideally recapture them to present to Luo Binghe. It was criminal! Criminal!

Shen Qingqiu was still wallowing in remorse when he lowered his head and unexpectedly found himself looking at a familiar face. His heart thumped.

Fuck, fuck, fuck. It truly was an unlucky year. His enemies kept marching down that narrow road.

Qiu Haitang was huddled in the cage, staring at him with a bewildered expression.

Shen Qingqiu was stupefied for a couple of seconds, then feigned ignorance. He motioned for her to hurry out, then nonchalantly turned around.

With his current appearance, no one (should have) recognized him. Moreover, five years ago, countless pairs of eyes had witnessed the scene of Shen Qingqiu's self-detonation. There was nothing to worry about.

After coughing up blood, Sha Hualing remained sprawled on the floor in a daze for a while, then finally struggled into a seated position with great difficulty. She focused her gaze and yelled, "It's you?

Who the hell are you? You actually dared follow me here! You sure have some guts!"

Yang Yixuan looked like it had suddenly occurred to him to ask this question as well. So as he was setting people free, he asked off-handedly, "Oh, right, Senior, who are you?"

"Oh, right" my ass. Young man, your reaction time is way too slow! Also, what's with that tone, like you're asking something tangential and unimportant?!

Shen Qingqiu was considering whether to introduce himself with the title of Peerless Cucumber again when Sha Hualing humphed out a laugh. "Whatever, you've come this far—so don't imagine I'll allow you to leave."

She clapped her hands, bells jingling around her wrists. After a moment, Chi Yun Cave's guard regiment finally flooded into the hall from every corner.

Chi Yun Cave was Sha Hualing's private residence, so her regular underlings weren't around, and these useless troops were nothing to fear. Those minor demons circled around and around them, raising and lowering their arms, looking exactly like they were performing some kind of backwater dance ritual. Shen Qingqiu was mystified by the sight. But he was impatient, so he prepared to send them all flying with his fan when to his surprise, it seemed like countless strands of hair had fallen all over him, constraining his movements.

Immortal-binding cables.

Even though these motley troops didn't have much fighting ability, they were obviously trained. Each held a hair-thin immortal-binding cable, and they circled him nonstop, winding him into a giant ball of string until he was fully entwined.

Sha Hualing hadn't managed to cheer in victory before Shen Qingqiu laughed, then violently stomped on the floor. The air filled with the sound of snapping strings.

They had burst. The immortal-binding cables had been thoroughly snapped by this person who flooded them with spiritual energy!

More or less everyone there was so terrified, they completely forgot the task at hand. This really was the first time they had seen someone who could use spiritual energy to simply snap immortal-binding cables.

What a straightforward and brutal method of freeing oneself!

"Just run!" Shen Qingqiu yelled.

The freed cultivators didn't need additional encouragement; most of them were already long gone. Yang Yixuan and Liu Mingyan had just struggled free of their immortal-binding cables, and the circulation of their spiritual energy was still unstable. Knowing they would only get in the way if they stayed and seeing that Shen Qingqiu would likely be able to handle things, they retreated, leaving with only a "Senior, take care."

The underlings didn't know whether to chase them and remained stuck in place, waiting for their superior's orders.

Sha Hualing pointed at Shen Qingqiu, a strange gleam in her eye. "Catch him!" she shouted. "Don't worry about the others—just him! Hold him down, even if you die trying!"

A few hodgepodge soldiers threw themselves at Shen Qingqiu, and he sent them flying with his fan. Then something heavy pressed down on his head.

A giant net.

Countless immortal-binding cables, each the thickness of a pinky finger, had been woven into a giant net, which was draping down upon his head. When it settled over Shen Qingqiu, its weight alone forced his knees to fold, and he nearly fell flat on the ground.

Where did you get this kind of bizarre prop? With cables this thick, are you sure it's for binding immortals? Maybe you mean elephants?

Sha Hualing waited a while, and only after seeing that Shen Qingqiu was indeed unable to struggle free this time, she lazily approached.

Her previously wretched state had been swept tidily away. Sha Hualing felt that she had completed a momentous task and was wholly content. Even her reprimands took on a coquettish tone. "If a hundred immortal-binding cables can't hold you down, then why wouldn't I use a thousand, or ten thousand?" she chuckled. "This immortal-binding net wasn't originally prepared for you, and yet it was used on you, so you should feel supremely honored. Don't flail about! As long as you behave, I won't do anything to you."

"If you won't do anything to me, can I trouble you to withdraw this net?" asked Shen Qingqiu.

But the demon race's star employee Sha Hualing had jumped right back into her grand missionary sales pitch. "It seems that you were blessed with extraordinary talent," she said as she crouched down, though she was speaking mainly to herself. "If you were to surrender and pledge yourself to my people's banner, power and glory would be within your grasp. Of course, even if you won't pledge yourself, it doesn't matter. What should be done must be done; some suffering will be unavoidable. You should consider this carefully."

No wonder Sha Hualing had ignored the others fleeing the cave and concentrated all her firepower on him. Luo Binghe needed spiritually powerful human vessels, abundant in spiritual energy. Of all the cultivators she had captured, none could have been more spiritually powerful than Shen Qingqiu. So this brat was planning to offer him to Luo Binghe as a human vessel!

Releasing the three beautiful flowers had been a purely unthinking mistake. Shen Qingqiu had certainly never planned to fill in the gap they left behind himself. He had that old feeling of having accidentally picked up the wrong script—it made him vaguely suspicious that that scam of a System was still around.

Shen Qingqiu was thinking up escape plans when Sha Hualing fixed her slightly messy hair, and with a swing of her hips, forged ahead out of the hall.

From a distance, Shen Qingqiu heard the sound of her soft and delicate laughter. "My lord, it isn't the night of the full moon. Why did you think to visit this subordinate? Although you came at just the right time. As it turns out, I've prepared a special gift for you— it's right in here."

In a split second, a flood of hot blood mixed with cold sweat surged into Shen Qingqiu's head.

He didn't know where he found this burst of explosive power, but he grabbed the side of the net and sent the bottomless pool of spiritual qi in his body outward in the form of a spiritual blast.

Bang!

A giant boom sounded. Sha Hualing's smile became fixed on her face. She sprinted back to the inner hall in a panic and was left staring tongue-tied at the sight.

In the middle of the hall, every last one of Chi Yun Cave's minor demons lay sprawled every which way, all over the ground. In the center of the immortal-binding net, there was an immense hole, its edges still sizzling with flashing sparks, and wisps of white smoke drifted through the air.

That man was, in a word, terrifying. He'd rent a devastatingly large hole in this specially made immortal-binding net. And he was gone.

The person behind Sha Hualing passed her and strolled into the hall. Chi Yun Cave was lightless and dim; only his straight and slender silhouette was visible, along with the subtle silver light reflecting off the embroidered patterns on his black robes.

After a moment, Luo Binghe spoke with a tone that was neither pleased nor angry. "And this is your special gift?"

"Due to a momentary miscalculation, I let him get away!" Sha Hualing said bitterly.

Her distressed heart was dripping blood. An immortal-binding net woven from thousands of immortal-binding cables, originally meant to be used on those stinking cultivators from Cang Qiong Mountain Sect, had been torn open with a massive hole just like that. This wasn't something she could just sew and patch with a needle, then go back to using like it was nothing!

Luo Binghe's back was facing her. He lowered his head and looked over the wreckage as he said icily, "I seem to recall telling you that people from Cang Qiong Mountain Sect were off-limits."

Drops of cold sweat dripped down Sha Hualing's forehead. Luo Binghe had indeed told her this. However, the spiritual energy levels of Cang Qiong Mountain Sect's disciples were generally higher than those of other sects' disciples by a good margin, and so they were the most suitable human vessels for extraction. Clinging to wishful thinking, she'd just captured a few, thinking that maybe she could switch their clothes and slip them into the collection undetected. She hadn't expected that Luo Binghe would somehow still be able to tell who she'd captured, even after they'd all fled. Internally, she couldn't help but feel her blood freeze over.

"Don't be angry, my lord," she said hurriedly. "I accidentally captured two of them, but I released them right after. Rather, this time, this subordinate found someone exceptional. I've never seen a cultivator with more abundant spiritual energy. If you had that one person, you'd no longer need to switch to a new vessel every month." She bit her lip and added, "As long as you give me...a certain thing."

After waiting for a moment, she suddenly extended her hand to catch the object tossed her way. Securely clutching it in her palm, she smiled, determined.

At this time, Shen Qingqiu had already run miles away and was terrified out of his mind.

His terror wasn't because he'd just made an explosive getaway from right under Luo Binghe's nose, but rather because in that split second, he'd heard an exceedingly familiar and hateful voice.

A mechanical voice, with a tone like Google Translate.

Fuck, fuck, fuck, fuck. New hardware should be guaranteed virus-free! Where's my promised chance to turn over a new leaf, to henceforth be a bird, soaring high and free?!

Shen Qingqiu covered his ears as if, this way, he could pretend the voice didn't exist, and in this manner he dashed from the Demon Realm to the Human Realm as fast as lightning, tearing the entire way through from the desolate wastes to the borderlands. Yet that demonic sound poured into his brain unceasingly, as though it were stationed within his very psyche.

[Activating... Activating... Binding to soul...]

[Debugging... Contacting customer service...]

So because it was bound to his soul, the System had reactivated upon encountering Luo Binghe?

I switched bodies, so the connection is bad, and therefore you need to contact customer service, huh?

Luo Binghe was truly the bane of his existence!

Fortunately, aside from repeating those few keywords in a half-dead manner, the System was utterly incapable of forming complete sentences. Shen Qingqiu smacked his head the whole way, but upon seeing signs of human life here and there, he considered his appearance, then slowed his steps and strolled back into the garrison town.

This small border town seemed more alive during the day than it had at night. It couldn't be called flourishing—the streets were neither wide nor narrow, and the pedestrians were neither many nor few—but with the storefronts open, it could still be considered to be thriving.

Beside a tea shop with its flag fluttering in the wind, a young man and woman stood gazing into the distance, swords in hand.

"Why haven't you returned to Cang Qiong Mountain?" Shen Qingqiu asked as he walked over to them.

Liu Mingyan gave him a shallow bow.

"The disciples from the other sects have already returned," Yang Yixuan said hastily. "Seeing that Senior has managed to escape, we too are now at ease."

Shen Qingqiu entered the tea shop with them, finding a table at which to sit down. To the side, some people who had originally been idly chatting suddenly cried out in alarm upon glimpsing him.

"Ah, it's...it's..."

Shen Qingqiu turned around to look. It was those border guard disciples he'd saved the night he first crawled out of the ground. The person who had first seen him stammered, unable to call out a name.

"It's you, Peerless...-xiansheng!" Lu Liu rushed to say.

He mumbled another word after "Peerless," but it came out remarkably muddled, muttered from beneath his tongue. The others mimicked him one after another, with some degree of hastiness: "It's you, Senior Peerless...!"

Shen Qingqiu nodded his greetings, internally deciding that he really had to take up another title without delay.

"Senior, are you called Camellia? Commitment? Commander?" Yang Yixuan said blankly.

Shen Qingqiu coughed twice and mumbled, "It's..."

After using this ID for so many years, for the first time he finally felt a bit ashamed of it.

He put on a stern expression. "Last night, disciples from various sects saw me in Chi Yun Cave. Though I can't conceal the fact of my existence anymore, if other people ask about me, say as little as possible. It would be ideal if you could keep your lips sealed on this topic altogether."

"Why? Senior, aren't you familiar with my master?" asked Yang Yixuan.

"Uh, we are indeed quite familiar..."

While Shen Qingqiu was still unsure of what to say, the table to the side continued their conversation.

"Liu-ge, why don't you elaborate. What exactly is the alternative theory?" one person asked while spitting out melon seed shells.

"About that, it's really rather interesting," said Lu Liu. "This theory apparently originated with insiders and spread from there. So this Luo Binghe and Shen Qingqiu..."

Upon hearing these two names, Shen Qingqiu's heart thumped. He involuntarily straightened his posture, pricking up his ears to listen, and the motion of the fan in his hands slowed. The pair of disciples from Cang Qiong Mountain Sect also couldn't resist looking over.

Lu Liu drank a mouthful of tea. "This Luo Binghe and Shen Qingqiu were master and disciple, right? This Luo Binghe came from a humble family and had suffered the hardships of the world since he was young. After becoming a disciple of Cang Qiong Mountain Sect, he still went underappreciated for a while and was beaten down and humiliated by his peers. Fortunately, Shen Qingqiu treated him with great warmth and kindness."

He spoke with great flourish, his cadence rising and falling. With a traditional rosewood gavel in hand, he would have looked no different from a professional storyteller.

Shen Qingqiu inwardly nodded. Right, he too could agree that until he kicked Luo Binghe down into the Endless Abyss, he'd been quite kindhearted.

Yang Yixuan snorted. "What use was that warmth and kindness, didn't he still..."

"Doesn't this theory run absolutely contrary to the rumors that Shen Qingqiu abused his disciples?" one person asked, flabbergasted.

"You're already astonished at this point?" asked Lu Liu. "Then what are you going to do when I say that while this master and disciple were together, day and night, hidden feelings were born?"

The three people at Shen Qingqiu's table had each taken a mouthful of tea. Upon hearing this sentence, Shen Qingqiu and Yang Yixuan simultaneously spat theirs out. Though Liu Mingyan didn't spit out hers, her hand shook and her teacup tilted, spilling its contents all over the table.

Everyone at the other table sucked in their breaths, one after another.

"That's the theory?!"

"That's right!" said Lu Liu. "But strictly speaking, it was only Luo Binghe who harbored impure thoughts toward Shen Qingqiu—a one-sided delusion."

A one-sided delusion? A one-sided delusion?!

"What sort of person was Shen Qingqiu? Peak lord of Qing Jing Peak. What was the way of Qing Jing Peak? To be tranquil of heart and forsake desire, devoting all thoughts to the lawful path of cultivation. Shen Qingqiu rejected the mortal world and avoided entanglement with others, and so because Luo Binghe sought after the unattainable, love gave birth to hate!"

Blue veins rose on Shen Qingqiu's forehead and the backs of his hands.

"L-Love gave birth to hate?" Yang Yixuan asked, astonished.

"If you think of it this way, it's obscenely easy to explain everything else," Lu Liu said. "Without a doubt, the whole sequence of events at the Immortal Alliance Conference went something like this:

"Luo Binghe entered the battlefield as Qing Jing Peak's head disciple. Because of his remarkable performance, he was filled with confidence. Right then, the demonic beasts ran loose, the mountain was sealed, and Shen Qingqiu entered Jue Di Gorge to provide backup. Seized by a momentary fit of madness, Luo Binghe took the chance to confess his true feelings to his shizun."

Shen Qingqiu held his forehead in misery.

Why, why did it seem like for every ten lines this person said, nine would be about right, but the last one would sound so off?

And it was exactly due to that last sentence that the implications of the entire account became so bizarre!

"Shen Qingqiu was of noble and unsullied moral character, so naturally he delivered a firm rejection," Lu Liu said solemnly.

Shen Qingqiu was a little moved. Other than his bleeding heart of a zhangmen-shixiong, he'd never expected to hear someone else willing to use the phrase "noble and unsullied moral character" to describe him.

Who could have predicted that right after, the story line would take a nosedive?

Lu Liu continued, full of emotion. "Who could have predicted that after being rejected, Luo Binghe, in the grips of despair, would be overtaken by wicked thoughts to the point that he lost his mind and embraced the abominable. Out of lust, he tried to force Shen Qingqiu to submit!"

Shen Qingqiu dug his fingers into his head of messy hair, burying his face in his hands.

Yang Yixuan was thoroughly speechless. The gates of a whole new world had just been opened for this young man, assailing him with new perspectives.

Liu Mingyan, on the other hand, just let out a soft, "Ah," and said seriously, "so that's how it was."

What do you mean, "so that's how it was"?! What "that" is "that" referring to?! Don't think I won't rip you a new one just because you're the female lead!

Without his notice, a crowd of spectators had congregated at Lu Liu's table to listen to his gossip, their melon seeds and wooden benches littering the floor, their attention rapt. At this time they all sighed.

"A beast!"

"Not just a beast, basically worse than that..."

But within these sighs was a tone of incomparable satisfaction.

Da-ge, are you the captain of the border patrol squadron or the gossip brigade?!

Lu Liu abruptly slammed his teacup down like a gavel. "Of course Shen Qingqiu wouldn't submit! Master and disciple crossed swords, and in the end, the master still came out on top, so Luo Binghe retreated in defeat, leaving in sorrow.

"Though all pretenses had been shed, Shen Qingqiu still couldn't bear to ruin the reputation of his beloved disciple. He couldn't bear to be fully honest about what had happened and could only offer the excuse that Luo Binghe had died at the hands of the demon race. With this, he preserved the reputation of his disciple, being unwilling to cut him off entirely.

"So, this is the truth behind Luo Binghe's years-long disappearance after the Immortal Alliance Conference, as well as why he didn't return to Cang Qiong Mountain Sect despite having survived.

"It wasn't that he didn't want to see his Shizun—it was that he didn't have the face to!"

While the story was in full swing on Lu Liu's end, Shen Qingqiu's heart was flooding with tears on his.

What an intense story line!

This r- [beep–] *-pist and this white lotus Holy Mother—who are they?!*

The key point was that the r- [beep–] *-pe actually wasn't a successful r-* [beep–] *-pe. This is way too fucking off. How could that be Luo Binghe? If he wanted to r-* [beep–] *-pe someone, they would obediently spread their legs themselves, okay?!*

Lu Liu was still going on. "After his heartbreak at the Immortal Alliance Conference, Luo Binghe went on his own adventures.

He trained until he had a set of exceptional martial abilities to his name, and he even gained the favor of Huan Hua Palace's Old Palace Master. But he was still unwilling to give up on Shen Qingqiu, and so he staged a grand comeback. Thus came the events of Hua Yue City.

"Doesn't all of Cang Qiong Mountain Sect insist that Luo Binghe is a demon? I don't think that's necessarily baseless, or wind from an empty cave. Most likely, they discovered slivers of evidence that he was colluding with the demon race to slander Shen Qingqiu. After all, Shen Qingqiu stood high above him, aloof and untouchable. If Luo Binghe couldn't measure up in his eyes, he wanted to drag Shen Qingqiu down—make him fall from grace and shatter his arrogance!"

Shen Qingqiu didn't know what exactly he'd given up on, but either way, he suddenly felt his body and mind relax, and he no longer wanted to listen to or care about anything anymore.

"Let's order something," he said pleasantly to the other two.

"Peerless...*ahem*-xiansheng, you can count your table on my tab," Lu Liu seized the chance to say.

Then he turned back around and continued to sorrowfully lament.

"Luo Binghe thought of every possible method to shut Shen Qingqiu in the Water Prison of Huan Hua Palace. What do you think his goal was with this? His wicked ambitions were as clear as day. Huan Hua Palace had long been in his pocket; he had the entire sect dancing in the palm of his hand. They claimed to be keeping Shen Qingqiu in temporary custody, pending the four sects' joint trial, but it was no different from throwing a lamb into a tiger's den. For the couple of days Shen Qingqiu was shut in the Water Prison, he was bound with immortal-binding cables and completely without spiritual energy—who knows what that traitorous disciple did to him?!"

In perfect harmony, the crowd cried out one after another in disgust:

"A traitorous disciple indeed!"

"Raising a tiger invites calamity!"

Shen Qingqiu threw aside his menu. "How about we go somewhere else."

"Shen Qingqiu couldn't take this humiliation, and after struggling with all his might, he managed to escape. Little did he know that he would be cut off in Hua Yue City by the search party sent by Luo Binghe. From top to bottom, Cang Qiong Mountain Sect is of one heart, so the peak lord of Bai Zhan Peak, Liu Qingge, naturally came to provide assistance. This attempt to aid Shen Qingqiu was met head-on by Luo Binghe.

"Luo Binghe's jealousy overturned the heavens. He immediately took on Liu Qingge in an earthshaking battle, going all-out for the kill. With no other alternative, Shen Qingqiu could only self-detonate on the spot... And henceforth..."

Lu Liu stopped and waited with a meaningful silence, drawing a chorus of sighs from the crowd. Finally, he arrived at his conclusion. "And so, this is the alternative theory that's been widely circulated underground. Even though it sounds incredibly absurd, and some might treat it as complete nonsense, there are many details worth considering. Gentlemen, bear this in mind: When history is officially recorded, it's often whitewashed or embellished, the actual facts purposely withheld, and many times the unofficial version is the truth!"

Those details aren't the slightest bit reliable, okay?! "The truth," your sister! Even if I had no girls to fondle for twenty years, no matter how wretched I became, I wouldn't get so desperate that I'd get gay with a guy! Let alone get gay with the male lead!

The young waitress had finished gracefully weaving her way to their table and serving their dishes, but Yang Yixuan and Liu Mingyan were still in a daze.

"Hurry up and eat," Shen Qingqiu reprimanded them. "After you finish, you should hurry back."

If these children stayed any longer in this dangerous place, who knew what kind of assaults their views on life, the world, and morality would suffer?!

10
Huan Hua

A FTER ESCORTING the two juniors out of the borderlands, Shen Qingqiu picked a direction opposite to theirs.

He'd been walking until the moon was high in the sky when his terrifically keen hearing caught the indistinct peal of demonic bells.

"You're exactly like a ghost that won't move on," Shen Qingqiu said without even turning his head.

With her presence discovered, Sha Hualing didn't intend to keep hiding, and she confidently strolled into view, coiling red gauzy cloth around her fingers as she laughed. "Who taught this distinguished gentleman to make Ling-er so curious? You took such attentive care of those two. What sort of relationship does your distinguished self have with Cang Qiong Mountain?"

Shen Qingqiu turned around and wagged his finger. "I won't fight you, and you shouldn't try anything with me either."

Sha Hualing couldn't do anything to him with her current ability. He was just thinking about scaring her a little when, out of nowhere, his entire body jolted. It felt like a millipede was crawling through his internal organs. A familiar and frightening sensation began to unfurl from the pit of his stomach.

Sha Hualing's smile was sinister. "I'm indeed no match for you, but did you think that means I have no way to control you?"

For a moment, Shen Qingqiu's legs went soft, but he still managed to stand firmly. He clenched his teeth. "When did you make me eat it?"

"How was the food and drink in town today?" Sha Hualing asked coquettishly. "Was the waitress pretty? It's fortunate you ate at all. If you were more devoted in your cultivation, avoiding food and practicing inedia, you would have really given Ling-er a headache."

Fuck. In the moment, his entire attention had been comprehensively captured by the gossip brigade captain's beautiful and heartfelt performance. *Gossip kills, ah!*

"Do you know what's currently inside your body?" she asked as she circled Shen Qingqiu, overflowing with glee. "This is no ordinary poison."

Shut up! I'm more familiar than you. I've already eaten heavenly demon blood twice—twice! Normally, you eat it once and die once. Who's hit the jackpot as many times as me?!

No one was capable of controlling heavenly demon blood other than said blood's owner. As the blood mites were already starting to stir inside Shen Qingqiu's body, that could only mean one thing.

Sha Hualing bowed to someone behind Shen Qingqiu. "This subordinate did not fail your trust. I have already captured him."

Shen Qingqiu stiffly turned his head.

A rift that looked like dark lightning had split the air and was now slowly sealing back up, and behind him stood a tall and slender silhouette. As Shen Qingqiu turned, he met that stare head-on.

Luo Binghe was looking down on him from above. Though he had no expression, under those eyes, like twin cold pools, Shen Qingqiu could forget another layer of whiskers—even a more advanced disguise would have seemed to vanish into nothing.

Shen Qingqiu fixed his gaze on him.

While indeed cold, the Luo Binghe of the past had been like the reflection of warm sunlight on fresh snow. Even in Jin Lan City and the Water Prison, he had more or less possessed some traces of humanity, some faint expressions, and would lose control and grow angry. But this young man's countenance looked like a landscape of snowy wastes and glaciers that had been frozen for a thousand years. The sight of him chilled one to the bone.

Despite this, Shen Qingqiu's current state of mind was quite different from what he'd expected. It was difficult to explain; all sorts of emotions were tangled up in his head, but the single emotion that should have been most prominent was missing: fear.

Maybe it was because he'd failed to avoid Luo Binghe despite all his exhaustive planning, with a series of freak accidents sending him back to square one. Either way, he found himself calm and felt that none of this really mattered.

For a split second, Luo Binghe's expression was puzzled, causing his face to appear to soften, just a little. But soon this sliver of softness dissipated without a trace. His pupils contracted, and a red mark flickered at the center of his forehead in a burst of light.

Luo Binghe's sleeves hadn't even fluttered when Sha Hualing was abruptly hoisted into the air as if by an incorporeal hand squeezing her throat. She coughed painfully.

At the same time, that drop of heavenly demon blood in Shen Qingqiu's internal organs split into thousands of frenzied threads, boring through his insides. Cold sweat soaked his back.

"You certainly have some guts," Luo Binghe said breezily.

Though his tone was light, anyone could have felt the violent rage concealed beneath the surface.

You have some guts? Was he saying that to Shen Qingqiu or Sha Hualing?

Shen Qingqiu's brain shifted into high gear. Luo Binghe shouldn't have been able to recognize him, even though this current face did somewhat resemble Shen Qingqiu's. With Luo Binghe's observation skills and ability to notice details, he could effortlessly pick out the minute differences even through a layer of whiskers. But it looked like Luo Binghe had taken him for someone with a *similar* face...

Though that did fuck-all for him. Being recognized would indeed have been a disaster, but it turned out that not being recognized wasn't much better.

Sha Hualing didn't know why Luo Binghe had become so furious, and she struggled while frantically scanning the area through tear-blurred eyes, trying to figure out exactly what had brought on this punishment. When her gaze swept over Shen Qingqiu's face, she suddenly looked like she had seen a ghost.

"My lord, forgive me, this subordinate knows her mistake, but this subordinate swears that it was a complete coincidence!" she said in a terrified voice. "My lord, forgive me, I honestly didn't do it this time!"

Inside, Sha Hualing was bitterly grousing nonstop. You see, she had a rap sheet. Ever since joining Luo Binghe's forces, she had watched Luo Binghe spend all his time gazing at Shen Qingqiu's corpse and managed to more or less guess a couple of unspeakable things. Thinking herself clever, she'd found a person whose face was about similar to Shen Qingqiu's by about five parts of ten, then asked a capable demon to perform some minor modifications to make the fake perfectly match the original. One could have called it a work of otherworldly quality. Afterward, she'd sent the counterfeit to Luo

Binghe, and the result? Not only had it failed to make Luo Binghe happy, it had sent him into a terrible rage instead. He'd nearly wiped out the entirety of Chi Yun Cave in a horrible massacre.

Sha Hualing would never forget that, nor did she wish to see that expression of Luo Binghe's again. From then on, she was careful, not daring to touch on anything even slightly related to the subject. Who could have known that the vessel she had settled on this time would also coincidentally share some similarities with that fucking Shen Qingqiu's eyes and brows! This was definitely another violation of Luo Binghe's major taboo!

"I seem to have previously warned you not to try anything with this face," Luo Binghe said.

Strung up in midair, Sha Hualing's face was flushed red from asphyxiation. After a stream of choking noises, she said, pained, "This time...this subordinate truly didn't do it on purpose..."

Though Shen Qingqiu didn't know the ins and outs of the situation here, he'd pretty much guessed that it was related to this face of his. He shut his mouth, fretting inside. He'd already been dead for five years, and just looking at someone with a similar appearance still made Luo Binghe profoundly angry. It looked like he'd really left some severe scars on Luo Binghe's psyche.

Suddenly, a sharp pain assaulted Shen Qingqiu's abdomen, like tens of thousands of steel needles were piercing through his organs.

This time, no level of bountiful spiritual energy would help him. His vision darkened and he coughed up a mouthful of blood, red with a hint of black.

The air pressure around Luo Binghe had dropped to extreme lows, and his gaze was that of a person looking at something dead. At his waist, Xin Mo trembled in excitement while humming unceasingly, as if about to exit its sheath. His hand pressed down on the hilt, and an all-consuming red welled from the depths of his eyes.

Shen Qingqiu wiped at the blood by his mouth, a little stupefied by the sight.

Logically speaking, after starting the Demon Realm arc, Luo Binghe should have rewired himself into a relatively stable state. Sucking someone dry every month should only have consolidated him further. So why did he have the feeling that Luo Binghe's internal balance had, instead, worsened? It was even more turbulent than when Shen Qingqiu had incidentally helped suppress it after self-detonating.

As Sha Hualing was hoisted increasingly higher, she saw Shen Qingqiu cough up blood, and she knew that Luo Binghe had the intent to kill—that he was currently manipulating the heavenly demon blood within the vessel's body.

"My lord...you absolutely mustn't kill him..." she said, frantic. "Tonight is the full moon, and he'll undeniably be useful... There's no one more suitable than him..."

She wasn't really concerned about whether Shen Qingqiu lived or died. It was just that if she let Luo Binghe kill this weirdo in a rage, even if his body's demonic qi *didn't* suddenly surge and cause him to go berserk, his next step would have nothing good in store for her either.

As she thought this, Sha Hualing felt that her life was rife with misfortune, and she became even more desperate, shouting herself hoarse. "Even if you don't care about him and don't care about me, think about...think about your...the one who..." She threw it all out, raising her voice. "Think about the Holy Mausoleum!"

Upon hearing those last two words, Luo Binghe's movements slowed.

The Holy Mausoleum was the place where past generations of the demon race's ruling class were laid to eternal rest. Other than the current supreme ruler, the miscellaneous remainder of demonkind were, with no exceptions, forbidden from entering, and all violators were killed.

Within the Holy Mausoleum, the generations had accumulated various funerary treasures of rare quality in enormous quantity— talisman charms and spiritual artifacts, stuff that anyone would drool over. Rumor had it that within the Holy Mausoleum, there was even a mystical artifact capable of bringing the dead back to life in defiance of the natural order. With Sha Hualing as his double agent, the original Luo Binghe had successfully climbed to the top of the Demon Realm and infiltrated the Holy Mausoleum. Everyone knew whose hands those treasures had ended up in.

If Sha Hualing was mentioning the Holy Mausoleum now, was she reminding Luo Binghe that he still needed her for something?

Whatever it was, she'd obviously found the right angle.

On hearing those two words, a somber red still flickered in Luo Binghe's eyes, but Sha Hualing's body suddenly dropped a bit, and the tips of her feet could now touch the ground if she strained.

"You managed to remind me." Luo Binghe's fingertips languidly stroked Xin Mo, soothing the restless, agitated sword as he said in a low voice, "True, there's still the Holy Mausoleum."

Sha Hualing was about to gasp for breath when she heard Luo Binghe say, "Are you threatening me?"

Sha Hualing's soul almost fled her body. "This subordinate wouldn't dare!"

Just...tragic. All else aside, she was one of two main female leads of *Proud Immortal Demon Way*, who'd for years on end ranked in the top three of the (female) character popularity rankings—how had she ended up in this state?!

Shen Qingqiu hadn't managed to finish lamenting when it felt like someone was pulling on his front, and his entire body was abruptly hauled upward.

His vision blurred, and in an instant, his chest had chilled to the point of freezing. When he looked down, he saw Luo Binghe had pressed one hand against the left side of his chest.

The following sensation was like someone had fired a cannon into his chest, the ammunition being pure, black, demonic qi. Once it entered his body, it spread like an explosion through his limbs and bones via his meridians.

The System's jarringly clear, shrill notification made his head throb:

[Touch verification successful!]

[Connected to central power source, storing power!]

[System self-evaluation: all operations normal. Thank you for your continued patronage!]

Isn't this touch verification a little too advanced?!

The spiritual energy within Shen Qingqiu had started off as a full reservoir, but after this one brief link, more than half was sucked away.

But this depleted state lasted for only an instant. The flesh body formed by the Sun-Moon Dew Mushroom began to generate a rapid influx of spiritual energy. This influx was then absorbed even more rapidly by Luo Binghe.

Shen Qingqiu felt like a mobile power bank.

Okay, in my last life, maybe I ranted a little too much in the comments section, he howled internally, *but honestly, I only ranted about Airplane Shooting Towards the Sky's writing quality and never the male lead—so why is Luo Binghe always picking on me?!*

Luo Binghe made a sound of surprise and withdrew his palm.

This body differed from his previous vessels. He'd extracted the majority of its spiritual energy and poured an enormous amount of demonic qi into it, yet it could still rapidly and automatically replenish itself. It seemed that Sha Hualing's single-minded insistence on capturing this person, and all the great trouble she'd gone through to do so, had been justified.

With a thump, Sha Hualing fell to the ground in a seated position. She knew that she had been correct to capture this person and that she'd now survived great calamity and escaped death. Still terrified, she ignored how her knees were trembling and hurriedly corrected her posture to kneel on one knee.

"I don't care if you did it or not," said Luo Binghe. "Remember to never let me see him using this face."

Sha Hualing hastily bowed her head. "Understood!"

Luo Binghe casually sliced open a spatial rift and stepped inside. The flippancy with which he left as he pleased was practically infuriating—just up and dumping the two of them in the wastes, like he was altogether unconcerned with whether Shen Qingqiu went or stayed.

But true enough, he had no need to be concerned, since Shen Qingqiu had drunk his blood. Wherever he fled, he could never truly escape. With a flick of his fingers, Luo Binghe could appear in front of Shen Qingqiu and leave him mired in excruciating pain.

So...does this mean I've become Bing-ge's lackey? Shen Qingqiu thought.

Luo Binghe hadn't recognized him, so if he followed along and did his job properly, maybe his prospects would actually be pretty good?

(Like hell.)

Wasn't it just once a month? A couple more rounds of this, and he could get used to it!

Currently disoriented as he was, he was caught off guard when Sha Hualing moved to claw at his face. Shen Qingqiu blocked her with two fingers. "What are you doing?"

Sha Hualing clenched her teeth. "Didn't you hear? He said just now that he doesn't want to see your face!"

Shen Qingqiu stared at her, then reached out and tore a piece of gauzy cloth from her body.

"What are you ripping my clothes for?!" Sha Hualing shrieked.

Shen Qingqiu punched two holes into that cloth and covered his face with it, leaving only his eyes exposed. "My clothes are already ragged enough, so I'm borrowing yours. Is clawing faces your only solution to everything? Covering myself with a cloth does the job. Must you resort to disfigurement?"

If Luo Binghe hadn't needed to use this person once a month from now on—meaning she had to guarantee his absolute safety—Sha Hualing would have wanted to hack him to pieces. Though if she thought about it more, even if Luo Binghe hated counterfeits, he probably wouldn't have liked seeing this face drenched in blood either, so Sha Hualing could only swallow her anger and yell, "Go!"

No issues with that. After all, it would be the same wherever he went, so he figured he might as well take things step by step and observe.

By Shen Qingqiu's calculations, after Luo Binghe completely suppressed Xin Mo, he probably wouldn't need a vessel anymore. Then it'd be goodbye forever, and that day likely wasn't far off. He just had to be especially careful so Luo Binghe didn't discover that he'd pulled off a great escape using the Sun-Moon Dew Mushroom.

Having adjusted to his new role ridiculously quickly, Shen Qingqiu followed Luo Binghe's lead and stepped into that rift. Sha Hualing was the last to enter, and the opening slowly sealed up behind her.

The star employee of the demon race's ability to adjust her mental state wasn't too shabby either. After several deep breaths, Sha Hualing had calmed down and asked, "Your name?"

The other side of the rift connected to a long corridor, its two walls decorated in hundreds of complicated designs, though the lighting was rather dim. Shen Qingqiu was thinking that this place looked somewhat familiar as he said absentmindedly, "Peerless Cucumber."

Sha Hualing muttered, "Peerless Cucumber?" Then exploded in anger. "Are you mocking me?!"

The more Shen Qingqiu looked around, the more he felt that even if he'd never been here before, he must've at least heard the description somewhere, and in the process, he fully ignored Sha Hualing.

Having received no response, she threatened him angrily. "No matter where you're from, now that you've drunk heavenly demon blood, you henceforth belong to the lord. If you try to rebel, death and a desecrated corpse will be a kindness!"

After turning a corner and passing several disciples wearing familiar light yellow robes, Shen Qingqiu was finally certain: this was Huan Hua Palace, Luo Binghe's headquarters in the Human Realm.

But this was far too different from the Huan Hua Palace he knew. Huan Hua Palace was supposed to be resplendent and majestic, dazzling with gold and jade, each plank and stone grand and lavish to the utmost. But the architecture before his eyes could only be described with one word: lifeless.

Past generations of palace masters had to a one adored extravagance, and Luo Binghe was no exception; it was just that his love was for extravagant darkness. Even the two rows of oil lamps lining the corridor seemed on the verge of flickering out.

In the blink of an eye, Sha Hualing had changed into the apparel of a Huan Hua Palace disciple. When deliberately suppressing her demonic qi, she looked just like any ordinary, beautiful human girl. Luo Binghe passed through hall after hall like he was in a fugue before he sat down in the main palace hall.

Shen Qingqiu had wanted to go for a stroll elsewhere, but Sha Hualing grabbed him. "Where are you going? Don't wander around. Follow me!"

Shen Qingqiu didn't want to clash with her, so he could only line up beside her on the side of the main hall, back perfectly straight. Immediately thereafter, some disciples entered to make their reports. Several paid their respects to the throne, reverently relaying information.

At first, Shen Qingqiu listened without paying attention, but suddenly he heard a name that jabbed him like a needle.

"Palace Master," a disciple said, "during the time you were gone, that Liu Qingge came twice more. When he was unable to find you, he demolished Ling Hua Domain."

As Shen Qingqiu listened to this, his chest tightened, his gums aching slightly.

If Liu Qingge had done such a thing... *Surely he isn't taking revenge for my sake, right?*

The lack of concern on Luo Binghe's face said: Whatever, my

important self has plenty of money. "Let him demolish what he likes. Anything else?"

The disciple glanced at him, wiped at his cold sweat, and spoke his next words with excessive carefulness. "One more thing... The Little Palace Mistress...wants to see you."

Shen Qingqiu's first thought was that Luo Binghe was about to summon his beloved concubine to the hall with a doting expression on his face, but to his surprise, Luo Binghe remained frosty and indifferent. As if even speaking would be too much, he wearily waved his hand, implying rejection.

"But..." the disciple said awkwardly.

"But I'm already here!"

The mere sound of this voice made Shen Qingqiu's teeth and body ache. Before he knew it, the Little Palace Mistress had already stormily charged into the hall, her presence as forceful as spitting flames. Following alongside her was a comely, slightly older woman in a light yellow robe. Her eyes were hazy, as if on the verge of tears. It was Qin Wanyue.

Shen Qingqiu did a subtle double take, a little surprised.

At this time, these two maidens should still have been blossoming flowers in their prime, but when he looked at them, there was a clear impression of haggardness. The Little Palace Mistress was especially afflicted. Those two splotches of uneven crimson on her face were probably due to a rushed application of cosmetics.

No matter how he looked at her, she had not even the slightest bit of a well-pampered mistress's radiant glee.

The Little Palace Mistress lifted her chin, looking straight at Luo Binghe. "You've returned."

Luo Binghe glanced at her and didn't say anything.

"Little Palace Mistress, let's go back..." Qin Wanyue said quietly.

"Do you imagine I don't know who you think of, day and night?" the Little Palace Mistress asked caustically. "The reason you endure humiliation and remain by my side, exhaustively thinking and scheming—isn't it all to lay eyes on him again? So why are you retreating now that you finally see him, acting all fragile and pitiful? Why not try to stop me before we got here instead of only attempting to dissuade me now?"

Head lowered, Qin Wanyue dared not speak, her ears flushed.

The Little Palace Mistress clicked her tongue, directing it to the hall. "Have you found Daddy?" she asked.

"The Old Palace Master has gone into traveling seclusion," Luo Binghe said. "No one has seen a trace of him."

This was an incredibly egregious example of a stock insincere answer. As far as Shen Qingqiu understood it—and this went for various dramas and novels—it was widely accepted that anyone on the throne who said this line was the main culprit who had caused "no one to see a trace" of the previous leader.

The Little Palace Mistress laughed harshly. "That line again. Would you have to expend too much energy to even think up a new excuse for me? All right, I won't talk about Daddy. I'll just talk about myself—if I didn't come find you, would you ever come to see me?" she asked shrilly.

How dare you imply Luo Binghe is the kind of scoundrel who recklessly wastes resources? Who tosses his women aside without sleeping with them? Don't insult his dignity as a top-shelf stallion novel male lead!

Too bad Luo Binghe plainly didn't care to preserve that dignity.

Several Huan Hua Palace disciples appeared in the palace hall. Shen Qingqiu assumed they were going to console the Little Palace

Mistress, but in actuality they forcibly grabbed her and dragged her off. On the way, she screamed and yelled. Qin Wanyue followed alongside her, but sometimes she shot tearful glances at Luo Binghe out the corner of her eye, as if hoping for something.

Before this point, Sha Hualing had been staring straight ahead, her posture perfectly upright, but now she wrinkled her brow and followed them out, standing in the corridor to berate them. "What have you lot been doing? You were asked to keep an eye on her, and this is how you do it?"

Shen Qingqiu had always maintained a respectful distance when it came to the fights between female characters, but having observed this, he felt like the gap between his expectations and reality was too great to ignore. He hurried out after them, continuing to observe.

"I'm sorry, I neglected my duties," Qin Wanyue said while holding back tears. "I didn't stop the Little Palace Mistress..."

Sha Hualing swiftly cut her off. "It was entirely your fault! I've heard that saving face is especially important to Human Realm women, but even though you've failed to seduce the lord many times, you shamelessly refuse to leave—so that's all your face amounts to. Moreover, not leaving is one thing, but you can't even keep a proper eye on a single person. You're her shijie, so her cultivation is inferior to yours, yet you didn't stop her, and you even let her throw a tantrum before the lord. Who are you humiliating yourself and acting pitiful for?"

Listening to Sha Hualing point out her inadequacies to her face, Qin Wanyue wanted to die of shame and resentment. Even in the original work, Sha Hualing had deeply hated Qin Wanyue and always found fault with her. It seemed that though they hadn't entered the harem together this time, their relationship hadn't improved in the slightest.

Sha Hualing then turned her head and swapped out her entire expression. She spoke to the Little Palace Mistress while full of smiles. "These past few years, the Little Palace Mistress has lived a life of luxury, just like she did before. Other than the occasional house arrest, you've suffered no real mistreatment, right? So why are you so aggrieved?"

"Who the hell are you?" the Little Palace Mistress asked viciously. "How dare you, an indecent vixen seductress from heavens know where, speak like that to me in Huan Hua Palace! How is the way he treats me any different from a kept pig?!"

Sha Hualing pouted. "Then why doesn't the Little Palace Mistress tell me: What else can she do other than eat and sleep like the animal she brought up?"

Qin Wanyue sobbed. "Little Palace Mistress, let's go. Everything... has long since changed..."

"On what grounds can you make me leave?!" the Little Palace Mistress said hysterically. "This is my Huan Hua Palace—mine! Get out of my way! Traitors, the lot of you!"

The scene fell into complete chaos, with people sent flying every which way.

Shen Qingqiu had discovered a most shocking truth. He carefully counted on his fingers:

Sha Hualing: Was made not a wife but a subordinate. Toils to death on overtime, and her pay and benefits are nothing to write home about. From her boss's attitude, doesn't look like he wants an office romance either. X

Liu Mingyan: Didn't even exchange the sword tassel love token. X

Ning Yingying: After puberty, stopped demonstrating the fanatical love from her naive youth toward the male lead. Seems like her lovesick brain's been cured. X

The Little Palace Mistress: Bitter locked-up woman. She herself said that Luo Binghe treats her like a kept pig. X

Qin Wanyue: Bitter locked-up woman the sequel. Failed at offering herself countless times. Moonlights as the Little Palace Mistress's nanny. X

Qiu Haitang: After dragging Shen Qingqiu down, she's supposed to be happily going down to cuck town with Luo Binghe. Why's she still wandering about like a vagrant? X

The three Daoist nuns: A second in the spotlight, hello and goodbye. XXX

...

Looking down this list, Luo Binghe had really...ended up in an awful state!

As the hale and hearty male lead of a stallion novel, are you doing okay or not?

A perfectly good harem had been broken down to the point that it was coughing up smoke. If this were a novel, and the plot had unfolded to this point without the protagonist collecting a single wife, what satisfaction points were there to be had?!

Shen Qingqiu promptly called up the System to check the various categories' point values. Unexpectedly, he discovered that, beneath the B-Points, the protagonist satisfaction points not only hadn't decreased, they had actually risen to over nine hundred.

Because many of the points had been added while the System was offline and hibernating, he hadn't received the notifications. Shen Qingqiu prodded open the many new windows providing detailed calculations that he'd unknowingly received. Lined up within them were a bunch of new records.

[Ning Yingying: Subverted the trope of a female character being a brainless martyr for love. B-Points +100.]

[Ming Fan: Subverted the trope of a side character being an illogical idiot. B-Points +50.]

[Liu Mingyan: Subverted the trope of a female character being a nonsensical martyr for love. B-Points +150.]

...

The ubiquitous love martyr female characters and idiot cannon fodder: these two points together constituted the classic landmine elements of stallion novels. Now the female characters weren't relationship-based martyrs for the male lead, and the side characters' EQs and IQs had also risen, so naturally the B-Points had risen too. This Shen Qingqiu understood.

But while Luo Binghe hadn't bedded a single girl, the System hadn't deducted any of his satisfaction points—that part was unscientific!

Could it be that currently, the male lead's satisfaction points were no longer bound to the male lead himself? Or to say it another way, what determined the male lead's "satisfaction" no longer lay in such pleasures?

Could it be...

Shen Qingqiu couldn't resist the urge to raise his eyes and take in Luo Binghe's dismal expression. He suddenly felt that he couldn't stare straight at him anymore.

It was criminal, criminal—could it be that he'd raised an otherwise totally fine stallion novel male lead...to be asexual?!

Shen Qingqiu closed the windows, his feelings complicated. Then he realized that something about his location didn't seem quite right.

Just now he'd definitely been in Huan Hua Palace, minding his own business, so how had he ended up walking into a forested grove without noticing? And regardless of how he studied it, it was a strikingly familiar-looking bamboo forest.

The bamboo forest rustled as a gentle breeze blew through it.

Shen Qingqiu didn't even need to guess the identity of the location. Even if he'd been shown only a corner of this place, he'd know where he was.

Cang Qiong Mountain, Qing Jing Peak.

How could he not be familiar with the place where he'd thus far holed up for the longest period of time in this life?

[Your current location: the land of Luo Binghe's dream realm.]

When Luo Binghe's consciousness was unstable and its fluctuations were especially large, outsiders were often affected, sucked into a dream realm that was as vast as a deep-sea vortex. Or, you could say, they became collateral damage for Luo Binghe's incomparably huge black hole of an imagination For a specific example, please see the beginning of the Meng Mo instance from way back when.

Shen Qingqiu had run through the Meng Mo scenario with Luo Binghe at that time. This was operating on the same principle as "strangers the first time but familiar the second." It was similar to how, after connecting to a Wi-Fi network once, the second time you would connect automatically without needing to enter the password.

Shen Qingqiu quickly touched his own face and found no beard. Within the dream realm, he'd returned to his original appearance, leaving him with absolutely no sense of security. Just as he was thinking of finding a place to hide and wait for Luo Binghe to awaken by himself, some disciples walked toward him in twos and threes, and Shen Qingqiu jerked to a halt, wholly forgetting to conceal himself.

The problem was that although the expressions on these coming and going disciples were slightly wooden, every single one had noses and eyes, their facial features complete. Shen Qingqiu could even name quite a few.

Not even Meng Mo was able to simultaneously support a vast barrier while guaranteeing the facial features of the life forms within. Yet Luo Binghe could already do it, and to such a great level of detail.

Though Shen Qingqiu had long known that Luo Binghe's OP-ness could eclipse the heavens, he still couldn't help but let out a sigh. "Amazing."

After exiting the little bamboo forest, he came upon Qing Jing's Bamboo House. Between the scattered stalks of bamboo, some tall and some short, spring water flowed in a rush, tinkling rhythmically and reflecting the sunlight in a rainbow of colors. Shen Qingqiu was worried that Luo Binghe was inside the house and halted his steps. Having strolled this bamboo forest countless times while idling about, he easily found a place to hide and came to a stop within the shadows.

Suddenly, there came the sound of footsteps on fallen leaves, and from within the overlapping, verdant bamboo, out walked a youth in white, fifteen or sixteen years of age.

This youth's skin was fair, and he appeared to have run all the way here. A layer of sweat covered his forehead while his cheeks were rosy, which made for an incredibly adorable sight. The lines of his eyes and brows were precise without being sharp, and they radiated a sense of youthful inexperience.

Shen Qingqiu mourned despite himself. It'd been a long time since he'd seen the youthful Luo Binghe, that small, refreshing sun.

While cultivating on Qing Jing Peak, Luo Binghe had liked to wear white. But after his rebellious phase began, the devil incarnate Luo Binghe had come to wear only black, pretty much the polar opposite of before. This youthful tenderness was even more a memory, and it was no longer in evidence at all.

Luo Binghe strode forward, calling out in high spirits, "Shizun!"

Shen Qingqiu was hidden in the shadows, so naturally, this call wasn't for him. He turned his gaze, and as expected, he saw a form in teal robes standing at the far end of the cobblestone path.

The "Shen Qingqiu" forged from memories in the dream realm stood in the midst of a stretch of verdant, flourishing bamboo. His figure was slender, like unto a thin stalk of bamboo himself, and his expression was unperturbed, radiating the cool aura of an immortal, while his poise was veritably somewhat otherworldly. As a bystander, the current Shen Qingqiu judged him from head to toe and still had to applaud.

To be able to fake it to this level, he was really too superb!

Also, that Luo Binghe could perfectly restore all these tiny details—as expected of the man who would personally succeed Meng Mo!

The Shen Qingqiu in the midst of the bamboo appeared to have been lost in thought. He cocked his head and asked, "Finished running?"

Luo Binghe nodded. "Ten laps... All finished."

Shen Qingqiu finally remembered what slice of memory this was.

The "ten laps" Luo Binghe spoke of referred to ten laps around the fence encircling Qing Jing Peak. Shen Qingqiu had personally assigned him this task.

He hadn't done it because he had a twisted hobby of inflicting corporal punishment upon the great male lead, but because he just couldn't endure it any longer. After taking over Luo Binghe's education, he'd mulled it over and decided that since he was to be a role model and worthy teacher, he ought to at least do some proper teaching. This way, after they fell out in the future, he would be able to utter the phrase, "Within a master-disciple relationship lies the grace of knowledge passed down," without reddening from shame before the words left his mouth.

In his course curriculum, the first thing to correct was the absolute mess that was Luo Binghe's footwork and form.

As for the results, he'd mentioned it a while back. The most significant outcome was that Luo Binghe had repeatedly fallen into his arms for half a month.

"Once more," said Shen Qingqiu. "If you get it wrong again this time, it won't be only ten laps."

Luo Binghe obediently performed the maneuver once more. While he certainly didn't fall into Shen Qingqiu's arms this time, instead, his legs buckled and he ended up directly embracing Shen Qingqiu's waist.

Shen Qingqiu was silent.

"Shizun, this disciple is useless," Luo Binghe said bashfully. "After ten laps, my legs have no strength."

Shen Qingqiu sighed.

"This disciple knows," Luo Binghe said, fully aware. "Twenty laps."

"What laps? Go back and rest." Shen Qingqiu had no interest in abusing children.

At that time, he'd truly given up.

Let him do whatever he wants. No more teaching! There's no sense of accomplishment whatsoever. I'm throwing out the textbooks!

Luo Binghe failed to realize that he'd been declared a hopeless case.

"Thank you, Shizun!" he said in high spirits. "This disciple will absolutely make up the twenty laps tomorrow. Is there anything Shizun would like to eat tonight?"

To the side, Shen Qingqiu rubbed his forehead.

Luo Binghe in those days...had genuinely been naive and sweet to an exceptional degree.

Enduring labor, resentment, beatings, and verbal abuse, being stepped on, kicked, and made to cook... Ahem, of course Shen Qingqiu hadn't done most of those things.

After watching this artificial master-disciple pair, one tall and one short, walk off while conversing, Shen Qingqiu came out of his hiding place and lapsed into bewilderment.

Within the dream realm barrier Luo Binghe had constructed for himself, he would naturally choose to relive only his most wonderful memories. If any memories of Qing Jing Peak could occupy such a niche, they should have been the ones related to Ning Yingying. So why had this one played out?

The dream realm precisely reflected the truth of a person's heart—it would neither lie nor deceive. Within Shen Qingqiu welled up a thought he'd never had before.

This thought was admittedly a bit shameless, but...probably, maybe, possibly, those memories of this "master-disciple relationship" occupied a better place in Luo Binghe's heart than Shen Qingqiu had thought?

At the very least, it could be said that he'd given Luo Binghe a couple of moments that were decent enough to look back on. So perhaps the entire thing hadn't been *completely* unbearable.

However...was Luo Binghe a bit of a masochist? Shen Qingqiu didn't want to badmouth him, but normally a memory about being punished with ten or twenty laps could never have anything to do with the word "wonderful," right?!

Suddenly, a trace of chilly air unfurled over Shen Qingqiu's nape, as if a gaze both hot and cold was crawling upward along his back.

He unconsciously looked behind him. Luo Binghe, clothed in black, was leaning against a stalk of bamboo and staring straight at him.

The two of them stared at each other without speaking.

In the flesh...?

In the flesh!

Shen Qingqiu's initial reflex wasn't to make a break for it but to remain in place unmoving and adjust his expression to be as natural as possible.

This wasn't because he was scared stiff with legs too weak to run, more that he'd long since psychologically prepared himself to en-counter this kind of scenario. Running couldn't solve the problem at all. This barrier was Luo Binghe's home field, so he could run as fast as he could and it'd still be pointless.

That gaze being simultaneously hot and cold hadn't been his imagination, nor was it a mistaken description. Luo Binghe's ex-pression really did seem like both ice and fire—a deep chill within, as well as a burning heat. The two temperatures combined bizarrely and condensed within his eyes, which were locked securely on Shen Qingqiu's form.

Shen Qingqiu braced himself, letting their eyes meet.

After a long while, Luo Binghe sighed first. He murmured, "Being able to dream is also a wonderful thing."

When Shen Qingqiu heard this, he realized that he'd managed to get away with his risky maneuver.

By summoning his courage, he'd actually won the gamble. At this moment, Luo Binghe's absentmindedness had enabled Shen Qingqiu to be taken as a dream realm creation.

Shen Qingqiu studied Luo Binghe leaning against the bamboo, stare fixed on himself. He thought of Luo Binghe's numb appearance on the throne earlier that day, all alone. When he compared that to the scene in the original work of Luo Binghe surrounded by splendid luxuries, his every call answered by hundreds, Shen Qingqiu's heart throbbed a bit, though he tried to stop it.

Luo Binghe didn't have a single wife by his side to heal his injuries, to pamper and ask after him. How could his heart not throb? A perfectly fine stallion novel male lead had fallen to such a state. What man could bear to look?

"Shizun, won't you speak with me a little?" Luo Binghe asked.

At this moment, Shen Qingqiu's heart was full of sympathy for Luo Binghe. "All right," he said amicably. "What do you want to talk about?"

When he spoke, Luo Binghe unexpectedly went rigid, then straightened at once and left the bamboo stalk, the expression on his face one of slight disbelief.

Oh, no, Shen Qingqiu thought. *Was something amiss in the reaction I came up with?*

But since he'd already started acting, he had to act until the end; he absolutely couldn't give up halfway. Embarrassment was a small thing, blowing his cover was not. Shen Qingqiu smiled. "Didn't you ask this master to speak with you?"

He used the tone he'd often deployed in the past when interacting with Luo Binghe. The corner of Luo Binghe's mouth twitched, and he unhurriedly walked toward him. Shen Qingqiu kept his expression steady while casually and gently opening and closing the folding fan in his hand, using the small movements to alleviate his anxiety.

Luo Binghe was silent for a moment. "In the past, Shizun wouldn't even glance my way and would walk off without paying me heed—forget about talking to me. Perhaps my imagination today is a little too indulgent."

Shen Qingqiu's heart stirred.

Though he still felt that something was off, these words really did sound a tad pitiful. Could it be that within Luo Binghe's mind, "Shen Qingqiu" always treated him with indifference, and was lofty and unfeeling?

Luo Binghe really did have slight masochistic tendencies, huh...?

As Shen Qingqiu thought this, in his distraction, his hand unconsciously began to move, and in accordance with the natural order, he patted the top of Luo Binghe's head. He'd performed this action countless times. The saying went that it was forbidden to touch men's heads and women's waists, but the more something was "forbidden," the more he felt the urge to do it.

Shen Qingqiu especially loved patting people's heads. Unfortunately, as a grown adult, he couldn't often indulge this sort of rude impulse, and moreover no one would let him touch them however he wanted. Luckily, the Luo Binghe of the past hadn't minded when Shen Qingqiu placed his hands on his head, so Shen Qingqiu had aimlessly patted him whenever, until it had eventually become a habit. And now he was doing it again.

He had barely patted Luo Binghe two or three times when he was caught off guard. Luo Binghe lifted his own arm, his right hand grasping Shen Qingqiu's left wrist.

Shen Qingqiu's expression stiffened as he thought, *Isn't this a bit too close?*

Straight after, his right wrist had been firmly captured as well. Lifting his head in shock, Shen Qingqiu felt his vision blur.

Something like a feather delicately brushed his cheek. From on top of his lips came a foreign sensation, soft and slightly cool.

In this way, his eyes opened wide, and he met gazes with Luo Binghe's pair of pitch-black irises. His throat bobbed once with difficulty.

He wanted to speak, but he couldn't open his mouth. Because someone was biting down on his lips.

Luo Binghe shut his eyes, his jet-black eyelashes casting curved shadows on his cheeks; it made him look incredibly endearing, but his hands and mouth were a totally different story. He angrily held Shen Qingqiu's lips between his teeth, chomping, the action carrying a hint of childish resentfulness. His right hand released Shen Qingqiu's frozen limb and moved to the center of his waist instead, pressing Shen Qingqiu into his arms. Even though their builds were similar, he could still entirely enfold Shen Qingqiu with this simple one-armed embrace.

Shen Qingqiu's worldview repeatedly collapsed and re-formed, collapsed and re-formed, cycling infinitely at the speed of light.

What broke through his breakdown was a System notification, accompanied by celebratory background music:

[Satisfaction points +500! Congratulations! Congratulations! Congratulations! Important things must be said three times!]

"What the fuck?!" Shen Qingqiu snapped in his head.

He finally understood why, even though Luo Binghe hadn't slept with a single girl, even though neither hide nor hair could be seen

of his innumerable harem of beauties, his satisfaction points had never fallen.

Because he'd used Shen Qingqiu to make up for the deficit, ah!

The Shen Qingqiu who'd suddenly understood the truth was half-horrified and half-enraged. He raised his foot and kicked.

Luo Binghe neither ducked nor sidestepped and took the kick head-on, but he didn't retreat a single step. He even continued to hold Shen Qingqiu without letting go.

"I'm not even allowed to dream?" he asked, looking both angry and wounded.

Hurry and wake up! Even though this is a dream, you didn't dream up this big shot!

He couldn't slap Luo Binghe awake, but he couldn't let him continue this foolishness either!

This was the real being stuck between a rock and a hard place!

Shen Qingqiu hadn't figured out what to yell in order to calm himself down when his back was slammed into a stand of bamboo without warning, and he was pressed into it. Luo Binghe lowered his head and descended once more.

It wasn't Shen Qingqiu's first time being kissed, but it was his first time feeling the threat of someone going crazy and biting off his lips.

Between disordered breaths, Luo Binghe whispered, "Shizun, I was wrong..."

Shen Qingqiu managed to free one of his hands and pushed against Luo Binghe's chest. He really didn't want to do this kind of "woman from a good family resisting a ruffian" pose, but—

You fucker, does this look like you knowing that you're in the wrong?!

Shen Qingqiu was the one who had been wrong, really wrong, *completely* wrong. "Wind from an empty cave"—yeah right! There was a scientific basis to all that jianghu gossip. Every single gossiper must have been a fallen angel in their previous life, hence their ability to see past the surface to the reality beneath!

Shen Qingqiu hadn't raised the male lead to be an asexual, and it wasn't an issue of whether or not Luo Binghe was a masochist. The reality was much more terrifying: he'd raised the male lead to be gay—ahhh!

No wonder he hadn't collected a single wife! No wonder his harem was in shambles! Women could no longer attract his interest, and they were no longer linked to his satisfaction points!

What the actual fuck!

Shen Qingqiu absolutely refused to submit, tenaciously resisting and struggling with all his might. He was just considering which option would result in a worse conclusion, self-detonating again or kicking Luo Binghe's crucial bits, when Luo Binghe released him without warning. He looked at the sky above them with its swirling vortex of clouds, and his expression abruptly darkened.

In an instant, the scenery and people before Shen Qingqiu's eyes crumbled and dissipated, the illusion shattering into a thousand pieces. At the same time, on the roof of Huan Hua Palace's main hall, Shen Qingqiu sprang to his feet.

Now *this* was the real world!

Shen Qingqiu took in a series of violent breaths and finally managed to settle his mind. Suddenly, he realized that every area beneath the main palace had been lit, and the alarm bells were ringing together en masse. He poked his head over the edge, his clothes flapping ceaselessly in the night wind, and looked down from above. Countless lights were converging on the palace. Those were the disciples of Huan Hua Palace's various domains, swarming here from all directions.

"Stand guard! This is an order to all domains: stand guard!"

"Another breach," someone cursed. "How many times has he broken in by now? Have we managed to hold him off even once?"

Shen Qingqiu rejoiced. An invasion was ideal. It would let him escape in the chaos. Who cared about that heavenly demon blood or whatever? His integrity was more important. Leave first and worry later, goodbye! But in the end, he hadn't flown two steps before he heard someone say:

"He went in the direction of Huan Hua Pavilion. Form up and stop Liu Qingge!"

Shen Qingqiu's feet slipped out from under him, and he immediately turned around and ran back.

Dammit. Liu Qingge just *had* to come now. Shen Qingqiu couldn't just throw him to a wholly broken down and presently raging Luo Binghe, right?

Huan Hua Pavilion was where successive generations of Palace Masters had lived and cultivated, and it wasn't too far. With a couple of steps, Shen Qingqiu leapt off the roof, mingling with the main unit and hurrying over. They had yet to enter Huan Hua Pavilion when wave after wave of frigid, threatening wind assaulted them head-on. From within the structure there came an enraged shout full of murderous intent.

"Get out!"

When they'd heard the alarm bells, some ignorant disciples had burst in, and the several dozen people in front were sent flying by an enormously powerful wave of qi. Shen Qingqiu was in the wave after, so he managed to dodge this blow in time. Picking out a good position, he took advantage of the chaos and slipped inside. A freezing chill hit him the moment he entered, eliciting a wave of goosebumps.

It was as if the entirety of Huan Hua Pavilion had become an enormous ice cave. A single step inside was like entering a land of frost and snow. Chill wind flooded Shen Qingqiu's robes and sleeves, and the cold sweat on his back and forehead rapidly froze into a thin layer of ice. One could imagine exactly how inhospitable the interior had to be.

Not only was the temperature abnormally low, the doors were all sealed shut, the windows airtight. It was both freezing and *dark*. If it hadn't been for the intruder (that is, Cang Qiong Mountain's Director of Demolitions, Liu Qingge) forcibly blowing open a huge hole in the walls, the place would have been like a coffin made of ice.

The top of the sitting platform at the center of the pavilion was half-shrouded by curtains, and several black and white outer robes were messily piled beside it.

Luo Binghe was only wearing an inner robe, and he looked like he'd just gotten up from bed. His black hair was disheveled and his clothes were in disarray, the neckline gaping and crooked. His face was abnormally pale, yet his lips had color, while his eyes flashed with a cold light, the aura sinister and menacing. It seemed he was prepared to fight, his claws and fangs bared.

Liu Qingge faced him from seven steps away, the bones protruding on his sword-holding hand, his entire face ashen.

He stared at Luo Binghe, who calmly sat next to the platform, and enunciated each word: "You bastard."

11

Corpse

A VIOLENT SURGE of spiritual light and killing intent burst from Cheng Luan. Shen Qingqiu's guard was up as he glanced back and forth between the two, then suddenly, he looked in the direction in which Liu Qingge's sword was pointed. From his brain there came the sound of the last surviving shred of his worldview finally shattering.

Luo Binghe's right hand was on Xin Mo, which never left his side, the snow-white blade already almost halfway out of its sheath, yet his left arm was, in fact, holding a person.

Though Shen Qingqiu called it a person, it was more correct to say a body. It was completely lifeless, its head lolling and limbs slack, yet also completely pliable. It too wore a set of flimsy inner robes, the neckline having slipped past its shoulder, exposing half of a paper-white back.

"What have you done?" said Liu Qingge.

Liu Qingge would never forget the scene he had witnessed just seconds before. After Cheng Luan had torn open an entrance, he had found a room completely empty other than the overlapping silhouettes among the curtains. Liu Qingge knew that Luo Binghe definitely had to be in the pavilion, but he never could have imagined that he wasn't the only one within.

Luo Binghe raised his eyebrows, tugging the limp body in his left arm further into his embrace. "You tell me: What have I done?"

Shen Qingqiu was thoroughly speechless. Two people, or you should say, one alive person and one dead person, rolling off something similar to a bed together, in clothes that barely covered anything—it didn't look like something family friendly whatever way you spun it!

Without a single word from Liu Qingge, Cheng Luan shot forward. Xin Mo had yet to be drawn all the way, so using only the sheath, Luo Binghe blocked Cheng Luan's point. The energy from Cheng Luan's sword glares was overwhelming. Shifting sideways slightly, Luo Binghe blocked the bitingly cold energy attacks, keeping the body in his arms safe behind him as his expression grew angry.

Liu Qingge too had realized that if he deployed Cheng Luan within such a cramped chamber, a bit of carelessness might lead to his razor-sharp sword energy damaging that body. He instantly returned his sword to its sheath and began pitting his spiritual energy against Luo Binghe's.

As they tumbled around, locked in combat, the loose clothes on that body slipped completely down to its waist, and Luo Binghe's palm pressed flush against that fair skin.

"Beast! No matter what, he's still your shizun!" Liu Qingge said with bloodshot eyes.

"You think I'd do this with an outsider?" Luo Binghe asked calmly.

The Huan Hua Palace disciples who'd formed several circles around them were all dumbstruck. Luo Binghe paid them no attention, his entire focus on dealing with Liu Qingge. Spiritual energy roiled like boiling water in the air around them, shooting in all directions. As they clashed, their expressions worsened, each more frightening than the last. No one dared to step inside Huan Hua Pavilion for fear of being caught in the crossfire.

Shen Qingqiu, however, wasn't afraid of the crossfire. He was simply, merely unable to look at it straight on.

Too hardcore... Way too fucking hardcore!

Even if his imagination had been as vast as the moon was covered with craters, he had still never imagined that one day he would become a character in this kind of hardcore kink play. The thing Luo Binghe was holding in his arms—that...was indeed dead, right? He absolutely wasn't mistaken, because that was his corpse, okay?!

This had already surpassed the level of fridge horror. Even before he thought about it carefully, it was already beyond horrifying!

Even though he couldn't force himself to look directly, he hadn't forgotten his reason for coming back.

Shen Qingqiu flashed behind Liu Qingge. The latter went on guard, believing this to be an ambush, and let out a dark laugh, preparing to send his assailant flying with spiritual qi. However, instead, a hand pressed against Liu Qingge's back, and a stream of steady, gentle, yet powerful spiritual energy flooded into his meridians.

Once Liu Qingge received this aid, he could somewhat push back Luo Binghe. Liu Qingge dared not be careless, but he turned his head slightly. Out of the corner of his eye, he could only make out the muddled visage of the person behind him, as if there was something covering their face.

"Who's there?" Liu Qingge asked quietly.

Shen Qingqiu didn't answer and instead sent more force through his hand. The two peerlessly powerful streams of spiritual energy merged into one.

Though Luo Binghe could block it perfectly, this blast of offensive spiritual energy would travel down his body and into the corpse in his arms. He could dissipate the energy, but the dead could not; if he didn't let go, the shock would probably cause the body's facial apertures to rupture. Luo Binghe was unwilling to harm the corpse, so he could only release it. The body was shortly tossed away by the boiling spiritual field, flying outward.

Even after letting go, Luo Binghe's gaze remained firmly fixed on that body, his expression both helpless and reluctant. Shen Qingqiu suddenly found that expression of his unbearable. Using this method to force him to let go...somehow felt a bit like bullying?

Several disciples lacked sense and moved to take action.

"Don't touch him!" Luo Binghe yelled. Even from a distance, a wave of his sleeve filled that direction with screams.

Shen Qingqiu withdrew the spiritual energy he'd been applying to Liu Qingge's back. With a tap of his foot, he launched himself forward, catching the body within his arms.

The sensation of holding your own corpse definitely wasn't just an ordinary level of incredible. Shen Qingqiu gave it a couple of cursory glances: his old body's complexion was actually still decidedly rosy, its four limbs pliant. Other than the tightly closed eyes and lack of breath, it was no different from a living person in a deep sleep.

After self-detonation, one's spiritual energy was entirely dispersed; no cultivation remained within to prevent the corpse's decay. On top of that, more than five years had passed since his death, so just preserving the body with ice wouldn't have yielded this level of success. The body didn't smell of herbs, so it probably hadn't been treated with chemicals either. It was unclear what method Luo Binghe had used.

Shen Qingqiu dodged a spiritual blast strong enough to split stone and looked up. Luo Binghe was currently staring dead at him, his expression ferocious. Only now did Shen Qingqiu realize that this body's clothes had already slipped all the way down its torso, and that he was holding its naked flesh. Given how he had been touching and gazing at it, no matter how you looked, it was a...both incredibly disturbing and rather provocative sight.

He hurriedly pulled up the corpse's clothes, then sent this hot potato toward Liu Qingge. "Catch!"

Luo Binghe wanted to seize it, but he was intercepted by Shen Qingqiu. Originally, Shen Qingqiu had been worried that Luo Binghe would activate the heavenly demon blood mites, but whether murderous intent had gone to his head or his panic had sent him into a tizzy, he surprisingly didn't think to activate that trump card.

Liu Qingge caught the body with one arm and called forth Cheng Luan with his free hand, easily beating back the circle of attacking Huan Hua Palace disciples.

Due to being tossed back and forth between them, the corpse's top had finally ripped completely. When Liu Qingge caught it, he felt an expanse of smooth skin beneath his palm, both fine and cool, and the area where his hand touched seemed to skitter with a slight electric current. Liu Qingge's entire body froze. Finding no appropriate place he could hold the body, he almost sent it back once more.

Luckily, he managed to resist this impulse in the end and took off his outer robe, the white cloth spreading like wings, and bundled up the body in his arms. Cheng Luan flew back and steadily hovered before his feet.

Luo Binghe's eyes had turned fully scarlet. The entire Huan Hua Pavilion was like a tightly sealed box, and inside the box a bomb had been placed. When the bomb exploded, the walls collapsed with a loud rumble.

Falling alongside the flying sand and hurtling stones—aside from people, people, and more people—were two objects that hit the ground with a metallic clang. When Shen Qingqiu focused and looked, he saw they were actually two swords:

Zheng Yang, Xiu Ya.

These two swords had originally shared the same fate and broken into numerous sections of blade shards. It was unclear how they had been repaired, but they had been tied together and placed in Huan Hua Pavilion. Only with the pavilion's collapse did they once again see the sun and sky.

Seeing these two swords once more left an indescribable feeling in Shen Qingqiu's heart. He looked toward Luo Binghe, whose clothes had been disheveled from the start. After that wave of explosions, his clear-cut collarbones and chest lay entirely exposed. Near where his heart lay, there snaked a hideous-looking sword wound.

Luo Binghe's ability to regenerate was surpassingly powerful. Even if his limbs were chopped off, he could flawlessly reattach them. If you went a bit more hardcore, he could even grow new ones without problem. Unless he purposefully chose not to heal an injury, there were no wounds he couldn't mend and none that could leave a scar.

"Liu Qingge," Luo Binghe shouted, "for Shizun's sake, I've let you live over and over again. But since you want to die so badly, you can't blame me!"

The force of his subsequent eruption of spiritual energy and murderous intent almost made Shen Qingqiu's internal organs shift inside him. He knew Luo Binghe was furious, and he hurried to yell at Liu Qingge, "Still haven't left?!"

It felt like ever since he'd come to this world, he'd kept playing the role of the selfless rearguard who sacrificed himself for others! Liu Qingge gave him a glance, then was as decisive as expected—he left without delay, tucking the body beneath his arm and jumping onto his sword, then flying off at lightning speed.

Luo Binghe wanted to take action, but abruptly, a violent tremor shook his heart, and Xin Mo's sudden recoil forced him still for a beat. Due to this one missed beat, he could only watch helplessly as Liu Qingge flew off with Shen Qingqiu's corpse under his arm.

He remained in place in a daze, a blankness flickering over his face for an instant; he'd forgotten to even return fire. He had the appearance of a child who'd had his entire world, his most beloved thing, snatched away from him, whose sky was about to collapse and fall.

Shen Qingqiu had originally planned to take advantage of the chaos to slip away, but when he saw this, for some reason his feet remained stuck in place, and that unbearable flash from before grew ever stronger.

But even if he found the sight unbearable, it couldn't be helped. If he'd continued to let Luo Binghe embrace that corpse, who knew what gravely sinful and terrifying developments could have transpired?!

The real problem was that his heart had softened at such an inopportune time. He hadn't managed to slip away. Luo Binghe's head turned sharply in his direction, and those two severe red eyes locked on him.

Within its sheath, Xin Mo began to tremble with both joy and malice. Luo Binghe's expression clearly told Shen Qingqiu that he would absolutely, positively hack him into a thousand pieces. Shen Qingqiu looked at his eyes that were both furious and devastated and backed up two steps. Then all of a sudden, as if his mind had been bewitched, he wanted to tell Luo Binghe something true.

He wanted to say: "Don't be so sad, Shizun isn't dead."

Just as he moved his lips, a black shadow sprang out from the group of Huan Hua Palace disciples.

That silhouette was unbelievably fast and nimble. It snatched Shen Qingqiu up like a whirlwind and left just like that. Luo Binghe's eyesight and reflexes were exceptional, yet the spiritual blast he fired managed to miss.

He stood in place, emotionlessly looking at the ruins that remained of Huan Hua Pavilion and at the troops strewn everywhere. The entire time, the Huan Hua Palace disciples had been unable to interfere, but they too knew that Luo Binghe's mental state was unstable after this series of losses. He would definitely explode in a rage. They hurried to kneel en masse.

It also happened that Sha Hualing had finally made it to the pavilion. She rushed to the front, but Luo Binghe sent her flying the moment she arrived, and she coughed up three liters of blood.

She'd long known that Luo Binghe was temperamental, but not knowing what had enraged him this time, she said in terror, "My lord, calm down. My lord, calm down!"

"The person you brought back is really quite something," said Luo Binghe.

This "really quite something" was so fearsome that it would have been less scary if Luo Binghe had told her to commit suicide on the spot. Sha Hualing's soul almost left her body.

"This subordinate has something to report!" she said hastily.

"The moment the break-in occurred, this subordinate detected the problem and went to deal with it. Liu Qingge wasn't the only intruder! The peak lord of Bai Zhan Peak had scouted the palace's interior by cover of night, but he was unable to break the maze array. However, someone had broken the maze array beforehand, and using that, Liu Qingge also successfully infiltrated."

Luo Binghe gazed in the direction in which Liu Qingge had disappeared on his sword and slowly clenched his fist, the bones of his knuckles cracking.

Sha Hualing figured that Luo Binghe genuinely didn't care who the other intruder was; he was only concerned with Shen Qingqiu's body, which had been snatched away, so she hastily changed her tune. "Liu Qingge can't get far carrying that...that...by himself! This subordinate will take some forces and give chase!"

"No need," said Luo Binghe.

Sha Hualing shivered, her heart chilly, a vague premonition welling up within.

And indeed, she heard Luo Binghe coldly say, "I'll go myself. Call Mobei here."

At this time, Shen Qingqiu finally came to understand exactly how gentle Luo Binghe had been while controlling the blood mites in his body.

If Luo Binghe really wanted to kill someone with heavenly demon blood, the pain would in no way be only on the level of period cramps. He could make you wish you were dead, make it hurt until you couldn't stand straight, couldn't speak, until you could only roll around on the floor, and afterward, you'd lie there like a corpse, but the head-to-toe anguish wouldn't lessen even the slightest bit. There was no way you could last until it dulled, or until you got used to it.

Case in point: after his rampaging fury passed, Luo Binghe had finally remembered that he still had his heavenly demon blood.

The person who'd dragged Shen Qingqiu off in the midst of the confusion had probably reached someplace safe, as their pace slowed and they began to walk while supporting him. Shen Qingqiu wanted to sit, not walk, but he no longer had the strength to speak. He was dragged along half-dead for a stretch before that person finally realized something was wrong.

They lowered Shen Qingqiu to the ground. The voice they spoke with was both gentle and refreshing, the words measured. They seemed to be a young man.

"What's wrong?" the young man asked in a concerned tone. "Were you injured just now?"

Shen Qingqiu moved his lips, but he still lacked the strength to speak a single word. At present, it was like millions of blood mites were carousing in his capillaries, biting and swelling, squirming and twisting, the sensation both disgusting and agonizing.

This was teaching Shen Qingqiu that when Luo Binghe had activated the blood mites in his body before, he'd had no malice at all, and had basically been a hundred and twenty percent tenderhearted, more or less just briefly teasing him.

Shen Qingqiu rapidly ran through the various achievements and honors he'd earned under the System's coercion, and he honestly found it hilarious beyond belief. Exactly where had he gone wrong? How had his actions resulted in Luo Binghe's feelings of *that* for him?!

Shen Qingqiu searched himself and concluded that he'd been a staunch straight man from birth, and that all of heaven and earth could testify to this. There should've been no need to doubt Luo Binghe's orientation either. So exactly whose fault was this?

No need to wonder. If a character was derailed, it was of course the author's fault. Everything could be blamed on Airplane Shooting Towards the Sky!

Two dry laughs had just left Shen Qingqiu when there was another burst of excruciating pain, and he really did roll around on the ground a couple of times. It seemed that doing this could alleviate the agony a little.

He'd hardly rolled anywhere when he was held in place by the person who'd taken him. The young man touched Shen Qingqiu's forehead along with his cheeks. His beard had mostly fallen off, leaving it sparse and patchy, and cold sweat was everywhere. That touch trailed downward until it was at Shen Qingqiu's chest and abdomen.

For some reason, the places he touched felt a bit better. Shen Qingqiu sucked in a breath, and he couldn't help but say, "Eh, my friend, where...are you touching?"

Even a few hours ago, he genuinely wouldn't have cared where others (especially those of the same sex) touched him. They could touch wherever they liked, please go ahead. But ever since Luo Binghe had opened a series of gates to a new world for him, Shen Qingqiu's worldview, which had been set for the past twenty-plus years, had suffered a heavy blow. From now on, he needed to look at this world with a new gaze and more sensitive attitude.

Especially on the issue of befriending those of the same sex!

That person made an "ah" sound, then quickly let go and apologized. "Sorry. I...didn't mean to."

"No, no, no!" said Shen Qingqiu. "You can touch! Please continue! Thank you!"

It wasn't an illusion. When this person let go, Shen Qingqiu immediately began to hurt. It seemed like this guy...really could pacify the heavenly demon blood.

Shen Qingqiu turned his head. He couldn't see the young man's face clearly beneath the moonlight, but those features were more or less bright and refined, the eyes incredibly pellucid. They reflected Shen Qingqiu's silhouette and the crisp moonlight like dew water, the images overlapping within them.

Shen Qingqiu looked at those eyes and faintly recalled something, but before he could give it careful thought, something exploded within his brain, the pain so great that he groaned. Shoving his head downward, he curled his fingers into a fist and furiously bashed the ground.

Suddenly, Shen Qingqiu felt someone lift him by the back collar, his lower jaw throbbing as his mouth was forced open and a liquid poured in. His tongue was numb, and from the reaction of the acid in his stomach, though he couldn't tell what taste this liquid had, it probably wasn't anything delicious. Choking, he wanted to spit it out, but the young man covered his mouth. Though his movements were forceful, his tone was incredibly tender. "Swallow," he coaxed.

Shen Qingqiu's throat bobbed violently, and in a moment of haste, he ended up swallowing the liquid anyway. Rivulets of the unknown liquid trickled from the corner of his mouth. He lowered his head while coughing harshly, and the young man patted his back from the side, helping him breathe.

The shocking thing was that after this liquid entered his mouth and stomach, the pain from the blood mite bites, which had tormented him the entire trip, swiftly vanished.

Shen Qingqiu's body felt better, but the ground dropped out beneath his heart instead. He seized a fistful of the clothing at the young man's chest. "What did you make me drink?"

The young man pried open Shen Qingqiu's fingers one by one, bringing them away from his chest, and smiled. "Does it still hurt?"

It didn't hurt. It really didn't hurt. But the fact that it didn't hurt was what made it scary. He'd never imagined that something like heavenly demon blood could have an antidote!

As the sense of taste gradually returned to his tongue, Shen Qingqiu felt that the stench of blood within his mouth was also growing stronger—strong to the point that he felt nauseated.

The original work had said very distinctly that all medicines were ineffective against heavenly demon blood.

Only heavenly demon blood could keep heavenly demon blood in check.

Fuck.

Not only had he drunk it twice, he'd drunk heavenly demon blood from two different owners.

Shen Qingqiu really could fucking live up to the eight words: "Unprecedented and unparalleled, with none before or after."

After thinking this, Shen Qingqiu let out a cheerful whoop, then fell over face-first.

The sound of ripping flesh.

What's more, it was accompanied by hoarse, wretched screams.

Shen Qingqiu pressed on his temples, and the scene before his eyes slowly clarified and focused.

A sea of blood. A mountain of corpses.

Luo Binghe stood wooden in the midst of this purgatory of a scene. He wore black, so the blood couldn't mark his clothes, but half his face was splashed with specks of crimson, and he raised and lowered his sword callously and mechanically.

To start, when Shen Qingqiu first laid eyes on Luo Binghe, an image automatically surfaced in his mind: that of Luo Binghe holding Shen Qingqiu's corpse as he rolled off the bed in a heap. So it was hard to look at him directly.

But soon he realized that Luo Binghe was massacring his own dream realm constructions. What difference was there between this and stirring his own brains with a knife?

He's not an idiot who doesn't know better. Only a madman would do something like this!

Though Shen Qingqiu often loved to say that Luo Binghe was a masochist who liked to torture himself, there was no way he could squeeze out a couple of dry laughs over this level of self-torture, or even take the time to ridicule it.

Luo Binghe lifted his eyes to Shen Qingqiu, his gaze hazy, like his mind was unclear. But as soon as those eyes reflected Shen Qingqiu's silhouette, they instantly brightened, and he promptly tossed aside the longsword in his hand. He threw it far, far away and then hid his bloodstained hands behind him, calling in a quiet voice, "Shizun."

Then he remembered that his face was stained too, and as if to remedy this, he wiped at the blood washed over half his face with his sleeves. But the more he wiped, the dirtier it became, and like a child who'd been caught stealing red-handed, he grew increasingly distressed.

A stranger the first time, familiar the second. Shen Qingqiu had experience pretending to be a product of artificial intelligence, and he could still project an unperturbed image. He involuntarily softened his voice when he spoke. "What are you doing?"

"Shizun, I...I let you be taken from me again," Luo Binghe said quietly. "This disciple is useless and couldn't even hold on to your body."

This answer made Shen Qingqiu's expression and emotions became equally complicated.

So this cruel murder of his own dream realm constructions just now should be considered...self-discipline?

Given how deft Luo Binghe's actions had been, Shen Qingqiu feared this wasn't the first time Luo Binghe had done this. No wonder Luo Binghe had been unable to distinguish the difference between a product of the dream realm and an intruder from the outside the last time they met.

Shen Qingqiu sighed and deliberated for a while before gently comforting him. "What's lost is lost. I don't blame you."

Luo Binghe stared at him vacantly. "But that's all I have left now."

Shen Qingqiu suddenly didn't dare look him in the eye. Could Luo Binghe really have spent those five years clinging to a corpse—to an empty shell Shen Qingqiu hadn't wanted anymore?

Luo Binghe's voice abruptly chilled. "After Hua Yue City, I swore that in this life, I'd never let Shizun be taken from me again, but I still let someone else snatch you away."

The bitterness, along with the dark red color within his eyes, was both turbulent and deep-set. The longsword he'd tossed aside soared into the air on his command and pierced through the chests of several "people" who were on the ground in their death throes. Waves of wretched screaming filled his ears.

Shen Qingqiu hastily restrained him. "Don't be reckless," he reprimanded. "Even if you're dreaming, this is no different from self-harm. Don't tell me you've forgotten!"

Of course Luo Binghe wouldn't have forgotten. He stared straight at Shen Qingqiu, flipping his hand over and pressing it over the back of his old master's. Only after a long while did he say, "I know that I'm dreaming. Only in a dream would Shizun still scold me like this."

Upon hearing this line, Shen Qingqiu snapped back to his senses. He couldn't. This was wrong. He couldn't do this to Luo Binghe.

If you didn't have that kind of intention toward someone, you shouldn't give them hope. The larger the hope, the larger the disappointment. His confused state of mind would only continue, and it would increase the chance that he would lose all reason.

Even if this was a dream, he still couldn't drag his feet and pussy around like this. He had to be decisive. If he continued to indulge such ill-defined involvement, it would become an evil deed.

Shen Qingqiu firmly yanked his hand back and corrected his expression, adopting that which he was best at: an unapproachable countenance, austere and aloof. Then he turned right around and left.

Upon being shaken off, Luo Binghe was stunned for a moment, then dashed after him. "Shizun, I know I was wrong."

"If you know you're wrong, don't follow," Shen Qingqiu said coldly.

"I've regretted it for a long while, but I was never able to tell you," Luo Binghe said anxiously. "Are you still angry that I drove you to self-detonate your spiritual energy? I've already fully repaired the meridians in Shizun's body. I'm not lying either! As long as I can enter the Holy Mausoleum, I'll definitely find a way to awaken you again."

Shen Qingqiu didn't answer, hesitating over whether he should drop some harsh words to make Luo Binghe give up on this idea. But then Luo Binghe suddenly threw himself forward and embraced him from behind. He hugged Shen Qingqiu firmly, not budging an inch even if Shen Qingqiu were to thrash and flail like a madman.

Shen Qingqiu's entire body stiffened within the hug as if he had brushed up against some hairy thing, and the fine hairs on his body stood straight up. He gathered energy into his hand but still didn't truly attack, instead spitting two words between gritted teeth. "Beat it!"

It's supposed to be a guarantee that after blackening, Luo Binghe no longer goes down the route of misery! Take your hands off!

Luo Binghe turned a deaf ear to his demand. "Or is Shizun angry about what happened in Jin Lan City?"

"Correct," said Shen Qingqiu.

Luo Binghe still refused to let go. "When I first returned from the Endless Abyss, I learned that Shizun had told everyone else that I was killed by demons," he mumbled. "At first I thought it was because Shizun was kindhearted, that you still had some lingering sentiments and were unwilling to ruin my name. But after we met, I saw Shizun's attitude and became scared that I'd been too optimistic. I thought that Shizun hadn't concealed the truth for me but because he felt that having brought up a demon would ruin his reputation."

He cut a pitiful figure while speaking, the sentences tumbling out one after another, as if he was terrified that Shen Qingqiu would brusquely interrupt and not let him continue. "I really wasn't the one who arranged for the sowers. At that time, I was so angry, I couldn't think. That's the only reason I let them shut Shizun in the Water Prison... I've known I was wrong for a long time now."

There would probably never be a time where the Luo Binghe in reality could ramble nonstop, without caring for his image. In all likelihood, he would only dare prattle on like this within the dreams he created for himself. To push him away during this moment would be like giving a young maiden—one who'd finally worked up the courage to call and brokenheartedly weep to an older sister for comfort and encouragement—a face-turning slap. It was really a bit cruel.

Shen Qingqiu was filled with both deep compassion as well as a feeling that this was extremely absurd. What could be more absurd than discovering that the person from whom you'd exhaustively plotted to flee, and had indeed fled from for so many years, hadn't actually wanted to kill you at all, but wanted to do you instead? Though whether the desire was to kill or to fuck, the result was the same: Shen Qingqiu would still run away with all his might.

One party wanted to meet but couldn't, and so had clung to a corpse for five years. The other party avoided the first like the plague but still felt like he ran into him a great deal.

Shen Qingqiu's hands were stiff as he raised and lowered them, clenched them and relaxed. In the end, he let out a sigh anyway and patted that head above his.

Fuck, I've really lost! he thought.

Right now, forget about the harem: a perfectly fine, dark, and vicious stallion novel male lead was very possibly still a virgin. Luo Binghe had already put himself in such a state, so it would have been rather inhumane of Shen Qingqiu to shove another knife in. In the end, Shen Qingqiu lost to the deeply tragic act Luo Binghe had sold him, as well as to his own sense of sympathy.

Luo Binghe instantly clutched that hand of his. Shen Qingqiu felt that the skin on Luo Binghe's palm, which was pressing into the back of his hand, was uneven. When he looked closer, he realized it was a sword scar.

At first, Shen Qingqiu didn't understand why there were so many scars on Luo Binghe's body, but then he suddenly remembered. During their night encounter in Jin Lan City, for a stretch, Luo Binghe had played cat and mouse with him. When Shen Qingqiu was caught, he had stabbed at Luo Binghe, and Luo Binghe had caught Xiu Ya's blade point squarely in his hand.

As for the wound on his chest and close to his heart, Shen Qingqiu had even less of an excuse for forgetting that. It was from the Immortal Alliance Conference. While forcing Luo Binghe to fall, Shen Qingqiu had accidentally stabbed him.

It seemed like every time he'd tried to stab Luo Binghe, the latter had never avoided the strike and had instead always received it head-on, neither dodging nor evading, letting him hack away. Because of this, Shen Qingqiu had stabbed him twice, despite not wishing to either time. Furthermore, after being pierced by his blade, Luo Binghe hadn't healed either wound and instead had purposefully preserved them.

Only a short while ago, Shen Qingqiu could have matter-of-factly believed that Luo Binghe was nursing a grudge and keeping the scars to remind himself of his hatred at any time. But now Shen Qingqiu could no longer deceive himself about the exact meaning of these actions.

He'd finished reading the hugely long original novel and raised this child to adulthood, but he'd never realized that Luo Binghe was actually a purehearted young man. And as the deeply emotional stallion had turned gay, the "stallion" part had actually been summarily dropped. This Luo Binghe, who'd been bent to heavens knew where by his rearing, possessed a heart both masochistic and easy to harm, more delicate than a young maiden's.

Or maybe it wasn't that Shen Qingqiu had never realized it but that he'd never thought to *understand*. When all was said and done, he had still regarded Luo Binghe as a character in a novel and adopted an attitude that he was something to constantly observe and occasionally mess around with. Most of the time, he'd kept himself at a respectful distance. And Luo Binghe, who'd had the strongest presence in the original work, had ended up suffering most of Shen Qingqiu's assumptions about tropes and story formulas.

Faced with this true Luo Binghe, Shen Qingqiu felt it was all extraordinarily troublesome, and he truly was at a loss for what to do.

He was still racking his brain for solutions, so from his angle, he couldn't see the hint of a twisted smile lifting the corner of Luo Binghe's mouth.

12
Zhuzhi

AFTER WAKING, Shen Qingqiu opened his eyes to see a gauzy, snow-white canopy above him. Someone pushed open the door and walked in, then lightly closed the door behind them. "Are you awake?"

Shen Qingqiu rotated his neck back and forth, then looked at the asker out of the corner of his eye.

Under the light of the lantern, which was warmer than the light of the moon, that young man's looks were indeed good: the corner of his mouth held a smile, his appearance was peerlessly clever and handsome. His eyes especially exuded a kind of gentle and quick-witted air.

He'd seen this pair of eyes before. They were eyes that had been nurtured by the Dew Lake.

When Shen Qingqiu rolled into a seated position, a bag of ice fell from his forehead. The man stooped to retrieve it and put it back on the table, then replaced it with a new bag for him.

Upon seeing this, Shen Qingqiu was too embarrassed to voice all the "who are yous" and "what do you wants" he'd been holding within himself. Coughing once, he said in a reserved tone, "Many thanks for your assistance at Huan Hua Palace."

The young man stood by the table and smiled. "Humans have a saying: a drop of kindness should be repaid by a flood. Moreover, the kindness from Immortal Master Shen far exceeded a drop."

First of all, this gentleman was indeed that snake-man from Bai Lu Forest.

Second of all, this gentleman knew that the person inside this shell was Shen Qingqiu.

"Tianlang-Jun...?" Shen Qingqiu asked probingly.

The reason why that ancient line of heavenly demons was called "heavenly" was because, according to legend, their bloodline had fallen from the Heavenly Realm and become demons. Only a heavenly demon with a lineage purer than Luo Binghe's could suppress the blood within Shen Qingqiu's body. In that case, a problem arose. Of the heavenly demon lineage, Shen Qingqiu knew of only two who had been named in the original work: Luo Binghe and his dad. Who else could he guess?

But such things only came in threes. At this juncture, Shen Qingqiu's super unique riddle-solving method, which had succeeded every time to date, finally hit a wall.

The man shook his head. "Immortal Master Shen, taking me for my lord is truly an excessive honor."

When Shen Qingqiu heard that "my lord," he finally figured out which character this person was.

By the time of the original work's prologue, Tianlang-Jun had already been subjugated and imprisoned underneath a high mountain. However, that grand battle of many years past had little to do with the male lead's overpowered and stallion ways, and thus Airplane Shooting Towards the Sky had but roughly covered the affair. He said only that Tianlang-Jun was "no match for the combined siege of numerous top cultivators of the Human Realm, and he was imprisoned beneath XX mountain, never to be free again, his trusted right hand separated from him by injury or death."

Which mountain was XX mountain, exactly? Shen Qingqiu had never properly considered this question. But once his curiosity was piqued, he finally realized which one it was.

Bai Lu Mountain!

Bai Lu Forest on Bai Lu Mountain!

Shen Qingqiu looked the man up and down. So this was the "trusted right hand" of Luo Binghe's father!

But looking at him now, he could find no trace of that snake-man's deformed figure from their first encounter. Shen Qingqiu swallowed. "May I venture to ask this distinguished gentleman... What is your name?"

"Tianlang-Jun's subordinate, Zhuzhi-Lang," the man said courteously.

His words had only just left his mouth when the System gave a notification:

[Increased degree of story line completion and filled in hidden character list: B-Points +300. Activated plot hole-filling event: B-Points +100.]

A burst of uncontainable excitement suddenly welled up inside Shen Qingqiu.

"Plot hole-filling" definitely referred to those atrocities whose perpetrators had never been identified, leaving the reader defrauded and without leads, as well as the buggy setting details in the original work. This was precisely (one of) the greatest reason(s) that Shen Yuan had disdained *Proud Immortal Demon Way*. It was also a major reason why he'd been beating his chest, stomping his feet, and gnashing his teeth after finishing the novel.

Now he'd drawn out a character who had never directly appeared on stage, and the System had opened a plot hole-filling opportunity.

Could it be that next, he'd finally uncover the truth behind those giant plot holes ripping through the sky?!

"I saved you once, then you saved me once. We're even now," said Shen Qingqiu.

The "saved you once" he spoke of referred to that time he'd stopped Gongyi Xiao from killing the snake-man. But Zhuzhi-Lang shook his head. "There's more to it than that. If not for Immortal Master Shen, I'm afraid that even after many more years, I still wouldn't have been able to approach the Sun-Moon Dew Mushroom. How could you say we're already even?"

This sounded perfect to Shen Qingqiu. "All right then, let's discuss: Can't you just extract both influences from my blood? Must you let them remain?"

It was as if there had been a parasite within his body and the doctor's approach to treatment had been to place another parasite inside him to fight it. From every angle imaginable, his situation had only worsened.

"Um... It's this humble one's first time utilizing heavenly demon blood," said Zhuzhi-Lang. "I've never even heard of a means by which to dispel it."

Though this was disappointing, Shen Qingqiu still expressed his understanding. The blood had entered his body and dissolved without a trace, so separating it out again truly wasn't especially feasible.

"Though it cannot be dispelled, as long as this one's blood is also in Immortal Master Shen's body, the other heavenly demon blood will be ineffective," Zhuzhi-Lang said. "After we go to the Demon Realm, the tracking function will fail, and he will be absolutely unable to torment you any longer."

Wait.

"Hold on. When did I say that I wanted to go to the Demon Realm?" asked Shen Qingqiu.

"We're going very soon," said Zhuzhi-Lang.

Shen Qingqiu examined his expression. "The 'repayment' you spoke of, it wouldn't happen to be taking me there?"

Why go to the Demon Realm at all? It was short on supplies and natural resources, the culture and customs were incompatible with his, and the environment wouldn't suit him either. In addition, more urgent worries were still piled up in his forebrain. For one, there was his brain's new trauma-driven meltdown courtesy of Luo Binghe's near-necrophiliac behavior, and for another he'd let Liu Qingge run off with his original body. What if Luo Binghe exterminated Cang Qiong Mountain in a fit of anger?!

Shen Qingqiu had to get there before him and notify his comrades. He swiftly tossed his covers aside, planning to run away. But unexpectedly, just as he began to move, he felt something slimy, soft, and icy-cold slither up his leg.

A jade-green snake lazily poked its head out from beneath the covers and flicked a scarlet tongue toward Shen Qingqiu with a hiss.

This snake was three fingers thick, and at first glance it resembled the venomous bamboo viper of the Human Realm. Its eye sockets were horribly large while its pupils were disturbingly small—a ghastly contrast. But Shen Qingqiu wasn't afraid of this sort of soft-bodied animal. Regarding it coolly, he stealthily gathered energy in the palm of his hand, intending to catch it off guard and blow off seven inches of its body. Suddenly, the jade-green snake reared back, its red mouth gaping open.

It was merely a snake, but from its mouth came a shriek as ear-piercing as a human's. At the same time, a dense layer of countless green spikes exploded around its head like a blossoming flower. The sharp tips were suffused with scarlet—obviously poisonous even at a glance—and the snake's body also inflated several sizes larger, as if it had been pumped full of air. Just a moment ago, it could have been considered a cute, dainty ornamental snake, but now it was a real fucking monster.

The breeds of the Demon Realm were verily savage. Shen Qingqiu promptly dispelled any thought of touching it with his hands.

Zhuzhi-Lang poured out a cup of tea. "Immortal Master Shen, why would you try to leave before I finished my explanation?" he asked cordially as he placed the cup on the table. "This one sincerely wishes to repay you for not killing him in Bai Lu Forest; you even went so far as to assist him."

Shen Qingqiu chewed on his lip for a bit. "You want me to go to the Demon Realm, and when I don't want to, you put this thing in my bed. Is this your idea of 'repayment'?"

Zhuzhi-Lang smiled. "Not only in your bed."

Another small snake the width of a thumb slid out from Shen Qingqiu's clothes.

This snake had been coiled in his robes all along. Warmed by his body temperature, it had been nesting comfortably, not moving an inch, so Shen Qingqiu hadn't even noticed its presence. With an endless hiss, a flood of countless green snakes of various widths and sizes slithered out from under the bed, carpeting the whole floor.

Shen Qingqiu was silent for a long while, until he said, "The snake race?"

"My father was from the southern border," Zhuzhi-Lang said calmly.

No wonder his name was thus.

The demon race placed a great deal of importance on social class and lineage. Common demons or demons of lowly lineages could not append "Jun" to their name. This title was a suffix representing one's social status, similar to how the emperor's name was taboo and couldn't be infringed upon.

The reason Luo Binghe's path to ascension was slightly rocky in the original work was because the demon lords took issue with him being of mixed human blood. In the early stages of the Demon Realm arc, Luo Binghe had done in quite a few characters named in the fashion of "XX-Lang." Therefore, Shen Qingqiu had concluded that while names with this suffix weren't necessarily all from the slums, their origins couldn't be especially esteemed either.

Zhuzhi-Lang undoubtedly belonged to the heavenly demon bloodline, but he couldn't take the title of "Jun." The issue was evidently due to his mixed heritage.

The snake race resided on the southern border of the Demon Realm. Strictly speaking, they still counted as part of the demon race, but their true forms took on the appearance of giant snakes. They were born in this form, and as they grew in age and cultivation, a terribly small number would over time shed their scales and take on a human appearance. But even more stayed in the shape of a snake for their entire lives.

"Who is your mother?" asked Shen Qingqiu.

"Tianlang-Jun's younger sister," said Zhuzhi-Lang.

Tianlang-Jun's younger sister counted as something like the demon race's princess. How foolhardy was she, that out of all her options, she had to have a child with a snake? Way too fucking hardcore!

As Shen Qingqiu endured those two snakes creeping around his leg and stomach, he asked, "So you're technically Luo Binghe's senior cousin? ...I say, can't you tell these fellows to not...slither into my clothes?"

"If by 'senior' one only means older, that can certainly be said to be true," Zhuzhi-Lang said. "And they seem awfully fond of Immortal Master Shen, so there's nothing this one can do."

Who the hell would believe there's nothing you can do?!

Shen Qingqiu bore with it to ask, "Why were you at Huan Hua Palace?"

"Originally I went to take care of official business, and I never thought I'd see Immortal Master Shen," Zhuzhi-Lang said with great patience.

Shen Qingqiu's heart thumped. "Official business? This official business you speak of, does it have to do with Luo Binghe?"

To offer an alliance and rule jointly as overlords? Or had there been a falling out within the demon race? Or maybe it had been for a "Heartbreaking! Demon Family's Reunion After Many-Year Separation, Overcome by Tears of Emotion"?

This time, Zhuzhi-Lang smiled and didn't answer.

"I fear this official business wasn't as heartwarming as reconnecting relatives," said Shen Qingqiu.

"This one was only obeying his lord's orders," Zhuzhi-Lang said, unhurried.

"This body of yours, was it sculpted from the Sun-Moon Dew Mushroom?" asked Shen Qingqiu.

If Zhuzhi-Lang had used that one sprout for himself, it would make things easier. If he *hadn't* used it for himself, then it was possible that he'd used it to sculpt a body for Tianlang-Jun.

Tianlang-Jun had been imprisoned under a mountain, hanging on by a single breath for many, many years, and his original body was likely long ruined. But if like a cicada he shed his carapace, Shen Qingqiu really couldn't guess what sort of waves would result. He had an uneasy premonition that his own careless flutter of butterfly wings had released something monumental.

Having received no reply, his mind couldn't settle down and he continued. "Is taking me to the Demon Realm another one of your lord's orders?"

Whenever a question touched upon the subject of Tianlang-Jun, Zhuzhi-Lang clammed up and refused to answer, offering nothing but a polite smile; it was truly infuriating. Only when Shen Qingqiu finally withdrew in defeat did he open his mouth, retaining his usual refined and courteous manner. "Rest well, Immortal Master Shen. If there is anything you need, please say so, and I will certainly handle it for you. We will depart for the borderlands tomorrow at the latest."

Exhausted from all the talking, Shen Qingqiu asked, "Do you have money?"

"Yes," Zhuzhi-Lang responded.

"Can I use it?"

"As you wish."

"I want women."

Zhuzhi-Lang stopped, staring blankly.

"Wasn't it you who said that if there was anything I needed, I should tell you, and to feel free to do as I wish? I want women," Shen Qingqiu repeated. "Get rid of the snakes."

A small crack finally opened in Zhuzhi-Lang's smiling expression; after a long while, he did as instructed. Shen Qingqiu hummed a laugh and turned to get off the bed; he threw on his outer robes and tidied his clothing. For some time, Zhuzhi-Lang seemed to be hesitating, wavering over whether to follow. But when Shen Qingqiu stepped out the door, he tagged along after.

As peak lord of Qing Jing Peak, Shen Qingqiu had been obligated to be mindful of his image. Though a thousand curiosities had gripped his heart, he'd cleaved to the tenet that brothels were not to be entered. But now he had the opportunity. Shen Qingqiu acted as though his Zhuzhi-Lang-shaped shadow didn't exist, and after strolling through the streets once, he picked the Warm Red Pavilion for its more hospitable appearance. He strode in, expression utterly at ease.

Before long, Shen Qingqiu was surrounded by brightly colored decorations, his nostrils assailed by the scent of talcum powder. Zhuzhi-Lang took a seat beside him at a round table, as motionless as Mount Tai.

"What's with the look on your face?" asked Shen Qingqiu.

Zhuzhi-Lang averted his eyes. "It's just… I'm a bit surprised. That Immortal Master Shen would actually be interested in this place of prostitution."

"Wait a moment. You'll see what I'm interested in," said Shen Qingqiu.

Just as he spoke, a new songstress leisurely walked up from the side. She was somewhat older, and the cosmetics she wore were also quite colorful. She sat on a flower stool while cradling a pipa before meeting eyes with Shen Qingqiu and startling briefly.

Not comprehending, Shen Qingqiu nodded at her. "Miss?"

The songstress snapped out of it. "My apologies, sir," she said with an easy smile. "Your appearance is excellent and reminded this servant of an old acquaintance. My eyes deceived me."

When she had said her piece, she lowered her head and didn't mention anything further. Then, with a few plucks and strums, she began to sing.

At first, Shen Qingqiu just whispered into the ears of the girls next to him, not bothering to listen to the music, but after catching a couple of phrases, he suddenly felt that he'd heard two incredibly unbelievable things. He called for the songstress to stop. "Miss, what is this you're singing?"

"This servant is singing the popular new ballad, *Regret of Chunshan*,"[10] the woman said with a delicate voice.

"That's odd," Shen Qingqiu said, his face full of black lines. "Just now I seem to have heard you singing two names? Could you repeat those?"

The pipa player smiled behind her sleeve. "What's odd about it? Could it be that you've never heard it before, sir? The leading characters in *Regret of Chunshan* have always been Shen Qingqiu and Luo Binghe."

...

...

...

When did we get fucking turned into a popular ballad?!

Zhuzhi-Lang had originally been refusing all services, quietly sitting to the side and pretending to be the air itself, but he unfortunately exposed himself when his shoulders faintly shook.

"Uh... Could I ask...this *Regret of Whatever Mountain*, what story does it tell?" asked Shen Qingqiu.

---

10   春山很: Chunshan literally translates to "Spring Mountain," while 恨 can imply resentment, hatred, and/or regret, depending on context. Since the story seems to be about Luo Binghe's despair over losing Shen Qingqiu as told by the brothel ladies, "regret" seems closest to the intended meaning, though this is narrower than the original Chinese.

Several women next to him spoke with chirping voices. "Sir, you don't even know that? *Regret of Chunshan* tells of the poignant sentiments between Shen Qingqiu and his beloved disciple, Luo Binghe—the unspeakable and taboo..."

Shen Qingqiu forced himself to listen from start to end in a petrified state.

To summarize the plot: In short, this was a "shameless master and disciple pair who spent all day on some nameless mountain ignoring their duties to knock boots, who went down the mountain to fight monsters and take trips to pound town, who used two person push-ups to settle misunderstandings, who still needed to play a round of hide the sausage before dying, who continued to ride the bony express after death, and who after resurrection would still gleefully smack each other's salmons as before"...sort of story.

The pipa player sighed faintly, plucking a string with her fingertip. "Having never understood the affection in the other's heart in life, and lying with the body in death—this manner of abiding love is truly matchless in this age."

All the women followed up with incessant sighs and sobs, some already beginning to shed tears of emotion.

Shen Qingqiu buried his head deep into his hands.

Dammit, isn't this just some fucking porn? Who wrote these lyrics? What mountain is "Chunshan"? Qing Jing Peak? Cang Qiong Mountain? Cang Qiong Mountain Sect's gonna wipe out your entire family in a minute flat, okay?!

Exactly how was this gossip's reach so wide that not only had it infested the borderlands, even the over-the-top porn in bookshops was milking it for content—as if he and Luo Binghe had been caught rolling in the sheets in front of the whole world!

Zhuzhi-Lang let out a chuckle and turned. "Master Shen...are you...interested in this ballad?"

Shen Qingqiu looked at him coldly. Zhuzhi-Lang hurriedly corrected the expression on his face, but he still struggled to hold it in. "It... It would be best if I removed myself for a bit..." he said.

However, just as he was about to get up, his movements slowed, and he froze in his seat.

Shen Qingqiu observed his expression and smiled. "What? Finally starting to feel unwell?"

Standing up, he shook out his robes, and the green snakes that had been curled against his chest fell to the ground with a splat, rolling over to show their yellow bellies. The women in the hall began to scream, and the pipa player flung her instrument away altogether.

Holding his forehead, Zhuzhi-Lang stood while supporting himself against the table, swaying back and forth. Staring at Shen Qingqiu, he raised his right hand and grabbed a handful of the little snakes that had slithered forth from his sleeve, but they remained twined between his fingers, entirely impotent. Zhuzhi-Lang shook his head and said weakly, "...Realgar."

For a while now, without his notice, the entire brothel had been soaked in the scent of realgar wine.

"Top-quality realgar wine," Shen Qingqiu said approvingly. "All purchased with your money, by the way."

His assistants didn't need to be superhuman. With a couple of whispers, the brothel girls accepted Shen Qingqiu's money and secretly purchased the entire town's stash of realgar wine, then placed it all around the Warm Red Pavilion and fanned the fumes as it boiled. After it boiled all night, no member of the snake tribe would be able to resist swooning under its influence.

Zhuzhi-Lang's guard might have been up, but he'd been aiming to prevent Shen Qingqiu from contacting other cultivators, not these brothel girls. In the end, he'd been too careless.

When Zhuzhi-Lang raised his head, the whites of his eyes had turned gold, his pupils elongated into slits at a speed visible to the naked eye. His face had also begun to change shape.

Shen Qingqiu quickly opened the door. "Aren't you going to leave?" he asked the prostitutes huddled and shivering in the corner.

The women immediately began fighting to run outside; the pipa player was last, her movements deft. Shen Qingqiu stuffed a bag of silver in her sash, compensation for her pipa, then closed the door behind them. When he turned around again, where Zhuzhi-Lang had once stood, a giant, jade-green serpent was coiled, its body thick enough to be encircled by three men with their arms outstretched. The giant serpent's head was enormous and triangular, its large yellow eyes like copper bells, its pupils the finest of lines. It seemed dizzy, like its thin neck was unable to hold up that heavy head, which kept drooping.

The realgar wine's effect had exceeded Shen Qingqiu's expectations: it had forced Zhuzhi-Lang to reveal his original form.

Now this was a bit of a headache for Shen Qingqiu. He picked up a nearby folding fan that someone had abandoned and snapped it open, giving it a couple of waves. The giant serpent slithered toward him and looped around him twice as if to wrap him up, but Shen Qingqiu easily jumped free.

The giant serpent roiled and twined, then burst out of the building like it was drunk, crashing down into the middle of the street and alarming the passersby, who screamed and fled in all directions.

Shen Qingqiu followed it down from the upper floor and shouted, "Going outside is useless—the entire town is filled with the smell of realgar wine!"

A piercing shriek erupted from the giant serpent's mouth. It shook its head and thrashed its tail in its spot on the road.

Shen Qingqiu decided to draw it away from places with large volumes of people, and he flew to leap onto the serpent's head. Whenever it moved in the wrong direction or was about to crash into a passerby or residence, Shen Qingqiu jabbed the side of its head with his fan. The serpent's scales were like armor, and they made a great rumbling sound as it slithered over the ground. Shen Qingqiu often had to pour large amounts of spiritual energy into the fan before he could make the snake change direction. In this manner, he just barely managed to pilot it toward the edge of town.

After taking his money, the brothel girls had done their job with everything they had. No one could say how much realgar wine they'd boiled. Carried by the wind, the smell drifted far and wide. Even after finally arriving at the foot of a nearby mountain, it still continued to waft toward them from uphill. The giant serpent was overwhelmed by the smell to the point of agony, and moreover Shen Qingqiu had jabbed, poked, and ridden it all the way here. Exhausted and spent, it could no longer move.

Deciding they were far enough from the city, Shen Qingqiu finally jumped down. The giant serpent was weak and dispirited; its head sagged while its body was coiled like a meandering mountain road.

"Although I'm very interested in filling in plot holes, I have no interest in emigrating to the Demon Realm," said Shen Qingqiu. "Besides, I already have enough on my plate to drive me mad. Since you can't remove the heavenly demon blood, you can forget about the repayment or whatever. Xizhi-Lang,[11] goodbye!"

Shen Qingqiu was incredibly afraid that once the wine's effect dissipated, Zhuzhi-Lang would return to his original form and release another torrent of snakes to ensnare him, so he ran like the wind. Once he reached the next sizable city, he found an eminently reliable chain store and rented a flying sword.

Yes, that's right, he really rented one. Just like rental cars, immortal swords could be rented. And the prices were entirely fair and reasonable!

Basically, he was still using Zhuzhi-Lang's money, so Shen Qingqiu pressed both hands together and gave thanks to this benevolent brother. Then he sped off toward Cang Qiong Mountain Sect by sword.

After no more than half a day, a continuous, rolling jade-green mountain range with twelve peaks of irregular height appeared from within the sea of clouds and mist.

It's been a while, Cang Qiong Mountain.

Two characters rose to his mind as he thought that: "Chunshan." Shen Qingqiu silently crossed them out.

---

11 喜之郎, *SQQ's nickname for Zhuzhi-Lang is also a jelly brand in China.*

13

Coercion

A N AIR DEFENSE barrier surrounded the periphery of Cang
Qiong Mountain Sect. Immortal swords not of the sect
could not enter without prior notice, and those entering
without authorization would be knocked off course. Thus Shen
Qingqiu stopped at the foot of the mountain and sent the flying
sword back, using the chance to change his clothes and procure a
bamboo hat to wear.

Cultivators often passed through the little village at the foot of
the mountain, yet today he didn't see many. Shen Qingqiu was just
beginning to find it strange when someone asked, "This immortal
master, he... Is he heading up to Cang Qiong Mountain Sect?"

Shen Qingqiu nodded.

That person continued, "Surely going right now isn't a good idea?"

Shen Qingqiu's heart tightened. "What do you mean, it isn't good?"

That person and a few others looked at each other. "You still don't
know?" they asked. "This mountain has been under siege for two
days."

As Shen Qingqiu passed through the gates and climbed the tall
staircase, he failed to encounter a single disciple on watch. The ominous premonition in Shen Qingqiu's heart grew stronger and stronger. He leapt up multiple steps at once, dashing upward. The farther
up he went, the clearer it became that in many stretches of sky above

Qiong Ding Peak, thick black smoke roiled, intermingled with the flash of lightning and crash of thunder.

The summit of Qiong Ding Peak was an absolute mess. The mountain forests in flames, the ground littered with icicles, the eaves of roofs collapsed and destroyed like they'd been through multiple brutal battles.

Outside Qiong Ding Hall, two distinct factions faced each other. On one side were the human cultivators: some standing and some on the ground, while Mu Qingfang shuttled busily back and forth between them. On the other side were demon soldiers in black armor: a dense legion with an awe-inspiring presence.

Though there seemed to be a temporary ceasefire, the moment someone drew their sword even a mote, the tension that drifted in the air like gunpowder would reignite.

It looked like Luo Binghe was no longer bothering to hide his identity, and Shen Qingqiu was not surprised. Luo Binghe's blood-line reveal in the original work had been around this time as well. His momentum as he climbed to the top of demonkind was by this point unstoppable, and he had already thoroughly brainwashed Huan Hua Palace, reshaping them until they were perfectly submissive to him. With his footing secured, he of course no longer needed to be secretive. The only difference between this formal shedding of pretenses and the scenario in the original were the setting and synopsis.

Though the disciples on the peaks had to wear uniforms, there were also many acclaimed cultivators who weren't subject to these restrictions, and so no one paid particular attention to Shen Qingqiu's out-of-place attire. He squeezed his way through the crowd until he was standing before the hall entrance and peered inside.

Yue Qingyuan sat there with his eyes closed while Liu Qingge stood behind him, palm pressed against his back. The ripples of spiritual energy around their bodies seemed rather unstable. In all likelihood, neither of their situations were good. Shen Qingqiu had finally reunited with his zhangmen-shixiong and unfortunate shidi only to find them in such a sorry state—a state that he'd put them into. Guilt welled within Shen Qingqiu's heart, but when he turned again, his breath stuttered.

Luo Binghe was standing at the other side of the great hall, a heavy air around him.

He was wearing black, which made his skin shine translucently pale in comparison. His eyes were dark as pitch but also blisteringly bright, and his expression was cold and dispassionate, yet the air around him struck a fearful unrest in others. Mobei-Jun stood behind him. Though it was the position of a deputy, his head was slightly raised, like an ice statue to whom haughtiness was second nature.

Yue Qingyuan suddenly opened his eyes.

"Zhangmen-shixiong, you... Are you all right?" Qi Qingqi asked worriedly.

Yue Qingyuan shook his head, then looked at Luo Binghe. "In the past, when the demon race attacked Cang Qiong Mountain, your distinguished self met them head-on as part of the resistance while your shizun protected the entirety of Qiong Ding Peak alone. I never thought that you'd be the one leading the demon race to push Cang Qiong Mountain into such straits."

"If your sect hadn't pushed me so far, I wouldn't want to do the same," Luo Binghe said indifferently.

Qi Qingqi was so enraged that she ended up laughing instead.

"Ha ha! Cang Qiong Mountain has pushed you too far? The entire world should come hear this. Even if we put aside the matter of you being an ungrateful wretch who betrayed your sect, you forced your own shizun to self-detonate in front of you. Then you clung to him even after his death, doing heavens know what with his body. And now you strike back at us with false accusations! So just who is going too far?!"

Luo Binghe turned a deaf ear to her taunts. "Who's next?" he asked apathetically. "I'm taking this nameplate."

Shen Qingqiu startled and looked up. The nameplate Luo Binghe spoke of was the horizontal plaque hanging high inside Qiong Ding Hall. The two characters on it, "Cang Qiong," had been personally inscribed by the founder of Cang Qiong Mountain Sect. After so many years, it held extraordinary significance, and it was equivalent to a slice of Cang Qiong Mountain's dignity. Likewise, taking this inscription would be the equivalent of slapping Cang Qiong Mountain across the face. Back when Sha Hualing had impudently led an army to surround Qiong Ding Peak, her goal had been to take this same nameplate back to the Demon Realm to show it off.

"If you want to fight, then fight," said Qi Qingqi. "First you burn down one of our abodes, next you destroy a gate, and now you're here to take this nameplate. What are your intentions? To torment us methodically, bit by bit, and refuse us a swift release?"

"Qi-shimei, let it be," Yue Qingyuan said as he stood. Though he was at a disadvantage, his expression was as steady as Mount Tai so as not to undermine his troops' morale. "Qingqiu-shidi's immortal body has already been placed inside the hall. He is of my Cang Qiong Mountain, and more importantly, of Qing Jing Peak. After he passes, he must be interred among the graves of the generations of Qing Jing Peak Lords to rest in peace. Unless you slaughter the entirety of Cang Qiong Mountain, so long as anyone in this sect has a single breath left to breathe, regardless of how long it takes, Qingqiu-shidi's body will never again fall into your hands."

"Exactly so!" many of the others present chorused simultaneously.

Shen Qingqiu had known they would adopt this sort of attitude. It was precisely because he knew Cang Qiong Mountain would do anything to protect that body of his that he'd had to come back.

The corner of Luo Binghe's mouth tugged up into an icy-cold smile. He lowered his head and said in a measured tone, "I won't do anything to Cang Qiong Mountain personally. And I won't kill a single member of Cang Qiong Mountain Sect. But what I have plenty of is time—time to stall you out."

Those three words "stall you out," one by one, resounded clearly within Shen Qingqiu's ears. Suddenly, his entire heart sank.

Luo Binghe was not the kind of person to engage in polite debate. When he was at an absolute advantage in terms of pure power, he was disinclined to feign civility, and if there was a sect he wanted something from, he would employ the most direct and effective approach: bathe the sect in blood, slaughter all comers, and take the desired object away.

Yet in this case, Luo Binghe had possessed the patience to stall for two days thus far. It moreover didn't seem like he'd been taken by a carefree mood, but rather like he was waiting for something.

For example, waiting for Shen Qingqiu himself to appear.

Shen Qingqiu tightened his fist.

"Attack," said Luo Binghe.

Mobei-Jun let out an "oh," and stepped forward, before suddenly saying, "I already have, many times."

All those exploded ice shards, those holes pitting the walls and ground outside the hall, were his great works.

"Then get someone else to attack in your place," said Luo Binghe.

Mobei-Jun nodded, reached behind himself, and scooped up a cowering figure. He dangled this person like a little chick and tossed him into the large empty space between the two sides with a plop.

Shang Qinghua's soul was about to fly away. He crawled to his feet in terror, and when the people of Cang Qiong Mountain saw him, fire nearly spewed from their eyes.

It wasn't just them. Shen Qingqiu was also about to spew raging flames from his eyes and mouth. That trouble-causing fucker, "Great Master" Airplane Shooting Towards the Sky! Ah, fuck, fuck, fuck!

Qi Qingqi drew her sword with a whoosh and yelled, "Traitor!"

Shang Qinghua smiled obsequiously. "Qi-shimei, if you have something to say, say it properly. Don't wave your sword around like that. You're so pretty, if you were only a bit gentler—"

Qi Qingqi had already sent her sword flying in his direction, yelling in rage. "Who's your shimei?!"

Shang Qinghua hurriedly dodged, hiding behind Mobei-Jun. Devoid of sympathy, Mobei-Jun kicked him right back out.

"I was forced against my will, don't be like this," Shang Qinghua said with a long-suffering look. "If anyone sees us comrades fighting amongst ourselves, we'll be ridiculed."

Shen Qingqiu was flabbergasted. Shang Qinghua truly had even less integrity than he'd imagined, to be able to say something like that now. It was...genuinely a bit shameless...

"Who's your comrade?" Qi Qingqi yelled. "You let demonic beasts into the Immortal Alliance Conference. Did you think of how the dead and injured Cang Qiong Mountain Sect disciples were your comrades? You turned traitor and became the demon race's dog. Did you think of how *we're* your comrades? You fought up the mountain with the devil himself today, and you have the face to call us *comrades*?!"

The two of them chased each other around the hall in what was basically a screwball slapstick scene. Shen Qingqiu watched from the side, his heart rising and falling along with it. *Chop, chop, chop— oh, fuck, almost got him! Qi Qingqi, go for the crotch! Awesome!*

Liu Qingge withdrew the spiritual energy he was feeding into Yue Qingyuan's back, having finished the stabilization, and stood. Cheng Luan trembled in its sheath, letting out a buzzing cry.

Yang Yixuan cupped his fist. "Shizun, you've been fighting that demon for an entire day!"

"Stand down," Liu Qingge said heavily.

Luo Binghe gave him a glance, then smiled and said lightly, "Ah, the loser I defeated."

Though not loud, each word was enunciated clearly, the pitch rising, and so everyone in the large hall could hear. Liu Qingge's hand tightened on his sword, his eyes sparking with electric current. Nothing could humiliate the Bai Zhan Peak Lord more than the word "loser."

Yang Yixuan's temper flared and he shot back, "Demon mongrel!"

Luo Binghe didn't take it to heart. "Yes, I am a mongrel. The entirety of Cang Qiong Mountain was overwhelmed by a mongrel. Glorious, isn't it? And not just Qiong Ding Peak: I can conquer each of the remaining peaks one by one. Let everyone in all the realms know that Cang Qiong Mountain, the leader of the cultivation world, was slaughtered by a mongrel, powerless to fight back. How about it?"

"Luo...Luo Binghe," Ning Yingying cried, distressed. "Will you only be happy once you burn everything, Qing Jing Peak included, to ashes?"

Luo Binghe responded immediately, without a second thought. "Of course not." He frowned. "If anyone dares to touch a single blade of grass, a single tree, a single stalk of bamboo, a single building on Qing Jing Peak, I will not spare them."

Liu Qingge humphed. "How insincere."

Cheng Luan flared, its sword glare sweeping past Luo Binghe's cheek and whipping up his hair.

Luo Binghe put his hand on the sword hung at his waist, returning bite for bite. "You overestimate yourself."

In the end, however, the two swords failed to cross again. Shen Qingqiu stood between them.

Sword energy surged and collided from both sides, promptly splitting the bamboo hat he'd been wearing for appearances in two. With his left hand, he caught the point of Cheng Luan between two fingers, preventing Liu Qingge from advancing another mote, while his right pushed down on the hand Luo Binghe had placed on Xin Mo, preventing him from drawing it.

It's only a body, everyone, only a body. There's no need for this!

Shen Qingqiu looked to his left, then looked to his right, those words still unspoken on his tongue. Then Luo Binghe abruptly flipped his hand over and grabbed his wrist, fastening around it securely like a shackle of ice. The smile on his face looked almost twisted as he articulated each word. "Caught you, Shizun."

Even though Shen Qingqiu had long been prepared, he couldn't resist a chill of terror at seeing this face so close.

After a moment of absolute silence, a clamor rose in the hall.

Yue Qingyuan was astonished, his voice trembling faintly. "Are you...Qingqiu-shidi?"

Qi Qingqi forgot to hack at Shang Qinghua any further, and the latter hurriedly took the chance to scramble back behind Mobei-Jun.

Ning Yingying tugged on the battered and bruised Ming Fan. "Da-shixiong, did you hear?" she murmured. "A-Luo and Zhangmenshixiong are saying that person is...Shizun?"

"He looks like he is..." said Ming Fan. "But also not?"

However, Yang Yixuan's approach was entirely different. He said in shock, "These techniques, isn't it Peerless Cu...Senior Peerless? Senior...Peerless is Shen-shibo?"

Thank you for not saying the entire ID!

Liu Qingge's eyes suddenly went wide, his usual unaffected expression cracking completely. "...You're not dead?"

Shen Qingqiu's once guilty and grateful feelings shattered to pieces. "Liu-shidi, what's that look on your face?" he asked, disbelieving. "Aren't you happy your shixiong is alive?"

Liu Qingge's face flickered through an entire rainbow of colors: first green, then black, then white. It was quite a marvel to see, and many others looked about the same. Before Shen Qingqiu could respond, a hand tugged his face back around.

"At last you're willing to reveal yourself?" Luo Binghe asked.

Shen Qingqiu's bones felt like they were about to break under Luo Binghe's grip. The only things he could move were his legs, but it wasn't like he could kick Luo Binghe's crucial bits before the crowd. Faint flames of rage surged within him as he recalled every detail of what had happened.

"You did this on purpose," he said.

"What are you referring to, Shizun?" said Luo Binghe.

"Instead of directly butchering your way through the mountain, you chose to drag things out to this extent. You meant to draw me out."

Luo Binghe sneered. "So Shizun can, at times, guess what this disciple is thinking as well. This disciple is so overjoyed that he might lose his mind. I'm dying to beat my chest and stomp my feet, and I will certainly remember this moment until the end of my life."

Liu Qingge withdrew his sword, his body swaying like he was still a bit dizzy. He pointed it at Luo Binghe. "You, let go of him."

Luo Binghe dragged Shen Qingqiu into his arms and said irritably, "What did you say?"

His movements were forceful, and as Shen Qingqiu was pressed into his embrace, those simmering flames leapt into a towering blaze a meter high. He silently sucked in a breath. "When did you realize that it was the real me in the dreams?"

If Luo Binghe hadn't discovered that weak link, he could never have guessed that Shen Qingqiu wasn't dead, nor would he have been able to get Shen Qingqiu to deliver himself, free of charge, simply by waiting at Cang Qiong Mountain.

"Shizun, aren't you being a bit too condescending to me? Even if I didn't suspect it the first time, I really would have been a fool if I failed to notice anything wrong the second."

Shen Qingqiu's knees suddenly hurt. *You're not the fool,* he thought to himself, *I am.*

He'd known exactly how incredible Luo Binghe's cultivation was, how transcendental his control over the dream realm—and yet. Only Shen Qingqiu could have been fully aware of these things and still believed that Luo Binghe had been genuinely delirious, unable to differentiate between an intruder and an illusionary creation.

"If you'd already noticed something wrong, why not expose me?" Had it been fun playing along with the skit of a loving master and filial disciple?

Luo Binghe stared at him. "Why should I have exposed you? Didn't my sweetness make Shizun oh-so happy?"

Happy...?

Shen Qingqiu hadn't been even the slightest bit happy—he'd only been worried about Luo Binghe's emotional state. And this incident proved that even his worry had been a factor under Luo Binghe's control. After all, this was Luo Binghe, the male lead. How could a single blunder on Shen Qingqiu's bumbling part have turned him into a small, pitiful white lotus?

Shen Qingqiu was indeed the type who was open to coaxing over force, but you couldn't just slap him in the face afterward with an "I faked it."

"Wait," Qi Qingqi blurted out. "Exactly what is going on here?" She pointed toward the interior of Qiong Ding Hall. "Isn't that...that thing lying inside there Shen Qingqiu? How has another appeared?"

Luo Binghe appeared to be in a good mood. "Why not ask the former An Ding Peak Lord?"

Fucking hell, thought Shen Qingqiu. He should have known Shang Qinghua's slimy lack of integrity would come into play.

Shang Qinghua let out a weak laugh, and with a single sideways look from Mobei-Jun, he stepped forward without delay. Drawing a deep breath while raising his head and chest, he said in a clear voice, "Several years ago, in a certain place, Shen-shixiong happened upon and obtained a treasured item known as the Sun-Moon Dew Mushroom. This fungus has strong spiritual affinity and can recreate a flesh body. With this, Shen-shixiong pulled off a grand escape in

Hua Yue City by letting his soul leave his original form! Therefore, the one in the hall is him, though it's only an empty shell, and this one here is also him! Both are him!"

It was a succinct, crystal-clear summary. Countless pairs of eyes promptly turned toward Shen Qingqiu. Liu Qingge instantly pointed Cheng Luan at him, his new murderous intent even stronger than what he had directed at Luo Binghe.

"If that was the case, then why did you make no attempt to correspond with the twelve peaks for five years?" Yue Qingyuan asked quietly. "We received neither news nor sound from you. Could it be that, deep down inside, you see your fellow sect members as unworthy of trust?"

Harboring guilt within his heart, Shen Qingqiu's voice was weak. "That—Shixiong, hear me out..."

"Shen Qingqiu you...you!" Qi Qingqi raged. "Do you know how much suffering you've caused your shixiong? How much your disciples cried? They wept so much so constantly that Qing Jing Peak might as well have been cloaked in rain clouds for an entire year! It was unbearable to visit! And while the peak lord seat was empty, you were free as a bird, having the time of your life in the outside world!"

Shen Qingqiu was greatly afraid of the sharp-tongued Qi Qingqi jabbing at him and chewing him out. "I didn't do it on purpose, and I wasn't having the time of my life in the least," he hurried to say. "I was buried underground for five years and only woke up a few days ago! You tell me how that counts as free. It's all his fault!"

"How can you blame me?" Shang Qinghua said, indignant now that the heat was back on him. "You were the one who said to ripen it quickly!"

Liu Qingge held his temples. "Shut up!"

Shang Qinghua shut up. The ruckus they were making as a group would have been comical under different circumstances, but because the occasion was all wrong, Shen Qingqiu found the humor quite dampened.

The entirety of Qiong Ding Peak was awash with firelight and scattered with scorched debris. After two days of back-and-forth and siege warfare, it had lost its usual dignified grandeur. Both within and without the hall were bloodstained faces and disciples who had to be supported. The younger generation were worse off—constantly looking around anxiously, their complete exhaustion obvious, momentum spent like an arrow at the end of its flight.

Meanwhile, within the opposing battalion were demon generals and cavalry dressed in black armor, ready to move in a pincer maneuver. They glared like ravenous tigers, like freshly sharpened blades, the edges bright and gleaming.

Shen Qingqiu retracted his gaze. "Luo Binghe, you said you came to Cang Qiong Mountain Sect in order to capture me."

"Correct," said Luo Binghe.

"You've captured me."

And since he'd achieved his goal, it should be time to withdraw.

Luo Binghe stared at him. "You won't run anymore?"

Shen Qingqiu was silent, then slowly nodded. "I won't run anymore."

The corners of Luo Binghe's lips twitched and then pulled up into a helpless smile. It held none of the mocking sarcasm that had been plastered on his face until this moment. "I've believed Shizun so many times already," he said lightly.

"Shen Qingqiu, what's the meaning of this?" Liu Qingge asked suddenly. He stared at Shen Qingqiu as if he'd suffered some enormous disgrace. "The Bai Zhan Peak Lord is here, yet you throw yourself at another's feet before him?"

Shidi, I understand that as the Bai Zhan Peak Lord, you feel like your dignity has been violated, but please use a different phrase. Like hell I'm "throwing myself" at anyone! Use a different phrase, thank you!

"You fear becoming a burden to Cang Qiong Mountain," said Liu Qingge, "but Cang Qiong Mountain fears not your burden."

Luo Binghe sneered. "How many unbroken bones do you still have?"

Yue Qingyuan's hand grasped Xuan Su's hilt.

He'd barely done so when, next to him, Mu Qingfang anxiously said, "Zhangmen-shixiong, you were in secluded cultivation and forcefully interrupted your training, then faced these strong foes. It was already terribly hard on you. By pushing yourself to draw your sword now, I'm afraid your body will really..."

A burst of black qi rose from Yue Qingyuan's face, but he forced it back down. "Even if I can't, I must," he said in a strained voice. "Shidi has already died once, and at that moment, I was unable to protect him. How can I watch him go to his death a second time?"

At those words, turmoil surged within Shen Qingqiu's chest. When it came to the people whom Shen Qingqiu most admired and revered in this world, the one who placed first was none other than Yue Qingyuan. It wasn't so much because of his sincere desire to shield Shen Qingqiu but because of how he always put his entire heart and soul on the line for the sect.

Shen Qingqiu was too ashamed to let Cang Qiong Mountain and its sect leader continue to wipe his ass and pay the bill. He was the one who had dug his own grave, so he was also the only one who should suffer the consequences. "This is the disciple I taught, so it's only right for me alone to take responsibility. Zhangmen-shixiong is the head of this sect. On your shoulders rests the safety of every disciple on the twelve peaks. I trust you know what to choose."

The hall was dead silent. Yue Qingyuan's face froze, and the knuckles of his hand gripping the sword went stark white. Shen Qingqiu was reminding him: when in an unfavorable situation, the choice he should make as head of the sect went without saying.

The various peak lords had the exact same thought.

So instead it was Ning Yingying who ran out. She grabbed Shen Qingqiu's arm and yelled, "I disagree!"

"Ming Fan, take care of your shimei," said Shen Qingqiu.

"I'm no longer a child," said Ning Yingying. "I don't need to be taken care of! It's always Shizun taking on everything himself, whether it was that time with the demon woman or against Huan Hua Palace at Jin Lan City. So this time, why must it be you again? Why is it always Shizun who needs to suffer each and every time?"

Because this was the grave he'd dug. However, it seemed like he'd managed to raise a normal and filial girl after all. A portion of his remaining worries found release.

"Weeping at your age," he chided. "What sort of image are you projecting? This master won't die." Within his heart he added, *Probably...*

The next moment, Ming Fan spoke, his face full of sorrow and rage. "Isn't Shizun prostrating and submitting himself to the demons for Cang Qiong Mountain's sake a fate worse than death? The sayings only speak of throwing away all one has to give to accompany righteous men—never about doing it to appease demons!"

What are you even saying? Ming Fan, you little hellion, how about you speak human words?!

The situation had dragged on for so long that Luo Binghe had long lost his patience. He grabbed Shen Qingqiu with one hand, then put the other on Xin Mo's hilt. "I'll take Shizun's immortal body as well."

"You're going too far," another peak lord said angrily. "The person isn't enough for you, you also want the corpse? And for what?"

Luo Binghe didn't answer and only waved at Mobei-Jun, issuing the order. Just when things had calmed down after such difficulty, another wrong word would reignite the conflict.

Wanting to cut that off at the pass, Shen Qingqiu was about to tug on Luo Binghe's arm, but thought this too unsightly and switched to yanking on his sleeve. Only after mulling it over briefly did he steel himself and say, "I've already submitted to you. Why go so far?"

Upon saying these words, Shen Qingqiu felt deep shame.

He was a man, yet he had been forced to meekly tell another man that he would "submit to him," in front of so many people. And above all, the other man was his former disciple, which made it even more frustrating and shameful.

Nonetheless, displays of submissiveness had a guaranteed effect on any man. Luo Binghe's expression noticeably cleared quite a bit, and not only did his grip loosen somewhat, his tone even softened. Despite this, his words remained as forceful as before. "It's Shizun's original body, after all, so it's inextricably involved. And in the case Shizun tries to pull off another grand escape, this disciple would really be at a loss."

As soon as he turned his face away, his voice cooled. "Take it away."

Mobei-Jun had yet to move when Liu Mingyan suddenly appeared in the hall to whisper into Qi Qingqi's ear. The latter tilted her head to listen, and shock bloomed on her face before it transformed into calm.

"There's no need to fight anymore!" she called out. "Luo Binghe, there's no need for anyone to fight," she continued to say loudly. "Even if we agreed to let you take the body away, your wish would not come true."

Shen Qingqiu was well aware of Qi Qingqi's intense personality, and he figured that she was liable to do something extreme to enrage Luo Binghe. But just as he was thinking that this didn't look good, she surprised him by gesturing for Liu Mingyan to step forward.

"Mingyan, tell them."

"Shen-shibo's immortal body has disappeared," said Liu Mingyan.

After speaking, she stepped aside, and several disciples were brought in from the back of the hall. These were the disciples in charge of guarding the funerary platform, who watched over where the bodies lay. At this moment, they were all unconscious, and from their faces to their fingertips their skin was an eerie, bruised color.

The hall burst into an uproar. Yue Qingyuan's expression immediately changed, and Luo Binghe also raised an eyebrow.

"No need to look at me, Luo Binghe," Qi Qingqi said, unperturbed. "I indeed wanted to hide the body away, but by the time I sent Mingyan to the back to move it, the platform was already empty. It's as if the corpse we'd carefully preserved managed to fly off without wings."

Her mood and words were both overjoyed. It turned out she'd rather the corpse fly off than let Luo Binghe take it away.

Mu Qingfang was next to the disciples, examining them. "They're fully unconscious, but their lives are in no danger. They were poisoned."

"What poison?" Yue Qingyuan asked.

"At this point, I cannot come to a conclusion. They're also uninjured. Wait for me to draw some blood for tests."

"If it's a poison from the Human Realm, Mu-shidi would be able to identify it at a glance," said Qi Qingqi. "Since he can't, I have to ask: Was it you?"

"I dislike using poison," Luo Binghe said mildly.

This was the truth. Luo Binghe rarely killed with poison. On top of that, in a situation like this where he held the complete upper hand, Luo Binghe had no need to lie.

That was to say, some unknown party had taken advantage of the conflict between the two sides to slip onto the mountain entirely unnoticed. And this person had stolen away Shen Qingqiu's corpse from right under the noses of both the demon race and cultivation world while only a handful of walls away. How could anyone not be shocked?!

Shen Qingqiu was puzzled. Why would someone steal his corpse? How come no one had wanted him while he was alive, but now that he was dead, he'd become Helen of Troy?

Luo Binghe discerned that continuing to talk here would be pointless and frowned. "Fine. No matter who took it, I'll find it."

Xin Mo left its sheath and black qi streamed forth from it. An arcing crack split open where the blade sliced through the air.

"Drop the siege," Shen Qingqiu said to remind him.

Luo Binghe gave him a look, then said brusquely, "As Shizun wishes."

Cheng Luan's sword point hit the ground. Following it upward, Liu Qingge's hand was tightly clenched beneath his sleeve, and blood poured from a gaping open wound. It trickled down the length of the blade and dripped onto the floor. After a long second, he finally spat out: "Just you wait!"

These words were akin to an icicle launching forth, yet within it burned deep-seated flames of rage and a fighting spirit that could swallow the heavens.

Xin Mo was sheathed, but Luo Binghe sneered. "Come, try me."

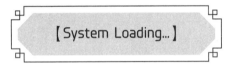

【System Loading...】

THE STORY CONTINUES IN
The Scum Villain's Self-Saving System
VOLUME 3

The Scum Villain's Self-Saving System

REN ZHA FANPAI
ZIJIU XITONG

‹◇◇◇◇›

Character
&
Name Guide

Characters

The identity of certain characters may be a spoiler; use this guide with caution on your first read of the novel.

Note on the given name translations: Chinese characters may have many different readings. Each reading here is just one out of several possible readings presented for your reference and should not be considered a definitive translation.

MAIN CHARACTERS

Shen Yuan (Shen Qingqiu)
沈垣   SURNAME SHEN, "WALL"

TITLE: Peerless Cucumber (web handle)

RANK: *Proud Immortal Demon Way*'s Most Supportive Anti

Probably the most dedicated anti-fan of *Proud Immortal Demon Way*, Shen Yuan was baited by its cool monsters and charming protagonist to read millions and millions of words of the hit stallion novel, though he cussed out the author's sellout tendencies the whole way. After his untimely death during a fit of rage over the novel's ending, he was rewarded with a chance to enter the world of the story and fix it his own damn self.

Having taken the place of the scum villain Shen Qingqiu, Shen Yuan strove to endear himself to Luo Binghe as much as he could to avoid a grisly demise. However, the System seems determined to make him retread the scum villain's most damning crimes, and when the grown-up Luo Binghe comes knocking on his door, Shen Qingqiu may have to resort to the nuclear option.

On top of that, more and more often Shen Qingqiu has to contend with the domino effects of his actions as the world around him grows beyond his recognition. He is coming to acknowledge that the residents of his new world have gained a life of their own beyond their roles as mere characters in a story. He'll just have to hope none of this throws a wrench in his plans before he figures out his escape.

Luo Binghe
洛冰河 SURNAME LUO FOR THE LUO RIVER, "ICY RIVER"

RANK: White Lotus Disciple (Qing Jing Peak)

SWORD (PRIOR): Zheng Yang (正阳 / "Righteous sun")

SWORD (CURRENT): Xin Mo (心魔 / "Heart demon")

As the protagonist of *Proud Immortal Demon Way*, the original Luo Binghe rose from humble origins to reign as tyrant over the three realms, his innumerable harem at his beck and call. However, in this story, when the transmigrated Shen Qingqiu offered Luo Binghe the love and acknowledgment he so desperately craved, he was diverted from his original dark path and instead turned his devotion toward his master.

Perhaps such a beautiful dream was never meant to last; a teenaged Luo Binghe received a sword to the chest when his beloved master sent him tumbling into the Endless Abyss. When he returns from his cheat-filled level-grinding and claws his way out of the Abyss two years early, he has become dark, mercurial, and thirsty... for revenge? Well, that's what Shen Qingqiu assumes, based on what he knows about *PIDW*.

The rift between them worsens with each clash. Luo Binghe's demands for answers go unfulfilled, and Shen Qingqiu realizes he no longer understands this person who is neither the protagonist he read about nor the sweet young lamb he shepherded. What does this new Luo Binghe want from his master, and will they be able to resolve their differences before it's too late?

CANG QIONG MOUNTAIN SECT MEMBERS

Shen Qingqiu (Shen Jiu)
沈清秋   SURNAME SHEN, "CLEAR AUTUMN"
沈九   SURNAME SHEN, "NINE"

TITLE: Xiu Ya Sword (修雅 / "Elegant and refined")
RANK: Peak Lord (Qing Jing Peak)

Shen Qingqiu, the refined and elegant peak lord of the peak of scholars, was also the scum villain who seemingly made it his life's mission to make Luo Binghe's life miserable in the original *Proud Immortal Demon Way*. He beat the young Luo Binghe for the slightest infraction and encouraged his peers to bully him. Furthermore, under his pure and unsullied exterior, he was (supposedly) a lustful degenerate who went so far as to target his own female disciple.

However, as the transmigrated Shen Yuan unlocks more and more hidden plot lines, he finds that the scum villain's original awfulness may be rooted in unspoken history...

Yue Qingyuan
岳清源   SURNAME YUE, "CLEAR SOURCE"

TITLE: Xuan Su Sword (玄肃 / "Dark and solemn")
RANK: Sect Leader, Peak Lord (Qiong Ding Peak)

As sect leader of the foremost major cultivation sect, Yue Qingyuan normally lives up to his responsibilities as a levelheaded leader and respected authority. But when his shidi Shen Qingqiu is the one asking for a favor, he can never deny the man anything...though this clear favoritism wasn't enough to keep the scum villain from causing

Yue Qingyuan's death in the original *Proud Immortal Demon Way*.

However, though the transmigrated Shen Qingqiu admires Yue Qingyuan more than anyone, he realizes he is no longer the intended recipient of this favor. As Yue Qingyuan continues to go to great lengths for someone who's no longer around to appreciate the sentiment, Shen Qingqiu must wrestle with his conscience: How long can he keep up this unintentional catfishing scheme?

Ning Yingying
宁婴婴 SURNAME NING, "INFANT"
___
RANK: Youngest Female Disciple (Qing Jing Peak)

Luo Binghe's shijie and childhood friend. In the original *Proud Immortal Demon Way*, she was the first maiden to be accepted into Luo Binghe's harem after she helped him confront his inner demons. As the world evolves away from the constraints of the stallion genre, Ning Yingying has grown up into a fine young woman who cares deeply for her peak and her shizun, and she is more than capable of showing some spine in a crisis.

Ming Fan
明帆 SURNAME MING, "SAIL"
___
RANK: Most Senior Disciple (Qing Jing Peak)

One of Luo Binghe's tormentors in *Proud Immortal Demon Way*, Ming Fan was a loyal lackey and co-conspirator to the original Shen Qingqiu. But aside from his worrying habits of antagonizing the protagonist, the transmigrated Shen Qingqiu finds him to be a promising young man who doesn't let his spoiled upbringing interfere with his respect for his master. Ming Fan helps keep the peak running in the wake of Luo Binghe's unfortunate departure, and he does his best to live up to his master's teachings.

Liu Qingge
柳清歌 SURNAME LIU, "CLEAR SONG"

RANK: Peak Lord (Bai Zhan Peak)

SWORD: Cheng Luan (乘鸾 / "Soaring phoenix")

Despite being a character who never made an official appearance in *Proud Immortal Demon Way*, Master Liu had a legion of fanboys for his legendarily unparalleled skill in battle. After the transmigrated Shen Qingqiu saved him from a lethal qi deviation, his opinion of his distasteful shixiong took a one-eighty, and he will now go to drastic lengths to fight for his shixiong's honor. What moving camaraderie between good martial brothers, right?

Yang Yixuan
杨一玄 SURNAME YANG, "ONE MYSTERIOUS"

RANK: Disciple (Bai Zhan Peak)

The son of a weapons shop owner from the plague-ridden Jin Lan City, Yang Yixuan is an energetic young man who inherited his father's courage. After encountering (and being solidly defeated by) the Cang Qiong peak lords on their rescue mission, he manages to convince Liu Qingge to make an exception and take him as a disciple.

Mu Qingfang
木清芳 SURNAME MU, "CLEAR FRAGRANCE"

RANK: Peak Lord (Qian Cao Peak)

A master of the healing arts, who feels a sense of responsibility for the well-being of his sectmates. His skills continue to be instrumental in solving medical dilemmas large and small, though even the most skillful healer has their limits.

Qi Qingqi
齐清蒦 SURNAME QI, "CLEAR AND LUSH"

RANK: Peak Lord (Xian Shu Peak)

A woman with a straightforward and fierce temperament; a sect-mate the transmigrated Shen Qingqiu gets along with well in his new world. Though she won't hesitate to speak her mind, she cares deeply for her sect.

Liu Mingyan
柳溟烟 SURNAME LIU, "DRIZZLING MIST"

RANK: Disciple (Xian Shu Peak)

SWORD: Shui Se (水色 / "Color of water")

The number one true female lead of *Proud Immortal Demon Way* and younger sister of Liu Qingge. Because of her peerless beauty, Liu Mingyan typically wears a veil to hide her face. She never loses her courage and poise as she grows into her own, and as an adult, she has begun to go out on her own adventures of all kinds.

Shang Qinghua
尚清华 SURNAME SHANG, "CLEAR AND SPLENDID"

TITLE: Airplane Shooting Towards the Sky
(web handle, 向天打飞机 / "beating your airplane at the sky")

RANK: Peak Lord (An Ding Peak)

Overworked and underpaid, the Peak Lord of An Ding Peak takes on a thankless job as the head of the sect's "housekeeping" department. Shen Qingqiu's fellow transmigrator may be rather shifty and unreliable, but sometimes a friend from the same "hometown" is just what he needs.

DEMONS

Many demons go by titles instead of personal names. Titles styled like XX-Jun are for high-ranking demon nobility, and some titles may be hereditary.

Tianlang-Jun
天琅君 "HEAVEN'S GEMSTONE," TITLE -JUN

RANK: Saintly Ruler (former)

Luo Binghe's birth father, a heavenly demon. He was sealed beneath a great mountain by the righteous sects, but is any cage truly eternal?

Zhuzhi-Lang
竹枝郎 "BAMBOO BRANCH," TITLE -LANG

RANK: Tianlang-Jun's Trusted Right Hand

Tianlang-Jun's nephew and subordinate, born to heavenly demon and snake demon parents. Sincere and straightforward, he is willing to repay anyone who shows him favor a hundred times over—including Shen Qingqiu, who spared him when he was still lurking as a snake-man in Bai Lu Forest. However, Zhuzhi-Lang is perhaps not the best at determining what repayment his benefactor would like to receive.

Sha Hualing
纱华铃 "GAUZE," "SPLENDID BELL"

RANK: Demon Saintess

A crafty and vicious pure-blooded demon who is eager to earn Luo Binghe's favor. However, her current role as an overworked and un-derpaid employee seems something of a downgrade from her original counterpart's status as a tyrannical member of Luo Binghe's harem.

Meng Mo

梦魔   "DREAM DEMON"

RANK: Luo Binghe's Teacher in Demonic Techniques

Once a legendary master of dream manipulation, Meng Mo is now Luo Binghe's underappreciated "Portable Grandfather." Oh, the things a teacher will suffer to pass on his techniques.

Mobei-Jun

漠北君   "DESERTED NORTH," TITLE -JUN

RANK: Demonic Second-Gen

Luo Binghe's eccentric sidekick. A proud ice demon turned plot device for Luo Binghe's plot-dictated power-up arc, as well as Shang Qinghua's demonic employer.

OTHER SUPPORTING CHARACTERS

Old Palace Master

RANK: Palace Master (Huan Hua Palace)

The master of Luo Binghe's birth mother. When he saw Luo Binghe for the first time, he seemed to recognize the shades of someone familiar in the young disciple's face...and he is now willing to offend even Cang Qiong Mountain for his new favorite.

Little Palace Mistress

RANK: Palace Mistress (Huan Hua Palace)

The Old Palace Master's spoiled daughter and a member of Luo Binghe's harem in the original *Proud Immortal Demon Way*; she likes to solve her problems with an iron whip.

Luo Binghe's Birth Mother

RANK: Former Disciple (Huan Hua Palace)

Expelled from her sect on suspicion of having secret ties to demons, Luo Binghe's birth mother set young Luo Binghe adrift on the Luo River before her death.

Gongyi Xiao

公仪萧   SURNAME GONGYI, "MUGWORT"

RANK: Head Disciple (Huan Hua Palace)

The former favorite of both the Old Palace Master and his daughter, Gongyi Xiao's star began to fall when the protagonist waltzed onto the scene. However, he is still an earnest and honorable young man who is willing to disobey orders to do the right thing.

Qin Wanyue

秦婉约   SURNAME QIN, "GRACEFUL AND SUBDUED"

RANK: Disciple (Huan Hua Palace)

A Huan Hua Palace disciple who tragically lost her younger sister during the Immortal Alliance Conference. She admires her new Luo-shixiong, though he doesn't seem to return her affections.

Qiu Haitang

秋海棠   SURNAME QIU, "CHINESE FLOWERING APPLE,"
FULL NAME TRANSLATES TO "BEGONIA"

RANK: Hall Master (some random sect)

The once-pampered daughter of the wealthy Qiu family, who met their end in a brutal massacre many years ago. Now a cultivator within a random small sect, she appears to share some unpleasant history with the original Shen Qingqiu...

Locations

CANG QIONG MOUNTAIN

Cang Qiong Mountain Sect
苍穹山派 "BLUE HEAVENS" MOUNTAIN SECT

Located in the east, Cang Qiong Mountain Sect is the world's foremost major cultivation sect. The mountain has twelve individual peaks that act as branches with their own specialties and traditions, each run by their own peak lord and united under the leadership of Qiong Ding Peak. Rainbow Bridges physically connect the peaks to allow easy travel.

The peaks are ranked in a hierarchy, and disciples of lower-ranked peaks call same-generation disciples of higher-ranked peaks Shixiong or Shijie regardless of their actual order of entry into the sect, though seniority within a given peak is still determined by order of entry. Disciples are separated into inner ("inside the gate") and outer ("outside the gate") rankings, with inner disciples being higher-ranked members of the sect.

Qiong Ding Peak
穹顶峰 "HEAVEN'S APEX" PEAK

The peak of the sect's leadership; the Peak Lord of Qiong Ding Peak is also the leader of the entire Cang Qiong Mountain Sect.

Qing Jing Peak
清静峰 "CLEAR AND TRANQUIL" PEAK

The peak of scholars, artists, and musicians.

An Ding Peak
安定峰 "STABLE AND SETTLED" PEAK

The peak in charge of sect logistics, including stock transportation and repair of damages.

Bai Zhan Peak
百战峰 "HUNDRED BATTLES" PEAK

The peak of martial artists.

Qian Cao Peak
千草峰 "THOUSAND GRASSES" PEAK

The peak of medicine and healing.

Xian Shu Peak
仙姝峰 "IMMORTAL BEAUTY" PEAK

An all-female peak.

Wan Jian Peak
万剑峰 "TEN THOUSAND SWORDS" PEAK

The peak of sword masters.

Ku Xing Peak
苦行峰 "ASCETIC PRACTICE" PEAK

The peak of ascetic cultivation.

OTHER CULTIVATION SECTS

Huan Hua Palace
幻花宫 "ILLUSORY FLOWER" PALACE

Located in the South, Huan Hua Palace disciples practice a number of different cultivation schools but specialize in illusions, mazes, and concealment. They are the richest of the sects and provide the most funding to every Immortal Alliance Conference. The Water Prison located beneath their foundations is used to hold the most notorious criminals of the cultivation world before trial.

Tian Yi Temple
天一观 "UNITED WITH HEAVEN" TEMPLE

Located in the central territories, the priests of Tian Yi Temple practice Daoist cultivation.

Zhao Hua Monastery
昭华寺 "BRIGHT AND SPLENDID" MONASTERY

Located in the East, the monks of Zhao Hua Monastery practice Buddhist cultivation.

MISCELLANEOUS LOCATIONS

Bai Lu Forest
白露森林 "WHITE DEW" FOREST

A forest on the edge of Huan Hua Palace's territory where the Sun-Moon Dew Mushroom can be found.

The Borderlands
边境之地

Areas where the barrier between the Human and Demon Realms is thin and it's possible to pass between them without crossing the Endless Abyss. Because this prompts frequent raids from the more opportunistic members of the demon race, the borderlands are sparsely settled by humans, with only a few garrisons of cultivators remaining as guards.

Hua Yue City
花月城 "FLOWER MOON" CITY

A city near Huan Hua Palace, located in a prosperous and densely populated area of the Central Plains.

Jin Lan City
金兰城 "GOLDEN ORCHID" CITY

Once a prosperous trade center at the intersection of two great rivers, Jin Lan City finds itself suffering from a mysterious plague. Its name, "golden orchid," is often used as a metaphor for "sworn brotherhood."

The Endless Abyss
无间深渊

The boundary between the Human and Demon Realms; the hellish location of Luo Binghe's five-year training arc before he reemerges as the overpowered protagonist.

Jue Di Gorge
绝地谷 "HOPELESS LAND" GORGE

A mountainous region with all sorts of treacherous terrain, perfect for adventure.

Name Guide

NAMES, HONORIFICS, & TITLES

Courtesy Names

A courtesy name is given to an individual when they come of age. Traditionally, this was at the age of twenty during one's crowning ceremony, but it can also be presented when an elder or teacher deems the recipient worthy. Generally a male-only tradition, there is historical precedent for women adopting a courtesy name after marriage. Courtesy names were a tradition reserved for the upper class.

It was considered disrespectful for one's peers of the same generation to address someone by their birth name, especially in formal or written communication. Use of one's birth name was reserved for only elders, close friends, and spouses.

This practice is no longer used in modern China but is commonly seen in wuxia and xianxia media; as such, many characters have more than one name. Its implementation in novels is irregular and is often treated malleably for the sake of storytelling.

It was a tradition throughout some parts of Chinese history for all children of a family within a certain generation to have given names with the same first or last character. This "generation name" may be taken from a certain poem, with successive generations using successive characters from the poem. In *Scum Villain*, this tradition is used to give the peak lords their courtesy names, so all peak lords of Shen Qingqiu's generation have courtesy names starting with Qing.

Diminutives and Nicknames

XIAO-: A diminutive meaning "little." Always a prefix.

> EXAMPLE: Xiao-shimei (the nickname Ming Fan uses for Ning Yingying)

DA-: A prefix meaning "eldest."

> EXAMPLE: Da-shixiong (how Ning Yingying addresses Ming Fan)

-ER: A word for "son" or "child." Added to a name, it expresses affection. Similar to calling someone "Little" or "Sonny." Always a suffix.

> EXAMPLE: Ling-er (how Sha Hualing refers to herself when she is trying to be cute)

A-: Friendly diminutive. Always a prefix. Usually for monosyllabic names, or one syllable out of a two-syllable name.

> EXAMPLE: A-Luo (the nickname Ning Yingying uses for Luo Binghe)

Formal

-JUN: A suffix meaning "lord."

-XIANSHENG: A respectful suffix with several uses, including for someone with a great deal of expertise in their profession or a teacher.

Cultivation and Martial Arts

ZHANGMEN: Leader of a cultivation/martial arts sect.

SHIZUN: Teacher/master. For one's master in one's own sect. Gender neutral. Literal meaning is "honored/venerable master" and is a more respectful address.

SHIFU: Teacher/master. For one's master in one's own sect. Gender neutral. Mostly interchangeable with Shizun.

SHINIANG: The wife of a shifu/shizun.

SHIXIONG: Senior martial brother. For senior male members of one's own sect.

SHIJIE: Senior martial sister. For senior female members of one's own sect.

SHIDI: Junior martial brother. For junior male members of one's own sect.

SHIMEI: Junior martial sister. For junior female members of one's own sect.

SHISHU: The junior martial sibling of one's master. Can be male or female.

SHIBO: The senior martial sibling of one's master. Can be male or female.

SHIZHI: The disciple of one's martial sibling.

Pronunciation Guide

Mandarin Chinese is the official state language of China. It is a tonal language, so correct pronunciation is vital to being understood! As many readers may not be familiar with the use and sound of tonal marks, below is a very simplified guide on the pronunciation of select character names and terms from MXTX's series to help get you started.

More resources are available at **sevenseasdanmei.com**.

Series Names

SCUM VILLAIN'S SELF-SAVING SYSTEM (RÉN ZHĀ FĂN PÀI ZÌ JIÙ XÌ TŎNG):
ren jaa faan pie zzh zioh she tone

GRANDMASTER OF DEMONIC CULTIVATION (MÓ DÀO ZŬ SHĪ):
mwuh dow zoo shrr

HEAVEN OFFICIAL'S BLESSING (TIĀN GUĀN CÌ FÚ):
tee-yan gwen tsz fuu

Character Names

SHĚN QĪNGQIŪ: Shhen Ching-cheeoh

LUÒ BĪNGHÉ: Loo-uh Bing-huhh

WÈI WÚXIÀN: Way Woo-shee-ahn

LÁN WÀNGJĪ: Lahn Wong-gee

XIÈ LIÁN: Shee-yay Lee-yan

HUĀ CHÉNG: Hoo-wah Cch-yung

XIǍO-: shee-ow
-ER: ahrr
A-: ah
GŌNGZǏ: gong-zzh
DÀOZHǍNG: dow-jon
-JŪN: june
DÌDÌ: dee-dee
GĒGĒ: guh-guh
JIĚJIĚ: gee-ay-gee-ay
MÈIMEI: may-may
-XIÓNG: shong

Terms

DĀNMĚI: dann-may
WǓXIÁ: woo-sheeah
XIĀNXIÁ: sheeyan-sheeah
QÌ: chee

General Consonants & Vowels

X: similar to English sh (**sh**eep)
Q: similar to English ch (**ch**arm)
C: similar to English ts (pan**ts**)
IU: yoh
UO: wuh
ZHI: jrr
CHI: chrr
SHI: shrr
RI: rrr

ZI: zzz
CI: tsz
SI: ssz
U: When u follows a y, j, q, or x, the sound is actually ü, pronounced like eee with your lips rounded like ooo. This applies for yu, yuan, jun, etc.

The Scum Villain's Self-Saving System

REN ZHA FANPAI
ZIJIU XITONG

◆◇◆

Glossary

Glossary

While not required reading, this glossary is intended to offer further context to the many concepts and terms utilized throughout this novel and provide a starting point for learning more about the rich Chinese culture from which these stories were written.

China is home to dozens of cultures, and its history spans thousands of years. The provided definitions are not strictly universal across all these cultural groups, and this simplified overview is meant for new readers unfamiliar with the concepts. This glossary should not be considered a definitive source, especially for more complex ideas.

GENRES

Danmei

Danmei (耽美 / "indulgence in beauty") is a Chinese fiction genre focused on romanticized tales of love and attraction between men. It is analogous to the BL (boys' love) genre in Japanese media. The majority of well-known danmei writers are women writing for women, although all genders produce and enjoy the genre.

Wuxia

Wuxia (武侠 / "martial heroes") is one of the oldest Chinese literary genres and consists of tales of noble heroes fighting evil and injustice. It often follows martial artists, monks, or rogues, who live apart from the ruling government, which is often seen as useless or corrupt. These societal outcasts—both voluntary and not—settle disputes among themselves, adhering to their own moral codes over the governing law.

Characters in wuxia focus primarily on human concerns, such as political strife between factions and advancing their own personal sense of justice. True wuxia is low on magical or supernatural elements. To Western moviegoers, a well-known example is *Crouching Tiger, Hidden Dragon.*

Xianxia

Xianxia (仙侠 / "immortal heroes") is a genre related to wuxia that places more emphasis on the supernatural. Its characters often strive to become stronger, with the end goal of extending their life span or achieving immortality.

Xianxia heavily features Daoist themes, while cultivation and the pursuit of immortality are both genre requirements. If these are not the story's central focus, it is not xianxia. *The Scum Villain's Self-Saving System*, *Grandmaster of Demonic Cultivation*, and *Heaven Official's Blessing* are all considered part of both the danmei and xianxia genres.

Webnovels

Webnovels are novels serialized by chapter online, and the websites that host them are considered spaces for indie and amateur writers. Many novels, dramas, comics, and animated shows produced in China are based on popular webnovels.

Examples of popular webnovel websites in China include Jinjiang Literature City (jjwxc.net), Changpei Literature (gongzicp.com), and Qidian Chinese Net (qidian.com). While all of Mo Xiang Tong Xiu's existing works and the majority of best-known danmei are initially published via JJWXC, *Scum Villain's* series-within-a-series, *Proud Immortal Demon Way*, was said to be published on a "Zhongdian Literature" website, which is likely intended as a parody of Qidian Chinese Net, known for hosting male-targeted novels.

Webnovels have become somewhat infamous for being extremely long as authors will often keep them going for as long as paying subscribers are there. Readers typically purchase these stories chapter-by-chapter, and a certain number of subscribers is often required to allow for monetization. Other factors affecting an author's earnings include word count which can lead to bloated chapters and run-on plots. While not all webnovels suffer from any of these things, it is something commonly expected due to the system within which they're published.

Like all forms of media, very passionate fanbases often arise for webnovels. While the majority of readers are respectful, there is often a more toxic side of the community that is exacerbated by the parasocial relationship that some readers develop with the author as they follow serialized webnovels. Authors will often suffer backlash from these fans for things such as a plot or character decision some don't agree with, events readers find too shocking (often referred to as landmines), writing outside their expected genres or tropes, openly disagreeing with another creator, abruptly pausing or ending a story, posting a chapter late, or even simply posting something on their social media accounts that their fans do not like. Fan toxicity can be a huge problem for web novel authors who are reliant on subscriber support to make a living. This abuse can follow them across platforms, and often the only way to escape it is to stay off public social media altogether, which is a decision often made by the most popular of writers.

In *Scum Villain,* Shen Yuan could be considered one of these toxic fans due to his scathing commentary against the author of *Proud Immortal Demon Way.* However he did seem to stop at criticism towards the story itself and continued to pay for all the content he consumed, making him a lesser evil.

TERMINOLOGY

ARRAY: Area-of-effect magic circles. Anyone within the array falls under the effect of the array's associated spell(s).

BLOOD MITES: Called blood gu (血蛊) in the original text, these parasitic insectile creatures that Luo Binghe fashions from his own blood are reminiscent of a curse in traditional Chinese witchcraft. According to legend, gu are created by sealing poisonous animals (often insects) inside a container and letting them devour one another. The resulting gu must be ingested by a target, after which the gu can be controlled remotely to harm or kill the host.

BOWING: As is seen in other Asian cultures, standing bows are a traditional greeting and are also used when giving an apology. A deeper bow shows greater respect.

BUDDHISM: The central belief of Buddhism is that life is a cycle of suffering and rebirth, only to be escaped by reaching enlightenment (nirvana). Buddhists believe in karma, that a person's actions will influence their fortune in this life and future lives. The teachings of the Buddha are known as The Middle Way and emphasize a practice that is neither extreme asceticism nor extreme indulgence.

CHINESE CALENDAR: The Chinese calendar uses the *Tian Gan Di Zhi* (Heavenly Stems, Earthly Branches) system, rather than numbers, to mark the years. There are ten heavenly stems (original meanings lost) and twelve earthly branches (associated with the zodiac), each represented by a written character. Each stem and branch is associated with either yin or yang, and one of the elemental properties: wood, earth, fire, metal, and water. The stems and branches are combined in cyclical patterns to create a calendar where every unit of time is associated with certain attributes.

This is what a character is asking for when inquiring for the date/time of birth (生辰八字 / "eight characters of birth date/time"). Analyzing the stem/branch characters and their elemental associations was considered essential information in divination, fortune-telling, matchmaking, and even business deals.

CHRYSANTHEMUM: A flower that is a symbol of health and vitality. In sex scenes, specifically for two men, it's used as symbolism for their backdoor entrance.

CLINGING TO THIGHS: Similar to "riding someone's coattails" in English. It implies an element of sucking up to someone, though some characters aren't above literally clinging to another's thighs.

Colors:

WHITE: Death, mourning, purity. Used in funerals for both the deceased and mourners.

BLACK: Represents the Heavens and the dao.

RED: Happiness, good luck. Used for weddings.

YELLOW/GOLD: Wealth and prosperity, and often reserved for the emperor.

BLUE/GREEN (CYAN): Health, prosperity, and harmony.

PURPLE: Divinity and immortality, often associated with nobility.

CONCUBINES: In ancient China, it was common practice for a wealthy man to possess women as concubines in addition to his wife. They were expected to live with him and bear him children.

Generally speaking, a greater number of concubines correlated to higher social status, hence a wealthy merchant might have two or three concubines, while an emperor might have tens or even a hundred.

CONFUCIANISM: Confucianism is a philosophy based on the teachings of Confucius. Its influence on all aspects of Chinese culture is incalculable. Confucius placed heavy importance on respect for one's elders and family, a concept broadly known as *xiao* (孝 / "filial piety"). The family structure is used in other contexts to urge similar behaviors, such as respect of a student towards a teacher, or people of a country towards their ruler.

CORES/GOLDEN CORES: The formation of a jindan (金丹 / "golden core") is a key step in any cultivator's journey to immortality. The Golden Core forms within the lower dantian, becoming an internal source of power for the cultivator. Golden Core formation is only accomplished after a great deal of intense training and qi cultivation.

Cultivators can detonate their Golden Core as a last-ditch move to take out a dangerous opponent, but this almost always kills the cultivator. A core's destruction or removal is permanent. In almost all instances, it cannot be re-cultivated. Its destruction also prevents the individual from ever being able to process or cultivate qi normally again.

COUGHING/SPITTING BLOOD: A way to show a character is ill, injured, or upset. Despite the very physical nature of the response, it does not necessarily mean that a character has been wounded; their body could simply be reacting to a very strong emotion. (See also Seven Apertures/Qiqiao.)

COURTESY NAMES: In addition to their birth name, an individual may receive a courtesy name when they come of age or on another special occasion. *(See Name Guide for more information.)*

CULTIVATORS/CULTIVATION: Cultivators are practitioners of spirituality and martial artis who seek to gain understanding of the will of the universe while attaining personal strength and extending their life span.

Cultivation is a long process marked by "stages." There are traditionally nine stages, but this is often simplified in fiction. Some common stages are noted below, though exact definitions of each stage may depend on the setting.

◇ Qi Condensation/Qi Refining (凝气/练气)
◇ Foundation Establishment (筑基)
◇ Core Formation/Golden Core (结丹/金丹)
◇ Nascent Soul (元婴)
◇ Deity Transformation (化神)
◇ Great Ascension (大乘)
◇ Heavenly Tribulation (渡劫)

CULTIVATION MANUAL: Cultivation manuals and sutras are common plot devices in xianxia/wuxia novels. They provide detailed instructions on a secret or advanced training technique and are sought out by those who wish to advance their cultivation levels.

CURRENCY: The currency system during most dynasties was based on the exchange of silver and gold coinage. Weight was also used to measure denominations of money. An example is "one liang of silver."

CUT-SLEEVE: A term for a gay man. Comes from a tale about an emperor's love for, and relationship with, a male politician. The emperor was called to the morning assembly, but his lover was asleep on his robe. Rather than wake him, the emperor cut off his own sleeve.

DANTIAN: *Dantian* (丹田 / "cinnabar field") refers to three regions in the body where qi is concentrated and refined. The Lower is located three finger widths below and two finger widths behind the navel. This is where a cultivator's golden core would be formed and is where the qi metabolism process begins and progresses upward. The Middle is located at the center of the chest, at level with the heart, while the Upper is located on the forehead, between the eyebrows.

DAOISM: Daoism is the philosophy of the *dao* (道 / "the way"). Following the dao involves coming into harmony with the natural order of the universe, which makes someone a "true human," safe from external harm and who can affect the world without intentional action. Cultivation is a concept based on Daoist superstitions.

DEMONS: A race of immensely powerful and innately supernatural beings. They are almost always aligned with evil.

DISCIPLES: Clan and sect members are known as disciples. Disciples live on sect grounds and have a strict hierarchy based on skill and seniority. They are divided into **Core**, **Inner**, and **Outer** rankings, with Core being the highest. Higher-ranked disciples get better lodging and other resources.

When formally joining a sect or clan as a disciple or a student, the sect/clan becomes like the disciple's new family: teachers are

parents and peers are siblings. Because of this, a betrayal or aban-
donment of one's sect/clan is considered a deep transgression of
Confucian values of filial piety. This is also the origin of many of
the honorifics and titles used for martial arts.

DRAGON: Great chimeric beasts who wield power over the weather.
Chinese dragons differ from their Western counterparts as they are
often benevolent, bestowing blessings and granting luck. They are
associated with the Heavens, the Emperor, and yang energy.

DUAL CULTIVATION: A cultivation method done in pairs. It is seen
as a means by which both parties can advance their skills or even
cure illness or curses by combining their qi. It is often sexual in
nature or an outright euphemism for sex.

FACE: *Mianzi* (面子), generally translated as "face", is an important
concept in Chinese society. It is a metaphor for a person's reputation and can be extended to further descriptive metaphors. For example, "having face" refers to having a good reputation, and "losing
face" refers to having one's reputation hurt. Meanwhile, "giving face"
means deferring to someone else to help improve their reputation,
while "not wanting face" implies that a person is acting so poorly or
shamelessly that they clearly don't care about their reputation at all.
"Thin face" refers to someone easily embarrassed or prone to offense
at perceived slights. Conversely, "thick face" refers to someone not
easily embarrassed and immune to insults.

FENG SHUI: *Feng shui* (風水 / "wind-water") is a Daoist practice
centered around the philosophy of achieving spiritual accord between people, objects, and universe at large. Practitioners usually

focus on positioning and orientation, believing this can optimize the flow of qi in their environment. Having good feng shui means being in harmony with the natural order.

THE FIVE ELEMENTS: Also known as the *wuxing* (五行 / "Five Phases"). Rather than Western concepts of elemental magic, Chinese phases are more commonly used to describe the interactions and relationships between things. The phases can both beget and overcome each other.
- ◇ Wood (木 / mu)
- ◇ Fire (火 / huo)
- ◇ Earth (土 / tu)
- ◇ Metal (金 / jin)
- ◇ Water (水 / shui)

FOUNDATION ESTABLISHMENT: An early cultivation stage achieved after collecting a certain amount of qi.

THE FOUR SCHOLARLY ARTS: The four academic and artistic talents required of a scholarly gentleman in ancient China. The Four Scholarly Arts were: Qin (the zither instrument *guqin*), Qi (a strategy game also known as *weiqi* or *go*), Calligraphy, and Painting.

GOLDEN FINGER: A protagonist-exclusive overpowered ability or weapon. This can also refer to them being generally OP ("overpowered") and not a specific ability or physical item.

GUANYIN: Also known as a bodhisattva, this is a Buddhist term whose exact definition differs depending on the branch of Buddhism being discussed. Its original Sanskrit translates to "one whose goal is awakening." Depending on the branch of Buddhism, it can refer to (among other things) one who is on the path to becoming a buddha, or to one who has actually achieved enlightenment and has declined entry to nirvana in favor of returning to show others the way.

GUQIN: A seven-stringed zither, played by plucking with the fingers. Sometimes called a qin. It is fairly large and is meant to be laid flat on a surface or on one's lap while playing.

HAND SEALS: Refers to various hand and finger gestures used by cultivators to cast spells, or used while meditating. A cultivator may be able to control their sword remotely with a hand seal.

HUMAN STICK: An ancient Chinese torture and execution method where all four limbs are chopped off. The related "human swine" goes a step further: on top of losing their limbs, the victim has their face and scalp mutilated, is rendered mute and blind, then thrown into a pigsty or chamberpot.

IMMORTALS AND IMMORTALITY: Immortals have transcended mortality through cultivation. They possess long lives, are immune to illness and aging, and have various magical powers. The exact life span of immortals differs from story to story, and in some they only live for three to four hundred years.

IMMORTAL-BINDING ROPES OR CABLES: Ropes, nets, and other restraints enchanted to withstand the power of an immortal or god. They can only be cut by high-powered spiritual items or weapons and often limit the abilities of those trapped by them.

INCENSE TIME: A common way to tell time in ancient China, referring to how long it takes for a single incense stick to burn. Standardized incense sticks were manufactured and calibrated for specific time measurements: a half hour, an hour, a day, etc. These were available to people of all social classes.

"One incense time" is roughly thirty minutes.

INEDIA: A common ability that allows an immortal to survive without mortal food or sleep by sustaining themselves on purer forms of energy based on Daoist fasting. Depending on the setting, immortals who have achieved inedia may be unable to tolerate mortal food, or they may be able to choose to eat when desired.

JADE: Jade is a culturally and spiritually important mineral in China. Its durability, beauty, and the ease with which it can be utilized for crafting both decorative and functional pieces alike has made it widely beloved since ancient times. The word might cause Westerners to think of green jade (the mineral jadeite), but Chinese texts are often referring to white jade (the mineral nephrite). This is the color referenced when a person's skin is described as "the color of jade."

JIANGHU: A staple of wuxia, the *jianghu* (江湖 / "rivers and lakes") describes an underground society of martial artists, monks, rogues, and artisans and merchants who settle disputes between themselves per their own moral codes.

KOWTOW: The *kowtow* (叩头 / "knock head") is an act of prostration where one kneels and bows low enough that their forehead touches the ground. A show of deep respect and reverence that can also be used to beg, plead, or show sincerity.

LILY: A flower considered a symbol of long-lasting love, making it a popular flower at weddings.

LOTUS: This flower symbolizes purity of the heart and mind, as lotuses rise untainted from the muddy waters they grow in. It also signifies the holy seat of the Buddha.

MERIDIANS: The means by which qi travels through the body, like a magical bloodstream. Medical and combat techniques that focus on redirecting, manipulating, or halting qi circulation focus on targeting the meridians at specific points on the body, known as acupoints. Techniques that can manipulate or block qi prevent a cultivator from using magical techniques until the qi block is lifted.

NASCENT SOUL: A cultivation stage in which cultivators can project their souls outside their bodies and have them travel independently. This can allow them to survive the death of their physical body and advance to a higher state.

NIGHT PEARLS: Night pearls are a variety of rare fluorescent stones. Their fluorescence derives from rare trace elements in igneous rock or crystalized fluorite. A valued gem in China often used in fiction as natural, travel-sized sources of light that don't require fire or qi.

NPC: Shortened for "Non-Player Character". An individual in a game who is not controlled by a player and instead a background character intended to fill out and advance the story.

Numbers

TWO: Two (二 / "er") is considered a good number and is referenced in the common idiom "good things come in pairs." It is common practice to repeat characters in pairs for added effect.

THREE: Three (三 / "san") sounds like sheng (生 / "living") and also like san (散 / "separation").

FOUR: Four (四 / "si") sounds like si (死 / "death"). A very unlucky number.

SEVEN: Seven (七 / "qi") sounds like qi (齊 / "together"), making it a good number for love-related things. However, it also sounds like qi (欺 / "deception").

EIGHT: Eight (八 / "ba") sounds like fa (發 / "prosperity"), causing it to be considered a very lucky number.

NINE: Nine (九 / "jiu") is associated with matters surrounding the Emperor and Heaven, and is as such considered an auspicious number.

MXTX's work has subtle numerical theming around its love interests. In *Grandmaster of Demonic Cultivation*, her second book, Lan Wangji is frequently called Lan-er-gege ("second brother Lan") as a nickname by Wei Wuxian. In her third book, *Heaven Official's Blessing*, Hua Cheng is the third son of his family and gives the name San Lang ("third youth") when Xie Lian asks what to call him.

OTAKU: Anime fandom slang for individuals who are deeply obsessed with a specific niche hobby, e.g., anime. Generically, refers to those fixated on anime.

PAPER TALISMANS: Strips of paper with incantations written on them, often done so with cinnabar ink or blood. They can serve as seals or be used as one-time spells. Distinct from talisman charms, which are powerful magical objects capable of subduing or killing monsters.

PEACHES: Peaches are associated with long life and immortality. For this reason, peaches and peach-shaped things are commonly eaten to celebrate birthdays. Peaches are also an ancient symbol of love between men, coming from a story where a duke took a bite from a very sweet peach and gave the rest of it to his lover to enjoy.

PEARLS: Pearls are associated with wisdom and prosperity. They are also connected to dragons; many depictions show them clutching a pearl or chasing after a pearl.

PEONY: Symbolizes wealth and power; was considered the emperor of flowers.

PHOENIX: *Fenghuang* (凤凰 / "phoenix"), a legendary chimeric bird said to only appear in times of peace and to flee when a ruler is corrupt. They are heavily associated with femininity, the Empress, and happy marriages.

PILLS AND ELIXIRS: Magic medicines that can heal wounds, improve cultivation, extend life, etc. In Chinese culture, these things are usually delivered in pill form. These pills are created in special kilns.

PINE TREE: A symbol of evergreen sentiment or everlasting affection.

QI: *Qi* (气) is the energy in all living things. There is both righteous qi and evil or poisonous qi.

Cultivators strive to cultivate qi by absorbing it from the natural world and refining it within themselves to improve their cultivation base. A cultivation base refers to the amount of qi a cultivator possesses or is able to possess. In xianxia, natural locations such as caves, mountains, or other secluded places with beautiful scenery are often rich in qi, and practicing there can allow a cultivator to make rapid progress in their cultivation.

Cultivators and other qi manipulators can utilize their life force in a variety of ways, including imbuing objects with it to transform them into lethal weapons or sending out blasts of energy to do powerful damage. Cultivators also refine their senses beyond normal human levels. For instance, they may cast out their spiritual sense to gain total awareness of everything in a region around them or to feel for potential danger.

QI CIRCULATION: The metabolic cycle of qi in the body, where it flows from the dantian to the meridians and back. This cycle purifies and refines qi, and good circulation is essential to cultivation. In xianxia, qi can be transferred from one person to another through physical contact and can heal someone who is wounded if the donor is trained in the art.

QI DEVIATION: A qi deviation (走火入魔 / "to catch fire and enter demonhood") occurs when one's cultivation base becomes unstable. Common causes include an unstable emotional state and/or strong negative emotions, practicing cultivation methods incorrectly, reckless use of forbidden or high-level arts, or succumbing to the influence of demons and evil spirits. When qi deviation arises from mental or emotional causes, the person is often said to have succumbed to their inner demons or "heart demons" (心魔).

Symptoms of qi deviation in fiction include panic, paranoia, sensory hallucinations, and death, whether by the qi deviation itself causing irreparable damage to the body or as a result of its symptoms such as leaping to one's death to escape a hallucination. Common treatments of qi deviation in fiction include relaxation (voluntary or forced by an external party), massage, meditation, or qi transfer from another individual.

QILIN: A one-horned chimera said to appear extremely rarely. Commonly associated with the birth or death of a great ruler or sage.

REALGAR: An orange-red mineral in crystal form also known as "ruby sulphur" or "ruby of arsenic." In traditional Chinese medicine, realgar is used as an antidote to poison, as well as to repel snakes and insects. Realgar wine—realgar powder mixed with baijiu or yellow wine—is traditionally consumed during the Dragon Boat Festival.

SECOND-GENERATION RICH KID: A child of a wealthy family who grows up with a large inheritance. "Second-generation" in this case refers to them being the younger generation (as opposed to their parents, who are the first generation) rather than immigrant status.

SECT: A cultivation sect is an organization of individuals united by their dedication to the practice of a particular method of cultivation or martial arts. A sect may have a signature style. Sects are led by a single leader, who is supported by senior sect members. They are not necessarily related by blood.

SEVEN APERTURES/QIQIAO: (七窍) The seven facial apertures: the two eyes, nose, mouth, tongue, and two ears. The essential qi of vital organs are said to connect to the seven apertures, and illness in the vital organs may cause symptoms there. People who are ill or seriously injured may be "bleeding from the seven apertures."

SHIDI, SHIXIONG, SHIZUN, ETC.: Chinese titles and terms used to indicate a person's role or rank in relation to the speaker. Because of the robust nature of this naming system, and a lack of nuance in translating many to English, the original titles have been maintained. *(See Name Guide for more information.)*

SPIRIT STONES: Small gems filled with qi that can be exchanged between cultivators as a form of currency. If so desired, the qi can be extracted for an extra energy boost.

STALLION NOVELS: A genre of fiction starring a male protagonist who has a harem full of women who fawn over him. Unlike many wish-fulfilment stories, the protagonist of a stallion novel is not the typical loser archetype and is more of an overpowered power fantasy. This genre is full of fanservice aimed at a heterosexual male audience, often focusing on the acquisition of a large harem over individual romantic plotlines with each wife.

The term itself is a comparison between the protagonist and a single male stud horse in a stable full of broodmares. *Proud Immortal Demon Way* is considered a prime example of a stallion novel.

SWORDS: A cultivator's sword is an important part of their cultivation practice. In many instances, swords are spiritually bound to their owner and may have been bestowed to them by their master, a family member, or obtained through a ritual. Cultivators in fiction are able to use their swords as transportation by standing atop the flat of the blade and riding it as it flies through the air. Skilled cultivators can summon their swords to fly into their hand, command the sword to fight on its own, or release energy attacks from the edge of the blade.

SWORD GLARE: *Jianguang* (剑光 / "sword light"), an energy attack released from a sword's edge.

SWORN BROTHERS/SISTERS/FAMILIES: In China, sworn brotherhood describes a binding social pact made by two or more unrelated individuals of the same gender. It can be entered into for social, political, and/or personal reasons and is not only limited to two participants; it can extend to an entire group. It was most common among men, but was not unheard of among women or between people of different genders.

The participants treat members of each other's families as their own and assist them in the ways an extended family would: providing mutual support and aid, support in political alliances, etc.

Sworn siblinghood, where individuals will refer to themselves as brother or sister, is not to be confused with familial relations like blood siblings or adoption. It is sometimes used in Chinese media, particularly danmei, to imply romantic relationships that could otherwise be prone to censorship.

THE SYSTEM: A common trope in transmigration novels is the existence of a System that guides the character and provides them with objectives in exchange for benefits, often under the threat of consequences if they fail. The System may award points for completing objectives, which can then be exchanged for various items or boons. In *Scum Villain*, these are called B-points, originally named after the second sound in the phrase *zhuang bi* (装逼 / "to act badass/to play it cool/to show off").

THE THREE REALMS: Traditionally, the universe is divided into Three Realms: the **Heavenly Realm**, the **Mortal Realm**, and the **Ghost Realm**. The Heavenly Realm refers to the Heavens and Celestial Court, where gods reside and rule, the Mortal Realm refers to the human world, and the Ghost Realm refers to the realm of the dead. In *Scum Villain*, only the Mortal Realm is directly relevant, while the Demon Realm is a separate space where all demons and their ilk reside.

TSUNDERE: Anime fandom slang for a character who acts standoffish (tsun) but secretly has a loving side (dere), similar to "hot and cold" in English.

TRANSMIGRATION: (穿越 / "to pass through") is analogous to the isekai genre in Japanese media. A character, usually from the modern world, suddenly finds themself in the past, future, or a fantasy world, most often by reincarnation or teleportation. The character often uses knowledge from their former life to "cheat" in their new one, especially if they've transmigrated into a novel or game they have recently finished and thus have knowledge they can use to their advantage. These individuals are referred to as transmigrators.

VINEGAR: To say someone is drinking vinegar or tasting vinegar means they're having jealous or bitter feelings. Generally used for a love interest growing jealous while watching the main character receive the attention of a rival suitor.

WEDDING TRADITIONS: Red is an important part of traditional Chinese weddings, as the color of prosperity, happiness, and good luck. It remains the standard color for bridal and bridegroom robes and wedding decorations even today.

A bride was always veiled when she was sent off by her family in her wedding dress. Veils were generally opaque, so the bride would need to be led around by her handmaidens (or the groom). The veil is not removed until the bride is in the wedding suite with the groom after the ceremony and is only removed by the groom himself. During the ceremony, the couple each cut off a lock of their own hair, then intertwine and tie the two locks together to symbolize their commitment.

WHUMP: Fandom slang for scenarios that result in a character enduring pain—emotional and/or physical—especially if the creator seems to have designed that scenario explicitly for that purpose.

WILLOW TREE: A symbol of lasting affection, friendship, and goodbyes. Also means "urging someone to stay," and "meeting under the willows." Can connote a rendezvous. Willows are synonymous with spring, which is considered the matchmaking season, and is thus synonymous with promiscuity. Willow imagery is also often used to describe lower-class women like singers and prostitutes.

YIN ENERGY AND YANG ENERGY: Yin and yang is a concept in Chinese philosophy that describes the complementary interdependence of opposite/contrary forces. It can be applied to all forms of change and differences. Yang represents the sun, masculinity, and the living, while yin represents the shadows, femininity, and the dead, including spirits and ghosts. In fiction, imbalances between them can do serious harm to the body or act as the driving force for malevolent spirits seeking to replenish themselves of whichever they lack.

ZHONGDIAN LITERATURE: Likely intended as a parody of Qidian Chinese Net, a webnovel site known for hosting male-targeted novels.

The
Scum Villain's
Self-Saving
System

REN ZHA FANPAI
ZIJIU XITONG

✦〈〉✦

Bonus Image
Gallery

Luo Binghe

Gongyi Xiao

Mobei Jun

Shang Qinghua

Mu Qingfang

Zhuzhi Lang

FROM BESTSELLING AUTHOR

MO XIANG TONG XIU

Heaven Official's Blessing

TIAN GUAN CI FU

Born the crown prince of a prosperous kingdom, Xie Lian was renowned for his beauty, strength, and purity. His years of dedication and noble deeds allowed him to ascend to godhood. But those who rise, can also fall...and fall he does, cast from the heavens again and again and banished to the mortal realm.

Eight hundred years after his mortal life, Xie Lian has ascended to godhood for the third time. Now only a lowly scrap collector, he is dispatched to wander the Mortal Realm to take on tasks appointed by the heavens to pay back debts and maintain his divinity. Aided by old friends and foes alike, and graced with the company of a mysterious young man with whom he feels an instant connection, Xie Lian must confront the horrors of his past in order to dispel the curse of his present.

Available in print and digital from Seven Seas Entertainment

聡美Danmei

Seven Seas Entertainment
sevenseasdanmei.com